Praise for Barbara Delinsky

"Delinsky is an expert at portraying strong women characters."   *Booklist*

"Delinsky is one of those writers who knows how to introduce characters to her readers in such a way that they become more like old friends than works of fiction."

Flint Journal

"Delinsky is an engaging writer who knows how to interweave several stories about complex relationships and keep her books interesting to the end. Her special talent for description gives the reader almost virtual references to the surroundings she creates."

Cleveland Plain Dealer

"Delinsky's prose is spare, controlled and poignant as she evokes the simplicity and joys of small-town life."   *Publishers Weekly*

"Delinsky steers clear of treacle . . . with simple prose and a deliberate avoidance of happily ever after clichés."   *People*

"Delinsky should touch even the most jaded of readers."   *Chattanooga Times*

"Delinsky creates . . . a remarkably beautiful story."   *Baton Rouge Advocate*

Books by Barbara Delinsky

Shades of Grace
Together Alone
For My Daughters
Suddenly
More Than Friends
A Woman Betrayed
Finger Prints
Within Reach
The Passions of Chelsea Kane
The Carpenter's Lady
Gemstone
Variation on a Theme
Passion and Illusion
An Irresistible Impulse
Fast Courting
Search for a New Dawn
Sensuous Burgundy
A Time to Love
Moment to Moment
Rekindled
Sweet Ember
A Woman's Place

BARBARA DELINSKY

Finger Prints

HarperTorch
An Imprint of HarperCollinsPublishers

HARPERTORCH
An Imprint of HarperCollins*Publishers*
10 East 53rd Street
New York, New York 10022-5299

Copyright © 1984 by Barbara Delinsky
ISBN: 0-06-104180-7

First HarperTorch paperback printing: November 2000
First HarperPaperbacks printing: May 1992

HarperCollins®, HarperTorch™, and ♦™ are trademarks of HarperCollins Publishers Inc.

Printed in the United States of America

Visit HarperTorch on the World Wide Web at www.harpercollins.com

30 29 28 27 26 25 24 23

To my husband, Steve, for his endless support and the brilliant career that inspired Finger Prints, and to my sons, Eric, Andrew and Jeremy, for their indulgence in repeating things twice to catch my attention.

One

tHE NOVEMBER AFTERNOON WAS GRAY, WITH dusk lurking just around the corner, waiting to ensnare the hapless passerby in its chilling shroud. Carly Quinn tugged the collar of her trench coat closer around her neck, then shifted the bag of books to a more comfortable spot on her shoulder without missing a step. She walked quickly. These days in particular, she didn't feel safe until she was home and the last of the three bolts on her door were securely thrown.

The tap of her slender heels on the sidewalk reminded her that she'd forgotten to change shoes before she'd left school, and she silently cursed the haste behind the lapse. But she'd worked late grading themes. And it was Friday. When she left the library her only thought had been of home.

Home. She gave a wry smile as she turned onto Brattle Street, waited for a break in the rush-hour traffic, then trotted across to resume her march among the smattering of pedestrians on the opposite side. Home. Strange how the mind could adapt, she mused. How utterly, unbelievably different her life had been a year ago. Now, Cambridge was home and she was Carly Johnson Quinn. She looked like a Carly, dressed like a Carly, was even beginning to dream like a Carly. Perhaps they'd been right. Perhaps she would adjust after all.

Momentarily lulled into security by the humanity surrounding her, she became mesmerized by the taillights of the cars headed into Harvard Square. She wondered where their drivers were going, whether to dinner at Ahmed's or Grendel's Den, for a beer at the Wursthaus, or to a show in Boston.

A car honked in passing and, stiffening, Carly jerked her head sharply to the left. When her gaze met the grinning faces of several of her students, her relief was immediate. They had just returned from a triumphant basketball game against their arch rival. She had talked briefly with them as she'd left the school and now tipped her head up to offer a smile. Then they were gone, swallowed up in the inbound traffic, leaving her to control the runaway beat of her heart. Oh, yes, she reflected, she might well adjust to a new life, a new identity. But she seriously doubted that this would ever change—the constant nervousness, the perpetual guardedness, especially now that the days were shorter and darkness fell that much earlier.

Quickening her step, she covered two more blocks before turning right and heading toward the river. Her apartment was no more than five minutes ahead. Yet this was the strip that always bothered her most. The side street was narrower and less traveled than the main one. It was darker too, barely lit by the streetlights that seemed lost among the network of tree branches and telephone wires. And there were any number of front doors and side paths and back alleys from which an assailant might materialize. An occasional car approached from behind, headlights slinging tentative shadows across the pathways ahead. Carly swallowed hard once, anchored her lower lip beneath her teeth and pressed onward.

There was nothing to fear, nothing to fear. She repeated the silent litany as she had so often in the past months, speeding it up in time with her pace. Perhaps, she mused, she should follow Sam's suggestion and take her car. But then she would have a parking hassle at the end of the day. Besides, the exercise was good for her, as was the crisp fall air.

She took a deep, restorative breath, then held it convulsively when a figure suddenly approached from the opposite direction. Only when she recognized the research technician who worked at the hospital did she slowly exhale. He was right on schedule, she realized, mentally calculating the time. She passed him whenever she left school at five-thirty, which wasn't more than once or twice a week and then always on random days. It was one of the things Sam Loomis had taught her. The more varied her existence, the more elusive a target she'd be. Not that she was a creature of habit. She'd been far more impulsive in the past, when she was driven by the demons within to prove herself as a journalist. Now, though, as a highschool English teacher, she led a life more conducive to order. Strange, she mused again, how things had changed.

The research technician passed on the opposite sidewalk without a word. But then, he'd have no reason to recognize Carly. She, on the other hand, had Sam, who had carefully checked out not only her neighbors, but the people they'd passed in those first few weeks when he'd been by her side walking her to school in the morning, then home at night. He'd been a godsend, given the circumstances.

Now, though, she was on her own and free to imagine all kinds of villains in pursuit on a dark and deserted street. But it wasn't really deserted, she chided herself. There were close-set houses on one side, low apartment buildings on the other. And there were cars lining both curbs as evidence of people nearby. Surely if she were in danger, she would only have to scream and there would be any number of people to help. Or so she hoped. In less optimistic moments she wondered if these urban dwellers would come to the aid of a woman they didn't know. She wondered if, with their doors and windows shut tight, they would even hear her.

When, silhouetted against the lights on Memorial Drive, the rounded turret of her building came into view, she felt momentarily lightened. Then she heard the crescendoing thud of footsteps behind and her calm vanished. Without thought to her heels, the broken sidewalk or the heavy bag that pounded her side with each stride, she broke into as steady a run as she could manage. Looking neither to the right nor the left, she sprinted forward with single-minded intent. Her breath came in short, painful gasps, intermingled with soft moans of fear. Through the wisps of auburn hair that had blown across her face, she saw the sanctuary of home drawing closer, closer. Ignoring the stitch in her side, she ran on, nearly there now, all but tasting refuge.

It was only after she'd turned in at the stone courtyard that, without breaking pace, she dared a glance over her shoulder. The look was ill-timed. She'd barely spotted the jogger who had turned onto Memorial Drive when she collided headlong with a firm wall of muscle.

Terror-filled, she caught her breath in a loud gasp

and would have fallen on the rebound had it not been for firm fingers gripping her arms. One part of her wanted to scream; the other part recalled what Sam had told her.

"You're Carly Quinn now," he'd said in that soothing voice of his. "Stay calm. Whatever you do, if someone approaches, don't make the mistake of assuming that Robyn Hart has been found out. You've got to act with confidence or you'll blow your own cover. Carly Quinn has absolutely nothing to hide, nothing to fear. Remember that."

It was easier said than done. Now, breathless from running and with the drum of her pulse reverberating in her ears, she raised panic-stricken eyes to those of her captor. He was large, tall and broad-shouldered, intimidating. In the relative light of the courtyard, she saw that he was dark—his full shock of casually mussed hair, the beard that stretched from ear to ear and parted only briefly at his lips, the worn sweat shirt he'd shoved up to the elbow. She knew she'd never seen him before; there was an intensity about him that she would not have quickly forgotten. Yet as a hit man he was questionable. His features were too gentle, as were, oddly, the fingers that seemed now to grasp her arms more in support of her shaking limbs than in any form of detention. And his voice, his voice, too, lacked the coarseness for which she'd steeled herself.

"Are you all right?" he asked, frowning at the pallor that the courtyard lights illumined.

Slowly, Carly came to her senses. His concern was as inconsistent with imminent attack as was the leisure with which he stood there holding her in the light, in view of any neighbor who cared to look. Panic yielded to caution, which was tinged with embarrassment when she forced herself to speak. She'd obviously made a foolish mistake.

"Yes . . . yes, I'm fine," she whispered falteringly. As unwarranted as her alarm had apparently been, it had nonetheless taken its toll. She was breathless from her dash, and felt weak and tired. And she wasn't yet home free. Scrounging odd fragments of strength, she tore her gaze from his and took a step back. The man's arms dropped to his sides. Then she turned her head and murmured a chagrined, "Excuse me," before sidestepping him and heading for the door, which was mercifully propped open with a carton, saving her the trial of having to fit her key into the lock. With the trembling of her fingers, she never would have made it.

Bent only on reaching total safety, she walked quickly through the lobby to the open stairs that wound broadly around the plant-filled atrium. She neither stopped nor looked back until she'd reached the third floor and her own apartment. Glancing around then to see that she hadn't been followed, she quickly punched out the combination to disengage her alarm, fumbled with her key for a minute and let herself in. Before she'd even crossed the threshold she flipped a switch to brightly light not only the small foyer in which she stood but also the sunken living room beyond. Everything looked fine. Wonderful, in fact. Stepping inside, she shut the door firmly, reactivated the alarm, drove home the bolts, then sagged back against the door with a long, shuddering breath. For the many times she'd felt herself a prisoner of circumstance, her cell had rarely been more appreciated than it was at that moment.

Home. She'd made it. Through the harrowing trek, her worst enemy had been her own imagination. Her lips thinned in self-reproach. Nightmares were one thing—those she couldn't help. Though they varied in specifics, their general content was the same. She was caught. Cornered. Doomed. Sometimes by fire, blazing hot and out of control. Sometimes by an obscured face, by a gruff, terrifying voice. Or by a hand with a small but deadly gun.

Suppressing a shudder, she silently scolded herself. No, she couldn't control the nightmares. But *this*? Running through the streets in a state of sheer panic? Shaking her head in dismay, she gazed around at the comforts of home and took long, purposeful breaths. With the gradual steadying of her pulse, she pushed away from the door, dropped her shoulder bag on the hall table, shrugged out of her coat and tossed it over the arm of the living-room sofa before sinking into the adjacent cushions. Their welcome was heaven. She eased off her heels to allow her feet play in the plush carpet and laid her head back, closing her eyes and breathing deeply. In the four months that she'd been on her own, she couldn't remember ever having panicked. Yet just now she'd totally, pathetically lost her cool, and it baffled her.

She opened her eyes, first looking down at the sophisticated sweater and skirt that so fitted the image of the modern English teacher, then letting her eyes wander over the apartment that similarly spoke of her new life. Given the bizarre circumstances that had brought her east, she had much to be grateful for. She had this beautiful home, a newly converted condominium with every convenience and then some. And she had a good job, one for which she was well trained, if a bit rusty. It had been more than five years since she'd taught, and she had been hesitant, to say the least. But it had seemed the perfect answer to her relocation dilemma and, once her teaching position had been secured, she'd spent the summer preparing her curriculum. It had taken hours upon hours, long days of reading and study and thought. As with everything she'd ever done, though, she had wanted to do this right.

Initially she'd been simply grateful for the diversion. With thoughts of Melville, Faulkner and Hemingway dominating her mind, there was little time to brood on Barber and Culbert. Gradually, she realized that she truly loved what she was doing, all the more when school began in September.

Stretching to further relax herself, she reached back to lift the weight of hair from her neck and expose lingering traces of dampness to the air. Yes, she did love her job. She loved dealing with literature itself, she enjoyed the give and take with her colleagues, and she particularly adored the kids. They were fresh and open, eager to learn. Many came from families who sacrificed to send them to private school. All were college-bound. Even given the free spirits, the noncon-formists, the occasional troublesome ones of the lot, their dedication to learning was a teacher's dream. She felt challenged and rewarded, far more than she'd imagined she would ever be when she'd been forced to abandon Chicago, and some of the happiest years of her life.

Happiest, yet most tragic. First Matthew. Then Peter. Two people she'd loved, though in very different ways, now dead. And she had lived to begin anew in a way that most people wouldn't, most people couldn't, dream of doing.

She wandered restlessly around the living room, trailing her finger across a white lacquered cabinet to the television, then on to the bookshelf where she paused for a moment's thought before padding to the kitchen for a glass of orange juice. That firmly in hand, she returned to the sofa, settling back into the cushions to cope with an all-too-familiar sense of emptiness.

The view that met her eye was comforting, though. Her apartment was a vision of subdued elegance, from the white-textured cotton of the modular sofa, with its gay throw pillows of mauves and pale blues, and the low sculpted tables of white marble, to the original silk-screen prints on the walls and the recessed fixtures overhead. It was easily something a decorator might have put together, yet Carly had done it all. For the first time in her life she had splurged indecently. But then, she'd reasoned, she owed it to herself, both in compensation for the years she'd worked nonstop and in consolation for her more recent heartache.

Helplessly, her thoughts turned to Matthew. He'd never have lived this way, in a spotless apartment, with everything in its place. The apartments they'd shared through six years of marriage had been older, more cluttered, eminently casual. She'd loved it then because she had been with him. How she'd loved him. How she missed him!

Sighing, she absently swirled her orange juice, then nearly spilled it when the jangle of the phone made her jump. Muscles that had just begun to relax tensed quickly. The phone didn't ring often. That too was a change. There was a time when it had never seemed to stop.

The second ring brought her to her feet. Once in the kitchen, she hesitated for an instant with her hand on the receiver before lifting it with a studied calm. "Hello?" she asked cautiously.

"Carly?"

She didn't immediately recognize the voice, yet it sounded friendly enough. "Yes."

"Carly, it's Dennis." Dennis Sharpe. Of course. History teacher at the academy. Coach of the basketball team. Tall. Good-looking. Personable. "I'm sorry I missed you this afternoon. I had hoped to catch you before you left, but you must have escaped before we got back."

Escaped. A potent word. With a wary smile, she stretched the phone cord toward the kitchen table, settled into one of its canvas director's chairs and forced a note of buoyancy into her voice. "I waded through your boys on my way out. Congratulations! Sounds like quite a win."

"The guys played a great game. Particularly against Palmer. I was proud of them."

"Are we in first place now?"

He chuckled. "The season's barely begun. I suppose you could say we're somewhere up there, for what it's worth."

"Dennis," she chided lightly, "where's that school spirit?"

"That school spirit is back at school. It's the weekend. Which is why I'm calling. I know it's late, and I've got to be on the road before long, but I thought I'd give it another stab. How about dinner? Something quick and light in the Square? I've got to have something to eat before I get going, and I'd hate to do it alone."

With a sad smile, Carly propped her elbow on the arm of her chair and rested her head on her hand. Poor man. He'd been trying for dinner since September. Without success. "Oh, I don't know, Dennis. It's been a long week and I'm really exhausted."

"That's why you need to get out. To unwind and relax a little."

She *knew* that she needed to unwind and relax. But "getting out," after the scare she'd had earlier, would never do. It was far safer to stay home. "You're sweet to call, but . . . I don't think so. You see, I've got this date with a hot bath. We were planning to lose ourselves in lots of bubbles and a good book."

"How can you do this to me, Carly?" Dennis kidded, his voice the faintest bit hoarse. "You mean to say that I'm competing with a bathtub? What kind of rivalry is that?"

She laughed, but refrained from comment. It was always easier to change the subject. "You're headed for the Cape?"

He gave a magnanimous sigh. "Guess so. I've got some work to do on the house before winter sets in. It won't be long now, and I'm really behind."

"Your cottage isn't winterized?"

"Oh, it is. Or it will be once I've recalked the windows and put on the storms, turned off the outdoor valves, oiled the furnace. That type of thing."

"You've got your weekend cut out for you," she commented, half in envy, despite the work involved. There was something to be said for physical labor as therapy.

"Want to come? You're welcome to, you know. In fact, I'd love it if you were along. It gets lonesome down there."

Carly grinned. "Come on, Dennis. Don't tell me that you aren't in touch with every neighbor for miles. You happen to be one of the most outgoing people I know." From the first, she'd been struck by his way with people, not only the kids at school, but the acquaintances he'd run into on the few occasions when they'd lunched off-campus. It would be easy to warm up to him, which was all the more reason for Carly to remain aloof.

"Yeah, but it'd be different if you were there. I really enjoy talking with you, Carly. You're one bright lady."

Her smile was gentle in its sad fashion. "Flattery will get you nowhere, my friend."

"Then what will?" he blurted out.

"Oh—" she rolled her eyes to the ceiling and offered a tongue-in-cheek quip "—maybe a yacht in the Caribbean or a villa in Majorca. I could use a little sun about now."

"First a bathtub. Now the sun. I can't win, can I?" When she remained silent, he sighed in resignation. "Well, I guess I'll be going. Sure you won't join me even for a pizza?"

Her eyes held a melancholy look. "Thanks, Dennis, but I'd better not. You have a good weekend, though. See you Monday?"

He paused, as if wanting to say more, then gave up. "Right. So long, Carly."

After a quiet "Bye-bye," she replaced her receiver on its hook, took a sip of juice, set the glass down on the counter again, then crossed through the foyer and short hall to her bedroom. When she returned to the living room, she was barefoot and wore a hip-length tunic and jeans. Turning the lights down low, she stood by the window. Traffic on Memorial Drive, and on Storrow Drive across the Charles, was at its peak, heavy in both directions, whipping commuters home to family and friends. How envious she was.

Slipping down onto the window sill, she drew the drapes around behind her, enclosing herself in a semicocoon of darkness to gaze out on the world unseen. These were the hardest times for her, these times of leisure when, alone and admittedly lonely, she inevitably looked back.

Warm images filled her head of the comfortable Lyons home on the outskirts of Omaha, of her parents standing arm in arm in the large front hall when her father returned from a day at the office, of her brothers' lusty squeals coming from odd corners of the house. The boys had been rowdy by nature. Three of them, all close in age and strapping. When she'd come along, far from being the demure little girl her parents had expected, they found themselves with a tomboy who matched the boys round for round. Her brothers were grown now, each married and with children of his own. Only she had failed to find that niche.

A tiny smile touched her lips as she thought back to the imp she'd once been. A child filled with laughter and joy. Until her mother had died. It had been hard on them all—on her father, on the boys. When a woman in her early forties died as suddenly as Charlene Lyons had, it was always hard on the survivors. But on Carly—then Robyn—it had been the hardest. She'd been twelve at the time, just entering adolescence. As suddenly as the mother she'd adored was gone, so was the mischievous child, leaving in her place a more serious teenager, industrious, responsible, ever pushing herself despite her father's and brothers' protests.

She hadn't been unhappy. Rather, she'd been busy, burying her private grief in a newfound existence. Much as she did now.

Against her will, her thoughts returned to the present. She struggled with them, fought them, suffered with them, then bolted from the window. With the quickest glance at her watch, she ran to the kitchen, picked up the phone and punched out her father's number. Her throat was tight, her gaze desperate. She needed him, needed to hear that familiar voice just now.

After five long rings, she was rewarded.

"Hello?"

To her ears, the sound of John Lyons's deep voice,

seeming immune to both age and a fragile heart, was golden. "Dad! You *are* home!"

"Of course I'm home!" His words were shaped by an audible smile. "You know what my orders are."

Carly breathed deeply, savoring this contact that had the power to defer the darker thoughts that plagued her. "Oh, yes, I know what your orders are," she countered smartly. "I also know that you've been regularly resisting them." Her tone lightened as her own smile flowed across the miles. "How are you, dad?"

"I'm fine, sweetheart. Just sitting here relaxing with my feet up and my daily allotment of wine in hand. How are *you*?"

"Not bad." The last thing she wanted to do was to burden her father with her woes. It was enough to talk with him, to draw from his indomitable strength. "What did the doctor say? You saw him yesterday, didn't you?"

"I certainly did."

"And . . . ?"

"And he says that for a man who had a major heart attack six months ago, I'm a wonder."

Carly gave a teasing guffaw. "We all knew that, even *without* William Drummond's medical wizardry. So he says you're doing well?"

"Yes, ma'am. I've been given the go-ahead to play golf. The proof of the pudding."

"No kidding? That's great!"

"*I* think so." He gave a dry laugh. "Too bad the season's just about gone. It's been bad enough having to stop smoking cold turkey, and Chablis isn't quite the Scotch I'd like, but it's my golf that's been most sorely missed."

"By whom?" Carly teased. "You or Uncle Tim? I half

suspect that *his* fun is in being able to trounce you on the course."

Her father came readily to his brother's defense. "He's damn good at it. I'm lucky he'll play with me. Besides, I've been that much more fortunate in business. It's the least I can do, letting him win once in a while." Carly's Uncle Timothy was as different from his fraternal twin as night was from day. He had shunned the business world in favor of a life of ease, and now his summers were spent as the golf pro at a suburban Omaha club, his winters in a similar role in Arizona.

"Will you go to Phoenix this year?" Carly asked.

"I'm planning to head there for several weeks after I see you in New York."

New York. Thanksgiving. Carly had been looking forward to it ever since she'd come east. Now it was barely three weeks away. She felt excited, and sad. More than anything, she would have liked to have gone home. But it wasn't to be, not for a while, at least. Swallowing the lump in her throat, she forced a brightness to her voice that told only half the story. "I'm really looking forward to it, dad. It seems so long." Gritting her teeth, she fought the tears in her eyes. She wasn't usually this sensitive, or rather, she was usually better able to hide her sensitivity. Whether this lapse had been caused by the afternoon's fright or simply the approach of the holidays, she wasn't sure.

"Are you all right, sweetheart?" her father asked quickly.

She squeezed her eyes shut. A small tear trickled from each corner. "Sure," she managed to reply. "I'm okay." She hadn't wanted to do this. Her father would know in a second that she was *not* okay. It was perhaps one of the reasons they'd always been close. He could read her well.

"You sound as though you're on the verge of tears."

Unfortunately she'd passed that point. Her eyes were brimming now, her cheeks growing wetter by the minute. She should have waited to call, she chided herself belatedly. But she'd needed him.

"I'm sorry," she whispered, muffling the receiver against her mouth. "I guess . . . it's just. . . ." What was it? Fear? Loneliness? A simple need to be held? Dissolving into silent weeping, she couldn't say a word.

Her father seemed to understand. "It's all right, sweetheart," he crooned, his voice, despite its undercurrent of pain, gently soothing her as his arms might have done had he been there. "You just let it out. We all need to do it sometimes."

"I'm sorry . . . I didn't mean . . . to burden you. . . ."

"Burden me?" he countered with such tenderness that the flow of her tears only increased. "You're my daughter. I love you. And you've never in your life been a burden to me."

"But . . . all this. . . ." She sniffled, waving her arm in a comprehensive arc her father could only imagine. "How did . . . I ever get myself . . . in such a mess?"

With a gentle, "Shh" every so often, her father waited until her quiet sobs subsided. "Don't berate yourself, sweetheart," he began. "I'm so very proud of you. We all are. You faced the worst of danger, yet you went out on a limb for something you believed in."

"I know," she whispered, extracting a tissue from its box on the kitchen counter. "But I sometimes . . . wonder what good it does. Sure, Barber and Culbert are serving time, but I feel as though *I'm* the one being . . . punished." Pausing, she dabbed her eyes. "If only I'd listened to the others. They told me not to push it."

"It *had* to be pushed, sweetheart. Arson is a crime. People died in those fires."

Oh, yes. People did die. She winced at the finality of it. "I know," she murmured, and she did. All too well. She also knew that, given the same circumstances, she would do it all again. Yet she couldn't contain the note of bitterness in her voice. Only with her father could she vent it. She could count on him to love her nonetheless. "It's just that there are times when I wish it had been someone else who'd been hellbent on righting the wrongs of the world. There are times when I don't like the consequences I'm stuck with, times when I feel so alone."

"You've got friends, haven't you?" her father asked. "I can't imagine you teaching at that school of yours without meeting people."

"Oh, yes, I've got friends. But it's different."

"You're still staying in a lot?" Now there was gentle accusation in his question. It was something they'd discussed before.

Carly dabbed at her nose and shrugged. "I get out. But I always feel as if I've got to be on my guard. It's so tiring sometimes." Her voice broke. Again, her father waited patiently until she'd regained her composure.

"It'll take time, sweetheart. They told you that from the start. You'll gain your confidence little by little. Look at me. When I first came home from the hospital, I was sure that each day would be my last, that any bit of exertion would bring on that next attack. Then I woke up the second day and the third day and the fourth. After a week, I'd begun to hope. After a month, I'd begun to believe. That's it, sweetheart. You've got to believe that you can forge a new life independent of the old." His voice softened even more. "You can't spend your days looking back. You've got to look ahead now."

This was what she loved about her father, under-

17

standing mixed with a gentle dose of reality. And he was right in everything he'd said. "You speak with such confidence," she quipped, retrieving her poise.

"I *am* confident. Look at your own life. Your mother died and you pulled yourself together to become someone she would have been proud of. When Matthew died, you did the same. You've got a strength that many people lack. Don't you see that? You'll survive this, too. Just wait. In a year or two you'll have found yourself. You'll feel confident. You'll be happy. You're that kind of person, sweetheart. It's in your nature."

Her lips grew tight. "Then why do I sit here feeling sorry for myself? Feeling sorry for myself! How does *that* jibe with the person you describe?"

"You're human. Like the rest of us. Self-pity is only natural once in a while. And it's fine as long as it doesn't become the major force in one's life. That will never happen to you. You're a doer. You'll move on. Just be patient with yourself. Give yourself time."

"Time." Sighing, she leaned back against the counter. "You're right, I'm sure. Besides, things aren't really all *that* bad." And her father deserved to hear a little of the good as well. She sniffled away the last of her tears. "You should see the themes those kids turned in this week. They're pretty exciting."

For a while longer, father and daughter talked on a lighter vein. When Carly hung up the phone at last, she felt better. Her father, on the other hand, had another call to make.

Two

tAKING A WORN ADDRESS BOOK FROM HIS DESK
drawer, John Lyons dialed the number he'd been given
to use in case of emergency. It was a Washington number. His call would be forwarded without his ever
knowing its destination. Glancing at his watch, he wondered if he might be too late. He was in the process of
reminding himself that he had twenty-four-hour access
when the switchboard operator's efficient voice came
on the line.

"Witness Assistance."

"Control Number 718, please."

"One minute." There was a click, a lengthy silence,
then another ring.

"Seven-eighteen."

"This is John Lyons calling."

After the briefest pause, Sam Loomis grew alert. It
wasn't often that John Lyons called, though they'd
struck a rapport from the first. Man to man, they had
a common interest. "Mr. Lyons. What can I do for you?"

"I just spoke with my daughter. She sounded upset.
Nothing's happened, has it?"

Sam frowned. He'd spoken with Carly himself a few days earlier, and she'd been fine. "No, nothing's happened. At least, not that I know of. Did she mention anything specific?"

"No. But something's shaken her. I'm sure of that. She's usually so composed. There's been no word on a new trial, has there?"

"Uh-uh. Nothing. And Joliet's got our men safely on ice." He pushed aside his papers and glanced at the clock on the wall. "Listen, I'm sure everything's fine, but let me give her a call."

"I'd appreciate that."

"And you relax." Sam was aware of John Lyons's precarious health. "I'll take care of things from this end."

"Thanks, 718."

Sam chuckled. "No problem." Pressing the button on his phone to sever the connection, he punched out Carly's number.

Carly hadn't moved from where she stood, deep in thought, against the kitchen counter. When the phone rang by her ear, she jumped. For a fleeting instant she wondered if her father had forgotten something, then she caught herself. He never called her. He didn't have the number. It was part of the scheme.

"Hello?" she answered slowly.

"It's Sam, Carly." He paused. "Are you all right?"

Instantly she knew what had happened. "Uh-oh. He called you, didn't he?"

"He was concerned. He said you were upset."

"I'm okay."

"Were you? Upset, that is?"

The deep breath she took, with its remnant of raggedness, bore confirmation of that fact. She twisted the telephone cord around her finger. "I guess I was. Something must have just hit me."

Sam Loomis was good at his job. He wasn't about to shrug off a vague "something." "What was it? Did something happen at school?"

"No, no. Everything's fine there. I . . . it was really nothing."

A fine-tuned feeler caught the sound of fear, very subtle but present. "Listen, Carly, I'd like to stop by. Maybe we can go out for a bite. Okay?"

"No, Sam. You don't have to do that. I'm really tired—"

"Then I'll bring something in."

"I'm not hungry. Sam—"

"Give me fifteen minutes in this traffic. See you then." He hung up the phone before she could renew her protest. Then, shuffling the papers he'd been reading into a semblance of order, he flipped the file folder shut and tossed it atop a similar pile.

"You're leaving?" came a voice from the opposite desk. Sam looked up. "Yeah."

"Problem?"

"I'm not sure."

"Carly Quinn?"

Sam's gaze sharpened. Greg Reilly had been with the service for less than a year and Sam's assistant for most of that time, yet there was still something about the younger man that made Sam uneasy. "Yeah," he said simply, unwilling to say more.

Greg shifted his trim frame in his seat and adopted a more idle pose. "I wouldn't mind it. She's a looker."

Stuffing a pen in the inner pocket of his blazer, Sam rethought his plans, picked up the file he'd just closed, put it in the lower right hand drawer of his desk and locked the drawer tight. "She's a case, Greg."

"A very sexy one. Man, you must be a saint to keep your distance. Either that—" his grin twisted "—or you're mad."

Sam headed for the door. "Not mad. Married. And respectful of Carly. *And* aware of the rules. *Capice?*" He was into the darkened hall before Greg's parting shot hit him.

"Anytime you need assistance. . . ."

"Thanks, pal," he muttered under his breath, "but no thanks. This one's mine."

Carly stared at the dead receiver for several minutes before putting it back on its hook. He'd had the final say. He was on his way. Not that she didn't want him to be. She was almost glad he hadn't let her argue him out of coming. Sam was always a comfort. Though she'd never have called him on her own for such a reason as this, she welcomed his company.

Fifteen minutes later the buzzer rang. Having sponged her face and freshened her makeup, she took a deep breath and pressed the button on the intercom panel beside the door. "Yes?"

"It's me, Carly. Buzz me in."

Recognizing his voice, she did as she was told, then opened the door and ventured into the hall to lean over the banister and follow his ascent. To this day, Carly believed Sam Loomis to be the least likely looking deputy U.S. marshal she'd ever seen. Not that she'd seen many. But there was a stereotype that Sam definitely didn't fit. A six-footer of medium build, he was dressed with a casual, style-conscious flair in navy slacks and a tan corduroy blazer with a white shirt and snappy striped tie. His hair was sandy hued and full, brushing his forehead as he trotted easily up the steps. There was nothing formal or stiff or somber about him. He easily passed as Carly's beau.

"You must just love this on a Friday evening," she began in subtle self-derision as he mounted the last flight. "Bet you didn't expect quite an albatross."

"Albatross?" Sam snickered. "You should only know." Putting a strong arm around her shoulders, he leaned low to whisper in her ear as he led her back into her apartment, "You should get a look at *some* of my charges. They're nowhere near as pretty as you are." To the onlooker, he might have been whispering sweet nothings. Her comely smile would have supported the suspicion.

Carly nudged him in the ribs. "That's the oldest line I've ever heard. Besides—" the door slammed behind them "—you've already told me that most of them are thugs. Compared to a guy who's had his nose broken twice, his cheek slashed, his forearm tattooed and his fists battered, I should hope I come out ahead."

Giving her shoulder an affectionate squeeze, he released her. The affection was genuine and mutual. In the four months since they'd met, Carly and Sam had found much to respect in each other.

" 'Ahead' is putting it mildly. It's sheer *relief* to get a call from you."

"From my father," she corrected him gently. "I wouldn't drag you out here just to hold my hand."

Sam was quick to respond to the apology in her eyes. "That's my job, Carly. It's what I'm here for. You don't call me half as often as most of my witnesses do." Gently grasping her shoulders with his hands, he was all too aware of her fragility. "And *I'm* sitting there in my office, trying to decide whether I should pester you or leave you alone. You've got to guide me. Besides, we're friends. Something really got to you today. You should have called."

"I'm *okay.*"

"But you've been crying."

She looked away. "My father shouldn't have told—"

"He didn't tell me. I can see for myself." Cupping her chin with his forefinger, he tipped up her face. She had no choice but to meet his gaze. When her eyes grew helplessly moist, she broke away and went to stand before the window. With one arm wrapped tight about her waist, she pressed a fist to her mouth. The reflection in the window told her of Sam's approach. "You don't want to talk about it?" he asked softly.

She held out a hand, her fingers spread, asking him to give her a moment. When she felt herself sufficiently composed, she took an unsteady breath. "I was walking home and I panicked. It was dark. I heard footsteps coming fast from behind." When she closed her eyes, the scene was vivid before her lids. "I just assumed they'd found me, so I started to run. And all the while I was waiting to hear a shot or feel a hand clamp over my mouth." Her eyes opened wide, bespeaking her fear. "It was a jogger, a stupid jogger. But I thought . . . I thought. . . ." She waved her hand suggestively as her voice cracked and her tenuous composure dissolved. Though the last thing she wanted to do was cry in front of Sam, she couldn't help herself. "What's the . . . matter with . . . me, Sam?" she sobbed, her voice muffled against the hand she'd put up to shield her face from him. "I never cry. And here I am. Twice in . . . in one day. It's disgusting."

Without a thought, Sam put his arm around her and drew her close. Of all the witnesses he'd dealt with in his ten years on the job, only she inspired this kind of protectiveness. Oh, yes, she was a woman. And a looker, as Greg had said. But she was different all around—her intelligence, her personality, the very nature of the case that had brought her to him. Holding her now, offering her a silent kind of comfort, he recalled the first time he met her, when she arrived four months before with the marshal from Chicago in that unmarked car. She had been frightened and vulnerable. He'd found it hard to believe her to be the journalist who had so systematically, so single-mindedly probed an arson conspiracy. *That* was before he'd gotten to know her. Through the months of July and August he'd witnessed her dedication firsthand, tracking her day after day to the library, aware of the other days she spent, holed up in her apartment preparing to teach in the fall. When she set her mind to something, she went after it determinedly. He respected her tremendously. He also respected the susceptibility that now reduced her to tears.

"It's only natural, Carly," he said soothingly, as he rubbed her back. The other nice thing about their relationship was that he *could* hold her, even dote on her, without misunderstanding. He was happily married and loved his wife. Carly knew this, seemed able to relax with him all the more for it. Never once had either of them felt threatened. Theirs was a rare friendship, one that went well beyond the rules of his trade. He knew that wherever she went, whatever she did in life, they'd keep in touch. They were truly friends.

"You've lived through something most people would only dream about if they tried to sleep on a stomach full of Guido's supersubs with fried onions, hot peppers, diced pickles and salami."

She answered with a groan. "It's not funny, Sam. I don't have to eat *anything* and I have nightmares."

"Still?" He drew back to look at her face. "You're not sleeping again? I thought that was better."

"Oh, it is usually. It's just . . . once in a while . . . I really shouldn't complain."

"Do you want something for it?"

"No! God, the last thing I need is something to knock me out. Then I might never know if someone had broken in until he was on top of me."

"Carly!" Sam gave her a punishing glower. "That's exactly the kind of thinking that'll get you into trouble. No one is going to come after you." He deliberately enunciated each word. "No one is going to break in."

"Then why am I in this program?" she countered, matching his glower with the fire of her own as she took a step back and blotted her cheeks with her hands. There was nothing like healthy debate to stem tears. "If there was no threat, I'd still be Robyn Hart living in Chicago working for the *Tribune.*"

"Your reasoning only goes half way. As Robyn Hart, you *would* be in danger. That's why you were admitted to the program. On the other hand, now you're Carly Quinn. No one knows that, or where you live, or what you do. That's the whole point. You have a new identity, a new background, a new life. Take my word for it, Robyn Hart has vanished. We've taken care of that. And we know what we're doing."

Carly eyed him, feeling guilty even as she cornered him. "That wasn't what Michael Frank said."

Sam stared for a minute, then raised his eyes to the ceiling in frustration. When he looked back down, his expression was one of regret. He should have warned her. "You saw the program last Tuesday." No wonder she'd been upset. That garbage would have been enough to frighten even the most uninvolved of viewers.

"How could I help it? It was advertised for a week, blasted all over the evening news."

"You didn't have to watch."

"Come on, Sam. How could I *not*? It was an intensive study of the Witness Protection Program, of which *I* am a part. I was curious."

"And you believed all that crap?" he growled. "I can't fathom that. You're an intelligent woman, Carly. You're *media,* for God's sake! You should know how the facts can be twisted, how they can be selectively used to make one point or another. Television is a medium of exaggeration, and that show was nothing but a crude distortion of the truth." He paused long enough to hear his own anger, then looked down, shook his head and let out a long breath. "I'm hungry."

Carly stared at him. "You're *hungry*? What does hunger have to do with anything?"

He looked around, then headed for the sofa to lift the coat she'd dropped earlier. "I can't think straight on an empty stomach. Let's go get a snack."

"We can't do that, Sam. Ellen is sure to be sitting home waiting for you. She's probably spent the afternoon planning dinner."

For the first time since he arrived, Sam smiled broadly. "You've never met Ellen or you wouldn't worry. Ellen is the perfect deputy marshal's wife. She knows *never* to expect me unless I call."

To Carly it sounded awful. She and Matt had prized their dinners precisely because their days were so busy and apart. "How does she stand it?"

He grinned then. "My charm. She's a sucker for my charm." He held the coat for her. "Come on, lady. We've got some talking to do." Had it been anyone else, Carly would have steadfastly refused. With Sam, though, she felt safe on every level.

Once in his car, they headed toward a deli on the fringe of the Square. There, over corned-beef sandwiches and beer, they very sanely discussed the program she'd watched. "It only spoke of the failures, Carly, and those are a ridiculously small percentage of the whole. Sure, there have been thugs who've been brought into the program, who theoretically then have a clean slate to launch a second lifetime of crime; there have been misjudgments here and there. In most cases though, it's been decided that the importance of the testimony outweighed the potential risk."

"I know, Sam, but that wasn't what—"

"Bothered you most?" When she nodded, he grimaced. "That's what I thought." He took a long swig of his beer.

"I mean, you have to admit that hearing about cases where the person supposedly under protection is discovered and—and killed—isn't terribly encouraging."

"But look at those cases, Carly. Those were situations where the witness was a crook himself, where he had a whole army of enemies. And the one most important thing that bastard Frank failed to point out was that in every one of those cases, the witness was himself responsible for his cover being blown. Think about it." He spoke softly, a gentle urgency in his voice. "Here you are. You've got an entire background fabricated for you—birth certificate, social security number, school and employment records, even a marriage certificate and phony newspaper clippings of your husband's death. We've given you a past that parallels the truth enough for you to feel comfortable with it. Names, dates, places may have been altered, but as Carly Quinn, you're a complete, believable individual. And there's no way, *no way* that anyone can connect Carly Quinn to Robyn Hart. In fact, wasn't that the main thrust of Frank's argument? In the few cases he chose to explore, when the local authorities would arrest our witnesses on suspicion of a crime, they were unable to get so much as a fingerprint ID from the FBI. These were *police officers*, unable to break through the cover." He straightened and offered a half smile of encouragement. "In some situations, where local police don't know and can't learn that they have a dangerous person in their midst, it may be counterproductive. In your situation, it should be comforting. No one can find out who you are. Not Nick Barber. Not Gary Culbert. *No one.*"

Carly winced at the mention of the names that had brought terror to her life, then reflected on Sam's argument as she idly rearranged the potato salad on her plate. Finally, setting down her fork, she looked up. "I suppose," she murmured, but her skepticism lingered. "It's just that I get so frightened at times."

"Is that what happened this afternoon?"

Puzzled and frustrated, she frowned. "I don't know *what* happened this afternoon. I must have been edgy for some reason."

"Do you think it was Frank's program?"

"Maybe." She shrugged. "I don't know. It could also be the holidays coming up. These will be the first. It's kind of hard not to look back." Though her eyes were averted, her pain was evident. "We used to all get together, my father and brothers and their families and me."

"None of your brothers can get to New York?"

"Naw." She made light of it, but she knew she'd miss them terribly. "It's an expensive trip with the kids and all. I think that we'll try to rotate visits. I'll see my father in New York at Thanksgiving, my brother Jim and his family down south at Christmas, Ted and Doreen and the kids sometime in the spring God knows where. Exciting, huh?"

She made it sound anything but. In total sympathy, Sam felt helpless to come up with a remedy. "You really want to go home, don't you?"

Looking as sad as he'd ever seen her, she nodded. "Yup."

"It wouldn't be smart, Carly."

"I know." She gave a rueful smile. "But that doesn't stop me from wanting it."

This time it was Sam who nodded. He'd feel the same way if, for some reason, *he* couldn't go home. The times he spent in Montpelier had become more and more special with the years. Beyond that, he had Ellen, not to mention Sara and another child on the way. Carly Quinn was alone.

After several quiet moments during which they were both lost in thought, Sam shifted in his seat. "Why don't we get going," he suggested, gesturing for the check. "You can make me a cup of coffee at your place before I hit the road."

It was back in Carly's kitchen, over a second cup, that he finally broached the topic that had been on his mind since dinner's end. "You still don't date, do you?" he asked, stretching back in his chair with studied nonchalance.

Her gaze narrowed in mock reproach. "You're not going to start in on that again, Sam Loomis, are you?"

"You have to admit it's been a while since I mentioned it last," he argued good-naturedly, feeling not at all guilty. "And I've been patient. I've given you time. But you *aren't* dating, are you?"

"You sound like an older brother," she teased.

But he was serious. "No, Carly. Just a friend expressing his concern. When you were in protective custody, you were isolated, in a kind of limbo. It would have been impossible for you to lead a normal life then. But that's over. The trial is over. It's time you returned to the real world. You're young and attractive. You've got so much to offer a man. And you *need* one."

In vain she fought the blush that stole to her cheeks. "I *need* one?" A single auburn brow ventured high beneath her bangs. "Do I look that desperate?"

"You know what I mean," he scolded. "You need companionship. For God's sake, you're afraid to go out at night! A man would be company, protection."

"Ahhh," she drawled. "A knight in shining armor."

"You're not taking me seriously, Carly."

"I am." And she was, suddenly as sober as he. "I've given it lots of thought, Sam. Believe me, I have. I'm busy. There are always things to do for school—reading papers, planning classes. I want to be a good teacher. Honestly, it's better this way for now."

"Better? To sit up here alone, night after night? Hell, you'd never have gone out tonight had I not come over and trundled you off!" He glowered. "Maybe I should turn you over to Greg, after all."

"Hmm?"

"Greg Reilly. My assistant."

She grinned. "That charming fellow with the hungry eyes?"

"You noticed?"

"How could I help but notice. Every time I walk into your office he all but strips me naked." She held up a hand against Sam's scowl. "Figuratively, of course. I certainly wouldn't have to worry about nightmares with Greg around, would I?" she quipped, tongue in cheek. Actually, had the circumstances surrounding her presence in the U.S. marshal's office been different, she might have found Greg Reilly's appreciation to be flattering. Not tempting—just flattering. He was young, perhaps a year or two younger than she was, certainly more appealing than Brozniak, the assistant state's attorney she'd had occasional dealings with in Chicago. "It must be something about law enforcement as a profession that does strange things to you guys," she kidded, then added whimsically, "Actually, I prefer older men."

Sam ignored her humor, picking up his thought where he'd himself broken it moments earlier. His gaze narrowed. "But it's not only the nights, is it? Your weekends must be gruesome. My guess is that in the four months you've been here you've seen just about as much of the area as *I've* shown you. Hmm?"

Carly fingered her spoon. "I've gotten around some."

"Where?" He wasn't about to let up. She wasn't doing much more than existing. It was a waste.

She met his gaze with hesitance. "I've driven down to Plymouth to see the rock, and out to Lexington and Concord. The area's chock full of history. And I've been to the Faneuil Marketplace. You'd never have the patience to let me idle through the shops."

"And you did it? Without getting nervous?"

"Of course." It was a wee stretch of the truth, followed by a regurgitation of the arguments he had given her repeatedly himself. "I'm not *that* bad. I mean, if nothing else, I do look different from Robyn Hart. She had blue eyes and superlong straight hair. There was something—" she searched for the word, recalling an erstwhile wardrobe of peasant shirts, flowing skirts, floppy blazers and faded-to-nearly-nothing jeans "—Bohemian about her. Carly Quinn, on the other hand, is more conventional. She wears her hair at shoulder-length and lets it curl the way God intended.

She has gray eyes. She dresses out of the career shop at Saks. It's not a bad disguise."

"That's the problem, Carly. You've got to stop thinking of it as a disguise. You *are* Carly Quinn now. If you're called back to testify, the *other* will be the disguise."

Those gray eyes widened in alarm. "They haven't contacted you, have they?" Her heart pounded against her ribs. "Will there be another trial?"

He reached across to squeeze her hand. "No. No word of a trial. Not yet, at least. You do know that it's a possibility though?" Without dwelling on it, he wanted her to be prepared.

"Yes." Barber and Culbert had both launched appeals after they'd been convicted. Though the judge had refused them immediate stays of sentence, their appeals went on. She closed her eyes over images of pain. "God, I don't want that. The courtroom. The crowds. The press. Culbert and Barber staring daggers at me. Their lawyers shooting question after question, putting *me* on trial, trying to get me to say that I simply wanted to do someone, *anyone* in because my husband had died in a fire." Her lids flickered up and she focused pleading eyes on Sam. "Matthew died in a hotel half a continent away. We'll never know if it was arson." Her tone grew more agitated. "But we *do* know that Culbert raked in hundreds of thousands in insurance money when he had those buildings burned in Chicago. And people died!" For an instant, she was in that other time. Her expression bore the agony of remembrance. "The smell. God, it was awful. Acrid. Suffocating. Terrifying. . . ."

Sam held her hand tighter. "Take it easy, hon. You're right. We all know what those two did. So does the judge, the jury, the public. But legal processes take strange turns. Even if there *is* a new trial, it doesn't mean the outcome will be any different." He paused. "You know you'd be safe, constantly guarded."

Shuddering with apprehension, she nodded. "Yes."

"Good." He sat straighter. "So. Where were we?"

She saw no point in discussing the possibility of a trial, which was sure to depress her, or in discussing her social life, which was sure to depress Sam. Much as she had to force it, her only out seemed to be in humoring him. "You were telling me that this pregnancy's been tougher for Ellen and that you really ought to head home."

"I never told you that. How come you know so much?"

"I have three sisters-in-law and ten nieces and nephews. It was a safe guess."

"And a definite hint."

She apologized with a tremulous smile. "I really shouldn't keep you any longer. Besides, even if Ellen's not tired, I am." Emotionally, she was beat.

With a sigh of lighthearted defeat, Sam pushed back his chair and stood, taking her arm when she joined him. "Then I'll leave you to your sweet but lonely virgin dreams," he drawled in her ear.

"You're terrible," she chided. "No wonder Ellen's pregnant again, and Sara not yet two."

"Did I tell you that?" he asked, his eyes twinkling. But before she could answer, the doorbell rang. Both heads flew its way. Both smiles faded. "Were you expecting someone?" It was nearly nine o'clock.

"If I was, I'd never have let you razz me as you did," she murmured under her breath. "I have no idea who it could be."

The bell rang again. Sam spoke softly. "It's not the intercom. Perhaps one of your neighbors?" He put an eye to the tiny viewer he'd had installed in her door and stared for several long seconds. Then, reaching a tentative decision, he held up a finger for her to wait while he nonchalantly took a seat in the living room. Then he motioned for her to answer the door. When she hesitated, he repeated the gesture more forcefully. Turning, she put her own eye to the viewer, and froze. But when she looked back Sam was vehement. "Trust me," his eyes said. The palms with which he patted the air told her to be calm, to act as she normally would.

Cautiously she released the upper bolts, leaving only the chain in place as she opened the door those scant few inches. In an involuntary flash, she relived the terror she'd felt in the courtyard earlier that evening. Her knuckles grew white, her knees weak. She was helpless to stem the race of her pulse. For before her, seeming to dominate that narrow slice of hall, stood the tall, dark stranger into whom she'd so unceremoniously barreled in her farcical escape from an imaginary hunter.

Three

"**Y**ES?" SHE ASKED SOFTLY, UNSURELY.

His voice was deep and as strangely lulling as it had been in the courtyard. "Uh, I'm sorry to bother you, but I wonder if I might use your phone. I've just arrived with another load of things and—" he grimaced in chagrin "—it seems that I've locked my keys in the car."

Unhinged, Carly stood stock-still. She had assumed him to be a delivery man, though why, she wasn't sure. Her mind drew up the fleeting image of a carton propped against the door. But it was Friday night. Another load of things? In his car?

Reading her confusion, seeing lingering traces of the fear that had so gripped her earlier, the man smiled. She was lovely. "I'm Ryan Cornell. We'll be neighbors. I'm moving into the apartment just under yours."

"The Amidons's?" She was perplexed. She hadn't known they'd been seeking a buyer, much less sold their place.

"That's right. Actually, I'm renting until they decide whether to live in Sarasota year-round." When she still seemed wary, he elaborated. "They'd been toying with the idea of moving. A place came through unexpectedly, and they felt they had to grab it. It was furnished, so they left most of their things here. If they decide to buy down there, they'll send for the rest."

Carly nodded, wondering how he could possibly have fabricated such a tale. She wanted desperately to believe him, yet she was, by habit, guarded. Standing there, silently staring up at him through the slim opening of the door, she was struck again by his aura of gentleness. A large man. Exquisitely soft brown eyes.

In the background, Sam coughed. Having momentarily forgotten his presence, she looked quickly back. Ryan's gaze flew beyond, only to be thwarted by the meager span of the opening. Not so his perceptivity.

"Oh, I'm sorry. You're not alone." A faint crimson blush edged above his beard. With a contrite grin, he started to turn. "I'll try elsewhere." But the sound of the chain sliding across, then falling, halted his retreat.

The door slowly opened and Carly offered a smile. Sam was there to keep her safe. Besides, Ryan Cornell, awkward in such an appealing way, seemed no more of a threat now than he had to her downstairs in the heat of her panic. She stood back. "Come on in. The phone's in the kitchen." When he hesitated still, she urged him on with a cock of her head.

He took a step forward, looking down at her in gratitude, then stepped into the foyer and, sending an apologetic glance Sam's way, followed her pointing finger to the kitchen. Feeling himself a perfect ass, he lifted the phone and punched out the number of the place he'd called home for the past year. Then he waited, his head down, one hand on his hip, for the phone at the other end to ring.

From an unobtrusive post by the kitchen door, Carly

studied him. Lit generously now, his hair proved to be more brown than black. Though full, it was well shaped and neatly trimmed, as was the close-cropped beard that covered his jaw. Both were rich and well groomed. Indeed, despite her initial, irrational fear when he'd caught her arms downstairs, there was nothing of the scraggly cur about him. Though his sweat shirt was dark and faded, she could now detect its legend. Stretched across the muscled wall of his chest and slightly battered from washing and drying, it read Harvard. Though his jeans were worn, they were clean and hugged the leanest of hips. His sneakers were on the newer side. Just as she paused to admire his height, he glanced over at her, softly, silently, and she sensed that same gentleness she had earlier. When he offered a self-conscious smile, she half returned it.

Then, with the abrupt shift of his expression, and after what must have been eight or nine rings, his call was answered. He tore his eyes away and focused on the floor.

"Yeah." The voice at the other end was hoarse and begrudging.

"It's me, pal. Sorry."

"Ryan? What the—"

"I need a favor." His jaw flexed. He spoke fast and low. "In the kitchen, the cabinet by the fridge. There's a slew of my keys still on the hooks. Find the spares for my car and bring them over?"

"But you've got the damned car, haven't you?"

"Not the keys." He didn't have to elaborate. His brother knew him too well.

"Geez! What did you do, lock 'em in again?"

Ryan tucked his head lower. "Spare me the speech, Tom. Can you run them over or not?"

"Damn it, Ryan." The phone was muffled, dropped,

then grabbed up again. "I thought I was free of you for the night."

"You are. I just need the keys."

"It can't wait till morning?"

"The car's running." Ryan forced the words out under his breath in the hope that Carly wouldn't hear.

With a pithy oath, Thomas Cornell sat up to cast a rueful eye at the woman by his side. "And you can't break in? You know, jimmy the lock with a hanger or something?"

"I've tried. It's not working." Ryan's patience waned. "Come on, Tom. I'm imposing on one of my neighbors—"

"You're imposing on *me*! Do you have any idea what you're interrupting?"

Ryan hadn't been blind to the fair-haired attraction of his kid brother's date. Nor was he blind to the fact that Tom was a skilled playboy who'd easily be able to pick up an hour later where he left off now.

"I think so. Don't forget, I've got a few years on you." He took a deep breath. "I'm parked right out in front. I'll be waiting downstairs in twenty minutes."

Tom tried to argue, but the phone was dead. Muttering something mercifully unintelligible, he rammed the receiver home. Then he looked down at the warm body in his bed. "He's done it again, babe." He sighed, feeling the last of his own passion fade as he lay back to stare at the mirrored image overhead.

The young woman snuggled closer. "Who was that?"

"My brother. You know, the guy who moved out tonight?"

"What's his problem?"

"He needs me."

"So do I." She slid one leg over his thigh.

Yeah, Tom thought, arching a brow, *but you'll forget me tomorrow.* Tossing back the sheet, he rose.

"Hey, you're not leaving me like this, are you?" came the sulky voice from behind.

"I'll be back."

"But, Tom—"

"I'll be back." Heading for his clothes, he crossed the black shag carpet to an oversize leather chair. It too was black, as was fully half of the room's decor. The other half was white. He'd thought it sleek and masculine when he'd done it up three years before. Ryan had thought it tacky from the start. But then, what did Ryan know, he thought angrily as he thrust first one leg then the other into his jeans.

What did Ryan know? A hell of a lot. Though absent-minded enough to lock his keys in his car on a regular basis, Ryan had always been the responsible one, the one with a solid career, the one with a wife and home . . . well, once. Tugging his sweater on over his head, Tom took his brother's side on that one. Alyssa had been a bitch, anyway. Spoiled and demanding. Not that she wasn't half right in her accusation that Ryan was wedded to his work. He was. He was dedicated. And a whiz when it came to the law. He'd certainly come through for *him* on that score.

"Tom . . . ?" This time it was a whining complaint.

He stuffed his feet into his boots, then knelt to rescue the denim from their clutches. "Yeah, babe?"

"Come on, Tom. He'll wait a few more minutes."

"You don't know my brother." *And I do owe him.* Running his fingers through his thick blond hair, he headed at a clip toward the door.

"And if I'm not here when you get back. . . ?" was the taunt.

Tom paused once on the threshold to cast an arrogant glance back. "Then it'll be your loss, babe."

Ryan turned back to Carly, who'd all the while stood silently by the kitchen door. "Sorry about that." He thrust his hands in the pockets of his jeans and looked decidedly sheepish. "I guess you're not the only one I've inconvenienced."

"Can your friend help?" she asked softly, her wariness now held in abeyance. The half of the conversation she'd heard had been utterly believable. Either he was a superb actor, or he had told the truth about his dilemma. Not to mention the fact that Sam remained where he was, sprawled casually on the sofa, apparently unconcerned.

"He'll help. Well—" he took a step toward the door, then cast another glance at Sam "—I'm sorry to have bothered you. With any luck my phone will be in on Monday." He reached the door when Sam finally came to life.

"Can I give you a hand with something?" he asked, rising from the living room to stand behind Carly.

Ryan raised an open palm. "Thanks, but no. I've disturbed you enough." His gaze dropped once more to Carly's face. "Have a good night."

As suddenly as he'd come, he was gone. Sam closed the door, then turned to lean back against it and stare pointedly at Carly. "You didn't know they were moving?" he asked in subtle accusation.

"The Amidons? How would I know a thing like that?"

"Don't you ever talk to your neighbors? You can't be *that* much of a hermit. For Pete's sake, we've checked them all out and they're safe."

She deftly reversed the argument. "Why weren't *you* on top of this? You're supposed to be the one keeping an eye on me. It's your job. Isn't that what you said earlier?"

Realizing he'd come on too strongly, Sam softened. "Of course it's my job, Carly. But I need your help. I can't possibly have people snooping around all the time. It's up to you to alert me to changes like this. Then I can take over and have things checked out."

Feeling duly chastised, she turned away and wandered to the living room to sink into the sofa. Eyes closed, she laid her head back. "You seemed to trust him."

"I know who he is."

Her head came forward, eyes open and wide once more. "You know him? It didn't look like he recognized you."

"I said that *I* know who *he* is." He came around to stand before her. "His name really is Ryan Cornell. He's a lawyer."

A moan slipped from Carly's lips. "Another one of those? I'm beginning to wonder if there isn't an epidemic. A new kind of plague. You know—" she illustrated the point with two walking fingers of one hand "—an onslaught of little men in their natty three-piece suits, all bent on finding the lowest common denominator of humanity."

Sam chuckled. "That's got to be the editorialist in you seeking release. Either that, or you've truly had your fill of the legal profession in the last year."

"A little of both, I'm afraid."

"Well—" he sighed, scratching the back of his head "—it seems that Ryan Cornell doesn't fit the mold. He's not a little man by any measure, and I find it hard to picture him in a natty three-piece suit after—" he tossed his head toward the door "—that."

If Carly didn't know better, she might suspect Sam

Loomis to be jealous of the other's rugged good looks. But she did know better. Sam would simply be doing his job, sizing Ryan up in advance of the phone call he'd be certain to make shortly. Sure enough, before she could begin to ask him what else he knew about her new neighbor, he headed for the kitchen to put through the call.

Fishing a dog-eared piece of paper from his wallet, he ran his eye down the list to one of the newest of the numbers. Then he punched it out. The phone was picked up after a single ring.

"Reilly."

"Greg. Bad time?" Much as he was unsure about his assistant, Sam respected his privacy. It was, after all, Friday night, and it had been a busy week.

Greg Reilly let his feet fall to the floor of the sofa and sat up. "Don't I wish it," he murmured, casting a melancholy eye around his slightly messy, thoroughly lonely living room. "Just catching up on some reading." He set the magazine aside. "What's up?" He knew that Sam wouldn't be calling to shoot the breeze, though at times he wished he would. Sam was a brilliant detective, able to find solutions to problems *he* wouldn't know where to begin on. But then, having served as a detective with the state police before coming to the marshal's service, Sam had ten years on him. As chief deputy, Sam had responsibilities that reflected his talent. It'd be nice to be in his inner circle.

As for himself, he seemed to be forever blowing it. Like today. He'd really hit a raw nerve when it came to Carly Quinn.

"Listen, can you do me a favor?" Sam asked.

"Sure."

"I need information on Ryan Cornell."

"The lawyer?"

"Yeah. You know something?"

Greg took a deep breath and let it out in a hiss between his teeth. "He's one bright man. And a damned good counselor."

"Who says?"

"Fitzgerald says. Dray says. I say."

Fitzgerald was the state's attorney general, Dray a justice of the Superior Court. Greg Reilly had come to the U.S. marshal's service with a load of clout in his back pocket. "You've seen him in action?" Sam asked.

Greg nodded. "Very smooth. Very sharp. Brilliant defense."

"And his character?" Sam's voice spoke of his concern. Greg picked up the ball.

"I know who to call. Where can I reach you?" He'd been on the verge of asking if Sam was still at Carly's house, but had caught himself just in time. The innuendo might have ticked Sam off again. Hell, he'd only been kidding before. He knew Sam was in love with his wife. He had eyes and ears and was vividly aware of those soft calls every day at four.

"I'll reach you," Sam replied, then gave a short, "Thanks," before hanging up the phone. Returning to the living room, he sat down across from Carly.

"Well. . . ?" she asked, tempering a fine line of tension.

"We're working on it."

"Do you know anything, other than that he's a lawyer?"

Sam shrugged. "Not much. I know he's handling more and more criminal work. That's why he looked familiar. Several months back, he defended a member of the governor's cabinet on charges of embezzlement. His face was all over the evening news."

"Did he get an acquittal?"

Sam scowled. "Yes."

"But you think his client was guilty?"

"From where I sat," which was only at his desk reading the newspaper, "yes."

"Then how did he get off?" It was a question born more of indignation than innocence.

"Very simply. The prosecution didn't have solid enough evidence to convince a jury beyond the shadow of a doubt. There wasn't any witness like you to make its case."

The terse reminder of her predicament brought furrows to Carly's brow. "Is Ryan a danger to me? Do you think he might have some connection to Culbert?" More likely Culbert, a high-placed political blackguard, than a lowly thug like Barber. Perhaps both. She wanted to believe neither. "He wasn't terribly threatening just now, even if he did give me a scare downstairs."

"Downstairs?"

Only then did it occur to her that Sam knew nothing of the blockbuster end to her fiasco. "I, uh, ran into him in the courtyard," she began, feeling foolish all over again. "I mean, *literally* ran into him when I thought I was being chased. I'd looked over my shoulder and wasn't watching, and wham. He caught me and kept me from falling." Recalling the events, she gave an involuntary shudder. "My first thought was that he was part of a brilliant scheme, that he'd been waiting right there to catch me. You know, the lamb being, in this case, chased to the slaughter? But he let me go as soon as I'd regained my balance. He was as harmless then as he seemed just now. Wasn't he?"

Pondering her vulnerability, Sam felt the full weight of his responsibility. How in the hell could *he* know about Cornell? If the guy were a faceless shoe salesman or the obscure manufacturer of computer parts, he might feel more confident. But a fairly visible criminal attorney might easily be the target of Gary Culbert's maneuvering. Culbert had been a state legislator before greed had taken over. Though none would admit it now, Sam was sure that he still had friends in high places. And friends in Illinois high places had friends in other high places who could feasibly make calls and pull strings and find weaknesses in a man as the grounds for blackmail. What were Ryan Cornell's weaknesses? He was human. Surely he had some, aside from a knack for locking his keys in his car.

Perhaps it was wishful thinking, but in his gut Sam agreed with Carly. On the surface, Cornell seemed innocent enough.

"I'm sure he is," he said, forcing a smile. Carly was already on edge. There seemed no point in feeding her dark imaginings. He would, however, stop at the office before heading home. With Cornell apparently already installed in the apartment just below hers, Sam wanted fast answers on this one. "We'll check things out. I don't want you to worry." He glanced at his watch. "I should be going."

Pushing herself up from the sofa, Carly walked him to the door. "Thanks for coming, Sam. I guess I did need someone to talk with."

He threw an arm around her shoulder and gave her a parting squeeze. "You get some rest, you hear?"

"I will. See ya."

With a final smile and a thumbs up sign, he was gone. Carly very deliberately bolted herself in and activated the alarm, then turned to clear the cups from the kitchen table.

In that most innocent of ways, Sam was good for her, she mused. He exuded the kind of confidence she needed, yet it wasn't a blind, macho thing. He was thorough. Ryan Cornell would be carefully scrutinized. If there were any possible connection between him and either Gary Culbert or Nick Barber, it would be found. *And what then,* she asked herself as she had so many times before. What if it was learned that her cover *had* been breached? She sighed, laying the cups and saucers in the dishwasher and closing its door. Another name? Another place? It could go on forever. She didn't think she could bear that.

It was like chicken pox, she mused, flipping off the kitchen light, doing the same to all but one of those in the living room, the one she'd leave burning all night, then seeking the haven of her bedroom. As a child she'd been exposed year after year, waiting to get ill, and by the time she'd reached her teens she'd begun to pray for the inevitable if only to eliminate the fear. Now, at times, she felt the same, half wishing Culbert would come after her as he'd threatened. At times, she simply wanted it over! But then, she'd never caught the chicken pox.

Lifting the bell-shaped lid of a round rattan basket, she retrieved her needlepoint, took refuge in the fortress of her corner chair with the phone in arm's reach, and began to carefully weave a silk-tailed needle through the network of ultrafine mesh. It was to be a Christmas gift for her father, a hand-painted canvas of wheat fields at sunset that, when covered with silk and framed in bronze, would capture the vibrant reds and the golden tones that so spoke to her of home. From the time she'd first spotted the piece in a shop on Newbury Street, she'd felt drawn to it. Even now, as she pulled the thread from front to back with slow, even strokes, she felt more peaceful than she had all day.

From the start, she'd found needlepoint to be therapeutic. She recalled vividly her introduction to it. She'd been sixteen at the time, a high-school senior living through the tension of college boards, applications and admissions. When she'd noticed the small eyeglass case in the window of the store in downtown Omaha that Saturday afternoon, it had appealed to her instantly. Not only was it practical, with her three pairs of glasses floating around the house at any given time, but the design had been too right to resist. A robin perched on a tiny branch—she'd loved it. How clearly she remembered the saleswoman's reaction.

"You've done needlepoint before, have you?"

"No."

"No? Then perhaps you ought to consider another design. This particular piece is quite delicate. It takes a lot of skill."

"I know how to sew. And knit. I can do it," she'd responded without hesitation. The thought of learning a new craft excited her. It would be something to divert her mind from the unsureness of the future.

The saleswoman had been far from convinced. "Did you look at the pillow kits on that shelf? They're perfect for a beginner."

But Robyn Lyons had known what she wanted. "I'll take the robin," she'd said gently but firmly. "If you have a good instruction book, I'll take that too. If you don't, I can get something from the library."

She'd left the shop that day with not only the eyeglass case, a supply of Persian yarn and needles and a how-to-book on basic stitchery, but a full stock of determination. In her wake she'd left one saleswoman smug in the conviction that the piece would be a disaster. When her young customer returned a week later, needing nothing more than instructions for blocking her skillfully completed work, the saleswoman had been duly put in her place. And when Robyn had proceeded to purchase a second piece, this time an Aran Isle pillow requiring no less than six different stitches, the saleswoman became the eager teacher. It was the start not only of a hobby that had carried Robyn Lyons through light times and dark, but of a close friendship as well. Sylvia Framisch saw her protégé only during college vacations after that first year, though the two kept faithfully in touch. Long after Robyn had married, she continued to return to the shop during visits home. In turn, Sylvia knew just which canvases to order with Robyn in mind.

Shifting to tuck her legs snug beneath her, Carly wondered how Sylvia fared. She missed her warmth, the friendly talk. It wasn't the same—the elegant Newbury Street shop she now visited once a month or so for supplies. Or perhaps it was she—Carly—who had changed. Robyn had been more outgoing, making friends easily. Carly was, of necessity, more cautious.

Perhaps Sam was right, she told herself. Perhaps she did need to spread her wings further. But it was hard, when she was always on her guard lest she say or do something to betray her true identity. Was loneliness something she'd have to learn to live with? Or would she, in time, feel comfortable enough with Carly Quinn to be able to open up?

There was more, though. It wasn't just loneliness or distrust that caused her to put distance between herself and friends and acquaintances. There was fear. Raw, recurrent fear. Memories of an inferno, a gun, a look of sheer hatred, a threat ground out by a violent soul. Though cloaked at times, the past was ever present.

Sam had asked if she'd explored the Boston area. Yes, she'd done her share of cursory sight-seeing. And she'd gone on occasional jaunts with friends from school. But most often she went out only when necessary, such as to go to the market, the cleaner, the drug store, the library. At other times it was simply safer staying home.

Hearing Sam's disagreement as though he were there, she shook her head sadly. No one could understand why she felt the constant need to glance over her shoulder. No one could understand why she stood far enough back from the trolley tracks to prevent someone's coming from behind and shoving her in front of an oncoming train. No one could understand that tiny flicker of doubt each time she turned her key in the ignition of her yellow Chevette, or why, when sitting in the midst of downtown traffic, she would check twice, three times within minutes to be sure the doors were locked. No one could possibly understand why she would pay more to park in an open-air lot rather than parking for less in a dark, enclosed garage.

No one could possibly understand these things, or feel the mindless terror that prompted them. The gun, the threat, the sudden conviction that death was imminent—even Sam could only begin to sympathize. After all, *he* wasn't the one being hunted!

Take Ryan Cornell. In other circumstances, she might have thought it exciting to have such an attractive man living nearby. Now she could only wonder whether his gentle facade hid another kind of man. What if he *had* been hired to find her? What if he'd taken the apartment below her with the purpose of penetrating the wall she'd built? What if . . . what if Gary Culbert had conjured a far more subtle, far slower, more painful means of revenge?

* * *

In his downtown office, Sam cradled the phone against his ear. "Sid? Sam Loomis calling. Sorry to bother you so late but I need information." Sid Aronski was one of the court officers with whom Sam had a working relationship—a lunch now and then, a bottle of whiskey at Christmas, in exchange for information.

"Who you after?"

"Ryan Cornell."

"Cornell?" There was a note of surprise. "What's he done?"

"That's what I want to know. What *has* he done?"

"Beats me," the court officer returned with a shrug, pushing the cat off the worn hassock to make room for his feet. "Besides win maybe nine cases out of the last ten he's tried."

"That good?"

"That good."

"Any monkey business with juries?"

"Cornell? Are you kidding? He's straight."

"Know anything about him personally?"

"Naw. He's a private guy. Doesn't open up like some of them."

"No lady friends sitting in the back rows drooling?"

"Not that guy. He's got this lady lawyer who assists him sometimes. And the she-reporters love him. Funny, though, but I can't remember him ever showing any interest. In the courtroom, he's got one thing in mind. Getting his client off. He's good at it. Too good. Many more goddamn felons back walking the streets, and we'd do better to lock *ourselves* up for protection."

Sam had spent more than his share of time listening to Sid Aronski's philosophy. He didn't have the patience for it tonight. "Is the guy married?"

"Maybe . . . no . . . hell, I dunno."

"Okay, Sid. Thanks. You've been a help. We'll have lunch sometime soon, yeah?"

"You know where to find me."

Sam had no sooner hung up when he punched out another number. As it rang, he glanced at his watch. It was getting late. He'd really feel bad about disturbing her.

"Hello?" came a groggy voice.

He'd done it. "You were sleeping."

Jennifer Blayne stretched, then blinked and looked around her in surprise. "Sam? Is that you?"

"It's me. Hey, Jen, I'm sorry. I thought maybe I'd catch you just before—"

"God, I'm glad you called." She sat up quickly and thrust a thick mane of hair back from her eyes. "I fell asleep out here on the sofa, fully dressed, every light on in the place."

"You must be exhausted."

"It's been one hell of a week. Between the chemical spill and the Chelmsford murders and that little kid who was pinned under the truck, the station's had me running all over creation."

"That's success." Jennifer Blayne was one of the most visible and popular members of the Channel 4 Eyewitness Team.

"Hah! That's insanity." She yawned. "And you too. What are *you* doing working at an hour like this?"

"Trying to learn what I can about Ryan Cornell."

"Ryan Cornell?" Sam imagined that her voice warmed just a bit. "What about him?"

"What do you know?"

"I wish I could tell you all kinds of spicy little tidbits like the kind of shaving cream he uses or the color of his briefs. Unfortunately, I can't."

Sam cleared his throat and drawled, "No problem, Jen. I really don't care what color his briefs are."

"What *do* you care about?" she returned more quietly, letting the reporter take an edge over the woman.

"That depends. How well do you know him?"

"I've interviewed him. I've seen him at receptions now and again."

"Is he married?"

"Not now."

"But he was?"

"Yes."

"Recently?"

"A year or two ago."

"Is he strapped for alimony?"

"Ryan?" She laughed softly. "Ryan's doing fantastically well. And besides, his wife *is* money. She doesn't need his. Oh, I assume he's giving her something, but it can't be anything hefty."

"Child support?"

"Uh-uh. No kids."

"Does he date?"

"So I'm told," she replied.

"What do you mean? You've never seen him with a date?"

"Nope."

"Think he might be gay?"

The laughter that met his ears this time was a helpless outburst. "Ryan Cornell? Oh, Sam, you're barking up the wrong tree. Ryan Cornell is quite a lover. *That* I got from a colleague of mine who went out with him once. *Just once.* No, there's nothing wrong with him in the lust department."

"Then what is wrong with him?"

"He's a private person. He's very self-contained." Her voice grew more pensive. "He's just come off a bad marriage and seems to want to avoid any kind of commitment to a woman. I honestly think that he's happy enough being a good lawyer. You know," she argued, only half in jest, "sex isn't everything. There are those of us, Sam Loomis—"

"Uh-huh," he cut her off with a smile, unable to resist teasing her for a minute. "You don't have to rationalize, Jennifer. I'm not about to pass judgment on you. If you're tired of being a sex object, that's your problem. If you're swearing off men—"

"Now, did I say that? I know that it's against the rules for you to tell me why you're asking all these questions, but I'll tell you this. If you're planning on taking Ryan Cornell into custody and need a playmate for him, I'll volunteer."

"He turns you on?"

"In many ways. He's a real nice guy."

Sam smiled, feeling more relieved by the minute. "And that's your final word?"

"It is."

"Go back to sleep."

"You bet. Take care."

His smile lingered as he hung up the phone. Jennifer Blayne was a sweetheart; Ryan Cornell could do much worse. But the issue wasn't Ryan and Jennifer, was it? It was Ryan and Carly. Grabbing the receiver once more, he stabbed at the buttons.

"Greg?"

"Yeah. Good timing. I just got through talking with Mertz."

"State committee?"

"Yeah."

"What've you got?"

Greg Reilly proceeded to give him a skeletal dossier on Ryan MacKenzie Cornell. By the time he'd finished,

Sam was satisfied. "Thanks, Greg." The genuine warmth in his tone said far more.

"No problem," Greg said, feeling eminently pleased. "Anything else?"

"Yeah. Have a good weekend."

"You mean you're calling it quits?" he teased gently. "Hell, Sam, it's only ten-thirty. I know you've been working since eight this morning, but—"

"Aw, shut up." Sam chuckled, deciding that the kid had his moments. "See ya." He pushed the disconnect button, then punched out a final call.

The jangle of the phone beside her gave Carly a jolt. Accidentally stabbing herself, she swore softly and whipped the injured finger to her mouth. Then she looked at her watch. She had no more idea who would be calling her at this hour than she'd earlier known who was at the door.

She took a deep breath before reaching for the phone. "Hello?" she asked, sounding miraculously, deceptively calm.

"It's me, Carly."

"Sam?" She exhaled. "You frightened me!" In truth, she'd frightened herself. It happened every time she let her thoughts run along the line they had.

"Nothing to be frightened of. That's why I'm calling."

"You're not home already, are you?" She knew that he lived on the North Shore, a good forty minutes' drive from her place.

"I'm in town."

"In town? Poor Ellen! *In town?*"

"At the office. I wanted to make another call or two about your neighbor."

Carly sat straighter. Strange how she'd been thinking of him too. "You were worried?"

"Not worried," Sam lied, knowing it was for the best.

"Curious. From what I've been told though, he's clear."

"What were you told?"

"That the guy's straight as an arrow. Graduated Harvard Law and has been practising here ever since. He's in his own firm—Miller and Cornell—with three other partners and some six or seven associates. He started out handling most anything that could take him into court, but he's been able to grow more selective. Does a lot of white-collar-crime work. Won't touch the mob with a ten-foot pole. And he's doing very well. Not much cause to suspect he'd resort to shady dealings in smoking out Robyn Hart."

A wave of relief swept over her, leaving her feeling strangely light-headed. "No, I don't suppose so. Well, then, if he comes up asking to use the phone again, I should let him in?"

"Would you let another of your neighbors in?"

"Yes."

"Then I don't see any problem. The guys here will do a more thorough check, and I'll let you know if I come up with anything. But the references were good from three sources just now. I doubt there'll be anything more."

"I can relax," she stated, having already begun.

"Yes." He chose not to enlighten her on the man's personal situation. As it was, he'd said enough on the matter of Carly's social life earlier that night.

"Thanks, Sam."

"No sweat, Carly. I'll be in touch at the first of the week. You'll remember to call me if there's any problem between now and then?"

"Sure. Take care."

She hung up the phone with a smile on her face, feeling buoyant despite the hour. There was, then, nothing to worry about. She'd needlessly gotten herself in a stew.

Setting her needlepoint aside, she ran a hot bath, which she proceeded to lace with a double dose of scented oil. Her clothes fell quickly to the floor. She piled her hair atop her head. Then she stepped in, sank down and stretched out in the luxurious liquid heat, breathing a long, lingering sigh of delight as she laid her head back and closed her eyes.

Security. Relaxation. What precious things they were. She'd been her own worst enemy today. She owed herself a treat tomorrow. A movie? She could take in a matinee. Or she could drive down to the waterfront and take a cruise around the harbor. Would it be too cold? The museum. That was it! If she did everything she had to by noon, she would take her life in her hands and go to the museum.

Four

SATURDAY MORNING DAWNED CLEAR AND SEA-
sonably warm, the kind of rich autumn day when anyone old enough to remember pined for the smell of
burning leaves. Ryan Cornell remembered. He'd been
raised in the verdant Berkshires and knew well the joy
of the leaf pile on the lawn, the delight of running and
jumping and vanishing in its midst, then sitting back to
breathe in that incomparable smell when the pile had
been raked to the curb and lit.

At times like these, he missed that simple life, so
pure, so straightforward, so filled with love. Sighing, he
opened the window farther and leaned out, inhaling
the fresh air; its scent was a poignant reminder of all
he'd lost. Before long would come winter, with its snow
and slush and mess. How he hated that time, coming in
tired and cold at the end of the day to a dark and empty
house. It was just as well Tom was back. It had been a
year, about time he got a place of his own. Perhaps
he'd enjoy city life. More action, more diversion, less
time to brood on all he couldn't change.

A movement beneath him caught his eye, the bob of

a thick auburn ponytail as a slender figure in a sweat shirt, shorts and running shoes moved down the front walk to the street then looked to either side before breaking into an easy jog and crossing to the river path.

Ryan whipped his head in, remembering to duck only after he'd hit the window with a thud. Blindly rubbing the injured spot, he ran to the bedroom and began to rummage madly through an open suitcase. Several knit shirts were tossed aside, as was a hapless pair of jeans. Fishing out his running shorts at last, he tugged them on, hopping precariously first on one foot then the other, then grabbed for his sneakers and laced them in record time. The sweat shirt he'd discarded the night before hung on the doorknob. He swept it up as he ran past and was halfway down the stairs before he'd managed to wriggle into it.

By the time he hit the fresh air he was well warmed up. Breaking into a run, he bolted down the walk, dodged his way across Memorial Drive, and lit into the river path with an enthusiasm he hadn't felt in months. He looked ahead, scanning the path in vain. He glanced down at his watch, only to remember that it was back on the bedside table. At a guess, she had no more than two or three minutes on him.

He quickened his pace, grateful that he'd managed to stay in good shape. But then, running had kept him sane. It was his outlet. Aggression, frustration, help-lessness—he regularly battered them into the ground only to find, with each new day, a rerun. Perhaps today would be different.

His eyes studied the path ahead as it gently rounded the river. To either side the Saturday-morning traffic had begun to pick up. Where was she? Had she possibly turned off and headed toward Harvard Square? But why would someone in her right mind do that, when the river run was straight and clear and, with its own path, far less hazardous than the side streets?

Then he saw her, a small figure ahead on the bridge crossing to the other side of the Charles. He ran faster, wondering whether he would collapse when he finally caught her, but pushing himself nonetheless. Her pace was steady. She seemed to be enjoying the day as much as he would have had he not been engaged in this absurd chase. He didn't know what had gotten into him. He'd stopped chasing women years ago. This one was his neighbor. That could be good news, or bad. C. J. Quinn, said her mailbox. Carly, said one of their neighbors, who had come up the front path the evening before as Ryan had stood staring after her.

"Uh, excuse me?" he'd called out as the older gentleman passed, a briefcase in his hand, the evening edition under his arm. "Could you tell me . . . uh, I wondered . . . the woman who just ran inside . . . does she live here?" The outburst had been impulsive, devoid of pride or pretense.

The gentleman stopped on the single stone step before the door. He looked once at the fast-disappearing figure within, then back at Ryan. "Is there a special reason you ask?" he countered tactfully.

It was enough of a positive response for Ryan—in fact, he admired the man's protectiveness. Casting an explanatory glance toward the carton by the door, he approached. "I'm just moving in myself. She, uh, she seemed frightened by something. I just wondered if she'll be all right."

"Just moving in? The Amidons's place?"

"That's right."

A firm hand was extended his way. "I'm Ted Arbuckle. My wife and I live in 103."

He met the clasp. "Ryan Cornell. And. . . ?" He cocked his head toward the lobby.

"Carly Quinn. She's in 304. Nice girl. Quiet."

"Will she be all right? I mean, is there someone up there waiting for her?"

"For Carly?" He shook his head. "Nope. She's alone. But she'll be all right. Seems pretty self-sufficient."

Self-sufficient, perhaps. Spry, without a doubt. He admired her stride as he slowly closed in. She ran lightly, with an athletic kind of grace. Not quite deer-like, since she was more petite than long legged, but then there had been sheer terror on her face last night, as though she were indeed facing the hunter with the bow.

Carly heard the rhythmic slap of his step as he approached and shot a wide-eyed glance over her shoulder. He felt a moment's remorse that he'd been the one to frighten her again. Then he moved forward, passed her, glanced back and slowed.

"Hi," he offered, relieved to be able to match her saner pace.

She stared at him for a minute, as though trying to control some inner urge to race onto Storrow Drive, arms waving wildly, to stop the nearest driver and seek help. He hadn't quite decided whether she was afraid of him, or of men in general when, with the faintest tilt of her head, she slowly smiled.

His day was made. "You do well," he said, dropping his gaze momentarily to the slender legs that hadn't broken pace.

Her smile lingered to soften her gibe. "For a woman?"

"Now, now, I didn't say that," he chided with the gentleness she seemed to inspire. "There's many a man who would have been sitting back there on the edge of the bridge trying to catch his breath after having come half the distance you have." He paused, then took the plunge. "I've been trying to catch you for a mile."

Her smile faded slowly as wariness returned. "You have? Do you run often?"

"Every day. But never here before. And never with someone else. Two firsts," he declared on a triumphant note.

She couldn't resist looking up at him again. His grin, a generous slash of white through his beard, was so hopelessly boyish that, quite against her will, her wariness seemed to lessen. Tearing her eyes away, she sought the path once more.

"You must run often yourself," he speculated.

"When I can." It was evasive enough, she mused, yet not far from the truth. She'd been running since Matthew's death, when she'd wanted nothing more than to exhaust herself into oblivion. It had worked at first, until she'd built up her strength and discovered the sheer exhilaration of the sport. Now she ran as often as possible. Since fall had come, though, the opportunity had grown progressively more elusive. She didn't dare run in the dark, thus precluding most school days. Which left the weekends.

Ryan was silent for a time, wondering how much he dared push. Arbuckle had said she was quiet. Ryan might use the words private, or aloof, even distrustful, or skittish, from the looks of the tightly clenched fists that moved back and forth with her steady stride. Somehow he didn't want to think she was simply disinterested. "You always run by the river?" he asked.

Carly looked up and around. The sky was a pale shade of blue, even paler where the sun skipped over the skyline of Boston, seeming to jump from building to building as her own perspective changed. "It's open here. And peaceful. I leave the cars to battle one another."

Ryan smiled his satisfaction. "I was counting on that. For a while I thought you'd turned off on a side street." At her look of puzzlement, then alarm, he quickly explained. "I saw you leave the building just as I was getting dressed." A slight fabrication, he reasoned, but harmless. "When I got outside, you'd disappeared. I thought that if I could catch up with you, you'd show me the best place to run."

"You found it yourself then, even before you saw me again. Your instinct was good."

He wouldn't tell her about the more lascivious instinct that had set him running double time. His thighs and calves would be telling enough later. For now, he simply wanted to get her talking.

"Do you ever race?" he asked.

"Running?" She crinkled up her nose and he felt a corresponding tickle inside him. "No. I'm not that good. I just do it for fun. You know, exercise, fresh air, 'sweeping out the cobwebs' kind of thing."

"How far do you go?"

She cocked her head toward the buildings rising ahead. "Boston University. I'm almost there."

"What is it . . . four miles round trip?"

Her ponytail slapped her neck with each stride, mirroring the gentle bob of her breasts. "I think so."

He focused on the ponytail. "You can do more, you know."

"Oh?" A smile played at the corners of her mouth.

"Sure. You're barely winded. Why not try for another mile?"

"There's still the return trip to make."

"You can do it. Come on."

She looked up at him. His good-natured smile egged her on. "What if my legs give out on me three-quarters of the way back?"

"I'll carry you."

"You're that strong?"

"You're that light."

When she would have asked him how he knew, she blushed and looked down. Not much was hidden by her running shorts, certainly not the slim, bare lengths of her legs. And she was indeed far shorter then he was. Oh, yes, he could easily carry her. Without the slightest effort, he could toss her over his shoulder and cart her to a van waiting somewhere ahead. Her blush washed out and disappeared.

Ryan instantly sensed the change. "Are you all right?" he asked, with the same soft concern in which he'd intoned those very words the day before.

Struggling against the silent demons that seemed to have struck again, Carly reminded herself of Sam's phone call. Ryan was honest. Safe. "Straight as an arrow," were Sam's precise words. It was time she stood up to her insidious suspicions.

"I'm fine," she murmured, forcing a smile.

"Suddenly tired?" he teased lightly. "Givin' up the race so soon? Tell you what. If you can keep up with me all the way back, I'll spring for breakfast."

"Don't eat breakfast." She returned his banter more easily, steadied by the cadence of her pace.

"Then lunch."

"Can't. Too much to do." If she hoped to get to the museum, she'd have to hustle through other chores as it was.

"You've got to eat sometime."

"I'll grab something on the run."

"That's not healthy."

She shrugged and dashed him a sheepish smile that made his insides tingle. "I'll live." Then she tossed her head back. "This is it for me." She made a wide circle around the lamp post she'd earmarked as her turning point, but was caught by the wrist and gently stopped.

"Dinner at Locke-Ober's?" His eyes gleamed. "How does that strike you?"

"Very extravagantly."

"It's yours for another mile in and then the return."

They stood facing each other, breathing deeply from the first leg of the run. "Why?" she asked softly, tipping her head up to eye him skeptically. "Why would you want to run with me? I'm sure you normally go much faster."

He shot her a mischievous grin. "Only when I'm try-ing to catch someone." Then the grin faded and he grew startlingly earnest. "I'd like the company," he said simply.

The cars whizzed by them on Storrow Drive, much as life did to two people marking time. Carly felt it then, a kind of kinship with Ryan. In his eyes was a warmth, a sincerity, a loneliness she would never have detected had she not been so thoroughly familiar with it herself.

"Locke-Ober's?" she asked with a hesitant smile.

"Ever been there?"

She shook her head.

"Lobster Savannah . . . shrimp mornay. . . ."

Her smile grew coy. "I'm listening."

"Caviar. Hearts of palm. Chateaubriand."

"Uh-huh?"

"A '79 Châteauneuf-du-Pape Blanc."

"Blanc?" She whistled. "You don't fool around."

"Nope."

She hesitated for a final minute, then cautioned, "I couldn't make it tonight."

"That's okay." He smiled, feeling suddenly victorious. "We could make it next week, the week after, any time that's good for you." Strange, he half wanted to put it off. The anticipation would be thoroughly enjoyable. It had been too long since he'd had something to look forward to. And, after all, there was no cause to rush. He wanted her to be comfortable, confident. Perhaps it was better to wait.

Carly's decision had nothing to do with caviar, lobster, or wine. It was based simply on that strange flicker of kinship she felt for Ryan Cornell. "You're on," she said quietly. Then, cocking her head toward Boston, she raised her brows questioningly. When he gave a smug nod, she broke into stride. He was right beside her. It was a surprisingly reassuring thought.

For the most part they ran in silence. Carly's thoughts were on the pleasure of the day and how secure she felt just then. Ryan's thoughts were on Carly and the world of questions he wanted to ask. But she seemed reticent even now to say too much. He couldn't help but wonder what made her so.

The extra mile he had suggested brought them in view of the first of the Saturday sailboats. "Look. Pretty, isn't it?"

She nodded and gave a smile that dimpled her cheeks becomingly. "You mean to say I've been missing this all along?"

"You bet. Actually, it's kind of late in the season. There won't be too many boats out. Most of them are already drydocked." They ran on for a bit, enjoying the view, before he ventured to speak again. "You ought to see it at the height of the season. On a clear day, especially at sunset, it's a beautiful sight."

"You've seen it at sunset?"

"My office overlooks the river."

She directed her bobbing gaze toward the downtown skyline. "Which one is yours?"

"You can't see it from this angle. We're too low. It's on the other side of the State House." He took a breath between strides. "If you'd care to run a little farther—"

Her sharp sidelong glance shut him up. The sight of an office building was obviously less enticing than Locke-Ober's. But then, he didn't really blame her. Though relatively new and elegantly decorated, it was . . . an office. Wasn't one law office the same as the next? It was, after all, what went on within its walls that set it apart. And Miss Carly Quinn certainly had no call to see that.

Miss? Or Mrs.? Ryan cast a fleeting glance toward her left hand, waiting for it to come forward in alternate rhythm with its mate. No. There was no band. But there . . . on the right . . . that wide gold band he'd seen last night. She'd obviously been married. A European arrangement? But she lived alone. Separated? Divorced? He found it hard to believe she'd failed at marriage. She seemed quiet and agreeable, far different from so many of the strident women with whom he worked each day. Could it have been her marriage that had instilled such wariness in her? It didn't seem possible. What man in his right mind would harm, even threaten, as gentle a creature as she? Unless her husband had not been all there. Lord only knew he'd seen enough of them!

On reflex, he raised a hand to rub his bearded jaw. Oh, he knew firsthand about crazy husbands. One had nearly put an end to his career, not to mention his life. As if he'd ever have considered bedding a client . . . and *that* woman? Never!

"Hello? Hello? Are you there?"

The breathy voice by his side brought him back to

reality. He looked down and smiled in relief. "Sure, I'm here."

"Could've fooled me for a minute there." She crinkled up her nose. Again it made him melt. "Can we turn yet?"

He looked around in surprise to find that they'd just about reached the spot he'd had in mind. "Uh, sure. This is far enough."

"Getting tired?" she teased in an effort to erase what had appeared to be anger from his face. It disconcerted her. She liked it better when he smiled, which he proceeded to do with devastating appeal.

"Tired? Me?" Taking her elbow, he propelled her around, dropping his hold when she matched his gait, heading home. "I'll have you know that you're running with none other than the star of varsity track and field."

"Harvard?" she asked as her eyes spanned his chest. Faint rivulets of sweat marked a charcoal path down its center.

Looking down, he ran his palm across the faded letters. "This thing has seen better days." He chuckled. "So have I, for that matter. There was a time when I used to marathon. No more."

"Are you sorry?"

He pondered the question for a minute, thinking how much more pleasant it was to run like this, totally relaxed, than to run with one eye on the clock. "Sorry? Not really. Anything like that involves a kind of obsession. It can be all-consuming if you do it right. But I had other interests that made their demands. I couldn't do it all."

She assumed he spoke of the law, an obsession in itself. Almost against her will, she felt herself stiffen. It seemed impossible that this man, as surprisingly companionable as he was, should be grouped with those others she'd had the displeasure of meeting during the trial. But of course he might be different. John Meade had been different. As the prosecutor assigned to the Culbert-Barber case, he'd been kind and fair to her. His assistant, Brozniak, was something else. He'd wanted nothing more than to get her into his bed. Some obsession!

"Hello, hello?"

At his miming call to attention, she dashed a glance up at Ryan, whose grin brought her quickly from her trance. "Oops, I left you for a minute there, didn't I?"

"Just so long as it's not *me* you're angry at."

"I may be furious at you later. I'm not used to running this far. I'm apt to be crippled when my calves stiffen up."

"Then we can share my Ben-Gay," he returned, undaunted. "Just stamp on the floor three times and I'll bring it up."

"Is that a promise?"

"You bet."

With a soft chuckle, he looked forward again. They were back in familiar territory now; it wouldn't be long before they reached the apartment and went their separate ways. It might be his last chance for a while to find out more about her. Then he looked to his side and saw the serenity of her expression and he didn't have the heart to disturb it. It beckoned to him, that light and billowy cloud of contentment that hovered above them, between them, large enough to envelop them both. Unable to resist, he yielded. For now, it was enough.

He didn't talk further, nor did she. Rather, they ran in time with each other, comfortably and easily, finding strength in silent partnership. Ryan touched her elbow once to guide her across the street, then dropped his hand as they entered the courtyard and slowed to a breathless walk.

"Good show!" he panted through a grin, leaning down to brace his hands on his knees. His hair hung wet on his brow, giving him an eminently masculine look.

Carly flexed her legs, walking in small, idle circles. "Not bad yourself," she gasped, then splayed her fingers over the muscles of her lower back in support. "Why is it . . . that it's easier to . . . talk when you're . . . running, than when you stop?"

Straightening, he mopped his forehead with a long, muscled arm. "I'm not sure . . . but you're right. I think it must be a . . . kind of illusion. You know, we assume . . . that the words will be broken when we run, so the mind and body make . . . their own connections. We can talk even though our breathing is choppy. But when we stop, our breathing by . . . comparison seems that much rougher."

Carly nodded. She stood taking deep, long drags of air in an effort to ease her laboring lungs. After a minute, when she seemed even shorter of breath, it occurred to her that something else was at work deep within. Apprehension . . . anticipation . . . she had no intention of sticking around to find out.

"Well," she breathed, with feigned nonchalance. Her voice seemed unusually high; she was grateful to be able to blame it on the run. "I'll be going."

Ryan reached out, pausing just short of touching her. "Look, Carly—"

Her sharp stare cut him short. "You know my name," she whispered, appalled. She hadn't told him; she was sure of that.

Unable to comprehend her sudden shift from calm to

coiled, Ryan eyed her in puzzlement. He kept his voice gentle. "Of course, I know your name. It's on your mailbox."

"Not my first name."

"Ted Arbuckle filled me in on that. Listen, it's no big thing. You would have told me your name, wouldn't you have? I mean, I hope you weren't going to have me call you Ms. Quinn," he drawled in soft mockery, "through an evening at Locke-Ober's." His lips twitched coaxingly at the corners.

He was right, of course. She was being oversensitive and suspicious. Always suspicious. She hated herself for it. Suitably chastised by Ryan's teasing, she looked away in self-reproach. "Of course not," she murmured. "It's just that I didn't expect you'd ask around."

"It was really only a fluke," he explained. "Arbuckle came up the walk yesterday right after we collided. I pointed after you, wanting to make sure you were all right. As a matter of fact, he wouldn't even admit that you lived here until I'd introduced myself. It was then that he called you by name.

It was all so perfectly logical. She grinned sheepishly. "If I didn't know better, I might suspect you'd hit him with a few of those leading questions you lawyers are known for."

"We lawyers?" As the tables turned, Ryan looked at her skeptically. "And how did you know I was a lawyer?"

Too late, Carly realized her error. She looked up at him, swallowing hard. "My, uh, my friend last night recognized you from some case a few months ago. You were on television a lot?"

"The Duncan case." He nodded. "And your friend? Who was he?" It was one of the questions he'd been aching to ask. Now she'd inadvertently given him the opportunity. He had to admit that he felt slightly guilty. His interest in her friend had nothing to do with the Duncan case or the fact that her friend had recognized him. It was pure jealousy.

Fortunately Carly had spent enough time with Sam, particularly when she'd first arrived, to know precisely how to introduce him. They'd been over it many times. It was nothing more than a version of the truth.

"His name is Sam Loomis. He's a good friend of mine."

"Do you date him?"

"Date? Not in the sense you mean."

"Then in what sense?"

"In the sense of friends. Period."

"And he doesn't want it differently?" Ryan couldn't believe it wasn't so. Even now, amid the compulsion that kept him questioning her when he knew he should let up, he wanted only to reach out and smooth a stray curl from her cheek. With her hair caught loosely up in a ponytail and her face damp and makeup free, she looked no more than twenty, until one looked into her eyes. They were older, more knowing. It was one of the things he found so intriguing. That fleeting look of sadness, of pain and fear and understanding. Once again he wondered what she'd been through in life to have been so thoroughly seasoned.

"What is this?" she teased uneasily. "An interrogation?"

The edge in her voice, underscoring the flicker of apprehension in her eyes, brought him to his senses. He dropped his head in an outward show of contrition, then sighed, looked up and smiled more gently. "No. We lawyer types get carried away every so often." When her lips remained taut, he went on. "Actually, it had nothing to do with lawyer types. That was *me* wanting to know about *you*."

"About Sam," she corrected softly.

"About Sam as he relates to you. What I *really* want to know," he murmured hastily, helplessly, "is why you wear a wedding band, and whether you're involved with Sam or anyone else. I want to know if you're free."

"Free?" Her voice was weak, seeming to come from far away. Her eyes grew sad beneath the weight of memories. As she looked away, her gaze fell to the leaves beneath the trees, leaves that had been alive and aflame with color mere days before, yet now lay drab and dried, like cold ashes in the hearth. "No," she whispered without looking up, "I don't think I am." Lost in a trance, she headed for the door.

She was through the lobby and on the stairs before Ryan went after her.

Five

"CARLY, WAIT!" CATCHING THE DOOR JUST before it closed, he ran through, crossing the lobby in two strides, taking the first three steps in another. Reaching up, he grabbed her hand. He spoke more softly then. "Carly, please. Don't just run off like that."

She kept her head tucked low. "I've got to go," she whispered, but didn't remove her hand from his.

"Not yet," he murmured, climbing another step just until they were at eye level. "We haven't set a date."

She raised her head slowly. "A date?"

"For dinner. Locke-Ober's?"

Her gaze dropped to the railing where her free hand had tightly anchored itself. "Maybe that's not such a good idea."

"Why not? It'd be fun. Don't you need that sometimes?"

"I do. And I have it sometimes. It's just that. . . ." How could she explain her sudden fear, when she didn't understand it herself? Ryan was no threat to her in the usual sense of the word. She accepted that, as Sam had told her to do, as her own instinct had told her to do.

But there was something new now, something related to the rapid beat of her pulse, to the warming feel of his hand on hers, to the fact that when she looked into his eyes she didn't want to look away. "It's just that I'm really *not* free."

Sensing her weakness, since it was his own as well, he offered a soft challenge. "Can you look me in the eye and tell me that?"

She hesitated, then her eyes slowly met his. Her expression was an amalgam of emotions, not the least of which was regret. "I'm not," she whispered in anguish.

Glancing down at her hand, he passed his thumb over her ring. "You don't live with your husband."

"No. And I'm not attached to anyone else," she added, anxious to head off the question she was sure would come. "But I have other things, other responsibilities. I really can't let myself get involved."

"It's just a dinner, Carly. What harm can come of that?"

But he knew. He felt it himself, lured and captured by something far deeper in her wide gray eyes than the promise of companionship, of easy conversation, of a smile. He'd never had quite this reaction to a woman before, this sense of glimpsing a true treasure worth seeking. He felt suddenly stunned and frightened in his way, though he couldn't turn his back as she had done. Very slowly, he climbed another step until he gazed down at her.

Carly tipped her head up as he rose, helpless to either look away or escape. Her mouth felt dry; she swallowed hard. She felt the warmth of his gaze as it seared her eyes and cheeks before sliding to her lips in a vibrant caress. Catching in a sharp breath, she silently pleaded for him to stop. She couldn't handle this kind of attraction, simply couldn't handle it.

But he didn't let go. His hand turned once on hers to cradle it protectively. His thumb moved lightly on her palm. "I won't hurt you," he murmured. "I couldn't hurt you. I don't want you to be frightened."

"But I am!" she countered in a frantic whisper, all too aware of his long, lean body mere inches from her own. "Please, Ryan. Please let me go."

He dropped her hand, but only to gently touch her face. "I can't do that. I'd never forgive myself."

"But I can't be who you need! You don't know me. You don't know me at all! Leave me be, Ryan. Please?"

He stared at her then for what seemed an eternity before slowly shaking his head. The backs of his fingers caressed her cheek; he ran a trembling thumb across her lips. He hesitated, entranced by the unadorned softness of her mouth. Then, yielding to a need as strong as any he'd ever known, he lowered his head.

But Carly's fingers were against his lips, holding him back at that last moment. "No!" she cried on the edge of panic, then forced her voice to a whisper when she felt his compliance. "I can't handle this now. I'm sorry, but I can't." She was aware of her fingers on his mouth and lingered for that briefest instant to savor his maleness, the soft bristle of his mustache and beard, the strength of his lips, before letting her hand drop to her side.

"Can you tell me why?" When she shook her head, he went quickly on. "How can I fight something if I don't know what it is?"

"I'm sorry," she whispered, finally managing to avert her gaze. Fearing that if she lingered she might never have the chance again, she turned and ran up the stairs.

Ryan's voice carried clearly upward. "I'll fight anyway, y'know!" He watched her round the second-floor railing and start toward the third, and raised his voice accordingly. "I don't give up easily!" Then he leaned over the railing with his head tipped way back, reluctant to lose sight of her. His voice echoed in the silence. "I can play dirty. . . . !"

If he'd hoped to appeal to her sense of humor, he failed. The quiet opening and shutting of her door was the only response he got. Long after he knew she was once again entombed in her private world, he stood looking up.

Finally, accepting temporary defeat, he dropped his head forward and began the slow climb. Whereas when he'd bounded in after her, he'd had all the energy in the world, now he felt drained, discouraged, impotent. That was it. Impotent. It was a chilling feeling, one he'd experienced only once before in his life. That had been the night Alyssa had miscarried. He recalled every agonizing moment, from the instant he'd come home to find her doubled over in pain to that later one, when the doctor had sadly shaken his head. He'd felt so helpless then, as he did now. And he barely knew Carly Quinn!

Eyes dark and puzzled, he let himself into his apartment, closed the door, then passed distractedly to the bedroom. It was nice enough, he mused. The whole place was nice enough. Clean. Comfortable. But it wasn't home.

Home was. . . . Where was it? It wasn't Tom's place, which he'd used only for the year. It wasn't the old house in the Berkshires where he'd grown up. And it certainly wasn't the house he'd shared with Alyssa. Not anymore, at least. He hadn't set foot there in a year. Nor did he miss it. With its four massive columns in front and its twelve silent rooms within and its three acres of land to keep mowed and limed and landscaped, it had been far too pretentious for him from the start. But Alyssa had wanted something befitting la crème de la crème of society. She had it now, for better or worse. Perversely, he wondered whether the termites had made headway on the gardener's shed. Then, feeling minor remorse, he headed for the shower.

An hour later he was buried in work in his downtown office, as he'd been every Saturday for years. It wasn't that the work couldn't wait. While that might have been true when he'd first started out, when he'd had to bust his tail to ensure the success of the firm, things had changed. His reputation was established. His practice thrived. He had reliable lawyers under him, hand picked, personally trained. Oh, yes, his work could wait. But there was nothing he rather do. He loved the law. Perhaps Alyssa had been right when she'd accused him of making his work his mistress.

It was late when he returned to Cambridge, later than he'd expected. He'd spent the afternoon in the law library plotting his arguments for an upcoming fraud case and lost track of the hour. Now, rounding the block a second time in search of a parking space, he cursed the impulse on which he'd accepted the Crowley's invitation. A dinner party. Black tie and tails, no less. It was the last thing he needed! No, he caught himself, the last thing he needed was the eligible female they would inevitably pair him with.

Thin lipped, he started around the block again, only to slam on his brakes when the taillight of a car by the curb lit up, telling of its imminent departure. Shifting deftly into reverse, he backed up and waited, watching with growing dismay as the driver proceeded to comb her hair and apply lipstick, then fiddle in her purse for an elusive candy before finally pulling out. Muttering snide remarks under his breath, Ryan quickly took the space, then slid from his silver BMW and headed down the block.

Halfway to the courtyard he stopped and looked up. That was his apartment on the second floor, hers on the third. It was at the windows of the latter that his eyes held.

Carly Quinn. The thought of her was like a gentle breeze, easing his tension instantly. She was different, refreshing, in spite of the mystery that seemed to haunt her. He'd have given up work today for *her*, had she agreed to let him take her to lunch.

Her living-room light was on, shining warmly through the woven drapes. As he watched, a shadow passed before them. His gaze sharpened, but there was nothing more. Lowering his eyes at last, he resumed his walk. In the courtyard, his pace quickened. By the time he reached the stairs, he was filled with resolve.

Bypassing the second-floor landing, he was on the third in no time. He rapped lightly on her door. Then he waited, staring down at the leather of his loafers, listening for any sound that might come from within.

From her comfortable perch in a deep corner of the sofa, Carly stared at the door. She wasn't expecting anyone. She wasn't dressed for company. Her eye fell to the long terry robe that covered her legs curled beneath her. Then the knock came again, and she slowly put aside the needlepoint she'd picked up moments before.

Padding barefoot to the door, she laid a timorous hand on the jamb and put her eye to the viewer. Her heart began to hammer. It was Ryan. Resting her forehead against the wood, she sighed in frustration. If she were in her right mind, she would return to the sofa and let him knock until his knuckles grew sore. But he wouldn't give up, and she would only have more explaining to do when she finally opened the door.

Slowly, she released the bolts. Then she inched the door open, using her body as a shield to her apartment. It would be a none-too-subtle hint that he wasn't invited in, a hint in keeping with the hours of contemplation she'd put in that afternoon. To her dismay, she'd thought of little else but him as she'd wandered from room to room in the museum. None of the American painters or the French or the Dutch had distracted her for long.

Her conclusion? Ryan Cornell was a dangerous man.

She was never more sure of that than when she gazed out at him now. Standing as tall as ever at her door, he wore a shirt, tie and slacks. One side of his blazer was pushed back to allow his hand burial in his pants' pocket. He looked calm and relaxed, and unconscionably handsome.

"Ryan?" She greeted him warily.

"Hi, Carly." He grinned, as though unaware that there had ever been an iota of tension between them. "Listen, I hate to do this to you again . . . but I wonder . . . I've got to make this quick call. Would it be too much of an imposition if I used your phone again? I mean, I won't be long. I know you've got plans."

The first of her deceptions had come back to haunt her. She'd been vague enough, if misleading. The plans she had were for a safe, quiet evening at home. Ryan must have assumed she'd put on her robe as a prelude to dressing up. Even now, she didn't have the courage to correct his misconception. Yet she felt contrite.

"It's all right," she murmured, standing back for him to enter. It was the least she could do to make up for the deception. "Help yourself."

He tossed a light "Thanks" back over his shoulder as

he made for the kitchen. In a moment's indulgence, she watched him go, admiring the way his blazer fit his broad shoulders to perfection, the way his slacks moved with his stride, falling to just the right spot at his heel. She wondered if he'd been working. No natty three-piece suit? Then she tore her gaze away and retreated to the sofa to pretend nonchalance to match his calm.

In the kitchen, Ryan lifted the phone and punched out the number of his office. The connection clicked, then rang. As a matter of show, he held the phone to his ear, while his eye closely studied his surroundings. Everything was new and clean, from the round butcher-block table with its white director's chairs and the Plexiglas napkin holder with its mated salt and pepper shakers, to the shining copper-bottomed pots and pans suspended from a pegboard panel. It was a bright and airy kitchen, fresh out of *Metropolitan Home*, very beautiful, very proper. Something was lacking, though. He couldn't quite put his finger on it. It didn't look . . . lived in. It lacked the small personal touches he would have expected from a woman as intriguing as Carly. It lacked . . . history.

Puzzled, he turned his gaze toward the living room. She sat on the sofa with her back to him, occupied with whatever—was it sewing—she'd apparently been doing when he'd knocked on her door. His eyes wandered, taking in the room at a glance. Again, everything was perfect. Modular sofa, marble tables, wall prints, plush carpet. Too perfect. Where was *she* in all of it? If he'd hoped to learn about her through her home, it seemed he'd been thwarted again. Other than that she could afford to live in style, he knew nothing more now than he had before. And he grew all the more curious.

Replacing the receiver on its hook, he entered the living room just as Carly looked up from her work.

"No luck?"

He shook his head. But then, he hadn't expected luck. The office would have been dark and locked up hours ago. "I guess I've missed them. What's that you're doing?"

"Needlepoint."

He took a step closer, coming up behind the sofa to lean over her shoulder. "It's very pretty."

Not trusting the tremor in her hands, she spread the canvas flat on her lap to examine her progress. "I'm working with silk. It's a challenge. The threads separate and the stitch can come out lumpy if you don't pull the strands evenly." She ran a slender finger over the field of gold. "It's rewarding, though."

Ryan was as intrigued by the piece as he was by the finger that caressed it. "What will you do with it when you're done?"

"Have it framed. It's a gift for my father."

"He lives nearby?"

"No." Willing her hands to steadiness, she picked up her needle once more. Though she'd probably have to rework each stitch when he left, it suddenly seemed safer to have her hands and eyes occupied.

"Then you don't see him often?"

She shook her head, but didn't look up. She heard Ryan's sigh, knew that he'd straightened and was looking around the room. There was nothing here to betray her. There was nothing *anywhere* in the apartment to betray her.

"Well," he breathed softly, "I'd better be going."

"On your way out?"

"Actually, in. I've been working all day."

She looked up then and caught a glimpse of fatigue

in the depth of his gaze. "Do you always work on Saturdays?" she heard herself ask, knowing she should let him go, yet reluctant.

"It's a good time to get things done. The courts aren't open. The office is quiet. Clients are too busy doing other things to keep me on the phone for hours. I rely on my weekends to clean up the mess of the week."

"I know the feeling. You work Sundays too?"

"At home. I've got a pile of papers that I've got to get to tomorrow. But first I've got to make some headway unpacking the boxes of clothes and other things I moved in yesterday." He rubbed the taut muscles at the back of his neck. "Your place looks a damned sight better than mine at this point."

She grinned. "I have this terrific vacuum cleaner with a self-drive feature. You turn it on, sit back on the sofa with your feet up—" she added a lower aside "—it tends to munch on toes—" then returned her tone to its normal pitch "—and watch it do all the work."

"Does it pick up clothes from the floor?"

"None you'd want to wear again."

He waved his arm in disinterest. "Then you can keep it. I need something that will *really* clean."

"It sounds like you need a personal maid. Used to the fine life, are you?"

He saw the teasing in her eyes, heard the warmth in her tone and found infinite pleasure in having been able to make her relax. "The fine life?" he asked, his lips twitching. "The fine life makes for idle minds, double chins and very boring dinner conversation. As far as I'm concerned, you can take the fine life and shove it. And with that bit of opinionated drivel, I'll take my leave." He paused. "Will you be running tomorrow morning?"

"Yes." It slipped out before she realized what she'd done.

His brows rose in question. "Would you like to . . . ?" He cocked his head toward the door, his invitation obvious.

"Uh, I'm not sure. I don't know just when I'll be going."

Reluctant to push his luck, Ryan nodded. Then he opened the door. "I'm planning to head out at eight, then pick up the newspaper on my way back. I know it's kind of early for a Sunday morning, but if you feel like the company. . . ." His voice trailed off. The invitation could stand by itself. With a wave and a prayer, he shut the door behind him.

Carly gave it much thought. Ryan appealed to her. He intrigued her. He amused her. He also frightened her. Since Matthew's death, she had never been as naturally drawn to any person. Her relationship with Peter had been different—deep and meaningful, if devoid of heat. But heat was an early sign of fire. At the thought, she shuddered.

With the struggle she was waging to adapt to her new life, involvement with Ryan was the last thing she needed. She'd had Matthew and the all-abiding love they'd shared. She'd had Peter and the warmth of an affection based on similarity of interest. She'd had more in the past ten years than many a woman had in a lifetime. More love. More grief. It always seemed to end badly. She couldn't let Ryan in for that.

What the mind resolved, however, the heart could overturn in no time. It was actually several minutes after eight the next morning when Carly found herself on the front walk approaching Ryan, who was very diligently occupied tying the laces of his sneakers for the third time.

He looked up, straightened and offered her a self-conscious smile. "I wasn't sure you'd come."

"Neither was I." Having spent half the night debating the wisdom of joining him, of fostering *any* kind of relationship with him, she looked mildly tired.

"Late night?" he asked cautiously. Her light had been on when he'd returned at one. He couldn't help but wonder if she'd been alone.

"Uh-huh." It wasn't wholly a lie.

He glanced toward the river, shaking off that glimmer of jealousy, then returned a more placid gaze. "Shall we?" When she nodded, they took off slowly, reaching pace only when they turned onto the river path. They went for several minutes in silence, before Carly felt herself begin to relax. There seemed no point in rehashing the pros and cons of her decision. She knew that she was far too susceptible to Ryan's charm. She also knew the danger entailed. But damn it, she *wanted* to run with him. She felt safe and happy. She deserved a splurge now and then. After all, they were only running.

With several successive deep breaths, she shifted her awareness from the tall, lithe man by her side to the fresh, clear world all about. "Another beautiful one, isn't it?"

"Yup. Won't be too many more."

"I wonder whether this path will be cleared in the winter."

"You've never run in the winter?"

"I've never run *here* in the winter."

"You mean along the river?"

"I mean in Boston."

"Then you're new to the area?"

"Uh-huh."

"From . . . ?"

For the briefest minute she felt a pang of guilt. But she'd been given a past, an authenticated one at that, and it behooved her to use it. "San Diego."

"You grew up there?"

"No. I worked there."

"Doing what?"

"Teaching." It came out more easily than she'd expected, the staccato exchange facilitated by the rhythm of the run. Had they been sitting over coffee, looking at each other, she might have had more trouble.

"Is that what you do now?"

"Uh-huh."

"Where?"

"Rand Academy."

"Rand?" He shot her a sidelong glance underscored with a grin. "No kidding? Several of my partners' kids go there. It's supposed to be top ranking."

"We do well in college admissions."

"How long have you been there?"

"Since September."

"And in Cambridge?"

"Since July."

They ran on, reaching the bridge, crossing over to hook onto the river path by Storrow Drive. The traffic was even lighter than it had been the day before. It was as though they had the world to themselves.

"How about you?" she asked between breaths.

"Yeeeeesssss?" he drawled.

"Where did you live before yesterday?"

"In Winchester. About half an hour thataway." He flicked his head northward.

"An apartment?"

"A house."

"All by yourself? I mean," she hastened to add, "You're not married or anything, are you?" She'd just assumed him to be single. Now, posing the question, she wasn't sure whether to be disappointed or mortified.

The punishing glance he gave her precluded both. "If I were married," he stated firmly, "I'd never have come on to you the way I did yesterday. As for 'or anything,' the answer is no."

"Strange," she mused, thinking aloud as, side by side, they followed the curve of the path.

"What is?"

"That you're not attached. I would have thought—"

"—that a dynamic, witty, handsome devil like me would certainly have been caught by now?"

She saw the dark brow he arched in self-mockery and couldn't help but smile. "Not exactly the way I would have put it, but the end result is the same."

"The end result. Ahh. I have to confess that I have had my experience with that end result."

"You've *been* married?"

"That's right. Like you."

At first she said nothing in response to his bait. Then, feeling particularly bold, she took it. "I'm not divorced."

He frowned. "But you live alone. Separated?" When she shook her head, he felt something freeze up inside. The European connection. A right-hand wedding band. "Then your husband is away?"

Carly looked out across the water. Its surface mirrored the few, still clouds, peaceful until the silent rush of a lone racing shell cut an even slash through its plane. "He's dead."

Ryan's pace faltered. A *widow?* At her age? Of all the

possibilities, it hadn't entered his mind. "I'm sorry," he murmured, readjusting his stride. "Was it recent?"

Her eyes were distant. "Four years ago."

"Four years?" From mind to tongue, the words spilled out. "You were so young."

"I was twenty-five."

"What happened? Uh—" he shook his head, appalled at himself "—strike that. I shouldn't have asked."

"It's all right." For some reason that she didn't stop to analyze, she wanted him to know. It was the one part of the fabrication that wasn't fabrication at all. "He was in a hotel." Her phrases were clipped by her bobbing pace and that something else that seemed to grip her each time she allowed a return of those thoughts. "There was a fire. He was on the fortieth floor. He couldn't get out."

She was barely aware of the hand on her arm until it tightened to slow her up. Startled back from images of hell, she came to a stunned stop facing Ryan.

"I'm sorry, Carly. That must have been very painful for you." It certainly accounted for the anguish he'd seen in her eyes. Even now, they bore a tortured look.

"Painful for me?" she gasped in a whisper. "Painful for him! The smoke . . . and flame. He tried to reach the stairs, they said. He nearly made it. . . ."

Ryan wasn't sure whether she was on the verge of tears or whether the raggedness of her breathing was due to exertion. But he knew that over the past four years she must have tortured herself many times. It was the torment of the survivor to imagine the terror of life's last moments. He'd been eyewitness to that torment once before, in the grief of a mother whose young daughter had drowned in an improperly attended municipal pool. Then his case had been for negligence. Now, beyond the law and the courtroom, he had no case save compassion.

Bidden by the overwhelming need to comfort, he put his hands on either side of her neck and gently massaged the tight muscles. She seemed far away still. It frightened him. "It's all right, Carly," he began softly. "Things like that just happen sometimes."

"But to Matthew?" Her husband's name was supposed to be Malcolm. Lost in the world of memory, she was oblivious to the slip. "He was so kind and good."

"Tragedy doesn't discriminate. Kind, unkind, good, bad, we don't have any control over it."

Her eyes grew misty, yet there were no tears. "I know. But there are still all those What ifs. What if he'd been out drinking with the rest of the guys? What if he'd been on the third floor? What if the department had never authorized the trip in the first place?"

"But it did," he countered gently, able only to guess that her husband had been on a business trip, perhaps at a convention. "He wasn't on the third floor. And he wasn't out drinking. Don't you see, you can't agonize over what might have been. What's done can't be changed. You can only go on living. You can only look ahead."

Above and beyond his words, it was the glimmer of hope in his eye that captured Carly's senses. Very slowly, she returned from that charred hotel room to the present, to the comfort of this man, to the long fingers that moved gently on her neck. With the sound of approaching footsteps, another runner passed them with a salute. Occasional cars sped by on Storrow Drive. A flock of geese winged southward. Ryan's head shaded her from the rising sun, whose vibrant rays shimmered around the richness of his hair.

"I know you're right," she whispered, lost in his gaze.

"And I do try." It was hard to look ahead at times, when so much of the past was a consuming flame. Reason dictated she look ahead, echoing not only Ryan's, Sam's and her father's advice but her own common sense. And though her heart didn't always cooperate, she tried. She did.

Ryan smiled then, feeling pride in the spunk that had raised her chin a fraction of an inch. "It'll work, Carly. You'll see. You're strong and bright."

His eyes held hers, melting her to the core. Then, struck by a sudden wave of self-consciousness, she tore her gaze from his and focused on the drying grass by the side of the path. "I'm sorry."

"For what?"

"Blurting all this out. I usually have better control."

"Maybe that's why it came out. Maybe it needed to come out."

"But to you?" She raised her eyes, perplexed. "We're strangers," she argued in stark reminder to herself.

"Not really," he said gently. "There are times when I look into your eyes and feel I've known you all my life."

"But you haven't."

"Not yet." He smiled again. "Speaking of which—" he tipped her face up with his thumbs "—you never did tell me what you teach."

For a final moment they stood there, looking at each other in silent awareness of something very special that had passed between them. For Carly, it was the sharing of her grief, something she hadn't done in quite that way to any other human being. She had offered Ryan a bit of Robyn. And in that instant, rather than feeling duplicitous, she felt strangely whole.

For Ryan, it was something else. For a few moments at least, he'd penetrated Carly's shell, glimpsed a part of her that he sensed few people saw. She'd kissed him back . . . that was it . . . their lips had never touched . . . yet she had kissed him back.

His thumb moved from her jaw to the softness of her mouth. Entranced, he slowly outlined its sensuous curve, feeling her lips part beneath his touch. His eye sought hers then, and he knew that she was, at that moment, as open to him as she'd ever been. His heart-beat sped; the pulse at her neck kept time. If it was the present he advocated, he had a point to make.

Six

WHEN HE LOWERED HIS HEAD THIS TIME, THERE was no hand to block his lips from hers. He kissed her in a whisper, barely touching her lips at first, then very slowly, very carefully deepening the touch. Her warmth was intoxicating, every bit as sweet as he'd imagined it to be when he'd lain in bed last night, frustrated and taut. He took his time; there was no rush. In a rare instance in his life, he simply closed his eyes and enjoyed the sensation with total satisfaction. There seemed no goal more precious than this simple tasting of lips, this simple act of acquaintance.

Carly felt it too. Time seemed suspended. Yielding all thought of consequence, she ventured into a world of pleasure. She felt Ryan's lips against hers, firm and manly yet gentle and undemanding. There was a drugging effect to their movement. They were enticing, irresistible. As she opened her lips, she was aware of the tickle of his beard. It was nearly as heady a sensation as the deepening of his kiss.

And she surged with it, surrendering to its lure, feeling lazy and lavish and light. Then his tongue joined the play and she felt something far deeper. It was an aware-ness, an awakening. She was a woman. For the first time in months and months, she felt her femininity.

With a gasp, she tremblingly pulled back. Her eyes held longer though, clinging to the firm lips that had brought her to such a floating state, then, with a tight swallow, meeting his gaze.

Words were unnecessary. He saw her stunned sur-prise, felt a bit of it himself. Those brief moments of contact had been more forceful than anything he'd ever felt. Even now his body was a tight coil, not so much in anticipation of what might have come next as in shock at what had just gone by.

Carly caught her breath. "Ryan?" she whispered.

"Shh." He pressed a finger to her lips and gently shook his head. It seemed all wrong to try to analyze what had happened, just as it would have been a travesty to apologize for it. It was one bright moment, over now but leaving in its wake a vibrant memory. Slowly he dropped his hand, then cocked his head toward Boston. With one last steadying breath, she nodded and they resumed the run.

If anything, their pace was faster. When they reached the point where Carly normally turned, Ryan shot her a glance.

"How're ya doin'?" he ventured.

"I'm okay."

So they ran on, turning by unspoken consent at the point to which Ryan had urged her the morning before, then making the round trip with nothing more than an occasional exchange.

"What *do* you teach?"

"English."

He took that in, then cast her a glance. "Speciality?"

"Creative writing."

When a pair of cyclists came toward them, Ryan dropped back a step to fall into single file behind Carly until they passed. "Do much yourself?"

"What?"

"Creative writing."

She released a terse, "Some."

He left it at that, wondering if she was one of those teachers who could teach but not do. He recalled his highschool diving coach. The man was brilliant in explaining technique, in analyzing strength and spotting weakness. Yet he could barely do a simple jackknife, let alone a half gainer with a double back twist. With a fond smile, he refiled the memory in its bank and glanced down at Carly.

"You're happy at Rand?"

"Uh-huh. The kids are great."

"Grades. . . ?"

"That I teach?" She returned his gaze, helpless to ignore the swath of sweat that dampened the front of his sweat shirt. When he nodded, his hair clung to his brow. He looked disturbingly masculine. "Sophomores and juniors," she supplied abruptly, then poured herself into the run.

Ryan quickened his step accordingly. Though warm, he was far from tired. There was a release in pounding the pavement this way, a relief from the urge to ponder the "what now" of things. He'd kissed Carly; she'd kissed him back. They'd shared something he felt was unique enough to pursue. Yet he sensed he was on shaky ground. He had to tread carefully.

As they ran on, Carly wondered what he was thinking. Captured in a surreptitious glance, his expression was intense and calculating. She assumed his mind had turned to his work. Didn't she often use her running time to mentally outline lectures or plan upcoming assignments? If only she could do that now! But her lips still burned from Ryan's kiss and the trail of fire lingered lower. In a bid for diversion, she turned her thoughts to New York.

It had been several years since she'd been back, and even aside from the excitement of seeing her father, she was looking forward to it. The years she and Matthew had spent there had been delightfully irresponsible. He had been an assistant professor of economics, she his student. They had married in the middle of her sophomore year, before she'd reached the age of nineteen. Very much in love, they had been convinced that their fourteen-year difference was irrelevant. And so it had been. They went to school together and studied together. When she graduated, they moved to Chicago, where he was offered a full professorship. There had been more pressure after that—greater responsibility for Matthew, hard-won assignments for Carly—all of which made her memories of New York that much sweeter.

And now she would return. She and her father would eat in style, stroll the avenues together, perhaps take in a show or two. Was it safe? A spasm flicked across her brow. Sam said it was. He had been the one to promote New York from the start. Anonymity in crowds, he'd said. She supposed he had a point. At least, she was determined to believe it. She needed this trip. She needed to see her father's familiar face. For those few days, she would be Robyn again. It would be odd. . . .

When they reached the small incline to the bridge, Ryan took her elbow. They slowed until the roadway cleared, then jogged across and resumed their trek on the other side of the river.

Well after he released it, Carly felt his touch on her

arm. How would he take to a deception of the sort she practiced? He was a lawyer; perhaps he would understand. But when his eyes took on that smoldering gleam, he was first and foremost a man. He would expect honesty from her—which was precisely why he was dangerous. Of the men she had met since she'd begun her new life, it seemed that only Ryan had the potential to reach her. That much had been obvious from the very first when he'd caught her in the courtyard and spoken so gently. With Ryan she felt guilt at the dual nature of her life. Guilt. She neither wanted it nor needed it. But she'd made a decision long months ago; now she intended to abide by the consequences.

Feeling suddenly tired, she fell back a bit. Ryan slowed immediately. He watched her closely for several paces, noting the faint drop of her shoulders.

"Are you okay?" he asked softly.

Startled, she looked up. "Hmm? Sure."

"You looked a little sad there."

She shook her head in denial and made a concerted effort to maintain a steady pace.

"Game for trying the Square?" he asked when they neared the side street he wanted to take. At her questioning glance, he explained. "The newspaper. I wanted to pick one up."

The sensible thing, given the train her thoughts had just taken, would have been to go on straight while he made his detour. She could return to her apartment, shower and make breakfast, then sit down with her own paper, which would have been delivered by then. But the air was so fresh and home was so lonely. For just a little longer she would indulge herself.

"Lead on," she said, and he did, guiding her across Memorial Drive to the narrow side streets that zigzagged into the Square. Signs of life were scarce, as was usual on a Sunday morning. But Harvard was everywhere—in the brick buildings that lined the streets, in the Beat Yale decal that graced more than one bumper, in the bevy of deserted sandwich shops that by afternoon would be crowded with students.

At the kiosk in the center of the Square, they stopped. "Want one?" Ryan asked, eyeing the papers stacked into a miniature skyline of newsprint.

She shook her head with a smile. "No, thanks."

"You're sure?" He extracted money from his sock.

"I've got one waiting at home."

Nodding, he paid for the paper, passing a glance at its headline before tucking the thick wad under his arm.

"How about a doughnut?" he asked, spotting a sign at the corner coffee shop.

"Nope."

"Some coffee?"

"Uh-uh."

"A cold drink?"

She shook her head.

"The afternoon?" What the hell. He had nothing to lose.

She sent him a good-humored frown. "What do you mean, the afternoon? It's for sale?"

"I could be bargained down to a very reasonable price."

She chuckled. "You're impossible."

"No. Just lonely. I was planning to work, but. . . ." Tipping back his head, he looked at the sky. "It's such a beautiful day. It's a shame not to take advantage of it. Given New England weather, we'll have snow within the week."

"Go on! It's got to be in the midsixties by now." Her skin felt damp; her pale blue running shirt clung to her chest. As they turned and began to walk in the general direction of home, she savored the stirring of air against her face. "You really think it'll change that quickly?"

"It usually does. Something about the sea breeze, I think." He paused, then sprang. "So, how about it? We could take a ride to Gloucester and spend the afternoon walking the beach."

But she shook her head. "I can't. I've got to work."

"Work? You do that all week. Don't you owe yourself one afternoon of relaxation?"

"I *had* one afternoon of relaxation. Yesterday."

"What did you do?" He remembered going to her apartment when he'd gotten back from work and finding her sitting curled on the sofa in her long white robe. He assumed she'd just showered and was waiting to dress for the evening. Again, he wondered with whom she'd been. But his feelings of jealousy were minor in comparison to those other feelings she evoked. She'd looked so innocent, so appealing, so thoroughly sensuous—even now he fought the urge to reach out and touch her.

"I went to the museum."

"You did?" he asked, diverting ardor into enthusiasm. "The Museum of Fine Arts?"

"Uh-huh. You approve?"

"I suppose."

"What do you mean, you suppose?"

"It depends who you were *with* at the museum."

With a coy smile, she ticked off her companions. "Let's see, George Washington was there, John Hancock, Ben Franklin, Auguste Renoir, Vincent van Gogh—"

"Any *live* males?"

"Several. I didn't know their names. None of them were alone."

"But you were?"

With a sigh, she reluctantly left the banter behind. "In the way you mean, yes." Passing Ferdinand's and The Blue Parrot, they continued on at a comfortable walk.

"Does that bother you?"

She looked at him in surprise. "To go places alone?" It was a loaded question. On the one hand, she had never been one to shy from striking out on her own. On the other, she had indeed been gun-shy since the run-in with Gary Culbert's thug that had resulted in her acceptance into the Witness Protection Program. "No," she began, careful to choose words that weren't a total lie, "I'm used to being alone. Not that it isn't nice to have company sometimes." Fearing that Ryan would hear an invitation she hadn't intended, she rushed on in a higher voice. "So that was for relaxation's sake. Today I work."

"What do you have to do?"

"Grade a stack of essays, make up an exam."

"You have exams coming up already?"

"We're on the trimester system. By Thanksgiving the first term will be over. Exams begin in a week and a half. I have to get my rough copy in to the office by Wednesday so the secretary can get to work. Fortunately I've only got one left to do."

They walked on. In the absence of conversation, Carly realized how much she seemed to have told Ryan, rather than the other way around. But then, the less she knew about him the better. They had no future together.

She was unaware how somber her expression had

grown until Ryan caught her on it. "There you go again. Tuning out on me."

Looking quickly up, she forced a smile. "I'm sorry. I was just thinking about exams and all."

He suspected the "all" had nothing to do with exams, but couldn't force the issue. Rather, he concentrated on how best to worm his way into her life. When inspiration hit, his eyes lit up. "Listen, I've got work to do today too. We could work together. I mean, we could work on our own things together—in the same room."

She conjured up an image of them at her kitchen table, knees touching beneath the butcher block, and knew in the instant that she, for one, would never be able to concentrate. "I *really* need to work."

He followed her thinking, but was far from defeated. "Then the library. Harvard Law is as quiet as they come. We wouldn't dare talk there."

But it wasn't the talking that frightened her as much as the looking, the sensing, the savoring of companionship. One such working date could lead to another, then coffee during, then dinner after. It would be all too easy to get used to that kind of thing.

"Thanks, Ryan, but I'd better stay home."

He eyed her askance. "You're sure?" With her nod, he dropped it. For now. There had to be a reason for her reticence. He couldn't believe that she still mourned a husband who had been four years dead. Nor had he found an explanation for that look of abject fear he'd seen in her eyes more than once. He wished he had the courage to ask outright. But he doubted she'd answer, and he feared he'd only jeopardize the frail bond between them.

When the courtyard came into sight, Carly took a deep breath. "This was nice. Thank you."

"I didn't do anything."

"Well, it was fun running anyway." It would have to last her all week.

They walked up the path to the front door. "It *was* fun," he said quietly, then drew the door open and let her pass. Looking down at her, he felt drawn once again. She barely reached his chin, even to the top of the loose ponytail into which she'd gathered her hair. Stray tendrils had freed themselves as she'd run and now clung damply to her neck. In her running shorts and sneakers she seemed small, vulnerable and . . . brave. Brave. The word popped unexpectedly into his mind. He was pondering it distractedly when she stopped at the foot of the stairs and turned to regard him in question.

"Aren't you going to get it?"

"Get what?"

"That note sticking out of your mailbox."

He looked back toward the foyer." Sure enough, a piece of paper had been folded and worked into the narrow slit of the box, with just enough showing to attract his attention.

Carly watched him unfold it and read a brief scrawled message. When he frowned, she momentarily forgot her need for distance.

"Is something wrong?" she asked, coming closer to where he stood staring at the slip of paper.

"I don't know." His eyes were troubled. "It's from Howard Miller, my partner. He wants me to call him right away."

"Does that mean trouble?"

"I'm not sure." He looked again at the note in a futile attempt to uncover some hidden meaning. "If he made the effort to drive all the way in from Wellesley, there must be *something* on his mind." His dark brows knit in the struggle to guess what it was.

"You can use my phone," Carly heard herself offer. Turning, she headed up the stairs, knelt at her door to gather up her newspaper, and let herself in without looking back. Ryan materialized in her foyer moments later.

"I really apologize for this," he said, going straight toward the kitchen, pausing only to drop his paper on the table before lifting the receiver. "I'm giving your phone quite a workout."

She smiled. "It'll survive." Then she set her own paper in the living room and headed down the hall. When she returned, she carried two clean towels, one of which she offered to Ryan before settling on the sofa to mop the sweat from her forehead and neck as she eyed the Sunday headlines. From where she sat, she couldn't help but hear Ryan's half of the conversation.

"Sandy?" He ran the towel across his brow. "Is Howard around?" There was a pause; Ryan worked the towel around his neck. "Yeah, Howard. What's up?" The silence was prolonged and ominous. *"What?"* His voice held disbelief, then shock. "My God."

Twisting in her seat, Carly looked back to find his face a study in pain. Her heart began to thud as she listened to his terse questions. "When?" then, "Where?" and finally, "How?" Then he came alive. "What do you mean, they won't say? We have a right to that information!" His partner tried to calm him, but his anger raged. "Damn it, Howard, the bastard got to him! Suicide, my foot! I'm calling the D.A.—"

Unable to politely ignore what she'd heard, she slowly came to stand at the kitchen door. Ryan was too embroiled in his fury to notice. His brows knit low over his eyes, which were dark and threatening. One hand savagely gripped the phone, the other pressed hard against the wall. His lips were taut. Even his jaw, buffered by the thickness of its beard, seemed set in steel.

"That's a crock of bull! I want an autopsy! They'll rush him through the morgue and get him buried before anyone's the wiser. I'm telling you—"

He was loudly interrupted. Even Carly heard it, though Howard Miller's specific words were indistinct. But Ryan listened, very slowly calming down. When he spoke again, there was an element of defeat in his voice.

"Okay, okay." He sighed, his voice lowering to a murmur. "I'll call you back in ten minutes. Fifteen, then." Replacing the receiver on its hook, he closed his eyes. He looked distraught.

Carly took a step closer. "Ryan?" she said softly. "What is it?"

He looked up in surprise, having momentarily forgotten her presence. At her concern, he was doubly distressed. She didn't need to hear this; Lord knew she'd lived with death too closely already.

Thrusting his fingers through his hair, he scooped it back from his brow. "Nothing you should be bothered with."

"You'd rather not talk about it?"

"I'd rather not burden *you* with it."

She chided him gently. "I'm not fragile. Sometimes it helps to share things. Besides, after the way I dumped it all on you a little while ago. . . ."

He held her gaze then, seeing something he hadn't seen before. She wanted him to talk; it was no empty offer. And it was the first such open invitation she'd made.

He straightened and dropped his head back, then slowly raised it and looked down at her again. His eyes were clouded. "I've been defending a fellow on charges of dealing."

"Drugs?"

"Heroin." His taut-knuckled hands gripped the ends of the towel. "He was a nineteen-year-old kid who's been on the wrong side of the law for years. Very bright. Has run the cops around in circles time and again. But stupid enough to think that a little more money, always a little more money, would get him over the hump."

"But it didn't."

"Not this time. They found him dead in his cell last night. His mother was notified. When she couldn't reach me, she fished Howard's number from the book." He lowered his eyes and scowled at the floor. "It's criminal. Prison is criminal. Totally lawless as we know the law. A guy like Luis needed help. He was lost and desperate. His childhood alternated between running away from home and protecting his mother from beatings by a drunkard of a husband. The kid had nothing going for him but misguided intelligence and a mother who loved him. There's the shame. It was his mother who first called me. I swear, she would have sold herself into bondage if it would have meant raising the money for Luis's defense."

"How *did* she raise it?"

"She didn't. I'm not—I wasn't charging her."

"You do that then?" Not all lawyers did. Another something to respect.

"If I think the case merits it." He paused to rub the end of the towel along the line of his beard beneath his chin. "Sometimes a lawyer takes a case *pro bono* as a favor to someone else. Sometimes he takes it because he believes the client deserves representation. Then there're cases that offer an opportunity to break ground on a legal issue. And there are those cases that are simply interesting or exciting enough for a lawyer to want to handle, whether he's paid or not."

"And Luis's?" Carly prompted, absorbed in Ryan's philosophy.

"Luis," he sighed, "was just someone who needed a helping hand. One helping hand. Life had been tough on him; it didn't seem fair. Not that I felt I could 'save' him. He was what he was, shaped by nineteen years of hell." He raised his eyes, his voice deep and hard. "He was an addict. Do you have any idea what happens to addicts in there?" Carly had read her share on the subject, but he went quickly on. "It's a fate worse than death. Especially where Luis was, in that limbo between the cops and the guys on the inside who could either make or break him." With a muttered "Damn," he looked away in anguish. "I can't believe he killed himself."

"That's what they're saying?"

"That was what they told his mother. Howard's trying to contact someone in the prison." He looked at his watch. "I've got to try him in another ten minutes." He hesitated, cocking his head toward the phone. "Would you mind—"

"Of course not," she said, with a dismissing wave. Her thoughts had already moved on, the investigator in her at work. "But the alternative is murder, isn't it?"

"That's right."

"Do you really think it could be that?"

"He'd been getting his stuff from someone pretty powerful. It's been known to happen," he gritted.

"Committed by an inmate hired by the supplier?"

"Or the cops."

His words hung in the air like sulfur fumes around a rubber plant. Carly couldn't help but stare. Though the police she'd come to know through her own ordeal had been relatively innocuous, she knew well enough of those who weren't. Still, murder? Oh, it had happened. Just the year before, there had been an incident in Chicago. Then the cop had been convicted of manslaughter, a lesser degree, on the grounds that in a scuffle the cop had used undue force that had resulted in the man's banging his head against the back of a truck. The cop had lost his job, but hadn't served a day in jail. The case had pitted the community against the department; its disposition had been a no-win compromise.

"I'm sorry, Ryan," she whispered, returning to the present and his somber expression. "Will you be able to find out?"

"That's what I don't know. That's why Howard is getting onto it." He sent her a wry smile. "He figured that I'd go off the handle with accusations."

"Would you?"

"If I smelled a cover-up, you bet. It *could* have been another inmate, with a guard in the system protecting him. Hell, it *could* have been suicide." His voice dropped. "I just don't know." He looked at his watch again, then grew silent.

"How about some coffee?" she offered, wishing she could ease his wait.

"Hmm? Oh, no, don't go to any trouble for me."

"I was going to make a pot anyway. Would you like some?"

He shrugged, then nodded but said nothing, content to watch her remove a can of coffee from the cabinet, measure the prescribed amount into a filter, and set it into the coffee maker. She moved with a steadiness that was comforting. Strangely so. As though she'd always be there to lend an ear, to offer support. Alyssa would have never thought to ask about his legal life.

She had wanted it left in the office, appropriately filed and forgotten after business hours. And he'd done just that, though "business hours" had grown longer and longer. She had refused to accept his love for the law; he had refused to accept her refusal. It had been a standoff, one of the many irreconcilable differences that had led to their divorce.

And now there was Carly. Quiet and alone. Interesting and interested, though fiercely protective of her privacy. He could easily open up to her, as if *she'd* been the one who had vowed to take him for better or for worse, when in fact he'd known her less than two days. She seemed to have so much to give.

"How do you take it?" Her voice broke into his thoughts, and he realized he'd been staring. With a start, he shifted his gaze from her face to the coffee, which had already begun to drip.

He cleared his throat, needing the minute to refocus. "Black is fine." Then he leaned back against the counter, not far from her, and looked around the room. Immaculate, as always. Neat, sparkling. His gaze wandered into the living room to encounter the same. What *was* it that bothered him?

Leaving the kitchen, he idly approached the sofa, rounded it and sidestepped the pair of sculpted tables. His feet took him to the white-lacquered wall system, where he studied the bouquet of silk flowers in their elegant vase, the silent face of the television, the fine collection of books—literary works as well as volumes on art and drama and photography.

Something was missing. Puzzled, he reviewed what he'd seen, then returned pensively to the kitchen in time to see Carly remove two mugs from the cabinet. She was lovely. Lovely and intriguing. But her home? It lacked . . . it lacked . . . fingerprints. That was it. There was nothing in her home to brand it hers, to mark it as unique in the very way she was. It was strange.

Carly offered a gentle smile along with the mug of coffee. He took the brew with a murmured, "Thanks," and leaned back against the counter again. He was eminently aware of Carly, and she of him. When the phone jangled, they were both startled.

On reflex, Ryan reached for it as though it were his own. Carly held her hand suspended. "Hello?" she heard him say, then saw him frown and eye her questioningly. "Robyn?" Stifling a gasp, she managed to shrug. "There's no Robyn here," he responded offhandedly. "You must have the wrong number."

Replacing the receiver, he darted a sheepish gaze Carly's way. "Sorry about that. I guess I'm a little preoccupied. Kinda forgot this wasn't my phone."

Had Carly not been slightly preoccupied herself, she would have been susceptible to the half smile that gave his lips a roguish twist. But her mind was on the call itself, on the name that had passed through those lips moments earlier.

She tossed her head jerkily in an attempt at nonchalance. "No problem. A wrong number's a wrong number." But it hadn't been. Someone had called for Robyn, yet no one who would normally do that had her number. Apprehension sent a chill through her. She had to call Sam. But with Ryan here? Not wise.

But then, Ryan's presence offered a certain solace: protection at its most innocent. The blank look on his face when he'd repeated the name Robyn had seemed authentic enough—unless it was all part of a skillfully slow regimen of psychological torture.

"Hey, I've upset you," he said softly, intruding on this most gruesome of thoughts. "You look like you've seen a ghost."

The ghost of Robyn Hart—close, she thought. "Of course not. Must have been the running. Six miles two mornings in a row. I guess I'm not used to it."

He brushed his fingers against her cheek while his gaze seared her heart with an irresistible tenderness. "You're sure I haven't upset you with talk of my case?"

For an instant, she nearly forgot her own. The thudding of her heart could as easily have been caused by Ryan's touch. In defiance of the worst of her fears, she allowed herself to feel warm and safe and very much cared for. But she mustn't forget, she told herself. A phone call for Robyn was real and serious; Ryan Cornell's appeal was a passing thing, in all likelihood a fabrication of her own emotional need. Rationally, though, what she needed was to contact Sam, but she was hamstrung until Ryan made his call and left.

Tearing her eyes from his, she glanced at the phone. "I'd have to be made of stone not to be affected by your case. Who is your partner calling now?"

"He's seeing what he can get from the warden."

"Then what? If you want an autopsy performed, won't you have to go through a medical examiner?"

Ryan arched a brow at the extent of her knowledge. "If we're in luck, the warden will request the autopsy himself. Most likely we'll have to do the demanding. And yes, the medical examiner will be the one to contact."

"What about the district attorney?" she asked nervously. "You mentioned him before. If you suspect murder, will you go to him?"

"I'll go to him if I suspect *any* foul play." He paused to take a drink of coffee, then took a deep breath and looked at the ceiling. "I don't know. Maybe it was suicide. The guy had a raw deal in life. Who could blame him if he wanted to escape once and for all?" He gave his watch an impatient glance, then snatched up the phone and punched out his partner's number. Taking a seat at the table, Carly watched and waited. When he replaced the receiver a few minutes later, he wore a weary expression.

"What did he say?" she asked, curious enough about Luis's fate to ignore the fact that any conversation would prolong Ryan's stay and delay her call to Sam.

"The warden is convinced it was suicide. He claims there were no suspicious marks on the body."

"Do you believe him?"

Ryan frowned. "Luis had so many marks on him anyway—who knows? Howard's calling in for the autopsy, though. That should tell us something." He stared pensively at the last of his coffee before downing it in a gulp and putting the cup in the sink. Then he turned to Carly.

"Thanks," he said simply.

She stood as he retrieved his newspaper from the counter and headed for the door. She understood that his appreciation was for the phone, the coffee, the sympathetic ear, but she wanted no further sweet words. His compellingly masculine presence was far too potent as it was. Against her will she recalled the kiss they'd shared earlier that morning. Then she thrust it from her mind. She had a phone call to make. And the reason behind that phone call was precisely the reason why it behooved her to keep Ryan Cornell at a distance.

At the open door he eyed her with resignation. "Sure you won't change your mind? I'd much rather spend the afternoon with you than have to see Luis's mother or stop by the prison."

"You'll do that anyway," Carly declared softly, with

more admiration than criticism. "I know your type. Work before play. True?"

He hesitated a minute, wishing it weren't so but finally offering a "True" as softly, before giving her a sad smile and starting down the stairs.

Pulse racing, Carly closed the door quietly before bolting for the phone and punching out Sam's number. It was Ellen who answered.

"Hello?"

"Ellen? It's Carly Quinn. I'm really sorry to bother you on a Sunday morning, but is Sam around?"

"Oh, Carly, he's gone to pick up some milk for me at the store. I expect him back any minute. You sound upset. Is something wrong?" Though Ellen knew nothing of Carly's real name or the case that had brought her to Boston, she was well aware that Carly was part of the program and knew enough to be concerned.

"I don't know," Carly murmured. "I got a strange phone call a little while ago. I just wanted to run it past Sam."

"You're at home now?"

"Uh-huh."

"Got the door locked?"

"Oh, damn. Hold on a minute." She started to put the phone down, then raised it again. "Do you want to just have Sam call me back?"

"No, no, Carly. Go bolt the door. I'll hold on."

When Carly returned she was slightly breathless. "There. Thanks, Ellen. God, how could I have done that? I must be going soft!" She paused. "Any sign of him yet?"

"Not yet. I'm at the window watching. He'll be right along. In the meantime you can tell me about school. How's it going?"

"Not bad. Busy right about now." And the last thing

on her mind at the moment. Better to shift the conversation back to Ellen, who might be feeling a bit more talkative than she was. "But how about you? How are you feeling?"

"Pretty well. A little tired. The first time round I didn't have a toddler to watch. Sara's into the terrible twos three months before her time. She can't quite understand my being under the weather now and again."

"Jealousy before its time?" Carly ventured sympathetically.

Ellen chuckled. "Could be. Sam tells me you've got a load of nieces and nephews. This must be old hat for you."

"I've never had one of my own. It's always pretty exciting when someone's having a baby."

"Did you want to—have one of your own, that is?"

Carly sighed. It was something she'd asked herself more than once in the past four years. "I don't know. I was so young when I first got married and we were each busy with our careers. If Malcolm—" her voice broke slightly, only in part due to the use of a name so strange to her tongue "—had lived, I'm sure I would have wanted a child by now. I often wonder what would have happened if I'd had one. This relocation would have been that much harder with another person involved, I suppose. On the other hand, it would have been nice to have had someone with me, particularly with my husband gone. Then again, if I'd had a child I might have been more cautious about things to begin with. All this might never have happened." She gave a snort of disgust. "Am I rambling! See what happens when you ask a creative writer a simple question? They say that a born writer is one who is never satisfied with a single side of a story but keeps looking to the far end of the issue. I think they're right."

"Have you had a chance to do much writing?"

"No. School's been too demanding so far. Maybe when things settle down some I'll try."

"It'd be a great outlet, Carly."

"But far too revealing. In the wrong hands. . . ." Her words trailed off, their implication obvious.

"You shouldn't think that way," Ellen scolded gently.

"That's what Sam says."

"Well, he's right. Your cover is so tight nothing can possibly leak out. I'm always amazed when Sam talks about—hey, speak of the devil, there he is. Hold on, Carly. I'll go yell for him before he starts dallying with Sara."

The phone hit the counter with a clatter. Carly heard the fading patter of footsteps, then a muffled, "Sam! It's Carly," then, after a pause, louder, more solid steps returning.

"Carly—" Sam's voice came with reassuring calm over the line "—what happened?"

"Somebody called, Sam. Somebody asking for Robyn."

"Did you recognize the voice?"

"That's the worst part! I didn't hear it! Ryan was here waiting to make a call and when the phone rang he picked it up without thinking."

"Carly—"

"He told whoever it was that there was no Robyn here. I didn't even want to ask whether it was a man or a woman for fear of arousing suspicion. And I couldn't call you until he'd gone. Who could it have been, Sam?"

"Car—"

"Anybody who calls me here knows me as Carly!

Anybody who would use the other name doesn't call me here! *Who could it have been?"*

"Sheila."

The babble of chatter gave way to complete silence.

"Sheila?" Carly half whispered.

"Yeah," Sam said with a sigh. "And, boy, am I sorry. I knew at first glance she'd be trouble."

"Sheila who?"

"Sheila Montgomery."

"Sheila?" Carly's face lit instantly. "Sheila's here?"

"I'm afraid so."

"Sam, that's great! Sheila's terrific!"

"That was what her transfer papers from the marshal's office in Chicago said, and that was what I believed when I gave her your number. She already knew your name and that you were under my jurisdiction. Did you tell her before you left?"

"She was in on the planning back there."

"Hoffmeister may have been right when he suggested it'd be good for you to have someone to talk to, especially a woman, but now I'm not so sure. She seemed scatterbrained to me. To have called you and asked for Robyn, *particularly* when someone other than you answered the phone, only proves it."

But Carly was full of forgiveness. Sheila had been with her during the entire stint in protective custody. They'd begun as allies and ended fast friends. "She'll be working here?"

"Looks that way," Sam grumbled. He'd have to pair her up with Greg. Let old bedroom eyes tame her.

"When did she get in?"

"She stopped by the office early last week on her way to visit a cousin or someone on the Cape and wasn't due to begin work until a week from Monday. I had no idea she'd contact you so soon or I would have

warned you. She must have gotten tired of her cousin."
He gave a snort. "Most likely the other way around."

"Sam, Sam, where's your sense of humor? Here I was
scared to death that the *wrong* someone had my name,
and it's only Sheila. She's not scatterbrained. That's
just her personality. Bubbly and enthusiastic. Believe
me. I've seen her in action. She's smart as a whip and
thorough. And she can be one tough cookie when the
going gets rough." Her thoughts slipped back. Her
voice grew softer. "I don't know what I would have
done without her through those months."

Sam sighed. "Well, it looks like you're going to have
her again. At least the friend part of it. She'll be working
on other things for us, though you can be damn sure I
plan to give her a lecture about watching her tongue."

"I'm sure she was just excited. Go easy on her, Sam.
She's been through a lot in life. She's earned her
stripes."

"That's a recommendation?"

"Very definitely."

"Then I guess it'll have to do. At any rate, see if she
calls again. If she doesn't—" his tone grew momentarily somber "—let me know. She's the only one I can
think of who might have—"

"Wait, Sam. There's the intercom. Hold on." Setting
the phone on the counter, Carly ran to the panel by the
door and pressed the button. "Yes?" she asked, her
customary caution softened only by a definite suspicion.

"Carly Quinn?" came a voice made tinny by the
mechanism. "This is Sheila Montgomery. Now I know
you've got a guy up there with you because I called and
completely forgot who I was calling when I heard his
sexy voice, but I've just driven up from Provincetown
and wanted to say hello. Hello? Are you there?"

Carly grinned. It was Sheila, all right. "I'm here, Sheila. Come on up." Holding the front door release long enough to allow Sheila entry, she returned to the phone. "Sam? It's Sheila. She's on her way up. Hey, I'm sorry to have bothered you. Seems I jumped the gun and got scared. If I'd been a little more patient I guess the mystery would have solved itself."

"No problem, Carly." And well there wasn't, since Carly seemed pleased and no apparent harm had been done by Sheila's carelessness. Sam still vowed to take Sheila down a peg, but another time. "Go greet your friend. Maybe *she* can coax you out on the town. Hey, that's not a bad idea. Why don't you show her the sights? Explore together. As long as she's there, make good use of her."

"Oh, I will," Carly said with a smile. "I will."

Seven

SHEILA MONTGOMERY TUGGED AT THE BUZZING door and entered the atrium duly impressed with the surroundings of Robyn Hart's new home. Carly Quinn. Carly Quinn. Damn it, she'd have to remember. One slipup was bad enough. But it was hard. The woman she'd known, a frightened woman caught between two lives, had been Robyn Hart. Carly Quinn was someone new—new career, new apartment, new boyfriend.

At the thought of the last, Sheila felt a twinge of remorse. Perhaps she should have waited. But she only wanted to say hi. The Cape had been lonely all by herself. And Boston was as new to her as it had been to Rob—to Carly.

Pushing her windblown mop of raven hair back from her face, she started up the stairs. Not bad, she mused again, noting the fine carpeting on the stairs, the brass railings, the lush plants hanging hither and yon. Not bad at all. Certainly a sight nicer than the studio she'd rented on Beacon Hill. Though she'd definitely bought the location, the apartment itself left something to be desired. But, she reasoned morosely, she was used to it. *This* place, though, was something else.

Rounding the second-floor landing she headed for the third, then tipped her head back and caught sight of the face grinning down at her.

Carly leaned on the railing, forearms propped on the brass, and watched with pleasure as her friend met her gaze. "Sheila Montgomery, you haven't changed a bit."

Sheila returned the grin and spoke with the faintly nasal twang that was uniquely hers. "You, Carly Quinn, have." Running quickly up the remaining flight, she slowed as she approached Carly. "Wow, have you!" She ran an eye over the smart running suit Carly still wore, then took in the mass of curly hair that had escaped its ponytail, the flushed cheeks, the light gray eyes. For an instant she held back. There was something about this woman, something richer, something more sophisticated that put her in a class above. In that instant Sheila felt every bit the bodyguard, the woman who'd crossed from the wrong side of the tracks to make it in the world of law enforcement. In Chicago, with a very vulnerable Robyn, it had all seemed irrelevant. Here, though, with this elegant backdrop, with the knowledge that Carly Quinn was an established person, she felt distinctly inferior.

It was Carly who took the final steps and embraced Sheila warmly. "It's great to see you, Sheila! I had no idea you'd be in town!"

"Hey," Sheila began apologetically, "I know this is a bad time." She cast a skittering glance toward Carly's open door. "Maybe I should come back later."

"Don't be silly! I'm alone." Looping her arm around Sheila's waist, she guided the woman toward her apartment and spoke in a softer, more conspiratorial whisper. "He left. Sexy voice and all. You missed him."

Sheila managed a chuckle as she retrieved her bravado. "Damn. And here I thought I'd finally get a look at your type of man. Hey, this is gorgeous!" Inside the apartment, she slowly scanned the room. "My word, you really did it right, didn't you?"

Closing the door, Carly followed Sheila's gaze. "They suggested I change my image. I guess I did. I've never quite lived this way before. I mean, when I was growing up the house was beautiful in an old and elegant kind of way. This is more—"

"Chic. Modern. Perfect." Sheila's eyes took in the stylish decor before returning to Carly. "It's lovely," she said quietly. "You're very lucky."

Feeling suddenly awkward, Carly glanced away. Her home was a luxury, something she doubted Sheila could afford. "Listen, can I get you some coffee? I've got a fresh pot brewed."

"Sure. That'd be great."

Heading for the kitchen, Carly called over her shoulder, "Sam tells me you've been transferred to the Boston office."

"Sam Loomis? He told you I'd seen him?"

"Only when I called him a few minutes ago." She pulled a fresh mug from the cabinet for Sheila and filled it, adding hot coffee to her own, the one she'd used when Ryan had been there earlier. His stood cold and lonely in the sink, a stark reminder that he'd been and gone. "You really gave me a scare. When the phone rang and you asked for Robyn—"

"Listen, I'm sorry about that. I guess I wasn't thinking."

"Don't tell Sam that," Carly advised, arching a brow as she handed Sheila the coffee. "Tell him you thought you recognized *his* voice at the other end of the line or something."

"He was ticked?"

Carly shrugged, then led the way back to the living room. "Only because I was frightened. I was sure that someone had penetrated my cover and I couldn't call Sam until Ryan left—"

"Who *is* Ryan?"

"My neighbor," she said as she sank onto the sofa.

Sheila settled in the armchair across from Carly. "Is he as good-looking as he sounds?"

"He's good-looking."

"Boy, you didn't waste any time! Tell me about him."

"There's not much to tell." At least not much she wanted to tell. "I just met him. He moved in last weekend. His phone isn't going in until tomorrow, so he's been using mine. He was standing right next to it when you called. That was why he answered."

Feeling more bold now that they'd begun to talk, Sheila's eyes narrowed. "I hope you're going after him."

"No, I am not *going after him*. You know my situation. It's shaky, to say the least."

Sheila gave another envious glance at her surroundings. "Doesn't look shaky to me. You've got a new town, a new career. How's the teaching going, by the way?"

"Great. Busy. I enjoy it."

"Then you've got it made. What's to be shaky about?" It sounded like a perfect life to Sheila. What with a husband's life insurance, a job that paid well, plus money from Uncle Sam to work with, Carly had it easy.

Carly didn't see it quite that way. For a minute she was surprised at Sheila's lack of understanding. For a minute too she had forgotten Sheila's lot in life, compared to hers.

"Things aren't that simple," she said quietly. She sipped her coffee and gazed toward the window. "There's still the fact of where I've been, who I've been. If you think *you* had trouble remembering to call me Carly, just think about what it must be like for me. Twenty-nine years as Robyn, four months a Carly—it's an adjustment."

"But it's a fact," Sheila countered. "It's done. Robyn Hart has been wiped off the map. Carly Quinn has been put on it—and in style, I might add." Dryly, at that.

"Mechanically, yes. Emotionally, only maybe. It's been a lonely four months."

"Which is where sexy-voiced gentlemen come into play. You mean that you haven't begun to sow those wild oats of yours?"

"Wild oats?" Carly laughed. "Not quite. I've turned conservative, or hadn't you noticed?"

"You were always conservative—at least while I knew you. But not before. I got the impression you were a spitfire back then."

Carly nodded, smiling. "A spitfire . . . I suppose that's a good way to put it." Then she sobered and her eyes grew distant. "But that's changed. When Peter died, I guess. Or maybe later, when Culbert's thug came after me with a gun." She shivered. "In many ways I'm back where I was as a teenager. Quiet. Private."

"Then you'll just have to bloom all over again."

Carly studied her friend, taking in at a glance the light wool tunic, tights and calf-high boots. She'd always thought of Sheila as a character, a free spirit straitjacketed into an oddly controlled job. More than once she'd wondered if Sheila wouldn't have been happier as an aerobics instructor or a salesgirl at a specialty boutique. Her clothes were usually startling in either color or combination—exotic verging on the garish. It was as though she wanted to shock people into seeing her, then pull out her ID and put them in their place. Though Carly didn't agree with the philosophy, knowing Sheila's background made it no great surprise.

"How about if I let you do the blooming for me?" she teased. "Tell me about this transfer. How did it come about?"

"I requested it."

Carly frowned. "You wanted to leave Chicago? I thought you liked it there."

Sheila made an impish face. "I'd been there for seven years. Time to move on."

"What about Lee? And Harmon? And Mickey?" Sheila's social life had been a constant source of amazement to Carly. It seemed she never had an evening off without a date. The phone calls coming in to the house had been endless.

"Nothing special."

"With *none* of them?"

"Nah. It was going nowhere. I needed a change of scenery."

"Why Boston?"

Sheila eyed her sheepishly. "Because you made it sound so good. Remember those days we spent poring over maps and brochures and real-estate magazines when you were trying to decide where you wanted to go?" Carly remembered and felt a return of the camaraderie revealed in Sheila's smile. "Boston was perfect for you. Not too big, not too small. Lots of schools and universities around." She lowered her voice to a deep drawl. "Lots of up-and-coming businessmen and professionals."

"Wait a minute," Carly reminded her, with a chiding grin. "I never said that. You were the one with the eye out for social possibilities. All *I* wanted was an interesting place to live and teach. Where are you living, anyway?"

"I've taken an apartment on Beacon Hill."

"Not bad."

Sheila gave a comical scowl. "Not great. It's a studio. Subbasement. Kinda small and dark."

"But a good location."

"Hmmph. That's what I'm paying for."

"And lots of interesting guys living nearby?" Carly interjected with a sly smile.

"Damn it, I hope so." Sheila sat back in her chair and took a pose of idle indulgence. "What I'm looking for," she said airily, "is a tall blond with a great physique and a bulging wallet who'll fall madly in love with me and devote the rest of his days to showering me with lavish gifts and his undivided attention."

"Sounds good."

"But it's a dream." She sighed.

"Maybe not."

"Do you dream?"

"Sure. About fires. And guns. And people chasing me."

"Still? Oh, Robyn—"

"Carly."

Feeling a touch of impatience, Sheila ignored the correction. "Don't you know how safe you are?"

"It's one thing to say it, something else to believe it."

"Are you in touch with . . . anyone?"

"From Chicago?" Carly shook her head. "No. That was part of the deal, remember?"

"I know. But you had so many friends. I can remember the calls you used to get. They were all very concerned."

A flicker of pain crossed Carly's brow. "I know. It

helped. But I made a choice when I decided to testify for the state. My life—a new life—for that one."

"Are you sorry?"

"Sometimes." She shrugged. "But I can't change things. And I've been lucky."

"You must have new friends—"

Carly's smile was a weary one. "Now you're starting to sound like Sam. And my father. Sure I have friends. But friends do nothing for the dreams, the fear. It's always there, Sheila. What can I say?"

Sheila wished she could feel more sympathy. In her heart, she supposed she did. In her mind, well, looking around and at Carly, the woman had a lot going for her. Good background. A loving family. Memories of a husband who adored her. And financial stability. Bingo.

As though attuned to Sheila's thoughts, Carly threw a hand into the air. "Listen to me. I sound positively morbid. It must be because with you I can air those things I can't with another friend. I'm glad you've come, Sheila," she said more softly. "It'll be nice to keep in touch."

"Speaking of which," Sheila bubbled, leaning forward in her seat, "why don't we celebrate and go out for brunch. I hear there are some terrific places near Faneuil Hall."

Carly grimaced. "I'd love to, but I have to work."

"Today? It's Sunday!"

"What else is new?"

"Come on, Carly. You've got to take some time off."

Where had she heard that before? Thank you, Ryan Cornell. "I took yesterday off. Today I have to work." She was beginning to sound like a broken record.

"But it'd only be for an hour or two."

"I've already *taken* an hour or two," Carly overrode Sheila's coaxing with her own gently teasing tone. "And

I've got a good six or seven hours of work to do before tomorrow. Really, Sheila. We'll make it another time, okay?" She put her mug down and stood with Sheila.

"Promise? After all, you've got to show me around. You must know all the ins and outs of Boston by now."

Carly had no intention of getting into *that* particular discussion. The go-round with Sam on Friday night had been enough. "Knowing you, there will be a slew of men to show you the town by the end of the week." Then she thought of something Sam had said. "Hey, weren't you supposed to be staying on the Cape for a while? With a cousin?"

That was what she'd told Sam, Sheila mused. But there wasn't any cousin she'd been visiting on the Cape. They were all back in L.A. getting into one sort of trouble or another, and even if they weren't, they'd have to steal the money to fly east. "I came back early. Just wanted to get settled." She moved to the door. "You're sure I can't change your mind? It'd be fun. Like old times."

Fun? Another discrepancy in perception, Carly mused. True, she and Sheila had done any number of things while Carly had been in protective custody. After all, she hadn't been a prisoner. Well, not in the criminal sense, at least. The Marshal's Service had been most solicitous, planning dinners out, movies, yachting adventures on the lake. To Sheila, it must have seemed a pleasant turn in a job that had to be monotonous at times. To Carly, it was a consolation prize. Not that she hadn't enjoyed Sheila's company. Far from it. But regardless of how lavish the dinner, how engrossing the movie, how exciting the yachting adventure, she could never quite forget why she was where she was. Even in hindsight, her stomach knotted up.

"Maybe another time," she said, accompanying Sheila to the hall.

Sheila swung her large leather bag lithely to her shoulder. "I'll hold you to it, Carly Quinn." She grinned mischievously on her way down the stairs. "While you're doing your work, think of me breezing through the marketplace spending madly, fending off the most handsome of men—" Abruptly she stopped speaking, her attention caught by a most handsome man on the flight below her.

Curious, Carly stepped to the railing and followed her gaze. A tall, blond-haired man with the broadest of shoulders and a cocksure gait had approached the second landing as Sheila reached it. Even from where she stood Carly could see the smile he cast toward Sheila as he made his way down the hall. Eyebrows raised suggestively, Sheila looked up at Carly, tossed her head toward the bold figure as a quiet knock echoed through the atrium, shook one hand in mime of something hot, beamed at Carly again and was on her way.

Shaking her head with a helpless smile, Carly returned to her apartment to shower, then dressed in jeans and a sweater and headed for the kitchen. It was nearly noon and she hadn't eaten a thing. Making a cheese omelet and toast, she let her mind wander to the events of the morning. Sheila. Sam. Ryan.

Ryan. Her gaze fell once more to the cup he'd used. Lifting it, she held it to her, wondering what it was about the man that affected her so. Then, with a burst of determination she thrust the cup under the faucet, rinsed it and upended it in the dishwasher.

For four hours she worked without a break, finding solace in the intense concentration demanded by the papers before her. It was only a faint stiffness in her legs that brought her from her place on the living-room floor. Papers were strewn atop both of the low tables. The Sunday *Globe* lay unread at the end of the sofa.

Walking idly through the apartment, she paused in front of the window and gazed out at the Charles. It looked cold. Strange, when the air had been so warm that morning. But it was nearly dusk now, and morning was long gone. Then she'd been with Ryan. Now she was alone.

She was in very much the same circumstance the following evening, reading through a new batch of papers, when the phone rang. She had been expecting a call from Bryna Moore, an art teacher at Rand and a friend with whom she'd spent an hour that afternoon discussing a possible collaboration in an art-and-writing course. It wasn't Bryna, though. She instantly recognized the deep male voice by the involuntary flutter it sent through her.

"Carly? It's Ryan. How are you?"

"I'm fine," she answered softly, fearing she was better than that now that he'd called. She'd thought of him that morning when she'd left for school, and again when she'd paused in the downstairs foyer to get her mail on her way home. "Are you home?"

"Yup. My phone's in." He chuckled in self-derision. "Obviously." He paused for a minute. "I thought I'd test it out. You're the first person I've called."

She smiled, feeling suddenly warm. "Thank you. I'm honored. But how, uh, how did you know my number?" It was unlisted.

"It was printed on your phone. I have a good memory." He'd made a point to have, where Carly was concerned. He remembered every detail of the precious short time they'd spent together since Friday night, had relived those minutes repeatedly. And repeatedly he'd asked himself what it was about her that had instantly struck such a chord. He'd known his share of women over the years, both before and after his wife, yet none had seemed to have the need, or the reluctance, that Carly Quinn did. Among the many feelings she inspired, curiosity remained high on his list.

Aware now of the silence on her end, he cleared his throat. "I thought you might want to know that we got the autopsy done."

"What did they find?"

"I won't know for sure until the final report comes through in another couple of days. At least it was done. It's a start."

"Were you able to learn *anything*?"

"Just that he did have some signs of recent injury. How recent remains to be seen."

"Is the warden doing any checking on his end? You know, questioning guards and other inmates."

Ryan sighed. "He says he is. But he'll hear what he wants to hear, if you know what I mean."

Indeed she did. "He'll be hesitant to admit that any wrongdoing took place in his facility."

"Which was why the autopsy was so critical. All we can do is wait now for that report."

She nodded, but was silent. When Ryan spoke again, his tone held that something that tugged at her heart.

"I missed you this morning."

"This morning?"

"When I ran. I thought you might be out."

"My God, you must have been up early."

"I was out at six-thirty."

At six-thirty that morning she'd been in the shower, wishing she could have run even as she nursed tired hamstrings. "It's pretty dark then."

"All the more reason why it might have been nice to have you with me. Did you run after school?"

"Actually, no. The traffic was so heavy and it was pretty cold and I was tired." And it was dark then too. "I usually stick to the weekends."

"The mornings are nice. Other than being lonely, that is. But if you came with me it wouldn't be lonely. How about it?"

She twisted the telephone cord around her finger. "I don't know, Ryan—"

"Come on," he coaxed, and the thought of running tempted her nearly as much as the softness of his tone. "It'd be good for you. Fresh air. Exhilaration. It's a great way to start the day, particularly when you have to be cooped up in school."

"But I'm not cooped up," she argued. "I'm forever walking from one classroom to the other. Even outside." She hesitated. "Have you ever seen the school?"

"No."

"It's really beautiful, on the grounds of an estate with four separate buildings. My office is in one, the classrooms in another, the cafeteria in a third. So I do get exercise. Besides, I have to leave here every morning by seven-thirty. And if I've got to shower and dress and dry my hair and put makeup on. . . ." She realized she was babbling and caught herself. "Well, I'd really have to run at six. That'd be pretty early."

"Not for me. I'd be game."

"Thanks, Ryan," she murmured softly, reluctantly. "But I think I'll pass."

"For now. I'll give you that. But I'll keep after you, Carly. You won't know what you're missing until you've tried."

Oh, she knew what she was missing, all right. More

than anything she'd like to run each morning with Ryan. But it wasn't wise. It just wasn't wise.

At least, that was what she told herself all week. By the time Saturday morning rolled around, however, she was up early and eager to go. Unfortunately, it was raining. More disappointed than she might have wished, she returned to bed, wondering whether Ryan was in bed just below her, imagining him all warm and mussed from sleep, deciding that he'd most probably taken one look at the swelling puddles, turned over and gone back to sleep.

In fact, he was up at seven, staring gloomily at the rainsodden street. Wearing a pair of blue briefs and a look of disgust, he cursed his luck. He wandered to the living room, as though that window might reveal a ray of sun, then, thwarted there too, returned to the bedroom and thrust a hand through his hair in frustration. Pivoting on his heel, he backtracked to the kitchen, poured a tall glass of orange juice from the carton that looked as lonely in the otherwise empty refrigerator as he felt in his strangely empty life, and faced the window as he drank.

He hadn't planned to run until eight. That was the time he'd met Carly last Sunday. There was always the chance it would clear up. Leaning forward, he looked at the sky. It was dark gray and ominous, heavy, thick. Still, there was always that hope. . . .

Dragging the newspaper in from the hall with one arm and mental thanks that his home delivery had finally begun, he returned to bed to read. But he was restless. Headlines were about all he took in before he put the paper down atop the scattered sheets with an impatient rustle. Lying back on the pillow, he eyed the ceiling. He wondered what she was doing, whether she was awake, whether she'd planned on running, whether she was as frustrated as he. Most likely, he decided, she was sound asleep.

Bounding up, he looked outside again. It was pouring harder than ever. "Hell," he muttered, looked at his watch and sank back down on the edge of the bed. Pulling the paper closer, he extracted the editorial page, spread it with an agitated crackle of newsprint, and focused in on a column written by a colleague of his. Creative sentencing in the courts. An idealistic practice at best, at worst a mandate for discrimination. The piece was well conceived, if written with the verbosity that plagued so much of legal writing. When it was his turn to write an editorial, he'd make certain he consulted an English teacher.

Closing the paper impatiently, he went into the bathroom, quickly showered and put on his running suit, then returned to the window. He could try. Hell, he could always position himself downstairs on the pretense of debating whether to run or not, and wait for her. If she didn't show by eight-fifteen or so, he'd know.

Just then, a blur of yellow caught his eye and, squinting, he leaned forward. Some madman was actually running, if that was what could be called the dodging act he was doing round and about the obstacle course of puddles on the river path. Man, it was teeming! But maybe, just maybe, she'd be as crazy. After all, she hadn't run since last weekend.

He was about to head downstairs when a car approached, speeding eastward along Memorial Drive. Standing at the window in anticipation, he watched the car whisk by the runner, splattering him mercilessly, causing him to lose his stride. With that, Ryan Cornell unzipped his jacket and threw it onto the bed.

A floor above, Carly did the same. It was insane. She

didn't know why she'd even bothered to dress. The rain hadn't let up for a minute since she'd awoken. No one in his right mind would be running. The muddy yellow jogger she'd seen could have the path to himself. Much as she wanted the exercise, she wasn't *that* mad. Perhaps there was a message somewhere here. She looked heavenward. The weather was only another of the reasons she shouldn't see Ryan.

With a sigh of defeat, she returned to the bathroom to dress properly. Rain or no rain, she would have to go out later. Her refrigerator was nearly empty. There were clothes to be left and retrieved at the dry cleaners'. She had to pick up a few last skeins of silk thread to finish the needlepoint for her father. Not to mention a luncheon date with Sheila and a hair appointment at three. It was a lousy day for all that, but she would manage.

When Ryan knocked on her door, it was late afternoon. He'd spent the day working. Strike that. *Trying* to work. Something had to give. Patience was one thing, masochism another.

Hearing a faint sound from within, he stood straight, knowing that Carly would be looking out to see who was there. When the door slowly opened, he relaxed.

"Hi," he said with a smile, the simple sight of Carly Quinn melting his heart.

"Hello," she answered shyly. Her own heart beat double time.

"Just wanted to return this." He held out the towel she'd tossed him after they'd run on Sunday. "I finally did my laundry. It's clean."

She put a hesitant hand out to take the towel. "I'd forgotten all about it." Not quite the truth. In the back of her mind there had been the subtle awareness that

Ryan had something of hers. It had been reassuring. "Thanks."

"My thanks." Not knowing what else to do with them, he stuck his hands in the pockets of his jeans. "Crummy day."

Hugging the towel to her chest, she chuckled. "Tell me. I've been dodging the raindrops all day, what with a million things to do. I feel a little like a drowned rat." Her newly trimmed hair was damp. Her stocking feet hadn't quite dried out.

"You don't look it," Ryan said softly. She was the image of femininity, wearing a pale pink sweater and a plaid skirt of a matching pink and gray. She seemed small and fragile. Once again he felt a surge of protectiveness. And more. With her hair spilling in damp curls to her shoulders and her expression shy, verging on the self-conscious, she was as desirable as she'd ever been. "You look pretty," he whispered.

He didn't look bad himself in his jeans and dark sweater, she decided, before she looked away in sheer self-defense. "Anything inside and reasonably dry looks pretty on a day like this," she murmured. Then, helpless to resist, she looked back up at him. His hair, too, was damp, looking all the more vibrant. "You were out?"

"Uh-huh."

"Working?"

"This morning."

She nodded and swallowed hard. Her insides were astir with something she begrudged but couldn't shake. Ryan was too intense a man to take lightly, too quietly sensual to ignore. Against her will she responded to the heat of his gaze, the headiness of his presence. She swallowed again.

"Ah, hell," he murmured, stepping quickly into her

apartment, closing the door behind him and reaching for her before she could think to flee. He whispered her name as his lips opened on hers. Drawing her body against his, he kissed her deeply.

Carly reeled. Given the caution with which he'd approached her in the past, she hadn't expected this suddenness. Yet it was phenomenally exciting, for the need was there in them both. Minutes, hours, days of denial couldn't alter the fact of the raw biological attraction existing between them. And where more rational thoughts might have intervened had there been time, Ryan's aggression took the choice from her hands.

His lips were warm and moist, his tongue a welcome interloper. He was as thirsty as she, drinking of everything she gave, and she gave mindlessly. Her mouth opened to him, her tongue mated eagerly with his. She'd never known such gentle fire, and it seared her with startling force.

"Ah, Carly," Ryan moaned against her cheek when he finally released her to allow for the air both badly needed. "This is what I've wanted all week." His voice was hoarse, the arms strong that circled her and held her, trembling within bounds of steel. He buried his face in her hair and ran splayed hands up and down her back as though to reassure himself that she was there. "I've wanted to talk with you and hold you and kiss you. I've thought about you so much."

Carly's own arms were around his neck, her face tucked against the warmth of his throat, her brow cushioned by the thickness of his beard. She felt light and secure, at home for the first time in years. But she couldn't find the words to echo his. With the ending of his kiss, the choice was hers once more. And she knew for a fact that sensasions of happiness, of security, of homecoming, were cruel and taunting luxuries.

Clinging to the illusion for just a minute longer, she breathed deeply of his cleanly masculine scent. Then, slowly, she lowered her arms to his shoulders and levered herself away.

"You shouldn't," she whispered, eyeing him timidly.

"Shouldn't think of you? Shouldn't want you?" He locked his hands at the small of her back and kept her lower body pressed to his. "Why not?"

"Because I'm not right for you. You're not right for me."

"Are you kidding? After that kiss?"

Pain welled in her eyes. "It's physical, Ryan. That's all."

He was shaking his head before the last word was out. "No, it's not. Well, maybe it is. But the force behind it—that's far from physical. Physical is only the outlet. If you'd spend time with me, work with me, run with me, go out with me, you'd see."

Sadness mixed with pain in her soulful gaze. Looking up at Ryan, she believed what he said. Which made it all so much harder, so much harder. He didn't know who she was. He *couldn't* know who she was. And in that sense she would be forever deceiving him.

Lowering her eyes, she slowly shook her head. When she pushed against his arms, he released her. Turning her back, she silently walked to the window where, staring out at nothingness, she wrapped her arms around her middle. She felt cold and alone, that much worse for the warmth she'd known in Ryan's arms moments before.

"Carly?" His voice came from across the room, then again, more intimately, when he approached. "Carly? What is it?" he asked, directly behind her now. She could feel the heat of him, though he didn't touch her. And she wanted nothing more than to lean back against him, to be enveloped in the safe harbor of his arms once again. When he kissed her, he made her forget. For a split second she wished he would kiss her and never stop.

"Nothing," she said quietly.

"I know better than that." He slid his hand beneath the fall of her waves and lightly worked at the tautness of her neck. "I've seen it, Carly."

She cast a frightened glance over her shoulder. "Seen what?"

"That haunted look in your eyes. And desire." When she jerked her eyes forward again, he simply continued to stroke her neck. She didn't pull away, a fact that gave proof to his words. "You feel it, too. I know you do. But something's holding you back. I saw it on the stairs that day. You wanted me to kiss you, but you were afraid. Then, when we were running and I did kiss you, you opened to me with the same desire you felt just now. Then, too, something came between us as soon as you could think again. What is it?" he asked with such need that she nearly crumbled.

Which was precisely what she feared the most. Surrender. Confession. Discovery. Not that she doubted Ryan's integrity any longer. She trusted him fully. There was no way he could be faking the emotion she saw in his face. But her cover was something for which she'd given up her job, her friends and, in many respects, her family. To spill all to Ryan would be to poke a hole in that cover. She simply couldn't.

Which left her with the pain of deception.

"Tell me, Carly," he pleaded, his voice low and gravelly. Slipping his hand down her back and around her waist, he came to her side and looked down at her. "Is it your husband? Was your love for him such that you feel guilty experiencing something you might have shared with him?"

"No," she said quickly, then hastily qualified herself. "I did love him. Very deeply. Our marriage was something special. But, no, I don't feel guilty."

Ryan pondered her words and the urgent expression she wore. "It's been four years, you said. Has there been someone else since?"

She hugged herself more tightly, as though to ward off the heartrending concern that even now threatened to make her cave in against him. "There was," she said softly, unable to lie.

"Did you love him?"

"Not in the way I loved Ma-Malcolm."

"Then in what way?"

"Peter was a friend. A co-worker."

"A lover?"

She caught in her breath, then released it with a quiet, "No." What she'd felt for Peter hadn't ever approached the romantic, yet given what he'd sacrificed—in large part at her instigation—she felt nearly as attached to his memory as she did to Matthew's.

"Is he still back in San Diego?"

Involuntarily she winced. "No."

"Then he's here?"

"No."

"Are you in touch with him?"

She paused. To tell Ryan the truth, that Peter had died, would make her sound like a walking jinx. Which perhaps she was. But she didn't want to go into that. "No," she said simply, the finality in her voice conveying itself to Ryan, who took a deep breath and hugged her more tightly to his side.

"What about Sam?"

She was taken by surprise, jolted from one arena to another. Her heart pounded. "Sam? What about him?"

"Are you sure he doesn't have a hold on you?"

"Sam's a friend. I told you that. A very good one, but just a friend."

Ryan studied her intently. "So there's no one else. Then why not me?" he asked. "There are so many things I'd like to do with you, things that are awful to do alone. There are plays and new restaurants opening all the time—you still owe me an evening at Locke-Ober's—and there's the North Shore and the Berkshires and the White Mountains—do you ski?" When she shook her head he went quickly on. "I could teach you." He paused on an up note, the look of pain on her face reminding him of what she'd once said about not being free. He couldn't figure it out. "You're human. You have needs and desires just like the rest of us." His mind continued to labor. "Is it . . . a family problem?"

"No."

"Something physical?" He studied her with sudden alarm, the arm at her waist drawing her around to face him. Perhaps she was trying to spare *him* some sort of pain. "Are you sick?"

She looked up blankly. "Sick?"

He completed the circle with his free arm. "You can tell me, Carly," he urged, though torn apart by the thought. "Maybe I can help. If it's a question of limited time—"

"A fatal disease?" For the first time, she laughed aloud, taken with his flair for drama. "Oh God, Ryan, no. I'm fine. It's nothing like that."

"Then what?" he came back instantly, relieved yet as curious as ever. "What could possibly have such a strong hold on you that it would keep you from feeling, from experiencing and enjoying?"

Her humor vanished as quickly as it had come. With her hands resting on Ryan's forearms, she was aware of their strength, as she was of that of his thighs bracing hers, of his chest, his jaw, his personality. He'd kindled a flame and refused to let it die, and her body was in complete accord.

For a minute she simply looked at him, her eyes brimming with an anguished regret. Her voice was little more than a shaky whisper when she finally spoke. "Please, Ryan. Please don't push."

He held her gaze, his deep brown eyes mirroring her anguish. He half wished she would yell at him, demand he mind his own business, bodily kick him out. At least then he might be able to fight. But looking up at him the way she was, that lost doe, cornered and helpless yet wanting so desperately to survive, he couldn't fight her. He couldn't risk hurting her.

Instead, he gave a low moan and brought her against him. His head lowered protectively over hers. His encompassing arms formed a shield against the world. Eyes closed, he held her tightly, wondering whether she would ever take all he wanted to give. No, he couldn't fight her. Not with force at least. But he was far from defeated. And she was far from immune. Even now he could feel her arms creeping around his waist.

"Okay," he whispered into her hair. "Okay." He kissed her brow, nudging her head back. "It's okay." His lips brushed her eyes, her cheeks, her jaw. "Come sit with me," he breathed against her ear. "Just for a little while. I won't ask for anything you don't want to give."

She slowly shook her head. "It won't work, Ryan. It won't work."

"Why don't we see?" he asked, pressing slow kisses

along the line of her jaw. His hands slid forward along her waist, lightly scoring her sides.

"No," she murmured, but her eyes were closed and she had unknowingly tipped her head to the side to allow him access to her neck. When his fingers skimmed the side swells of her breasts, she sucked in her breath. Then the fingers were gone, returned to her waist, leaving her with nothing to fear but frustration.

Framing her face with both of his hands, Ryan tipped it up. "A last kiss, then," he whispered, and took it before she could think. No, he wouldn't force her. He wouldn't ask anything more than she was willing to give. But he'd found the key to that willingness, and he had every intention of using it.

Eight

"**Y**OU NEVER DID TELL ME ABOUT THAT AUtopsy report," Carly said as they ran the next morning.

"No point," Ryan responded. "It was worthless."

"Didn't show *anything?*"

His teeth gritted, giving his voice an edge. "Nothing conclusive. The warden claims there had been a scuffle in the prison yard two days before Luis died. The medical examiner claims that the bruises on his body could have come from that."

She cast a glance up at his face. "What do you think?"

Only after several pensive strides did he answer. "I think we'll never know."

"And it ends there?"

"It's ended. Oh, hell!" His sneaker hit a puddle, spattering them both. "Maybe this wasn't such a hot idea. It's damn wet underfoot."

"You're just upset," she said softly, dodging a puddle of her own. "Isn't there anything else that can be done?"

"Luis is dead. The prime witness gone. Nothing came from the inmates. Or the guards. It's not surprising."

"But you still suspect foul play?"

"I don't know. If someone feared Luis would spill his gut when his case came to trial, there'd be good reason to have him dead. He may have committed suicide. Then again, he may have been forced into it by a strong enough threat. His mother was the only person he had in the world. If he had to choose between his life and hers. . . ."

Carly tugged her wool hat lower over her ears. It was cold. It had been so warm last weekend, yet today the wind was cutting and the sky was leaden. "I'm sorry," she said at last.

"So am I."

They ran in silence for a while. Carly wondered what she would have done if she'd been a reporter investigating the possibility of foul play. She would have gone to the warden, then to the files. She would have tried to interview convicts and ex-cons and guards and defense attorneys and the commissioner of corrections. Somehow she doubted she would have learned much more than that foul play was not unknown in correctional institutions. But would anything have come of it? Probably not.

Prison was hell. Ryan's Luis had found that out.

After waiting for a week for his lawyer to show, Gary Culbert was impatient. The guard escorted him to a small windowless conference room, then shut the door, leaving him to pace the floor much as he'd done in his cell for what had seemed fifty hours a day since he'd been incarcerated one hundred and thirty-three days before. He took a cigarette from the pack in the pocket of his regulation blue work shirt and hastily lit it.

In the middle of the room stood a weathered wooden table around which three straight-backed chairs were set at odd angles, left carelessly by whomever had been there last. Completing the stark decor was a scratched metal bookshelf, bare of books, as depressing as the rest of the place, he decided with a snort. At least it was quiet here, a break from the incessant echoes of clanking metal doors and bars and voices raised in barely leashed anger.

The door opened and Philip Mancusi entered. A tall, thin man with a receding hairline and wire-rimmed glasses, wearing his usual three-piece suit, he carried himself well, looking the part of the cocksure lawyer to the hilt.

"Gary." He nodded in greeting, then deposited his briefcase on the table along with an overstuffed brown envelope.

"Where the hell have you been? I've been trying to call you all week! In case you haven't noticed, I don't exactly have a princess phone in my cell!"

Mancusi cast a quelling stare over the rims of his glasses, clearly not intimidated by the outburst. "I've been in court," he said casually, seating himself in one of the chairs. "You're not my only client."

"But I'm sure paying you one hell of a lot!"

"And we both know where the money came from." In the silence that hovered, Culbert scowled, but had no further retort. His lawyer proceeded. "Have a seat, Gary."

Angrily flicking his cigarette in the direction of the tin ashtray, Culbert sat. "What's happening? Are you getting me out of here or not?"

"You were convicted of murder," Mancusi reminded

him with a steady gaze. "All I can do is take the appeals step by step. You know that. You're a lawyer."

"Was. Was. That's the operative word. My license was revoked—or had you forgotten?"

"No, I haven't forgotten. But all that can be reversed. You can't give up hope."

"I haven't!" Culbert growled, taking a long drag on his cigarette. "It's the only thing I've got left, which is why I sit here wondering what's going on."

"We were denied the formal motion to stay execution of sentence."

No bail. No freedom. There was a silence, then an explosive "Damn it! Why didn't you tell me?"

"The written decision came down from the appellate court the day before yesterday. I thought it better to tell you in person. I've already begun preparing papers to file a motion for a new trial."

"On what grounds?" Culbert shot back.

Mancusi's shrug belied the pinched look around his mouth. "That's what I'm trying to decide. We could always claim that the prosecutor never fully revealed the extent of the promises made to his witness. The argument could be made for excessive temptation."

Culbert was as dubious as his lawyer. "Flimsy. What would our chances be?" It was a rhetorical question. He knew the score. Standing, he paced to the corner, then turned. "I want that new trial, Phil. This place is driving me insane."

"What did you expect?"

Storming the few feet to the table, Culbert put both hands down flat. His eyes were hard. "I expected you to get me off in the first place. That was what you said you could do. That was what I paid you for."

"That was before the state came up with Robyn Hart. She was a good witness."

"She was an ambitious bitch who latched on to a cause and was determined to use it as a stepping stone in her career."

"She's relocated now."

"Yeah." Culbert straightened. "Probably sniffing around in someone else's dirty laundry."

"If there's a new trial, she'll be back," Mancusi warned.

"And you'll just have to try again to show that she was too emotionally involved to be objective. Hell, the woman lost a husband in a fire. Of course she'd want to nail someone." He raised one hand. "Sure, sure, different fire, different city. But she was far from impartial."

"The jury didn't think so."

"Well, we'll have a different jury this time."

"But the same witness. I'm telling you, Gary, it may be tough." His gaze flicked to his papers, then back to Culbert. "There's one possibility we might explore. The guy who died in that last fire—Bradley? If we can show some involvement between him and Hart—"

"Involvement as in sex?" When the other gave an acquiescent shrug, he scowled. "Come on, Phil. How're you gonna do that?"

"There are ways. Vengeance can be a powerful motive in a woman's mind."

"But you said it yourself. She was a good witness. If you couldn't break her regarding her husband, how in the hell are you gonna do it regarding some two-bit photographer?" Breaking into a spasm of coughing, Culbert stubbed out his cigarette.

Mancusi watched his client, one brow raised. "You should give those things up. They're lousy for your health."

"It's this place that's lousy for my health. I'm getting high blood pressure climbing the walls." Calming himself, he sat back. "Without her the state hasn't got much of a case. Any chance she won't testify?"

Mancusi shrugged. "I don't know. If they've relocated her, she's given up a lot. So has the government. I doubt they'd *let* her renege. That was probably part of the deal."

"But if something happened to her, if she couldn't testify for some reason?"

"We'd probably get the case dismissed. Even with the notes she kept, I could make a case against her character. *If* something happened to her. But it depends what that was." He eyed his client cautiously. "Gary, Gary, I wouldn't even think it, if I were you. You're in enough trouble as it is."

"So what have I got to lose?"

"Exams beginning today?" Ryan asked as he and Carly set out on the river path. Though it was cold, the ground had completely dried. The weekend's rain had stripped the trees of the last of their leaves. Winter was on its way.

"Uh-huh. We had review days Monday and yesterday. I think the kids are ready."

"Will they study?"

A facetious laugh slithered from the back of her throat. "I hope so. Most of them will. I'm worried about a couple, though. One of the girls I counsel is rebelling against everything."

"You counsel?"

She nodded. "All of us do."

"Where do you get the time?"

"It's built into the day. I have four counselees. It's not bad."

"What do you do for them?"

"Get to know them. Keep in close touch. Watch for problems. Be on top of them when they occur."

"Hmmph. Sounds different from the guidance counselors I remember as a kid. Seemed like all they did was give summary approval to the courses I wanted to take, write recommendations, shuffle papers."

"Oh, I do my share of that too. But the theory at this kind of school is that the counselor is a friend."

"That was what they said then."

"But it's true. At least here it is, though come to think of it I didn't get a lot from my guidance counselors either. And they were working full-time at it."

"Maybe that was why they failed. You know, the typical middle-level bureaucrat who creates things to fill his time?"

She ran a bit, then smiled up at him and nodded. "Maybe you're right." She sighed. "Anyway, it's different at Rand. I think it works. The teachers are different. They're very dedicated. They genuinely like kids. And care about what happens."

"You do?" he asked, warmly meeting her gaze. He knew there was a reason he'd run at six since Monday. For every bit of time he spent with Carly, he learned—and liked—more about her.

"Yes. I do," she said conclusively.

"I'm glad." His voice lowered. "I'm also glad you decided to run during the week. Any regrets?"

She tossed him a single shy glance. "Sure. Sore muscles."

"You're doing fine, babe. Just fine."

Given the grin he sent her, she had no regrets at all.

On Thursday morning he had something else on his mind. They'd run in the dark to their usual turning point and were headed back as the sky began to pale.

"Just a week till Thanksgiving. It's hard to believe."

Carly didn't find it so hard to believe. Though the past ten days had zipped by, it seemed forever since she'd seen a family face.

"What are your plans?" Ryan asked.

She smiled. "I'll be with my father." She hesitated, on the verge of returning the question. As the days had gone by, as she'd run each morning with Ryan, she'd wondered more about him. She knew so little of his past. One part of her told her she didn't want to know. The less she knew, the less involved she'd be. It was the other part that goaded her on. "How about you? Will you be turkeying?"

"Of course. My brother and I are driving home for the day." Strange, he mused, how the phrase had slipped out. For Thanksgiving's sake, home *was* that grand old house in which he'd grown up. When he'd been married to Alyssa before things had turned sour, when a brood of kids had filled his mind, Thanksgivings had been in Milton.

"Where's home?"

His lips curved wryly. "Funny you should ask."

"I didn't mean—"

He squeezed her arm and chuckled. "No. It's all right. I was just pondering the same question. Home with a capital *H.*"

It was a poignant issue for Carly, yet she hadn't expected such a quandary in Ryan. "Did you find an answer?" she asked softly.

He raised his eyes to the far horizon. "Ultimately I guess it's where family is. Wherever that is. I used to think it was with my wife. Obviously, that's changed. For the holiday, it's back with my parents."

"Where's that?"

"In the Berkshires. The same old house where I grew up."

"Your parents are still there."

"Yup."

"That's nice."

Something in her tone brought his gaze around. "It is. I'd like you to come with me sometime. They're great, my parents."

"And your brother?"

"Well—" he let out a white huff of breath "—Tom is something else. A little wild. But he'll get there. It was his house I lived in before I moved into your building."

"He's not married?"

"Tom? Hell, no. He's a confirmed bachelor. What he *needs* is a woman to calm him down. But at the rate he's going, he'll never find the right one."

"Why not?"

"His taste is lousy."

"Oh." She smirked. "Must have been interesting living there with him."

"He wasn't there, thank God. He spent the year on the west coast."

"What does he do?"

"Do?" He cast a playful glance her way. For whatever differences he had with his brother, an obvious affection existed. "Tom dabbles here and there. He was into stocks and bonds when he, uh, ran into a little trouble."

"What kind of trouble?"

"A minor hassle about some misappropriated funds. Nothing a good criminal lawyer couldn't handle."

"He stole money from clients?"

"No. Just used what he thought to be investment genius to earn his clients a little more. It backfired."

"What happened?"

"There was an out-of-court settlement. He had to

pay them back with interest. Nothing he couldn't swing. Actually, the guy *is* a genius. He could probably be successful at any number of things. Maybe I was his problem. He's spent most of his life being unconventional to my conventional."

"But you're close."

"Closer as the years have gone by."

"What's he doing now?"

"He's writing computer software programs. Sitting at home. Working whenever the mood hits. Making a bundle. Like I said, he's a genius."

Amid his pride, Carly heard a total lack of jealousy in his tone. "You wouldn't be happy doing that."

"No." He met her gaze. "Like I said, I'm more conventional. I don't mind the hours I work. I love my job."

They ran together Friday morning, again silently most of the way. It was comfortable and, as Ryan had suggested, invigorating to start the workday this way. Carly felt fresher when she got to school than she had before, though whether the extra energy she felt was due to running or the company she kept she couldn't say.

"You're awfully quiet," she observed when their building came into sight once more.

"Just thinking."

"About?"

"Work. I've got a sticky trial coming up. A libel case."

"Interesting?"

"Very. My client is one of yours. Actually a college professor. He's being denied tenure because of personal differences between himself and one of the most powerful members of the board of trustees."

"Have you got a case?"

"You bet. The trustee was stupid enough to put it all in writing, then pass it around."

"Sounds pat. What's the problem?"

Ryan frowned. "My man isn't the most diplomatic, which is probably what got him in trouble to start with. I'd give anything to keep him off the stand. He's apt to blow it under cross-examination."

"Can you keep him off?"

"I'm gonna try. But the guy insists he wants to speak for himself." He eyed her askance as they ran up the steps. "You know these professorial types. They like to lecture."

Carly nudged him in the ribs and ran ahead to the door, only to be caught in the foyer in a playful embrace.

"What was that for?" Ryan asked. His grin was only half concealed.

"That was for taking a swipe at my profession."

She had time to say no more, for Ryan dipped his head and captured her open lips. His kisses were playful at first, warm jabs in deference to the panting bequeathed by their run. As their bodies quieted, though, the kisses grew slower, deeper, stimulating other senses, causing a breathlessness of their own.

When he finally released her lips, he pressed her ear to his heart. Carly's own was thudding at the pleasure of his touch.

"Dinner tomorrow night?" he murmured softly.

Eyes closed, she reveled in his scent, sweaty but all male and terribly arousing. "Umm."

"Eight o'clock?"

"Mmm."

"Great." He set her back, took her hand and led her into the atrium just as she was realizing what she'd done. When she would have drawn back, he only held her hand tighter. She had to scramble to keep up. Passing his own floor, he continued straight up to hers. At her door, he turned to her, placed a fast peck on her cheek and was off.

"Ryan!" she called, leaning over the railing.

He put one long finger against his lips. "Shh. It's a godawful hour. Everyone's sleeping."

"That wasn't fair!" she whispered loudly. "You took advantage of me!"

Directly beneath her, he craned backward against his own railing, grinning broadly. "I warned you."

"You're impossible!"

He shrugged, then disappeared. She leaned farther forward, saw nothing, heard his door open, then close, and knew she was trapped.

As Saturday evening approached, Carly grew nervous. She hadn't wanted to be involved with a man, at least not on a romantic level, not yet. With Dennis Sharpe or Roger Hailey or any of the other men who'd asked her out, a date might have been a simple evening spent together. Intuitively she knew it would be more than that with Ryan. Ryan turned her on, emotionally and, yes, physically. Just thinking about him sent tremors of excitement through her body, leaving her with a knot of desire deep down low. When she was in his arms she seemed to forget everything. Therein lay the danger.

Bucking the tide of reason that told her to call him or leave a note, to plead a sudden rush of work or even illness, she indulged in a long bath, took special care with her makeup and hair, then spent forever choosing a dress. By seven-thirty she was ready. Ignoring sweaty palms, she sat down at the kitchen table with a pile of half-corrected exams and tried in vain to apply herself. At seven-forty she returned to the bedroom to comb her hair again. At seven-fifty she ran to the living room to make sure she'd laid out the right bag and coat. Back at the kitchen table she cursed herself for having left so much time. When the doorbell rang at seven fifty-five, though, she took it back.

He looked breathtakingly handsome in a suit and tie, his dark hair neatly combed, his brown eyes sparkling. "Hi," he said, his own breath taken by the vision of beauty he beheld. "You look fantastic."

Hand on the doorknob for support, she smiled shyly. "A change from running gear and six-in-the-morning muzzies, eh?"

"You look great then too. This is just different." His eyes glowed their appreciation. In the mornings she'd been fresh and unadorned, sexy in the way women are when they've just rolled out of bed. Now she was sexy in another way. Her makeup was perfect, accenting her high cheekbones and deep-set eyes. Spilling around her shoulders, her hair looked rich and thick, gloriously tempting. Her dress, a subtle plaid of hunter green and plum with a high neck, long cuffs, wide belt and an array of tiny covered buttons from throat to waist, gave an air of regality. The sheerest of stockings, high-heeled pumps. . . . He caught his breath. She stood straight, almost awkwardly, before him and was dressed as conservatively as possible, yet she couldn't have been more alluring if she'd been preening in a slinky off-the-shoulder gown of red silk with a slit up the thigh.

He began to speak, then cleared his throat when his voice emerged hoarse. "Do you have a coat?" His own, a double-breasted navy topcoat, was slung over his arm. He shifted it when she returned to the sofa for her things, helped her on with her coat, let his hands linger on her shoulders for an instant. "You smell good too."

His fingers tightened. "What are you trying to do to me, Carly?"

She cast him a half-fearful glance, then was relieved to see his broad white smile. "You were the one who hoodwinked me into this. You can still get out—"

"No, no." He released her shoulders and held up a hand. "I'll gladly suffer." Shrugging into his coat, he found some solace in the admiring nature of her gaze. He offered her an elbow. "Shall we?"

Sliding her arm through his, she wondered just who would be doing the suffering.

As he had promised that first morning, Ryan took her to Locke-Ober's. Standing at the door of the downstairs grill, the men's only room that had been one of the last bastions in Boston to yield to women's liberation, he cast a despairing eye at the crowd. "I made reservations for us here. The atmosphere is more interesting. But it looks as though every politician in town had the same idea. Locke-Ober's is infamous for its gatherings."

The maître d' approached with a broad smile and an outstretched hand. "Mr. Cornell! Good to see you!"

Ryan warmly met his clasp. "Same here, John. But things are pretty busy down here." Even as he spoke, he raised his free hand to acknowledge several acquaintances who sought his eye. "I was hoping for something a little quieter."

"Shall I give a call upstairs?"

"It's more touristy there."

"There may be something in the back room. It's smaller and quieter."

At Ryan's nod of interest, John picked up the phone on his desk. Within minutes they'd climbed the stairs to the upper enclave and were seated at an intimate table for two in a room that was indeed smaller and quieter. Even then they'd had to pass through a larger dining area. Twice Ryan had nodded to familiar faces.

It occurred then to Carly that she was with a person well-known in Boston circles. Previously she'd been with Ryan only in isolation—her apartment, the foyer and atrium, the paths along the river, at bizarre hours, no less. While on the one hand it was flattering to be with a handsome man who obviously had so many friends, on the other it was downright intimidating. Since she'd come to Boston she'd maintained the lowest possible profile. She didn't want that to change.

Eyes downcast, she took a seat as the upstairs maître d' held her chair. Tucking her purse on her lap, she focused on the single rose in its bud vase in the middle of the table. Ryan settled on her right.

"Enjoy your meal, Mr. Cornell, ma'am."

Ryan smiled. "Thank you, Henry." The maître d' moved off, and Ryan turned his gaze to Carly. "Is this okay?" he asked, puzzled by her sudden unease.

Stifling her qualms, she turned to him with a gentle smile. "This is lovely, Ryan." Her eye skimmed the room. "It's a beautiful place."

He nodded, following her gaze. "Old Boston at its best. Locke-Ober's has been a favorite of mine since my parents brought me here when I was sixteen."

"You must come a lot. They all know you." Even then, the wine steward was approaching, wearing a smile of recognition.

"Good evening, Mr. Cornell. How are you tonight, sir?"

"Fine, Gray. Just fine."

"Would you like anything from the bar?"

Ryan sent Carly an assessing glance, "I think we'll order a bottle of wine. A Montrachet will be fine."

Carly noted that he refrained from pronouncing either of the *t*'s in his extravagant choice of wines.

Where she felt awkward, though, the wine steward did not. "An excellent choice, sir," he said with a broad smile, and left.

Ryan's eyes were on Carly. Strangely though, he seemed content just to look. Or maybe it was that for the life of him he couldn't think of anything he wanted to say.

Carly was no better. She returned his gaze, then looked down, then across the room at the other diners. They were a well-dressed lot, exhibiting proper decorum to match their attire. Conversation was kept at a low hum.

"So you've never—"

"So you often—"

They looked at each other and laughed. "You first," Ryan said.

Carly blushed. "It wasn't important. What were you going to say?"

"I was going to say that I'm pleased to be the first one to bring you here. Have you been around much since you arrived in Boston?"

"I've seen more of Cambridge—the restaurants, that is. Closer to school and all."

He wondered whom she'd been with but refrained from asking. Instead he just nodded.

She fingered the edge of the thick linen tablecloth. "You came into Boston often as a boy?"

"My parents believed in culture. They took us all over, wanted us to know everything about the city, even though we were always very happy to go home again."

"Yet you decided to settle in the city."

"The opportunities for a law practice were better

here than they would have been in the Berkshires. And then when I married . . . well, it all made sense."

She wondered about his marriage, but refrained from asking. "Have you ever regretted it—settling in the city?"

"No. I like the city. And Boston is more manageable than some. Not too big, not too small, lots going on." When she chuckled, he tipped his head in an endearing gesture of uncertainty. "No?"

"Oh, yes. I was just thinking that those were some of the same reasons I chose Boston." Instantly she regretted her choice of words. To her relief Ryan took them at surface value.

"Why did you? I mean, why did you decide to leave San Diego?" He'd wondered about it more than once. She'd said that her husband—Matthew, or was it Malcolm, he frowned, confused—had died four years before. And her family was from the mid-West—Des Moines, she'd told him in a breezy reference during one of their morning runs. "Was it because of Peter?"

It took Carly a minute to get her bearings. It was so hard vacillating between Carly and Robyn. When she was with Ryan, she wished Robyn had never existed.

"No." She met his gaze as levelly as she could. "I just wanted a change. When the opening at Rand came up, it seemed perfect."

"But you'd looked into various areas?"

"To settle? Yes."

"I'm glad you chose Boston."

"So am I," she conceded softly.

The effect of their eyes locking was warm—too warm—yet Carly couldn't look away. The steward's arrival with their wine was some diversion, as was the subsequent arrival of their waiter with menus. It was only after they'd ordered that the silence set in again.

Ryan sipped his wine. Carly did the same. She felt his presence through every fiber of her being. Even as she cursed herself for being conned into this dinner, she knew that she hadn't put up much of a fight. What she *really* wanted was to be even closer to Ryan.

As though attuned to her thoughts, Ryan took her hand from the fork she was nervously fingering and held it in his. He ran his thumb over her knuckles, caressing her fingers, polishing the gold of her wedding band in a way that should have been sacrilegious but seemed all the more intimate.

"You're not sorry you've come, are you? You seem uncomfortable."

She could feel her heart thudding. "No. I'm. . . ." But she didn't know what to say. Uncomfortable seemed wrong, yet awkward or confused or excited or frightened seemed no better.

He brought her hand to his mouth. The soft bristle of his beard was as stimulating as the light brush of his lips. "Don't be, Carly. Please. I want you to enjoy yourself."

"I am."

"You're shaking."

She gave a half smile. "You're kissing me." That said it all.

Ryan laughed softly, a deep, rolling sound from his throat. "Not the way I'd like to," he said, then lowered her hand to the table, keeping it tucked in his. He took a deep breath. "Tell me about your childhood," he began, determined to put her at ease. "I can picture a little girl with curls all over her head, wearing pink tights and ruffles up to her chin."

It was Carly's turn to laugh, indeed more easily. "Not quite. I was a tomboy."

"You're kidding."

"No. I had three older brothers. It was a matter of survival."

"Were they close to you in age?"

"Pretty much so. We were each two years apart. I was the last." She smiled. "After me, I think my parents gave up on sweet little quiet things."

"Must have been some household."

"It was." Her smile warmed with memory. "We had a lot of fun. My brothers decided early that I was just another one of the guys. They led me into more than my share of mischief." Her eye fell on Ryan's hand holding hers and she recalled one brother holding her hand, inching her up the old elm tree from which she'd been able to descend only with the help of the firemen, another brother holding her hand, tugging her through a maze of gravestones at dusk, a third brother holding her hand, pulling her to their hideout in the crawlspace beneath the house. Ryan's hand was different, though. His fingers were long, strong but gentle. Soft dark hairs were sprinkled on richly bronzed skin, peering from the crisp white cuff that edged beyond his navy jacket. His hand was that of a man, and she was mesmerized by it as she never had been by her brothers'.

"But your parents held up fine."

She shook off her thoughts. "They loved it. Not that there wasn't a load of yelling and screaming. It seemed that my mother had no sooner washed the kitchen floor than one of us needed drinks for the bunch. Do you know what it's like for a five-year-old to try to juggle four glasses of grape juice? Or what it's like when even one of those glasses spills?"

Ryan chuckled. "Grape juice? I can imagine. Your mother must have had her work cut out for her."

"She did," Carly said more softly. "Poor woman. It wasn't until after she died that we got a housekeeper."

His hand tightened. She had never spoken of her mother before. She had only mentioned her father when she'd talked of Thanksgiving. Though there had always been the possibility of divorce, Ryan had more or less assumed her mother had died. "How old were you when it happened?"

"I was twelve."

He winced. "It must have been very hard."

"Yes. We'd all been pretty happy-go-lucky children. Our parents had provided a warm, loving home. Nothing could go wrong—until it did. It was a shock."

"Very sudden."

"Uh-huh." She gave a sad laugh. "Quieted me down some, I can tell you that."

He ached for her as he had when she'd told him about her husband. "No more tomboy?"

"No. I suppose it was about time anyway. I was—" she made a gesture with her free hand and blushed "—growing up."

He admired the blush, his suggestive gaze fueling it. "I bet you had a line of suitors to keep your brothers jealous."

"Not quite. I started to study and spent hours reading in my room. I suppose that was the beginning of my interest in literature. And writing. I kept a journal. It was an outlet."

Imagining the pain she must have felt with her mother gone and in a household of men at such a critical point in her development as a woman, Ryan wanted to take her in his arms and comfort her. Something in her expression, though, defied pity. She was proud. And self-sufficient—from the start he'd been aware of her self-containment. Now he could begin to understand its roots.

He was about to speak when a couple that had entered the room moments before detoured to their table. The man was tall, bespectacled and distinguished looking. The woman was striking. As a pair they had an intensity that struck an immediate chord in Carly.

When Ryan stood to make the introductions, she felt an irrational discomfort. It was one thing to have him merely nod at acquaintances as they passed, another to hear her name on his lips, spoken softly but clearly, announcing to the world who she was. Swallowing her deepest of fears, she managed to smile and return the warm greeting she was offered. Even as the couple had moved off she was chiding herself for her sensitivity. There was no possible way that anyone could recognize her. Surely she had only imagined that the woman had eyed her particularly closely.

Ryan's soft elaboration on their identities did nothing to ease her mind. "Mark is the executive producer of the evening news on Channel 4. Jennifer is his star attraction."

"She's a reporter," Carly stated, her voice miraculously warm, given the ice suddenly flowing through her veins.

"A good one. And a nice person at that. Some of them are impossible. Pushy and totally egocentric. Jennifer is different. I like her."

Quite unexpectedly, it was Ryan's praise that gave Carly a viable reason for the woman's interest in her. Jealousy, curiosity—either would do. "She likes you too," she said, much relieved. "Have you ever dated her?"

Ryan leaned closer, his voice low, if animated. "Dated Jennifer Blayne? Are you kidding?"

"I thought you said you liked her."

"I do. But liking her is one thing, wanting a relationship with her another. She's not my type at all."

"What is your type?" Carly asked on impulse.

His gaze didn't waver. "A woman who has time for me, for one thing. Jennifer has a career to attend to."

"Don't we all?"

He arched a dark brow. "There are careers . . . and there are careers. For women like Jennifer, a career is the be-all and end-all. Oh, they're fun to be with, I suppose. But I, for one, could never compete with a career that demands that kind of commitment."

"Do I detect a trace of chauvinism?" she couldn't help but tease.

"You bet you do," he countered, undaunted. "And I'm not ashamed of it. At least I recognize what I need. It may not be right, but it's a fact. I respect women like Jennifer. But my type—the type that really turns me on—is softer, more private, more home-oriented. She's interesting and may have a successful career of her own, but there's room for more. She needs me." He held her gaze with a force that nearly stole her breath. "She needs me more than she needs any other person on earth."

Once again Carly's heart was drumming. This time it was the arrival of their meal that softened the edge, steering conversation to a lighter track. Startled by his own intensity, Ryan shook himself out of it by making small talk about the food and the restaurant, relating anecdotes of times he'd been there before. Then he asked Carly about her exams. In turn she pumped him for information on his libel case. With the earlier discussion temporarily shelved, each seemed to take as much interest in hearing the other speak as in speaking.

Drawn into the web of Ryan's congeniality, Carly

enjoyed herself. The food was delicious, the wine superb, and Ryan was as attentive a companion as she might have dreamed.

As they ate and talked, though, she had the uncanny sensation of being watched. She ignored it at first. But when she dared cast a glance to the side of the room where Jennifer Blayne was seated, she imagined the woman looked quickly away. It was in a second such glance that Carly's eye caught at another table, another woman. This one didn't look away. Another admirer of Ryan's, Carly wondered? But this one was different. Darker, more serious looking, attractive, but in an ultrapolished kind of way. . . .

"Is something wrong?" Ryan asked, turning his head to follow Carly's gaze. When he turned back, his expression was placid.

"She's staring. Even now. Do you know her?"

"Uh-huh," he said calmly. "She's my ex-wife."

Nine

CARLY'S GAZE SWUNG TO RYAN. "YOUR EX-WIFE?"

"Uh-huh."

"Oh." She clamped her jaw shut.

Ryan grinned mischievously. "Is that all you have to say?"

She shrugged. "What else should I say?" Her gaze slid back to the woman. "She's stunning."

"Uh-huh."

"So's the man she's with."

"I hadn't noticed."

"Then you don't care?"

Ryan's good humor ran deep. With Carly by his side, he felt perfect. "We're divorced. Alyssa can do whatever she wants with whoever she wants. If you're looking for jealousy, you're in for a disappointment."

"How about curiosity? Aren't you that teeny bit curious about who she's with?"

"I'm sure I'll find out. She'll be over here in a minute."

"She will?"

At Carly's sudden look of dismay, Ryan grinned. "Alyssa is the one who's curious. That's why she's been staring at you. Social climbing is her speciality, gossip an integral part of that. Right about now she's wondering who you are, where you come from, whether you've got a pedigree and who she'll call first when she gets home."

She sounded precisely like the kind of person Carly could do without. "Doesn't that bother you?" she asked, put out that she seemed to be the only one to feel annoyed. "I'd think you'd resent it."

"I might have at one time." Since he'd met Carly— was it only two weeks ago?—he realized all he'd been missing. With Carly he could talk about anything and everything, knowing she cared. He felt closer to her than he had to anyone in years. Remarkable, given the questions that still lurked in his mind.

"You're right," Carly muttered, straightening. "Here she comes."

Ryan squeezed her hand. "Relax. She won't bite. She's all talk."

That was what bothered Carly. Nonetheless, she gathered her composure and produced a smile when the other woman and her companion arrived at their table. Again Ryan stood to make the introductions. Again Carly felt a sense of unease when the couple left. It wasn't that she was ashamed to be with Ryan. On the contrary. Even with Alyssa Cornell standing not three feet from her, Carly felt proud and confident. No, embarrassment was nowhere in the picture. What bothered her was her own visibility. It was good for her, she could hear Sam Loomis saying. There was nothing to fear, nothing to fear. Why, then, did she half expect the evening to be topped off with a photographer popping up to take pictures to splash all over the local rag?

"There, that wasn't so bad," Ryan said when they

were alone once again. His eyes toasted her, boosting her spirits some.

"She seems nice enough."

"She is."

"Then what happened?" Instantly she blushed. "I'm sorry. That was inexcusable. It's none of my business."

"I don't mind," he replied softly. "I'd be disappointed if you didn't ask. Alyssa and I just went in different directions. That's all."

"You must have loved her once." She couldn't imagine his having married without that—not Ryan, who seemed to have so much to give.

"I did. When we were first married I thought she was the next best thing to a hard-fought first-degree murder conviction."

Something in the crooked tilt to his mouth spurred Carly on. "And?"

"That was just it. She was the next best thing. Only the next best thing. My work came first. She couldn't accept that. And I don't blame her," he added with a sigh. For the first time that evening he seemed troubled. He lifted his wineglass, drained its remaining drops, put the glass down and studied its slender stem. "I guess I'm no better than a Jennifer Blayne."

"In what sense?"

"My work has always been my life. My career really is the be-all and end-all."

"I don't believe that for a minute, Ryan," Carly chided with a conviction that astonished even her. "I've heard you talk of too many other things, and with feeling. If the law came between you and Alyssa, there had to be something amiss in your relationship from the start."

Ryan raised his eyes to hers. "I suppose there was. When I first met Alyssa, she was quiet and agreeable.

Her father was a very wealthy man, as well as an autocrat. She'd been pretty much dominated through life, but she had definite ideas of what she wanted."

"Which was?"

His words flowed. He hadn't shared his feelings so honestly before, and there was a strange relief in it. "A husband who, with the help of her money, would sit back, work part-time, spend every free minute with her. She desperately wanted love." He took a breath. "Unfortunately, when the honeymoon was over and she realized that I intended to work, she felt cheated."

"Didn't she go off on her own—I mean, find things to keep herself busy?"

"If only. No, her solution was to try harder. She was constantly in the office expecting a three-hour lunch. Or she was picking me up from work, taking me to one engagement or another. Or she made plans for the two of us to join a bunch of others for the weekend in New York or a week in the Bahamas.

"It became impossible. I was trying to build my practice, needing to work every free minute, and she fought me every step of the way." His lips thinned. "I tried to give her everything she wanted. Bought her a huge house in Milton. A Mercedes. A fur coat. And since I refused to take the money her father offered, I had an excuse to work all the harder. Then she wanted to have children."

"Didn't you?"

"Oh, yes. Very much." His eyes lit at that particular dream, then dimmed. "But for different reasons than Alyssa's." At Carly's questioning gaze, he explained. "I've always loved kids. Often when we went to friends' houses, I found the kids more interesting than their parents. Alyssa wasn't dumb. She sensed it. She hoped a child would keep me home more. So we tried. And things went from bad to worse. When she didn't become pregnant, she compensated by clinging all the more. Finally she conceived. In her fourth month she miscarried." He stopped talking then and stared darkly at the table.

Carly put her hand on his. "I'm sorry, Ryan."

He turned his palm up to twine her fingers in his, studied them, then shrugged. "Maybe it was for the best. We had so many differences. Her possessiveness was doing to me what my work was doing to her. It was mutual overkill. Things went downhill from there. I started working all the harder. Gradually she withdrew. From me, at least. Alyssa is, above all else, a very social being."

"And you're not?"

"Not in the same sense. Alyssa's life is a show. It's her place in society that gives her pleasure. I don't care about that. I like being with people purely for the enjoyment of it. If the company I keep is boring, I want out."

"There's nothing wrong with that."

"If you're married to Alyssa, there is. Toward the end it was a constant struggle. Our final parting was remarkably amicable, a relief on both sides. I think she's much happier now."

"And you?"

He looked her in the eye. "Right now? Without a doubt."

"In general," she prompted.

His gaze grew melancholy. "Yes, I'm happier. Which isn't to say that I don't want a wife and family. I want those more than anything. It's just that now I've got my eyes wide open. There's more to happiness than the mere fact of family life. It's the quality of that family life that's important. Come to think of it, marriage is almost inconsequential. It's who you're with that counts." He quirked a sudden smile. "Wanna come live with me and have my kids?"

"Ryan," she chided, "you're awful. If you go around asking women questions like that, you're apt to find yourself in a worse mess than you were in before."

"But I'm serious."

"You're not. You barely know me."

"I like what I see."

"You don't know the half."

"Which is why we should live together for a while. Hey—" his eyes sparkled "—I've got a great idea. We could cut through my apartment's ceiling, put in a spiral staircase and have a big place for ourselves."

Carly smiled. "You don't even own your place yet."

"But I will. The Amidons are sure to find something in Florida. It's just a matter of time."

"Then why don't we wait," she teased with a good-natured crinkle of her nose. "There's no rush."

"No rush? Hell, I'm pushing forty. *You* may have time. I don't." As though to make his point, he signaled for the waiter. Within seconds he'd ordered dessert to go. Then he turned back to Carly. "Let's get out of here. I think I've about had it with the public eye for one night. Besides, I have to show you what a mean cup of coffee I make. Maybe that'll convince you."

"Don't hold your breath," she scoffed. But it was her breath being held when they entered his apartment half an hour later. Ryan disappeared into the kitchen to dispense their dessert while she looked around his home. "This is nice," she commented when he returned to place two plates on the coffee table.

"It's okay," he shrugged. "A little staid."

"No, it's fine."

He stood straight and looked around. "Maybe it's that it's not mine. I don't feel at home."

She knew what he meant. The furnishings were pleasant and in good condition, but more befitting the Amidons than Ryan.

"Anyway," he went on, "it serves my purpose. Everything's here, if a little bland."

Carly was intrigued. "What would you do if it were yours?"

"Get rid of pea green, for one thing," he stated with his hands on his hips. "It needs character. I'd start with something vivid on the walls. Maybe burgundy . . . or navy."

"Paint the walls navy?" she asked.

"No, no. Art. Something bold and contemporary. I'd throw a rya rug on the floor, chuck those curtains for Levolors to pick up one of the other colors, replace the sofa and chairs with endless sectionals, put a tree over here—"

"A *tree*?"

"Sure. It'd add life, no?"

She couldn't suppress a chuckle. "That it would."

"Well?" He turned to her expectantly. "What do you think? How would it all look?"

"Interesting."

"You don't like it."

"I do. I do."

"Say that again," he said more quietly, thoughts of decorating fast fleeing from his mind. He came to stand before her.

"I do," she murmured, the softest expression on her face as she was caught up in his web of enchantment.

Wrapping his arms around her waist, he drew her into his kiss. His lips were warm and inviting, pleading for an acceptance she didn't have the strength to deny.

It seemed the entire evening had led to this moment; she'd been lost from the instant he'd shown up at her door. Aloof and reserved? Poised and in control? No longer. Carly felt that she was a tree in springtime, coming alive, blossoming in his arms.

When he suddenly bent over and swept her off her feet, she felt a vague inkling of fear. "Ryan," she whispered, clinging helplessly to his neck, "what are you doing?"

"Carrying you off," he murmured, setting her half reclining on the sofa, resuming his kiss before she could protest. Her inkling of fear dissolved into pleasure. There seemed no finer dessert than Ryan's warm lips, his moist tongue, the hands that firmly held her face, the strong body hovering very, very near.

She returned his kiss with a taste of the excitement that shot through her body. Long-dormant desire flared. She basked in the luxury of it. When he pulled back and sat up, she moaned in soft protest. Eyes holding hers, he shrugged out of his coat and unknotted his tie. In fascination she watched him release the first few buttons of his shirt. Then he lifted her, shifted her, until she sat sideways on his lap.

"You're lovely," he murmured as his head lowered, and then he was drugging her further, honing her senses, heating her blood.

Her breath came in short gasps. She felt his hands on her back, caressing her. Her own grew more bold, slipping forward to his chest, charting its manly contours. From the first, Ryan had inspried her curiosity. And she'd fought it. To some extent she still did. But the lure of his body, magnificent as far as she'd seen it, was too much. She wanted, she needed, to know his virile shape.

When his hands touched her breasts she cried out.

Her body responded; it seemed she'd been waiting forever for his touch. It had been so long since . . . since. But she hadn't missed a thing until she'd met Ryan. He alone had the power to ignite her senses and stir her to action.

Leaning forward, she put her lips to his throat and placed small, seeking kisses against its racing pulse. He tasted fresh and clean. Swept up in a realm of glorious sensation, she inched lower. Fine hairs began where his shirt parted. Her mouth explored their texture, sampling him with barely leashed hunger. His skin bore a faintly musky smell, very healthy, very male. Eyes closed, she savored it, breathing deeply, losing herself. After everything she'd lived with—and without—for too many years, this sensual delirium was heaven.

"Oh, babe," Ryan groaned thickly, burying his face in her hair. It seemed he'd been waiting forever to touch her this way. His hands roamed in ardent progression, leaving her breasts to trace the curve of her hips and thighs, returning to learn more of her womanly grace. He found her nipples hard even through the material shielding them. Encouraged by her small whimpers, he rubbed them with his thumbs. "God, I need you," he rasped. "You're so special, so special. . . ."

Consumed by the pleasure of the moment, Carly barely heard his words. Never in her life had she known this kind of fire. She'd been a virgin when she'd come to Matthew, and he'd been her teacher, her mentor in every sense. He'd acquainted her with her body and its capabilities, yet he'd always seemed older, more knowing than she was. As lovely as it was, there had been something onesided about their lovemaking; Matthew had been the masterful leader, Robyn the delighted follower.

It was Ryan who sought her as a partner, an equal. His intense need fueled the flame that drove her on.

Pressing kisses to his chest, she released first one button, then another and another, until his shirt was open to his waist. Tugging his shirttail from his pants, he watched, entranced, as she slid the last button from its hole and gave her fingers access to his flesh. They wandered restlessly, delighting in discovery. She spread her palms over an expanse of firm muscle, moving them in erotic circles while her mind spun dizzily. His ribs expanded with each labored breath; his stomach was lean and hard. The pelt of hair, broader, then tapering, lured her senses again and again in agonizing temptation.

Ryan needed her; her touch set him afire, sending live currents to a gathering point in his groin. In a bid to ease the ache, he shifted her to her back and moved down over her. When her arms encircled him, he held himself on an elbow and impatiently tackled the small buttons at her throat with his free hand.

Hot and constricted, tormented by desire, Carly welcomed the air that met her flesh. She arched closer to Ryan, seeking the feel of his hard length against her, simultaneously shocked and exhilarated by his throbbing, his outer show of all she felt inside.

Breathlessly she cried his name, only vaguely aware that her dress lay half open, though she was acutely conscious of the hands that forayed within its soft wool folds. His strong fingers were electric, sizzling her breasts, her ribs, her waist. Then he lowered his mouth and nibbled hungrily at her flesh, whispering her name, lifting her higher.

Greed surfaced; he couldn't get enough of her. His lips savaged the silk of her bra, the lace at its top, finally the turgid bud at the center of her breast. In unison they moaned, Carly as wild with need as he. His fingers fumbled with her bra's front catch, released it, peeled the fabric to either side. He buried his head between her breasts, turning it this way and that as though to devour all of her at once.

The brush of his beard against her flesh was new and infinitely arousing to Carly. Thrusting her fingers into his hair, she urged him on, seeking to ease her ache. But there was only fire, and it raged hotter. When his mouth closed over her nipple she cried out, then sobbed softly as the tip of his tongue pebbled it and his teeth took it ever so devastatingly in fever-provoking love play. Her hips began to move, undulating in instinctive response to his tentative thrusts.

"Ryan! My, God!" she whimpered, each shuddering breath feeding the flame.

His rasping response fanned it all the more. "Oh, babe!"

Displaced by gentle writhings, Carly's skirt was wrapped high around her thighs. Angling himself just enough, Ryan slid a hand beneath it, along the silken expanse leading home. Arriving with precision, he shaped his palm to her, groaning his desire when she bent her knee in welcome.

His vibrant caress, though, provided only brief solace. Aroused to a state of near oblivion, she strained against him, needing far more than even the thinnest silk bonds allowed. When he sought the waistband of her panty hose, she sucked in her stomach to show him the way. He needed little guidance. Her heat was a potent beacon. His fingers drew tiny circles on her skin, working downward, probing deeper.

Carly squeezed her eyes shut and gasped. Then, while her pulse raced out of control, he opened her, found her moisture and began to stroke it.

Suddenly she was scorched. Flames surrounded her. She could barely breathe.

Reacting as one being burned alive, she stiffened. Images from the past arose with a raging vengeance, a redhot conflagration threatening to engulf her. In a panic, she grabbed fistfuls of his hair to pull him away, then screamed in utter terror.

"No! No! *My God, don't!*"

Ryan went rigid. His breath came in great gasps. His head brought painfully up by the force of Carly's hands, he stared down at her, uncomprehending at first, then disbelieving, then with a stark terror of his own. Her eyes were wide, panic filled, unfocused and sightless. She was in another world, another time, experiencing an abject horror that stabbed his gut with ice.

"Carly?" he whispered hoarsely. "Carly! It's me. It's Ryan. *Carly!*" Frantic at the sight of such raw pain, he only knew he had to get her back. His hand trembled as he lifted it to stroke her cheek. "It's all right, Carly," he murmured shakily. "It's all right."

Her eyes shifted to his then, and she blinked. Tiny creases puckered her brow. Her fingers slowly released his hair. Her hands fell to his shoulders. She swallowed hard.

Yes, there'd been fire. First from Ryan's heat, then, in a flashback so startlingly intense that her skin felt blistered. But there was more. There had to be. A deep-seated fear of closeness, of commitment. A subconscious realization that, after months of hiding, years of avoiding intimacy, she *just wasn't ready.*

Helplessly she began to shiver. Her eyes filled with tears and Ryan thought he'd die. Sitting up, he took her into his arms and held her tightly, burying her face against his chest, absorbing the silent sobs that shook her. She felt chilled to the bone now, a far cry from the heat of moments before. Heartsick, Ryan could only hope to share his warmth.

"It's all right, sweetheart," he murmured, the ache of unfulfillment quickly forgotten. He rocked her ever so slowly and pressed his cheek to her hair. He didn't try to caress her, simply offered his best shot at comfort.

It worked. Her tears slowed, then stopped. She sniffled and eased herself back from him, chin tucked low, fists clutched knuckle to knuckle holding her dress closed.

"I'm sorry," she whispered raggedly. "So sorry. . . ." She shook her head in dismay, but a strong finger tipped it up.

"Don't be," Ryan said, holding her moist gaze with the gentleness echoed in his voice. "It's all right. You were frightened. That's all. Maybe it happened too fast." Even as he said the words, he knew they were simplistic. She wasn't a virgin, and nothing she'd ever said had led him to suspect that her husband had mistreated her in any way. But he'd seen that distant look in her eyes—and not for the first time. He wondered if she'd been raped, perhaps recently. Yet he couldn't make himself ask.

She lowered her eyes. "Too fast. It was. I wasn't prepared." But that, too, was false. He had felt her body's most intimate response. Still he didn't argue. "I didn't expect. . . ."

Her words trailed off, and she shuddered with the aftershock of terror that shot through her. No, she hadn't expected it. She wouldn't have believed it possible for the past to intrude that way. Well, she'd told Ryan that he didn't know half of it. Maybe now he'd think twice before pursuing her.

* * *

It didn't quite work that way. Later that night, lying sprawled in his bed, his arms pillowing his head, Ryan ran through the events of the evening. With the exception of that final .debacle, it had all been wonderful. He'd been proud to be with Carly at the restaurant. He'd enjoyed her company from the first. She was warm and receptive, interesting and interested, poised, playful and very, very pretty.

And she had a past. But he'd known that. She'd warned him at the start when she'd said she wasn't free. He hadn't been discouraged then; he wasn't discouraged now.

With a smile he recalled how gallantly she'd pulled herself together after what had happened on the couch. Her struggle had been obvious. But she'd done it. She'd adjusted her clothing as he'd watched, had finger-combed her hair and, blushing, swiped at the last of the tears on her cheeks. She hadn't moved far from him, as though she truly wanted to stay. Miraculously they'd even eaten the dessert that had been witness to their sensual disaster. Disaster? Hell, no. Right up to that last heart-wrenching moment, she'd been his ideal. She still was. If there were hang-ups to overcome, they'd do it together. For the battle, their relationship would be that much more precious.

For a moment he frowned. Was he a starry-eyed idealist, recklessly dreaming dreams destined never to come true? Perhaps, he admitted with a hard swallow. But he couldn't deny the dreams any more than he could deny his feelings. Carly Quinn had a place in his future. He'd find that place, or be damned.

One floor above, Carly lay pondering many of the very same issues. She flipped restlessly from side to side, finally switching on the light and going into the bathroom for a drink of water. Above the sink, the mirror reflected her image. She stood and stared, amazed at how different she looked without the contacts that turned her blue eyes gray. She rarely removed them; they were long-wearing lenses. But the evening's tears had irritated her eyes and she hoped to give them a rest.

Smoothing her hair back from her cheeks with a hand at either side, she studied those vivid blue eyes with which she'd faced the world for more than twenty-nine years. Strange sensations stirred within. She felt momentarily suspended, caught between two worlds. In the mirror was Robyn, so familiar yet distant. She let her hair fall back into waves. Here was Carly, newer, yet with definite merit.

With a frown, she turned from the mirror, padded back to bed and switched off the light. Her problem, she decided, was in trying to cling to Robyn. As usual, Sam was right. She couldn't be both. She had to release the past. But it was easier said than done.

Realizing she hadn't taken her drink, she bobbed up and flicked the light back on, grabbed a pair of oversize tortoiseshell glasses from the nightstand and put them on, then headed for the kitchen this time and warmed a cup of milk in hopes that it would help her relax. Her mind and her body were too keyed up to sleep. Perversely she put the blame on Ryan's coffee, which, as he'd promised, had been good enough for seconds.

She returned to bed with the cup of milk in hand, propped herself against the pillows and sipped the warm liquid. But her thoughts remained jumbled and, try as she might, she couldn't chase the furrows from her brow.

Sensing that sleep was a long way off, she reached for her needlepoint, a new canvas she'd bought just that morning, and spread it flat on the bed. It was a simple scene, an abstraction of whites and browns, blues and grays, a modern depiction of what she imagined to be a typical New England winter. She wasn't quite sure why she'd fallen for the scene. In the past she'd preferred warmer ones, such as the wheat field of gold she'd just finished for her father, or more vivid tones, such as those splashing from the multitude of pillows in her bedroom, or canvases with elaborate detail, such as those with the intertwining of family members' names that she'd given in past years to each of her brothers.

Her glasses slid down her nose. Absently pushing them up, she studied the new piece. It was more calm, more peaceful. It appealed to her need for serenity, perhaps represented a certain acclimatization. What little she'd seen of New England she liked; perhaps it would truly be home one day.

Threading her needle with a strand of steel gray Persian wool, she began working on the roof of the free-form cabin in the woods and imagined it done up inside with bold burgundys or navys, with sectionals from wall to wall, with rya rugs on the floors, and, yes, a tall fig tree at the window facing south.

Sighing in exasperation at the direction of her thoughts, she put the canvas down in her lap and looked up. Ryan's face was foremost in her mind, and with it a world of conflicting emotions. Biting her lip, she raised canvas and needle and applied another diagonal row of stitches, tore half of them out when she realized the tension of the wool was uneven, then dropped the work again and stared at the far wall in frustration. Rolling the canvas loosely, she leaned over to toss it into its basket. Her glasses clattered to the nightstand. She flipped the light off.

Forty minutes later, it was on again and Carly was sitting in the middle of her bed, emotionally exhausted but unable to sleep. Her mind was in a state of turmoil—*I want him, I want him not, I need him, I need him not. How can I, how can I, especially after what happened tonight?* One minute she rued the day she'd met him, the next she saw him as the bright light of her life.

With a small cry of confusion, she abandoned bed once more, to seek a measure of peace beneath the pulsating spray of a warm shower. It was, without doubt, relaxing. She stretched, rolled her head around, hoping to ease tension's grip, and felt generally better when she turned the water off.

Sleep came quickly after that, but it was shallow and troubled. Twice she awoke to squint at the clock. The third time, it was nearly dawn and she found herself tangled in the bedsheets in a cold sweat, with the tail end of an all-too-familiar nightmare horrifyingly fresh in her mind.

Sitting bolt upright, she switched on the light and tried to catch her breath. Fire. So often fire. In one dream she was in its midst; in another, the victim was someone she loved and she stood helplessly outside the flames, screaming, straining at hands that held her, fearing that it had all been her fault, her fault. She didn't need a psychiatrist to find hidden meanings. It was all very obvious.

Eyes wide, pulse racing, she gave a groan of defeat and got out of bed. She doubted she'd sleep now; it was starting to get light. To lie in bed would only mean further annoyance. Far better to wash up and *do* something, she decided. After all, it was Sunday. She'd nap later.

With her contacts in place once more and a fresh cup of decaffeinated coffee—the last thing her overactive nerves needed was stimulation—she sat on the living-room couch with a stack of exams to correct. She soon put them down, though, for concentration eluded her. Fetching the needlepoint from the bedroom, she began to work.

Yes, it was Sunday. She wondered if she should run, if Ryan would be expecting her. Probably not, after last night, though he'd been ever so kind with a kiss to her brow when he'd finally returned her to her apartment. She wasn't sure if she could face him again.

It was nearly eight-thirty when the soft knock came at her door. Curled in the corner of her sofa with the needlepoint crushed beneath one limp arm, she barely stirred. Exhaustion had taken its toll. When the knock came again, she slowly emerged from the deep sleep that had eluded her through the night. Stretching, she opened one eye, then both. She raised her head, tried to place what it was that had disturbed her, shot a guarded glance at the door. Heart pounding, she jumped up, then paused, hoping she wasn't right in her assumption. Perhaps he'd simply go away if she didn't answer.

Tiptoeing to the door, she peered through the tiny viewer, then closed her eyes and rested her forehead against the cold white metal. True, she could play the coward now, but sooner or later she'd have to face him.

Slowly she opened the door to look up at him. Dressed for running, he wore a long-sleeved all-weather suit. He held a wool cap and gloves in his hand.

He smiled cautiously. His voice was soft. "Hi." Then he took in her rumpled hair, the redness on her cheeks, the hint of grogginess in her eyes, and his smile faded. "I woke you. God, I'm sorry."

When she would have denied his charge, she couldn't. "It's all right." Nervously she tucked a handful of wayward curls behind her ear. "I should have gotten up to run. You, uh, you weren't waiting, were you?"

"I was late myself. I thought I might have missed you." He studied her too closely for comfort. "You look tired. Didn't sleep well?"

Three hours? Maybe four? She averted her gaze. "No."

"Listen, I'm running into the Square to get fresh doughnuts. Make us some coffee, okay?" He was at the stairs before she could stop him. "Be right back."

She opened her mouth to protest, closed it when she realized her protest would be in vain. What Ryan wanted, it appeared, Ryan got. A running mate, a dinner at Locke-Ober's, a kiss, far more. Doughnuts and coffee were the least of it.

Closing her door, she realized that he'd not been at all put off by what had happened last night. Albeit reluctantly, she was glad.

"Are you all set to go?" Sam asked as they strolled side by side through the Public Garden. It was Tuesday. Carly's exams had been given and corrected. After faculty meetings Wednesday morning, she'd be on her way to New York.

"I think so," she said, wrapping her scarf more tightly around her neck. It was sunny but cold. The wind raced in from the harbor, choreographing a lively dance of dried leaves by their feet. "I'm looking forward to it."

"Any worries?"

"Always worries."

He waited for her to go on. When she didn't, he prodded. "Well, what did you decide? Will it be Robyn or Carly?" They'd discussed the issue at length. The woman who would meet John Lyons at LaGuardia could be straight-haired and blue-eyed under the premise that Carly should be kept hidden from her family. Or she could have gray eyes and curly hair, in keeping with Robyn's demise. In the end, Sam had left the choice to the one who struggled with them both.

"It'll be Carly," was the quiet response.

He smiled his approval. "I'm glad. What made you decide?"

She looked up at him then. "I'm tired, I guess. And you're right in everything you've said. I've got to make the break. I've got to forget about Robyn. She's gone. Erased. A nonperson. I can't straddle two identities when one of them is no longer viable. Maybe if I share the new me with my father, it'll make it all easier to accept."

"You'll tell him your name?"

"Yes. I have this need to. And besides, if anyone does follow us—"

"No one will."

"But if anyone does, it'd all be blown if he called me Robyn. Anyway, he'll see that my plane's come from Boston. He still won't know my address. For his own safety, the less information he has the better." She gave a sarcastic laugh. "Maybe we'll pretend that he's taken up with a younger woman. He's booked a suite at the hotel. The clerks will never know the difference."

"Sounds cagey."

"I'm learning."

Lapsing into silence, they crossed the footbridge over the duck pond. Had it been summer they might have leaned on its rail to follow the swan boats with their contingent of riders. They might have tossed peanuts to the mallards, might have bought balloons from a vendor and let them sail from their wrists. But it was near winter, and the only movement on the pond was that inspired by the wind.

"Sam?"

"Uh-huh?"

"I went out with Ryan Cornell last weekend."

"Good girl."

"You didn't . . . you haven't come up with anything on him, have you?"

At her slight stammer, he eyed her intently. "No. Why?"

"Just wondering."

"You like him?"

"He's nice."

"Will you be seeing him again?"

"I suppose." She took a breath. "We run together every morning."

"Sounds serious."

Only when she cast him a defensive glance did she see he was teasing. Somehow she couldn't laugh. "I don't know. It could be. And it scares me to death."

"Why should it? You've got nothing to hide."

"But I do," she argued, eyes wide. "I've got a whole past. It's fine and dandy to want to live in the present, and I do, to an extent, when I'm with Ryan. But what do I do if he sees me without my contacts? What do I do if I have a nightmare and wake up screaming?"

Man that he was, Sam heard Carly clearly. "It *is* serious, isn't it?" If she was thinking of sleeping with the guy, it had to be. Sam knew her well enough to know that.

Awkward, she looked away, wishing for an instant that she hadn't said anything. But she had to talk to someone, and Sam's advice was always sound. "Let's talk hypothetically. What do I do if I *do* get involved with someone?"

"You give him answers."

"But my cover—"

"It doesn't have to be sacrificed."

"But my eyes—"

"You're near-sighted, and you also want to tone down your blues."

"And the dreams?"

"Your husband died in a fire. That's part of the story. It'd be very natural for you to have nightmares. You loved him."

"And my family—what about them?" She had got to thinking after Ryan mentioned meeting his folks sometime. "I mean, if I ever was really serious about someone, I couldn't very well hide my family away. They're a vital part of me. And they call me Robyn."

"After this weekend your father won't."

She regarded him skeptically. "But my brothers will. And the kids. I've always been Aunt Robyn to them. How do you tell a child that his aunt just . . . decided to change her name? Can you actually expect him to remember to call her by something new?"

"Maybe. Maybe not. Anyway, there's always the chance, if you're that deeply involved with a man, that you'll decide to tell him everything. If that man is someone like Ryan Cornell, I believe he could be trusted. And if it was a situation where you'd be forever worried that he'd find out anyway. . . ."

"Damned if I do and damned if I don't, eh?" she muttered.

Sam threw an arm about her shoulder. "It's not that bad, Carly. Take it one step at a time. Time does amazing things. If the time is ever right to reveal everything to a special someone, you'll know it. Hasn't the decision about your father come fairly easily?"

"I suppose."

"Then let it ride. See what happens."

Another thought popped into mind. While they were discussing the matter, Carly rushed to air it. "What about Sheila?"

Sam drew a blank. "What about her?"

"What do I tell Ryan? He knows your name and that we're good friends. And your occupation is no secret; sooner or later he'll know you're a federal marshal. But how do I introduce Sheila? I mean, she's dropped in on me twice now, and Ryan lives right downstairs. He's bound to bump into her at some point. What do I tell him? And won't he think there's something strange about both of you doing what you do?"

"Tell him she's a friend of mine, that you met her through me."

"By the way, how did I meet you?"

"I went to school with one of your brothers. You and I met way back and renewed the friendship when you moved here."

"God, you're good at this," Carly said, admiration mixing with dismay. "You've got all the answers."

"I've been at it a while longer than you have. Speaking of which, I'd better be heading back. *Our* friend Sheila is spending the afternoon with me."

"You're a busy man."

"Yeah. This one's apt to drive me to my grave."

"How could that be? She only started work yesterday."

He shook his head slowly, his sandy hair blown by

the wind. "I don't know, Carly. You may like the woman, but I still think she's a flake."

"You just got off on the wrong foot with her."

"Maybe," he grumbled, not at all looking forward to the afternoon. Sheila Montgomery had already made it clear that there were certain cases she'd handle and certain ones she wouldn't. Had hers not been a civil-service position, he'd have canned her on the spot. For the umpteenth time, he reminded himself of the recommendations she had. "What about you?" he asked Carly. "Have you enjoyed seeing her?"

It was only for an instant that Carly hesitated, but it was long enough. "Yes."

"You don't sound convinced."

She tried to put into words what had been nagging at the back of her mind. "I am, I guess. It's just strange. When I'm with Sheila, I feel torn. She's such a blatant reminder of my past. I mean, it's nice not having to hide anything, and she's great fun to be with. It's just. . . ."

"You're ready to move on."

For his faultless insight, Carly sent him a look of gratitude. "I think so."

Not far away, in a Newbury Street café, Sheila Montgomery drained the last of her coffee and turned her full attention to her date. She'd met him the Wednesday before in a bar at the foot of Beacon Hill. Originally from Virginia, he'd said, he was with one of the larger banks in town and was the newest on a long roster of vice-presidents. He was good-looking, smartly dressed and sexy. They'd met at her apartment for a brief but intimate interlude late Friday afternoon, then again on Monday. She liked him. "Thanks, Jordan. This has been lovely."

"My pleasure," he said, eyes gleaming. "It's the least I could do. You've been good to me." His expression elaborated.

She blushed becomingly and spoke more softly. "Will I see you later?"

He glanced at his watch as though it held his appointment calendar. It didn't, but it might have for his response. "I can't make it today. I've got a meeting at five. How about tomorrow?"

"Same time, same place?" she drawled seductively.

Leaning forward as though to whisper, he nipped her earlobe. "You got it."

"Jordan?"

He was still by her ear, lingering at the shot of Shalimar she'd applied in the ladies' room moments before he'd come. "Mmm?"

"How about Thursday? I've got a turkey just right for two, with stuffing and sweet-potato casserole and cranberry sauce—the works. It'd be pretty lonely to eat all that by myself. Join me?"

He took a deep breath. Sheila sensed it had nothing to do with the Shalimar. "Oh, darlin'. I'm sorry. I can't." Straightening in his seat, he waved for the waiter.

"You've got other plans? Hey, listen, if it's a question of time, I could make it earlier or later."

He smiled less comfortably. "I really can't. Another time, huh?"

"I'll even throw in the TV. You can watch the damn games—"

"Sheila, I can't," he said firmly. Pulling out his wallet, he studied the bill set down by the waiter, placed three crisp tens on the tray and stood.

Sheila lingered for a minute, studying his set features, then joined him. They said nothing until they got to the street, where he caught her hand and gave it a squeeze. "Tomorrow . . . your place?"

When she nodded, he flashed her a lascivious grin, winked, turned and headed east down Newbury Street. Walking stiffly, Sheila headed west.

Ten

CHEEKS RED, RYAN AND CARLY SAT AT THE BOT-tom of the atrium stairs. In deference to the cold, they hadn't run as far as usual. Each seemed abundantly aware, though, that it was the last run they'd have together for several days. They lingered.

"That was good," Ryan said. He leaned back on his elbows and flexed one leg.

"Mmm." Sitting with him, looking over at his dark head, his solid frame, Carly knew she'd miss him.

"What time is your flight to Des Moines?"

"I'm not going to Des Moines," she said softly.

"No?" Beneath the random fall of his hair, his brow creased. "I thought you were spending Thanksgiving with your dad."

"I am. I'm meeting him in New York."

"Oh." He thought on, still puzzled. "Then you won't be seeing your brothers and their families?"

"They can't make it."

"I'm sorry, Carly. You'll miss them."

Her eyes acknowledged this, though she tried to make light of it. "I'll see them another time. Dad hasn't been to New York for a while. We thought it would be fun."

"It should be. New York's a fun place."

She nodded.

"What time's your plane?"

"Four o'clock."

"I'll come by for you at three. That should allow plenty—"

"Ryan, you can't do that!"

"Why not?"

"Because you've got work to do. It'd screw up your whole afternoon!"

"It's my afternoon, isn't it?" he asked, eyes twinkling. "And I choose to take you to the airport."

"But the traffic will be awful."

"I don't care."

"Really. I can take a cab."

"Over my dead body." Standing, he grabbed her hand and pulled her up; she fell gently against his muscled length. "Besides," he murmured, his gaze sliding from one to another of her features, "I want to see you safely on that plane. Airports can be decadent places, and a beautiful woman alone is a likely target. All I need is for some guy to pick you up. . . ."

Prickles of fear raised the hair on Carly's neck. Ryan was thinking of something relatively innocent; she was not. For the first time, she wished she weren't going anywhere. Cambridge, this building, Ryan himself seemed suddenly safe and comforting. "No one will pick me up," she asserted mechanically, her focus on Ryan's warm, firm lips.

"I'll see to that." He kissed her boldly, released her reluctantly. "Three o'clock?"

Just then, Carly wanted to throw her arms around

his neck, to kiss him madly, to cling to him until she missed her plane. Instead she simply nodded.

Ryan drove her to the airport, insisted on parking and walking her to the gate, then waited with her until her flight was called. They sat quietly, each with so much to say, neither speaking. When it was time, they stood and waited until most of the other passengers had moved through the gate. Knowing she couldn't postpone the inevitable, Carly turned to him.

"I'll see you when I get back?"

"What time . . ." he asked, then cleared his throat of its hoarseness. "What time does your flight get in?"

She saw the direction of his thoughts and began to slowly shake her head.

"What time, Carly?" he demanded more forcefully.

"Same time Monday. Four o'clock. Ryan. . . ." She drew his name out in subtle protest. School didn't re-open until Tuesday; she knew Ryan didn't have the extra day's grace.

"I'll be here."

"But—" Her words were dammed at her lips by his finger, which was as gently obstinate as his expression.

"Till four Monday." He leaned down and, putting his lips where his finger had been, gave her a last, soft kiss, then straightened. "Have a happy Thanksgiving."

She fought the tightness in her throat. "You too, Ryan." She forced a smile. "See you then."

'So, who is she?"

Ryan took his eyes from the road only long enough to shoot his brother a sharp look. "What?"

"Who is she?"

"Who?"

"Whoever it is that's put that expression on your face."

With a glance at the side mirror, Ryan pulled into the left lane to pass a minivan. He wanted nothing to obscure his view of the open road, wanted nothing to distract him from his thoughts. "What expression?" he asked innocently.

"The one you've been wearing for the past half hour. God, it's benevolent. Tender, if you care to be romantic. And don't tell me you're thinking about work. I know you love the law, but not like that."

Ryan waited to speak until he'd returned to the middle lane. Traffic was light, but then, it was barely nine. They'd gotten an early start. He had wanted to make the most of the day. And since he had nothing better to do in Cambridge. . . .

"Am I that transparent?"

"Who is she?"

"One of my neighbors."

His brother eyed him with sharpened interest. "The pretty one with long black hair and sexy legs?"

A smile played at the corner of Ryan's mouth. "She's got sexy legs, all right, but black hair? No way. It's auburn."

"Is the rest of her sexy?"

"What d'you think?" It was a turnaround, Ryan having the upper hand on his brother in the love-life department.

Tom rubbed the back of his neck and grimaced. "I dunno. Alyssa was beautiful enough, but sexy?"

"Carly's nothing like Alyssa."

"Carly it is then. Carly what?"

"Quinn. She's a teacher."

"A *teacher*? Geez, Ryan, a *schoolteacher*?" His voice dropped an octave. "Forget I mentioned sexy. Anyone who has to control thirty wailing banshees six hours a day, five days a week, hasn't got the energy left to be sexy." As though on cue they crept up on a station wagon filled with five such banshees and their parents. The kids were lined up at the back window as far away as possible from the adults. Their mouths were going, all in different directions. When one flashed a peace sign, Tom gave him a grin and returned the gesture, at which point Ryan pulled to the left again and passed them.

"Are you down on kids, or sex?" he teased.

Failing to see humor in the question, Tom scowled in disgust. "I met this great woman. Super lady. Real potential."

"But?"

"I had dinner at her place last weekend." He grunted. "Have you ever tried making love to a woman with three kids running in and out?"

"She didn't put them to bed?"

"Oh, yeah. She did. One came down for a drink of water. The second complained that the first one woke him up. Then the third threw up all over his bed and I had to keep all three of them occupied while she cleaned it up. Talk about a bucket of cold water. . . ."

Ryan laughed. "Where's your compassion? Sounds like the poor woman's got her hands full."

"That was what I told myself when I crossed her name out of my little black book. Anyway—" he drummed his fingers against his thigh "—there's a world of other women out there." The drumming stopped. "Just wish I could find a good one."

"Know what your problem is?"

Tom sent him a droll glance. "What?"

"You've got too much upstairs to be fixated downstairs, if you know what I mean."

"Ahh, hell." Lecture time. His gaze flipped to the window with imminent boredom. Then, in a burst of annoyance, he looked back at Ryan. "No, I don't. Spell it out."

"You're a bright guy. You need someone just as bright. But you're so hung up on sex that you walk right by some of the best women out there." He held up a hand. "Hey, so you don't get them to bed the first night. Maybe it'd be worth it for a woman you could talk to."

"Like a schoolteacher?" Tom drawled.

Ryan was about to correct his brother's misconception of Carly's job, then thought better of it. "Like a schoolteacher," he echoed and let the subject drop. He was in no mood for sermonizing, particularly when, at the moment, it would have been a case of the pot calling the kettle black. He wasn't sure how he was going to get Carly to bed; he just knew they both needed it badly.

Carly's plane landed on schedule Monday at four. Hoisting her bag to her shoulder, she waited behind the other passengers for what seemed an eternity until at last the line began to move down the narrow aisle. She was nearly as excited now as she'd been when she'd landed in New York. It had been a wonderful five days, filled with everything she'd expected and more. But she was glad to be home.

Her eye began to pick through faces the instant she stepped into the terminal. Many of the passengers were students who hurried through to catch the public transit or businessmen heading for cabs. Others were met by friends or relatives. Heart pounding, she stood still, searching the crowd for the one face she'd missed over the holiday. Passengers from behind circled her;

she took several slow steps forward and moved to the side and let her bag slide to the floor.

He wasn't there.

She checked her watch. It was nearly four-ten. Once again she scanned the room, its crowd thinning fast. Braced against a wall, she watched the crew filter out and disappear. Five more minutes passed. No Ryan.

Disappointment came in a crushing wave, offset only by a glimmer of fear. Airports were decadent places, he'd said, where a woman alone was a likely target. Not only, it seemed, was Carly alone, but she very definitely was also a likely target.

Shouldering her bag, she left the arrival gate and started down the long corridor. The sooner she got a cab, the sooner she'd be locked back in her safe cocoon. Safe, if alone. She sighed. She'd done it before, she'd do it again. If only she hadn't been so looking forward to. . . .

A tall, dark figure came into sight, running toward her, his topcoat flaring open. She stopped walking. Three weeks before she might have been terrified had such a ravenlike creature homed in. But much had happened in three weeks. Her hopes soared. This man had the steady gait of a runner. No way could that bearded countenance be mistaken for anyone but Ryan. Again her bag slipped to the floor. This time she didn't care whose path she blocked.

"Oh, hell!" Ryan gasped, skidding to a halt before her. Though his hair was blown every which way, he was dressed to kill . . . or to try a case. In either event, he looked thoroughly perturbed. "There was a breakdown in the tunnel. I sat honking my horn for twenty minutes, then was in such a rush that I took a wrong turn and drove in circles around the damn airport, trying to get into the parking lot." He raked his hair back from his brow with tense fingers, then held them at his neck, as though seeing her for the first time. "I'm sorry, babe," he whispered. "I wanted to be here."

A deep, deep affection stirred within Carly and she broke into a smile. "You are here," she breathed, reaching out as though to verify it. With exquisite tenderness, given his most recent state of agitation, Ryan took her into a close embrace.

"I am," he whispered against her hair, then held her back to look at her. "It's good to see you, Carly. I missed you."

"Me too."

His kiss was as urgently tender as his embrace had been. Strange, he'd spent so much time in the past few days thinking about getting Carly into bed, yet the only thing that mattered now was having her here by his side.

"Come on," he said softly, lifting her bag without once taking his eyes from her face, "let's go." He put his arm around her shoulder and they started forward. "I want to hear all about New York. Think you can put up with me for the next couple of hours?"

Her hand found a perfect niche at his waist; her steps matched his comfortably. "I think so." It was the understatement of the year.

The next few weeks flew. Carly would never have believed she could have been so happy, given the circumstances in which she lived. Sam saw the difference, as did her friend Bryna Moore.

"You look pleased with yourself," the other woman observed as the two sat in the school cafeteria one blustery mid-December day.

"Why not?" Carly mused. "We're doing *Pride and Prejudice* in my Lit II class. It's a favorite of mine."

Bryna waved aside the pat offering. "Besides that. You look more confident. Happier. Maybe you're finally feeling more at home?"

Carly knew it was true. Not only was she more relaxed, but also there was Ryan, always Ryan.

Sheila Montgomery, too, noticed Carly's glow. She pondered it as she paced her tiny apartment after returning from Cambridge one chilly Sunday afternoon. It wasn't fair. The woman had everything. And what did Sheila have?

She thrust back the simple cotton drapes on her single small window and scowled out at the street. Two pairs of denim-clad legs passed by, one masculine, one feminine, and she felt worse.

A little luck was all she asked. Where was it? New city, new assignment . . . and nothing. Jordan was married. She'd suspected as much when he'd brusquely refused her Thanksgiving invitation; she'd confirmed it the following day when he'd appeared at her door and she'd confronted him. So much for one up-and-coming bank executive.

Even her job grated strangely. Maybe it was Sam Loomis, always guarded, abundantly skeptical of her abilities. Oh, she was good. She didn't doubt it for a minute. She knew just how to handle her wards. Hadn't she proved it last week when the family of one of her charges had staged a near riot outside the courtroom? She'd been firm and in charge, and the clamor had died. But had Sam appreciated her efforts? No, sir.

Then again, maybe she was tired of the whole job. Maybe the real reason she'd requested a transfer from Chicago had been in hope of retrieving the spice that seemed to have vanished somewhere along the line. She was going nowhere. Turning, she made a despairing perusal of her apartment. Oh, she'd done it up well enough, with reds to brighten things. But aside from splurging on her bed—double job covered with ruffles and lace—it was bargain basement all the way. Not that there was much of a way to go. Perhaps she was lucky the place was so small. Less to furnish. Less to heat.

But she wasn't a pragmatist by choice. She wanted something better, damn it. Something better!

"I saw her again," Tom called, stretching his long legs over Ryan's coffee table.

Ryan came to the door of his bedroom. A thick towel was knotted low on his hips. He was drying his hair with another. "Saw who?"

"The black-haired lady with the sexy legs."

"Uh, yeah? Where?"

"Here. Downstairs. She was leaving as I was coming in. You're sure she's not your favorite neighbor in disguise?"

Ryan stopped his rubbing and draped the towel around his neck with a half laugh. "Carly? Fat chance. She's as straightforward as the day is long." As soon as he'd said it, he wondered why he'd felt so compelled. He should have left it at the half laugh. The fact was that there was a lot more to Carly than she let on. He'd seen that distant look in her eyes too often.

"Wonder who it could be," Tom said with deceptive nonchalance. For that matter, now that Ryan thought about it, his brother had been different lately. Since he'd returned from the coast? Since Ryan had taken his own place? There was this intense interest in a black-haired lady with sexy legs. . . .

"Beats me," Ryan said, as he made a note to ask Carly about that one. He raised the towel and rubbed his bearded jaw. "Listen, let me get dressed. I'm picking Carly up at two. Why don't you come meet her? Then you can scram." His pointed look elaborated.

"Goin' someplace nice?"

"I thought we'd go up to Rockport."

"On a day like this?"

"Sure. Tom, Tom, where's your sense of adventure?"

Tom grunted. "I think I've passed it on to you."

Carly was delighted to meet Ryan's brother, whom she instantly recognized as the blond-haired man Sheila had so expressively admired on the stairs several weeks before. Though she'd never seen herself as a matchmaker, she made a mental note of the definite possibilities. Later, alone with Ryan driving northbound on Route 128, she gently explored them.

"Tom is nice."

"Uh-huh."

"A real ladies' man?"

"He's lookin'. His latest fixation is some lady in our building. Black hair. Sexy legs. Do you know of anyone like that?"

"In our building?" Carly frowned. Unless there'd been another fast move, in which case Sam would have her head, there wasn't anyone fitting that description living in the building. "Not that I know of."

"How about visiting?"

The light dawned. "Sheila?"

"Hmm?"

"It might be Sheila." Propitious. "My friend. She drops in to visit at odd times. They passed on the stairs once."

Ryan suspected he'd hit on gold. Nothing would please him more than to do something for Tom. "Think you could arrange an introduction for me?"

"For *you*?" Carly arched a delicate brow.

"Sure," Ryan countered, a sly smile forming. "Got to check her out before I sic her on my little brother. He's at a sensitive time in his life."

"So's she." Carly had been well aware of the subtle restlessness in Sheila. "Maybe we can work something out."

Their afternoon in Rockport was wonderful. Though most of the small shops were closed for the winter, Carly and Ryan ambled down the narrow streets, admiring window displays, browsing through those craft shops that were open. They had steaming clam chowder in a restaurant overlooking the harbor and, arm in arm, admired Motif #1, the shed on the water that had become an art form extraordinaire. Then, driving farther up the coast, Ryan pulled the car to the side of the road, and they walked along the beach.

There was something breathtaking about the winter waves sloshing relentlessly against the shore. They were timeless, ever changing, never changing, their rhythmic force echoing the pulse of eternity. Robyn Hart . . . Carly Quinn . . . the tide was immune to such petty distinctions. The world went on, as it always would.

Mesmerized and slightly awed, Carly stood with Ryan in silent appreciation. When he put his arm around her shoulder and drew her close, she wondered if he felt it too, this sense of being something infinitely small in the face of perpetuity. They were a couple at that moment, finding strength in each other. Illusion, perhaps, but she liked the feeling.

Only when she spotted a piece of driftwood did she break away. "Look!" Running the short distance to where it lay, she knelt down, turned it, lifted it.

Ryan hunkered down beside her. "It's beautiful."

She fingered the damp, ridged forks of gnarled wood. "I'm bringing it home. It'll look great in my living room."

He smiled at her. It *would* look great in her living room. Had she not claimed it first, he might have done so. There was something terribly genuine about it, genuine as the wave of feeling that washed over him then. Taking the driftwood from her, he rose and tucked her by his side to walk the beach a final few minutes before heading home.

Only two things marred her total happiness during those weeks between holidays. The first was the physical frustration that had begun to haunt her. When she was with Ryan, she ached to be in his arms. His lean physique was a constant source of temptation. When she was away from him, the need was, if anything, greater. She found herself lying in bed at night thinking of him in the bedroom below, picturing his long limbs under the sheets, his muscled torso gleaming in the sliver of light coming in from the street.

She recalled every vivid moment of that night on his sofa, and wondered what it would have been like if they'd made love. She imagined his body all bare and hard and hair-spattered, imagined her slighter, paler body entwined with his. If she was tormented, she couldn't help herself. And if Ryan was tormented, he took no step forward. Oh, he was infinitely warm, touching her at every excuse—an arm around her shoulder, a hand in hers, a well-placed thigh, frequent kisses—but he made no attempt to go further. Much as she told herself to be grateful, the ache only grew.

She knew that he was waiting for a sign from her, yet she couldn't quite get herself to give it. Along with those fevered memories of the evening in his apartment went the stark reminder of what had torn them apart. She was frightened. She'd been totally out of control for those few moments when her mind had betrayed her. It could easily happen again. Moreover, lovemaking implied, at least on her part, a commitment that she wasn't yet sure she could make.

For there was still that other side of her that she couldn't ignore. Therein lay the second source of her turmoil as the days passed. Sam kept her up to date on the progress of things in Chicago. Gary Culbert had been denied bail pending appeal of his sentence, which meant that at least she wouldn't have to worry about his walking the streets in search of her. Now rumor had it that his lawyer was about to file a motion for a new trial, and if there was a new trial she would have to return to Chicago to relive her ordeal on the witness stand.

How could she explain it to Ryan? She saw him nearly every day. And what about the danger factor? It was always there, a new trial or no. And it was particularly frightening when she realized that it had been neither Gary Culbert nor Nick Barber who had come after her that dark night in Chicago. It had been a man with a gun and he'd never been caught. She didn't even know his name.

His name was Horace Theakos, better known in the trade as Ham, and he was admitted to the visitors' room after a cursory search by the prison guard. He sat down at one of the several tables and was satisfied to see that he had the room to himself. Culbert had promised that. A little palm money went a long way.

Culbert entered from a door on the opposite side of

the room and quietly took a seat. They wouldn't have much time. He'd get right to the point.

"We're filing for a new trial," he said in a very low, very even voice. "And I want something done about that witness." He might have been ordering a bologna sandwich.

Theakos was a large man with angular features. His full shock of black hair was slicked back. His business suit belied his pastime. His eyes were small, black and hard. Gary Culbert would have been the first to run from him in a dark alley.

"That's a tall order, Culbert," he replied under his breath. "I risked a lot las' time."

"That was your fault," Culbert murmured, his lips barely moving. "And you owe me. You let her get away."

"She's a fighter. I din't expect that in such a puny one."

"Such a puny one put me in this place. I want her taken care of."

Theakos didn't budge. "Don' know where she is. Don' know *who* she is. They got her hidden away. Ya' heard what they said at the trial."

"Yeah. I was the one sitting way up in front while you sat hidden in the back." Culbert stared across the table. "You know what she looks like. You know where she's come from. Find her. Just keep it quiet."

"Now you're really dreamin'," Theakos droned softly. "There's no way I can get close to her after las' time. I have to keep my distance. Y'll need someone else."

"*We'll* need someone else, you mean. You're in this over your head, Ham. Don't forget. I know who held the gun last time."

Theakos smiled and whispered through gritted teeth, "Y're a bastard."

"I'm in good company," Culbert retorted as softly. "I want it done right this time. Make it look like an accident. Self-inflicted, if possible. That'll muddy up the state's case but good."

"It'll muddy ya up, if anything leaks."

Culbert's eyes narrowed. "Then we'll go down together. Got that?"

"Guess what?" came the nasal voice over the phone. Carly instantly recognized it as Sheila's.

"What?"

"Harmon called."

"The Chicago Harmon? That's great!" she exclaimed, then caught herself. "Or is it? I thought you were done with him."

Sheila's grin was almost audible. "I was. But that was before he called last night. He wants to see me."

"No kidding? Is he coming to Boston?"

"Uh-uh. I'm flying out there."

"To Chicago? But when will you have time? With the holidays and all. . . ."

"That's when I'm going. Over Christmas. For the long weekend. Isn't it exciting, Carly?"

Carly hadn't heard quite as much enthusiasm in Sheila's voice since she'd first arrived in Boston. "I'm happy for you, Sheila." So much for matchmaking. "Listen, if I don't talk with you before you go, have a wonderful time. Okay?"

Two days before Christmas, Carly was off to the Bahamas to meet her brother and his family. As he'd done at Thanksgiving time, Ryan drove her to the airport.

"I wish you weren't going," he said, as once more

they stood at the boarding gate. "It'll be lonely here without you."

"I wish you were going to see your parents."

He shook his head. "Too much to do here. I'll call them, though." He paused. "Can I call you?"

"I'd like that," she said softly, pleased to have that to look forward to. Then she remembered. Jim was certain to have made reservations under his name, or, God forbid, under that of Robyn Hart. "But, uh, I'd better call you. I'm not sure exactly when we'll be at the hotel or out. You know how it is with three young kids to please?"

"Will you?"

"Please them? I'll try."

"Call. Will you call?"

"Yes," she whispered, feeling her insides knot. She hated goodbyes, particularly when it was Ryan she was leaving. Stretching up, she kissed him. Then, fighting the tears that might betray the depth of her feeling for the man, she turned and ran through the gate.

She called twice during the week she was away, both times at night, both times when she was lying in bed thinking positively indecent thoughts.

The first call came on Christmas Eve. Ryan was stretched out on his bed feeling sorry for himself. The loneliness was worse knowing that Carly was within his reach, yet not. When the phone rang, his heart thumped wildly.

"Hello?"

"Ryan?"

So soft, barely a whisper. Self-pity was forgotten amid the torrent of pleasure he derived from hearing her voice and knowing she was thinking of him.

"How are you, Carly?"

"Fine." She drew the phone closer and curled up around it. "The sun's great."

"Getting a tan?"

"Uh-huh. And a rest."

He angled himself up against his headboard. "Even with those kids?"

She chuckled. "Yup. They're more interested in the pool than the beach, which means that Sharon and I bask in peace."

"Sharon?"

"My sister-in-law."

He nodded, but his thoughts weren't of Sharon. He was picturing Carly on the sand. "What's your bathing suit like?"

"My bathing suit?" She blushed. "What kind of a question is that?"

"Indulge me, babe. It's cold and raw here. They're predicting snow for tomorrow."

"For Christmas? That's lovely!"

"It's a pain in the neck. Do you have any idea what a mess it'll be? The streets around here are narrow to begin with. If it snows, they'll be impossible."

"Playing Scrooge, are we?" she teased.

"Just missing you. It's Christmas Eve and I'm lonely."

"I thought you had a cocktail party to go to?"

"I did. I went."

She waited for the punch line. "Well?"

"It was boring. I didn't last an hour." He hesitated, then spoke again, this time more huskily. "Tell me about your bathing suit." If he was to die of frustration, he'd go out in style.

She lowered her eyes. "It's royal blue. . . ."

"Go on."

"With diagonal mauve-and-white stripes."

"Mmm. Sounds nice. Two-piece?" He pictured a long

slice of golden silk at her middle and shifted position to ease his burgeoning tautness.

"One."

"Ahh. You're saving it for me."

"Saving what?"

"Your middle."

"Ryan!" she whispered hoarsely. "What if this line is bugged?"

His eyes twinkled. "Then someone's getting horny. I know I am." Getting. That was a laugh.

"Ryan. . . ."

Suddenly he was sober. "We have to talk when you get back, babe. You know that, don't you?"

Her hand was suspended, holding the phone. Tremors of excitement blended with those of apprehension. Oh, yes, they did have to talk. She'd known it was coming, just hadn't been sure when. Since that night when she'd nearly flipped out in his arms, Ryan had been the essence of propriety. But he wasn't a monk . . . thank God. And they could only avoid things so long.

"Yes," she whispered.

"When you get back?"

"Yes."

"Well, then—" he sucked in his lower lip, let it slip slowly from beneath his teeth "—you have fun. You'll call again?"

"Uh-huh."

"And Carly?"

"Yes?"

"Merry Christmas."

Slow tears gathered at her lids. "To you too, Ryan." Her voice cracked. "Talk to ya later."

It wasn't visions of sugar plums that danced in Carly's head that night.

* * *

That was on Thursday. Knowing she'd be returning to Boston the following Tuesday, she called again on Sunday. Ryan was full of news.

"This place is mine! Isn't that great? The Amidons called this morning. They've bought something down there and want their stuff shipped as soon as possible."

"No kidding? That *is* great! But what are you going to do when everything's gone? You haven't got any furniture."

"Not yet. We'll go looking when you get back."

"We?"

"You'll help me do the place up right, won't you? I mean, your place is gorgeous. What do I know about decorating?"

"Seems to me you had some pretty solid opinions on that score."

"Yeah. Well. I was just talking. I don't know if any of that will look good." In fact, the one thing he *really* wanted for his new home would take some doing. He'd seen the finished needlepoint Carly had been about to send to her father. It was beautiful, from the subtle blending of reds and oranges to the tiny robin she'd set in the corner. Her mascot, she'd called it, passing it off as a personal quirk unworthy of notice. He'd noticed, and he wanted something with a robin in its corner, too. He wondered if she'd mind working in navy. "I need your help, Carly. And your company. Won't you like going shopping with me?"

More than she would have thought possible. "Of course. It'd be fun. Sure, I'll help you."

"Good. You get back on Tuesday. Maybe I'll take Wednesday off and we can spend the day together."

She couldn't resist teasing him. "And this is the man

who had so much to do that he couldn't get home for Christmas?"

Ryan took it all in good humor. "Heeeeey, there are priorities and there are priorities. I need a bed. I mean, hell, I'll be good for nothing in the office if I have to spend my nights on the floor." His voice lowered. "Unless, of course, my upstairs neighbor offered to share her—"

"Ryan." Tingles shot through her. Her whispered, "Please," was muffled into the phone.

Ryan stared down at the coiled black wire he clutched. He'd said they had to talk and precisely about this topic. In the face of Carly's reticence, he grew more determined than ever. But he didn't want to upset her. Not now. Not when she was so far away. If he had a case to argue, he wanted to do it face to face. "Okay." He took a breath. There was something else he wanted to tell her. "Anyway, I think I have an interesting new case."

She was more than willing to go for the diversion. Besides which, contrary to what she might have expected such a short time ago, she found Ryan's practice intriguing. "You think?"

"I have to do some preliminary work to find out if it's feasible."

"It's a good one?"

"Could be. I got a call from the president of a construction firm in Revere. He wants to take on the *Globe* and one of its reporters."

"The *Globe*? Really?" She sounded puzzled, as though she couldn't understand someone wanting to do a thing like that. Ryan found her puzzlement, and its suggestive naiveté, amusing.

"Uh-uh. The reporter did an in-depth story on my client's company. The article led to an investigation by the attorney general's office, indictments against the president and several of his top people and a trial. This week an acquittal came in. If I decide to take the case, we'll be suing for damages."

"Did you represent the company before?"

"No. The guy who did was a cousin of one of the vice-presidents. He did okay; he got the acquittal. But the president doesn't think the fellow is aggressive enough to successfully argue for the plaintiff." Left unsaid was that Ryan's reputation for aggressiveness in the courtroom had preceded him. "In the most general sense, forgetting sides, it'd be a fascinating exploration of the issues of freedom of the press and editorial responsibility."

"I'll say," Carly murmured. She pulled her blanket tighter around suddenly chilled feet. "Do you have much of a case?"

"That," he sighed, "is what I have to find out. According to the president, his company has suffered significant losses as a result of both the original publicity and that surrounding the trial. With the acquittal, the law states that he's not guilty."

"*Was* he innocent of whatever he was accused of?"

"Negligence and fraud. The jury said he was."

"The jury just wasn't convinced beyond a reasonable doubt of his guilt," she corrected, working to keep her voice light. "I don't know, Ryan. If that reporter came up with substantiated evidence, the paper may have been justified in printing its article."

"And," Ryan pointed out, playing the devil's advocate, "the grand jury did see cause to return indictments."

"Isn't it possible that the company's gone sanctimonious on the rebound? You know, the indignant rogue?"

Another time and with another person, Ryan would surely have argued, for the sake of argument if nothing else. Now, though, he was filled with generosity. "Mmm. It's possible. But I hope not. It'd be a fun case to try. The mood lately has been in favor of the press; we'd be the definite underdog, which makes it more challenging in a way. I'll have to go over the trial transcript in detail before I make any final decision." It suddenly occurred to him that he was talking on Carly's dime. "Listen, we can talk more when you get back." He gave a sheepish grin. "You're good to run things past. You think. For a layman," he drawled, "you seem to know the score. Are you sure you haven't got a law degree stuffed up your sleeve somewhere?"

Not quite a law degree, but certain other qualifications that would enable her to carry on quite a discussion. She would have to be careful. He was hitting close to home.

"I'm sure," she murmured. Wanting to change the subject yet not quite ready to let him go, she tried a different tack. "Did you get that snow?"

"Oh, yeah. Three inches worth. Not enough to ski on, just enough to snarl traffic."

"Poor baby."

"Don't 'poor baby' *me*. You'll have to deal with it in a couple of days." Two, to be exact. He was counting them closely.

"Maybe it'll be warm when I get back. After what you said about New England weather. . . ."

"Don't count on it, babe," he said softly. "Winter's here. It'll be a while before we're free and clear."

Those words would haunt Carly long after she hung up the phone.

* * *

Tuesday evening found Ryan sitting in a coffee shop at the airport sporting a frown. Carly's plane was late. It would be another thirty minutes at least. That much more time for him to brood.

Elbows propped on the table, he distractedly stroked the bristle of his mustache with his thumb. It had to have been a mix-up. That was all. He must have mistaken the name of her hotel. All he'd wanted to do last night was to hear her voice. It had seemed like an eternity since he'd spoken with her Sunday.

Sitting back, he raised his coffee cup, drained the last of its tepid contents, then shot a glance at his watch. Stretching his leg, he dug some change from the pocket of his pants, tossed it on the table and stood. Head down, he walked slowly toward the arrival gate, wondering how he could feel so very close to a person yet so distant. It was irrational, he knew, and thoroughly emotional. But then, Carly meant a hell of a lot to him.

The sight of her coming into the terminal, though, was enough to chase all brooding from his mind. Her skin a golden tan, she looked well rested and positively beautiful. She was here. And she was looking for him.

He waved once, then quickly wove through the incoming crowd. No less impatient, she did the same toward him. Then they were in each others' arms and Ryan was lifting her clear off her feet.

"Ahh, Carly," he moaned, "it's good to see you."

At that moment, Carly wondered if the whole purpose of her trip hadn't been to come home to Ryan this way. She held on for dear life, reacquainting herself with the feel of him, the smell of him, the wonderful warmth that had no rival in the sun she'd known all week. When he finally set her back down, the eyes that looked up at him were misted with happiness.

"You look great," she breathed.

"Not as good as you," he teased back. "Health personified. I'm jealous."

Her cheek dimpled becomingly. "No need. It'll fade in no time."

They stood there then, grinning at each other, happy to neither move nor speak. Later, in his apartment, when Ryan was to think back on that moment, he would be all the more perplexed. She'd been his then, fully his. Heart and soul. He was sure of it.

Until that phone call had come through.

Eleven

AFTER LEAVING THE AIRPORT, THEY'D STOPPED for a bite to eat downtown, then picked up fresh eggs and juice at the supermarket before returning to her apartment. Ryan had wanted to hear about her trip; Carly had wanted to hear about all he'd done while she'd been gone. They sat on the sofa facing each other, knees touching, arms and hands astir in tune with the discussion. Ryan felt as alive as Carly looked, their mutual animation reflecting the excitement of being together again.

Then the phone rang, and Ryan had watched the bubble pop. He could remember every word of that half conversation, as well as the slow crumble of Carly's features as she spoke.

"Hello?" she'd answered with a smile. "Sam! How are you?" Eyes on Ryan, she set her hand on her hip. "It was great! The weather was gorgeous!" Then she glanced at the wall clock and looked slightly puzzled. "Is everything okay?" As she listened to Sam's response, her brows knit, her hand fell to her side. When she spoke again, there was an incipient tension in her tone. "Oh." She slowly revolved until her back was to Ryan. Though she lowered her voice, he heard every word. "Oh, God. When? I know, I know. What? Tomorrow?" She shook her head and seemed to shrivel into herself. "I'm spending the day with Ryan." Ever so softly, the slightest bit apologetic. "No. Mmm. Are you sure? Okay." Barely a whisper. "Yes." Then, head down, she put the phone back on its hook, leaving her hand clinging there for several long moments before she turned back to him.

She'd refused to discuss the phone call, other than to acknowledge that it had indeed been her friend, Sam Loomis, that he had a personal problem, that she'd connect with him later. Though she made a valiant attempt to recover from whatever it was Sam had said, the moments of unblemished pleasure she and Ryan had shared were gone.

Thinking back now, Ryan paced to the window and planted both fists on its sill. He'd half hoped to be spending the night with Carly, but she hadn't been in a mood to discuss lovemaking, much less do it. Oh, she'd forced several smiles and had clung tightly to his hand when he'd finally walked to the door, but she'd been so obviously preoccupied that he hadn't had it in himself to push the issue. Instead, he'd simply kissed her goodnight and left, trying to curb his own mounting frustration, which was precisely the state he was in now, and in which he remained for a good part of the night.

Come sunup, in defiance of the slush outside, he stubbornly laced his sneakers and headed for the street. To his surprise, Carly materialized behind him on the stairs.

"It's pretty messy," he warned.

"That's all right," was her quiet response. "I need it."

And well she did. Jaws clamped tight, fists clenched,

she ran hard. It had been a horrendous night. She needed the outlet. Ryan's unquestioning if somber company was some solace. From time to time, when she felt his eyes on her and met his gaze, she consciously relaxed her facial muscles and gave a semblance of a smile. But inevitably, eyes back on the path, the tension returned.

By the time they returned home, sneakers wet, running suits filthy, they looked as though they'd been through a war. Panting, they walked idly around the front steps for a while before entering.

"Feeling better?" Ryan asked.

She nodded and shot him a look of gratitude. He was so good, she mused. And she'd hurt him last night. He was no fool; he had to know she was being more secretive than usual. Guilt consumed her. She and Ryan had come to share so many things. Having to shut him out now was an agony in itself.

"Are you still game to go shopping?"

"I'm looking forward to it."

He bit his upper lip for a moment as he studied her. "I wasn't sure. If you'd rather—"

"No, Ryan. I'd like to go with you."

"Then I'll come up for you at, say, ten?"

"That's fine." With a tentative smile, she headed into the building.

It was well after nine when Sam arrived. Having showered and dressed as soon as she'd come in from running, Carly was trying unsuccessfully to pass the time reading the morning paper when his quiet knock came. Running to the door, she peered through the viewer, then quickly released the bolts. Her barrage began the instant Sam was over the threshold.

"How did you get in downstairs?"

"Someone was leaving."

She made a face. "So much for security."

"It was only me," Sam offered gently.

"But it could have been *anyone*—"

"Which is why you've got a viewer and all these bolts. Listen, Carly, just relax. It was only a matter of time before they filed the motion for a new trial. We knew they were going to."

"But it's different, somehow, knowing it's done. What did John Meade have to say? He was the one who called, wasn't he?"

They sat on the sofa, facing each other as Carly had done last night with Ryan. Then the air had been charged with excitement; now it was filled with apprehension.

"Actually, my counterpart in Chicago called first. You remember Bill, don't you?"

"Of course I remember Bill," she countered with uncharacteristic gruffness. "He called the shots while I was in protective custody."

"Bill's got an ear to the ground, not to mention well-placed sources. He called me as soon as he heard. That was Monday morning. Meade called soon after that."

"Monday? But why didn't you call me? You knew where I was staying!"

"And ruin your vacation?" He tossed her a quelling glance. "Come on, Carly. What good would that have done? There's nothing for you to do just because they've filed for a new trial."

Her fear-filled eyes held his. "Then why are you here now?"

"To tell you what's happening before someone else does."

"Who else?" she shot back guardedly, at which point he leaned forward and patted her knee.

"Take it easy. Your father will have seen it in the paper. Your brothers—"

"It was all over the press? Damn it, I thought these things usually happened without a mess of fanfare."

"Remember, Culbert used to be a state legislator. And he still maintains his innocence. You can bet that his lawyer will try to soak the public sympathy for everything it's worth—which isn't much. But that means press conferences whenever possible, media leaks—"

Carly held her breath. "Will it work? I mean, I know the *Tribune* would never print anything even vaguely sympathetic about him after everything, but the *Tribune* isn't the only paper in Chicago." Her eyes widened. "Public opinion can be so fickle. Do you think there's a chance that the mood will sway in his favor?"

"Not a chance." Sam's firmness didn't waver. "If anything it'll go the other way. He was a legislator, Carly, a man whose salary came out of the taxpayers' pockets. As a legislator, he was given the public trust, and he violated it. Not only was he getting insurance kickbacks on the buildings he burned, but he was responsible for four deaths. *Four deaths.*" He shook his head. "People don't forget that kind of stuff quickly.

"Besides, in the end it doesn't matter what the public thinks. Culbert was convicted on the evidence before a judge and jury. Even if there *is* a new trial, and I can't imagine that happening, the evidence won't have changed. He'd be convicted a second time."

"Was that Meade's opinion too?"

"For starters, Meade can't envision a new trial being granted. He's been over the transcript from start to finish, and he doesn't see any possible error on which to base a new trial."

It suddenly occurred to Carly that a piece of information was missing. And in that instant she realized the true reason for Sam's visit. Pressing damp palms to the wool of her skirt, she fought to calm her stomach's slow churn. "What *have* they based their motion on? Mancusi would have had to cite something. What was it, Sam?"

Sam spoke more softly then, his eyes filled with a kind of apologetic haze. "They claim they have new evidence."

"What new evidence?"

"About you. They *claim*—" he emphasized the word "—that you were emotionally involved with Peter Bradley, and that that involvement warped your thinking."

"Of course I was emotionally involved with Peter Bradley! We were good friends. We worked together. He was the one person who was willing to work on the investigation with me."

"Romantically. That's the kind of involvement they imply."

"It's not true," Carly stated slowly. "There was never anything like that between us." There couldn't have been, though only she knew that. Her fingers clutched her skirt now for warmth. "What . . . evidence . . . have they got?"

Sam gave his head a quick shake. "I don't know yet. Neither does Meade. That's what we've got to find out. I just wondered—" he seemed to hesitate "—if you knew of any evidence they might have."

Those cold fingers suddenly clenched into fists. "If someone's given evidence of a romantic relationship between Peter Bradley and myself, that person is either mistaken or lying. Peter and I spent a lot of time together. We had to. If there were late nights at one or the other of our apartments, it was in his darkroom or in front of my typewriter. Never once did I wake up in his place; never once did he wake up in mine. I swear it, Sam."

Sam reached forward and, taking her hand, spoke gently. "I believe you, Carly. No need to get defensive. You're a free woman. You can do whatever you want with whoever you want to do it. No one's trying to pass judgment."

"Mancusi will!"

"Maybe, but that's beside the point. Meade just wants to be sure he's got the whole story so he can plan his offense if, and I do mean *if,* the motion for a new trial is granted. Besides, if he knows the facts, he'll better be able to ward off that possibility."

"Well, he knows the facts! There was nothing romantic between Peter and me! We were very dear friends. We thought the same way. I would be less than human if I didn't mourn his death, if I didn't feel guilty at having involved him in the arson investigation."

"Don't blame yourself. He knew the risks."

She sank against the cushions, her energy spent. "Oh, yes, he knew the risks. So did I, for that matter. But we were committed to getting that story. I wish—"

"Don't say it, Carly. What's done is done. There is no way you can bring Peter back. But you can help ensure that the men responsible remain in prison."

"What does that mean?" she asked.

Sam sighed, wondering if he was handling this all wrong. He'd come to see Carly in hopes of keeping her calm. His presence seemed to be having the opposite effect. "All it means is that you should be aware of what's happening. The more you can tell us about your relationship with Bradley, the better it'll be."

"But I've told you everything! There just isn't any more." Her face contorted in sarcasm. "I mean, I wish

I had it in writing. But Peter and I just didn't think to document the fact that we weren't lovers. It had nothing to do with our investigation. It was—it is—totally irrelevant!" Just then there was a knock at the door. Sitting forward stiffly, Carly lowered her voice. Her hands fidgeted in her lap. "That'll be Ryan. We're going shopping for furniture. The Amidons bought a place in Florida and want all theirs shipped down."

Sam stood and brought Carly up with him. "Good. Go with him, and enjoy yourself. Maybe he can take your mind off all this."

She raised timid eyes. "You'll let me know if you hear anything, anything at all?"

"Sure I will. You know that, Carly." He squeezed her hand and nudged her toward the door. "Go on. He's waiting."

Ryan was indeed waiting. He was about to ring the doorbell in the suspicion that Carly might not have heard his knock when she opened the door. The thought that she might still be finishing dressing was instantly dispelled by the sight of Sam at her side.

"I'm . . . early." His eyes held Carly's for a minute before sliding to Sam, who held up a hand on cue.

"I'm just leaving." Then, almost as an afterthought, he extended that hand. "Sam Loomis."

"Ryan Cornell." They shook hands. It was a formality. Each knew the other's name, though the benignancy in Sam's gaze contrasted with Ryan's more intense scrutiny.

Then Sam tossed Carly a gentle smile. "Have a good time. I'll talk to you later." Nodding toward Ryan, who took a step into the foyer, he left, at which point Ryan turned that intense scrutiny on Carly. Though she was outwardly calm, he knew her too well to miss the tension in her eyes.

"Is everything all right?" he asked cautiously.

"Just fine." Her response was a little too quick, too pat.

"Sam worked out his problem?"

She nodded. "For now."

"Are you all set to go?"

"Yes." Feeling terribly awkward and well aware of keen brown eyes following her every step, she got her coat and bag. They walked downstairs in silence and were at the front door when Ryan spoke. His head was down, one hand jammed in the pocket of his fleece-lined jacket.

"Listen, maybe we ought to forget this."

"Why?"

He looked up then. "It's obvious you're not in the mood."

"But I am—" she began, only to be interrupted by a deep growl.

"You're not! You're as coiled as a whip! What is it that happened, anyway? Is Loomis in some kind of trouble?"

She winced at the sound of his voice, in part because she felt responsible for his anger. Of course he would wonder. Seeing Sam this morning would only add to his curiosity. And since she had to be so tight-lipped about it all. . . .

"He's not in trouble," she began, drawing into herself. "I told you. It was a personal matter."

"Then there *is* something between you two? Hell, I've asked you that before and you said there wasn't. I thought we had something good going, Carly." The sudden softening of his voice cut through her.

"We do," she whispered. "There's nothing between Sam and me. We're just good friends. Don't you ever share your problems with friends?"

"Not usually. Not until I met you. I thought *we* were friends. What happened to *that* sharing?"

Sagging back against the wall in defeat, she put her hands in her pockets and pressed her arms to her sides. Head down, she studied the tile underfoot. "I'm sorry, Ryan. I'm not . . . free . . . to talk."

"You're not free. Not free. It all comes down to that, doesn't it?" When she didn't answer, but simply stared at the floor, he took a step closer and went on. "I'm still trying to figure it out. What is it, Carly? Why *aren't* you free? All right—" he raised a hand "—I know about your husband. His death must have been a trauma, and I fully sympathize. But that doesn't mean that you have to shut yourself off from the rest of the world."

"I'm not."

"From *me*, then." He took a breath. He hadn't meant to broach it quite this way, but he was helpless to stop himself. Sam's presence this morning, Carly's tension—it was as though a hole had been poked in the dam of his self-restraint and now the words spilled with gathering force. "Monday night I tried to call you in the Bahamas, but I couldn't get through. The hotel had no record of a Carly Quinn registered. Or of anyone by the name of Johnson. I *assumed* that was your brother's name, since it's your maiden name."

Her chest constricted. Things seemed to be closing in on her. Even as she tried to improvise, she fought a wave of growing panic. Damn it, Sam was so good at this type of thing. Where was he now and what would *he* have said?

She ran the tip of her tongue over suddenly dry lips. "I had no idea you'd called."

"Obviously."

Goaded by his sarcasm, she met his gaze. "And I have no idea why you couldn't get through. My room was registered in my own name." So far, no lie. Robyn Hart was her own, if no longer her legal, name. She didn't want to lie. Perhaps stretch the truth a little, but not lie. True, she'd had to show proof of citizenship at customs, but the hotel clerk had not thought to question—if he'd known of it at all—any discrepancy in names. "If the Emerald Beach—"

"Emerald Beach?" Ryan eyed her quizzically. "Weren't you staying at the Balmoral?" When she grimaced, he squeezed his eyes shut. "Damn," he murmured, "I can't believe I did that." There was distinct sheepishness in his eyes when he reopened them. "I was calling the wrong place. That was really dumb."

Carly felt doubly guilty. "No. It was an innocent mistake and may have been my fault at that. I may have mentioned different hotels. I was looking through so many brochures. . . ."

One more step brought his body flush to hers. He put his hands on the wall on either side of her shoulders even as crimson stained his cheeks. "I must be going crazy," he murmured hoarsely. "I'm such a fool. When I couldn't get through I thought I'd go out of my mind. And I've been stewing about it since then. If I didn't want you so much. . . ."

Needing to touch him, Carly put her hands on his waist, then slid them inside his jacket to his back. The tension in his muscles seemed to ease on contact. "I'm sorry," she whispered.

"No. I'm sorry," he said softly. "I've never been the suspicious type, or jealous, for that matter. Until I met you. What with not being able to reach you, then having Sam dominate your mind since you've been back—"

"Sam's not dominating my mind. And it was you I

thought of the whole time I was away. You were the one I looked forward to seeing."

He settled more snugly against her, holding just enough of his weight to keep from hurting her, not enough to keep from exciting her. "You mean that?"

She nodded, unable to tear her eyes from the compelling heat of his gaze. Only when his head lowered did her lids flicker shut, and then it was to more fully concentrate on the healing warmth of his lips.

He kissed her slowly at first, taking long, moist sips of her mouth. His senses, too, were centered there, his full concentration devoted to renewing the bond that, earlier, had seemed endangered. He found her mouth soft and sweet, trembling as he moved the tip of his tongue over its curves. When her own tongue emerged to touch his, his body quaked.

Bidden in small part by guilt at the pain she'd caused him, in large part by the wealth of erotic feeling he inspired, Carly met his kiss with a fervor to express all she couldn't say in words. She gave her hands play over the firm muscles of his back, drawing him closer as her lips parted widely in welcome. Her reward was the intense pleasure that spiraled through her limbs.

It was only the click of the front door as it opened that drew them apart. Ryan stayed where he was, gasping softly against her forehead, unable to step back for fear of embarrassing them both.

Eyes shut tight, Carly took short, shallow breaths. She heard the sound of a key in the lock then the pull of the inner door, and wondered which of her neighbors was witness to their impromptu surge of passion. But the door slid shut well before Ryan released her, so she was never to know. Not that it mattered. She'd paid for her place in this building, as had Ryan. If they wanted to neck in the lobby. . . .

Her muffled laugh was echoed by Ryan's.

"Hmm," he murmured, "got kind of carried away there. Wanna go back upstairs?"

"Now? But we're going shopping."

His hoarseness was telling. "The shopping can wait. Let's go to my place. You can get ideas in my bedroom."

"No way." She staved him off good-naturedly, a fast cover for her lingering hesitance. "You've taken the day off, so we'll go shopping. Who was the one who railed about not having any furniture?"

Slowly he pushed from the wall and levered himself straight. He took a deep, if unsteady, breath. "Why do I get the strange feeling you're putting me off?" When she put a hand against his chest and opened her mouth to argue, he raced on. He wanted nothing that hinted of tension to mar a day that had already had its share. "No harm. There'll be a better time." He held the door open. "Ma'am?"

Carly passed through with a demure smile, then took great gulps of the fresh, cold air. Though snow lay in random mounds on the grass, the walkway was dry. Yet she was walking on thin ice. She knew it and wondered fearfully when it would crack.

Sam propped his boot on the open lower drawer of his desk. "John? Sam Loomis calling. I spoke with Carly Quinn this morning."

John Meade cocked his head toward the door of his office, sending his assistant on his way. Then he swiveled in his chair until he faced the window. "How'd she take it?"

"She's upset. It'll be tough on her if that new trial is ordered. She doesn't relish the thought of facing it all again."

"If it's a question of facing it or letting the bastard go free, she doesn't have much of a choice."

The matter-of-fact way it was put rankled Sam. Carly had spoken well of Meade, expressing faith in his ability, an ability that would, of course, place prime concern on the legal issues involved. But Carly was a person, and it was Sam's job to understand her.

"She knows that. She won't fight you."

"What about her relationship with Bradley? She never said a word about it when she was here."

Sam scraped his thumbnail against the worn leather arm of his chair. "There was nothing to say. They were close friends and co-workers. That's it."

"You're sure?"

"I'm a pretty good judge of people. She wasn't lying."

Meade sighed. "Well, we may have to get her back here to go over her story anyway."

Sam wasn't thrilled with that idea. He could just begin to imagine what Carly's reaction would be. "Is that necessary?"

"I'm not sure yet. It depends what we can find out about this 'new evidence' Mancusi claims he's got. If it's anything, and I decide to run through the story with Robyn, we can fly her in for a couple of days."

"She works."

"So do I. Listen, I don't want to have to do it either. Hell, I didn't ask for new evidence; I thought we'd covered it all last time. Do you have any idea what it'll mean in terms of sheer man-hours if we have to go through the whole damn trial again? This isn't a joy ride for me, and I know it'll be tough on her, but it's all part of the deal."

Sam just grunted. It wasn't worth arguing. He was caught in the middle, feeling for Carly even as he knew that what John Meade said was true. All he could do was to hope that it would never come to a trip to Chicago, much less a new trial.

It was after he'd finished with Meade that a niggling thought bade him pick up the phone and punch out another number. Though he didn't know Bill Hoffmeister well, the little they'd dealt with each other had set the groundwork for a mutual respect. Sam wanted input on this one.

Having identified himself to the switchboard operator, he was in the process of mutilating a paper clip when Bill's hello came over the line.

"Bill? Sam Loomis. Got a minute?"

"Sure. What can I do for you, Sam?"

"It's about Carly Quinn. I have this uncomfortable feeling, maybe because she's so damned vulnerable. But with characters like Culbert and Barber, and considering what they tried to do before, do you think I should give her extra cover?"

"Assign someone to guard her? I don't know. I'm not sure we can justify that. There haven't been any threats."

"We won't be the ones to hear them. We have to anticipate them. I think what's got me nervous is the fact that Mancusi chose Carly as the focal point of the appeal."

"She was the star witness."

"Yeah. But they could have tried to find fault with the way the evidence was presented or looked for some technicality involving something the judge or prosecutor did or said. They chose Carly and they're trying to discredit her. If they think she's that crucial to the state's case, isn't there always the possibility that they'll try to find her?"

"There's always that possibility. But they won't be able to find her. We've made sure of that."

"Then you think I should hold off?"

"I don't think there's any cause to worry, not yet at least. Let me put someone on it here. We can monitor Culbert to a certain extent, find out if he has any suspicious visitors, if any sudden withdrawals are made from his bank account, that type of thing."

That was just what Sam wanted. "I'd appreciate it. Carly's tense enough about all this. The more reassuring we can be, the better."

"All the more reason not to put a guard on her. Speaking of which, Sheila Montgomery was in the other day. How's it working out?"

"Okay." Bill was one of those who had recommended her so highly. And though the woman had proved to be capable, there was still something about her that bothered Sam. "She was supposed to be back here Monday. I wasn't too thrilled when I got her call."

"She'll settle down," was the pacifying reply. "Give her time. As a matter of fact, if it ever comes to guarding Robyn, you've got the perfect one in Sheila. They're friends anyway."

"I'll keep it in mind," Sam said, and he did. He sat slouched in his seat with his fist pressed to his cheek for long minutes after Bill Hoffmeister had hung up. Then Greg barreled in, arms piled high with a conglomeration of papers and notebooks and files, and Sam's attention turned his way.

Greg hadn't been bad lately. He'd worked over the holidays without a murmur, had worked *hard*. He'd been more low key, less smart mouthed. He'd been a help.

"Greg," Sam began pensively, "how well have you gotten to know Sheila?" To his knowledge, and mild astonishment, there seemed to be absolutely nothing romantic going on between the two.

Greg eased his multilayered burden onto his desk, caught the stack when an avalanche threatened and looked up in surprise at Sam's question. "Sheila?" he managed a one-shouldered shrug. "Not well."

Sam recalled Greg's choice comments about Carly. Sheila was every bit as attractive in her way. "Any special reason?"

Greg darted Sam an oblique glance as he worked to distribute his goods into two more stable piles. "Any special reason you ask?" he countered cautiously.

"Just wondering. I thought you were into good-looking women—no pun intended."

"None taken. Sure, I appreciate them. And Sheila is good-looking—I have to say that for her." He settled into his chair and eyed Sam through the corridor he'd shaped. "But there's something about her." He frowned. "I'm not sure I can put my finger on it."

"Try."

The quiet command puzzled Greg. He half wondered if he was being baited and wasn't sure he liked the thought. "Why?" he asked with due respect. "I mean, she's a colleague. It's not my place to be analyzing—"

Sam cut him off with a wave of his hand. "Off the record, Greg. Strictly between you and me. Gut feelings. Nothing written. Nothing beyond that door."

"Gut feelings?" Greg echoed, pleased by the request only until he turned his thoughts back to Sheila. He let out a snicker. "Doesn't make it any easier. It's this vague feeling. I mean, she's friendly and all. She's bright. She's got a sense of humor."

"But. . . ."

"You're gonna think I'm nuts."

"We both may be. Go on."

Greg winced. "It's something in her eyes. A sharpness. She's looking at you, but she's looking past you.

And the whole time she's bubbling. It's like she's constantly . . . on. Maybe that's it. Nervous energy. It's unsettling." He paused. "What do you think?"

"I think," Sam mused in a slow, quiet voice, "that I agree with you. Unsettling. That's it. Listen, do me a favor?"

"Sure."

"Get closer to her?"

"How . . . closer?"

Sam appreciated his assistant's caution. "Nothing compromising. Just friend-wise. Get her talking. Find out what she does in her spare time, who her friends are, what she wants out of life. It may be that she's just different. Or—" he passed off a self-effacing smile "—that we're being chauvanistic. I mean, hell—" he sobered "—she does her job all right. I can't fault her on that. But I want to know more about her. Think you can oblige?"

"I'll try," Greg said. "When's she coming back, anyway?"

"Monday. Seems she wanted to spend more time with old friends. And since she's accumulated vacation time over the past few years, I couldn't exactly deny her. Didn't tell her I was thrilled, but then, I think she knew that." He was thinking aloud, feeling strangely free to ramble. "Come to think of it, maybe what bothers me about her is that she doesn't like me." He grinned and raised his brows in self-mocking speculation. "There's always that possibility, isn't there? Hey, maybe she'll decide to transfer back to Chicago. Now, that *would* thrill me."

By the time Carly and Ryan returned home, they were exhausted.

"I don't believe it," Carly moaned, bending to unzip

her boots the instant they reached the atrium's carpeted stairs. "My feet are killing me." She pulled off first one, then the other. "That's better."

Ryan, leaning against the railing, made no move to help her. "If you think your feet ache, you should feel my head." He turned and headed up the stairs, mumbling, "I need aspirin."

Making her slow way after him, Carly reached the second floor and glanced despairingly toward the third before deciding that the temptation of Ryan's open door was too great. With her feet finally free of the high-heeled demons she'd been walking on since morning, her legs themselves had begun to protest. Feeling like something of a zombie, she dropped her coat, boots and bag on a chair and went straight for the sofa, where she collapsed and gave a helpless moan as she gingerly stretched her legs onto the coffee table. Her head fell back and, eyes closed, she was in the process of massaging her throbbing temples when Ryan returned from the bedroom.

"Aspirin?" he offered.

She shook her head. "I'll be all right."

"How about a Scotch? My aspirin's not working."

Carly turned her head, opened her eyes and snickered. "You just took it." Then she winced and returned her fingers to her head. "Make mine heavy on the water and I'll take it."

He nodded and disappeared into the kitchen, then was back with two glasses, one of which he handed to Carly moments before he sank into the chair opposite her.

"I never thought it would be like this." He took a slow drink. "I feel like I've been through a wringer. When I close my eyes I see endless arrangements of sofas and chairs."

"Uh-uh." Carly moved her head in slow motion against the cushions. "Bedroom sets. If I see one more platform bed with built-in drawers and attached shelves, I'll scream."

"It was supposed to be fun. What happened? I feel dizzy."

"Burnout. In one day. Maybe we just did too much. Six stores in as many hours. . . ." With a grimace, she dragged her legs from the table and folded them by her side. "And we were supposed to be in such good shape." She sighed. "Well, at least you've got something to show for our pains."

"Yeah," he managed to chuckle. "Sales slips totaling half my life's savings."

"*You* were the one who chose those stores. Most people can't get into them. Where did you get those decorator's cards, anyway?"

"A decorator," he stated. "I represented her in a small matter two years ago. Nice lady. When I called her this week to ask where to go, she was more than willing to help. She wanted to come along." His eyes took on a mischievous twinkle. He was feeling better by the minute. Carly's presence had a way . . . or was it the aspirin . . . or the Scotch . . . ? "I told her that I was taking a very special lady with me and that she was somewhat shy and that I wanted to snow her with my quiet expertise."

" 'Somewhat shy'?"

"You are in a way. Anyhow, it worked. The cards were on my desk the next morning."

"Not bad. Are you sorry?"

"Sorry about what?"

"That you didn't let her take you around. You might have gotten it all a lot easier. She would have known just what to suggest. You probably would have gone to half the number of stores."

"Oh, sure. And the finished product would have had the stamp of a designer all over it. No, I'd rather have your stamp. I love what we bought."

"We did get it all, didn't we," she observed in self-satisfaction, stretching more comfortably. "Every major piece of furniture is on order. All that's left now is to pick up accessories."

"Accessories?" Ryan forced the word out as though it had a vile taste. His expression reflected that opinion.

"You know, art and area rugs and window treatments—all the stuff you've got such great ideas about. Since you've ordered the sectional and wall units in slate, you could use either navy *or* burgundy." She pondered the choice. "Burgundy, I think. Very rich, very masculine."

"How can you even *think* about that, after today? God, I need a while to recuperate. I don't think I want to set foot in—"

"Come on, Ryan," she coaxed, amused. "The hard stuff is done. What's left is the fun part."

"Fun? Hah!" he grumbled and took a drink. "I think I'll leave that up to you."

"No way. It's your place. You're the one who's got to live with it."

"But I want you to like it too." He paused, then dared a test. Despite its inauspicious beginnings, the day had been one of closeness and warmth. Even their exhaustion was shared. They'd been a couple shopping together. More than once a salesman had referred to Carly as Ryan's wife. One part of Ryan very definitely liked the way it sounded. "There's still the issue of the spiral staircase. . . ."

Carly sucked in a breath and gripped her drink more tightly. "Ryan. . . ." She slowly shook her head.

"I own the place now. I can do whatever I want."

"You don't own my place."

Though her voice was very soft, her meaning was clear. She wasn't ready yet. But after the day they'd spent together, one more in evidence of their true compatibility, one more cementing them together, Ryan felt positive. It was only a matter of time until she understood that their relationship was meant to be.

"Then how about tomorrow night?" he ventured, thinking how odd it was that he hadn't asked earlier. But then, he and Carly had for the most part taken things one day at a time. He'd been wary of scaring her off. Of course, there was always the chance that he feared rejection. Living together was one thing; he could appreciate her hesitance to commit herself to something as conclusive. But a date was simpler; he didn't want her to refuse.

"New Year's Eve?"

"Do you have plans?"

She paused. "A fellow from Rand is throwing a party. I told him I didn't think I could make it."

"But you don't have a date."

"No."

"Let *me* take you. I've got a party too—a bash being thrown by one of my partners. She's a swell person. You'd like her."

"I don't know, Ryan. I'm not big on parties."

"Neither am I. That's just it. If we were together, we could make an appearance, stick it out as long as we want, then leave. What do you say? It'd be perfect."

Carly drew herself up as though she were in pain. In fact the pain was there, but it was psychological. Ryan's urgent gaze told her how much he wanted to spend the evening with her. One part of her wanted it no less. But there was the part of her that shied from all unnecessary exposure. And there was that other part that feared what would happen after appearances had been made . . . and they left, together, alone.

A sliver of warmth stirred inside her. Oh, yes, there was the fear of what she knew would be inevitable. But for the first time there was a need that surpassed that fear, a desire that seemed to make the fear worth risking. New Year's Eve was a time for hope and joy, for kisses, for love. Damn it, she deserved to splurge.

A shy smile slowly curved her lips. "Okay," she whispered.

Having fully expected to be shot down, given that her expression revealed the war going on inside her, Ryan was momentarily stunned. "You will?" he asked in such surprise that Carly's smile widened.

"Yes."

"That's great!"

His reaction was ample justification for her decision, and, for the first time in four years, Carly found herself looking very much forward to New Year's Eve.

She might have been more wary had she known the scheme that even then Ryan was beginning to hatch.

Twelve

CARLY SPENT MOST OF NEW YEAR'S EVE DAY thinking, planning, dreaming. Running with Ryan in the early morning, she was attuned to the air of expectancy shimmering between them. His excitement was obvious. He dropped her at her door with a soulful kiss, the gleam in his eye speaking of his anticipation of the evening to come. Only later, alone, did she wonder if she'd made the right decision.

For the first time she would be introducing Ryan to her friends, to the people she worked with, to those who would know that Carly Quinn was coming out of her shell. For the first time she would be introduced to *his* friends, to the people *he* worked with, to those who would know the reason he hadn't lived and died the law, for a change, for the past month and a half. On all the mornings they'd run, they'd been alone. True, they had bumped into people when they'd gone to Locke-Ober's or, having spent more and more time together since Thanksgiving, caught a movie or strolled down Newbury Street. But New Year's Eve was something else.

At least it had always been so for Carly. She could remember when she'd been a teenager and her brothers had fixed her up. She'd felt awkward then, knowing exactly what she was missing when, on the stroke of midnight, bursts of glee had exploded, throwing people into one anothers' arms. Her dates had kissed her. She'd kissed them back. But the absence of genuine feeling had always grated. After several years, she'd taken to escorting her father to a grand dinner from which they returned well before the witching hour.

Then had come Matthew. They'd seen eye to eye on that particular night and its festivities, and had always chosen to entertain a few close friends at home. It had been warm and lovely ringing in the New Year that way. After Matthew died, she might have preferred to spend the night alone, but her friends wouldn't hear of it. There had always been some quiet get-together to which she was, not wholly against her will, shanghaied.

And now there was Ryan. She had no doubt the evening would be wonderful, even if—perhaps precisely if—it ended as she suspected it would. There was no better night to look toward the future. If she was ever to know whether she could be Ryan's lover, the time was right.

Yet even if things worked out well, she couldn't help but fear that she'd be leading Ryan on. They might well prove to be as wonderful lovers as they were friends, but what then? The spiral staircase Ryan had in mind? A commitment for something even more?

That was what frightened her. Ryan still didn't know. She wasn't free, she wondered if she'd *ever* be free of the dark cloud that hovered. Her life, as she'd chosen it, involved a danger she simply couldn't impose on anyone else, least of all him.

Sam's call brightened her.

"How're you doin'?" he asked gently.

"Fine. Have you heard anything?"

"Only that you're not to worry. I'm in close touch with both Meade and Hoffmeister. They're on top of everything."

"Good." She hadn't really wanted to talk about that, preferring to push it from her mind for the day, at least. "I hope you're planning something smashing with Ellen for tonight."

"Actually, we've hired a sitter. We're spending the night at the Ritz."

"Good for you! You deserve it!"

"Ellen deserves it," Sam corrected with a chuckle. "How about you? Any plans?"

"I'm going out with Ryan."

"Ahh. That does my heart good. Anywhere special?"

"To a party. Actually two."

"Sounds busy. And fun. Enjoy yourself, you hear? Live it up and don't worry about a thing. *You* deserve it!"

She laughed. "That's what I'm telling myself. That's what I'm telling myself."

Late in the afternoon, her father echoed Sam's sentiment. "He sounds like quite a man, this Ryan of yours. Go on out and have a good time. If anyone's earned the right, it's you."

That was the thought that kept a smile on her face. In a way it was defiance that gave backbone to her bravado. She *did* deserve it, damn it. She *had* earned the right to a good time. And a good time she was determined to have. She lingered in a bath, painted her fingernails and toenails a pale mauve to match her dress, took special pains with her makeup and hair, then dressed in silk. When Ryan appeared at her door looking debonair in a dark suit, crisp white shirt and boldly striped tie, she sensed she was in for a New Year's Eve not to be forgotten.

Whatever fears she'd once had of exposure were pushed aside by the sheer pleasure of being with Ryan. He was the consummate escort, mixing easily with her friends, drawing her into an easy mix with his. It wasn't boredom that moved them from one party to the next with speed; contrary to expectation, the company was relaxed and pleasant. Rather, their momentum was spurred by anticipation. When they hit the air after leaving the second party, that anticipation was enough to leave them breathless.

Wordlessly Ryan helped Carly into the car, circled to his side and joined her. Leaning over the center console, he kissed her once. His ardor was barely leashed; she could sense the tension in his body. Then he held back to look at her, giving her one last chance to demur. When she lifted a hand to stroke his neck, he had his answer.

He started the car and they were on their way. Reaching over, he took her hand and held it tightly. Carly's insides quivered. She clutched his fingers as though they were the only real things in existence and didn't take her gaze from his face until they'd left the lights of Boston behind and were headed down Memorial Drive. Then she closed her eyes and tried to contain the excitement that set each of her nerve ends on fire. She tried to blame her condition on the potent punch she'd drunk, but knew she couldn't. She tried to blame it on the fact of seeing Ryan with her friends, but struck out there too. There was one cause for the shimmering current of heat in her veins, and one cause alone. She was with Ryan now, for the night.

It was only when she assumed they were nearing home that she dared open her eyes again. To her surprise, they'd passed their building and were heading north on Route 2.

"Where are we going, Ryan?" she asked cautiously. He must have made reservations for a late supper. But she was stuffed. Between the two parties, there had been hors d'oeuvres to feed an army.

"You'll see," was his quiet reply. And he drove on, holding her hand, eyes glued to the road.

Carly's were too. They passed through Fresh Pond, ruling out two restaurants there that she knew, then sped through Arlington and Belmont to the northbound ramp onto Route 128.

"Ryan?" Looking at him, she thought his features were tense. In turn she was puzzled. But he simply lifted her hand to his lips and pressed a firm kiss to her fingers.

"Shh. Just relax."

"Where are we going?"

"Farther north."

"To a restaurant?"

"In good time."

If he'd meant to reassure her, his words did anything but. For an instant, Carly felt a surge of raw fear. Then, dismissing it as irrational, she concentrated on watching the highway. But when Ryan turned onto Route 3, still heading north, she couldn't contain her apprehension.

"Where are we going?" she demanded, tearing her hand from his as she sat straighter. She recalled the first time she had ever run with Ryan, when she'd been well aware of how easily he might hoist her over his shoulder and carry her off. Over the weeks, she'd come to trust him completely. Suddenly she wondered if she'd been wrong, if she'd misinterpreted every clue, if she'd seen and heard only what she'd wanted to see and hear. Heart thudding, she watched as he shot her a fast glance. Between her own terror and the dark, she couldn't see his perplexity. Only the tautness of his profile was clear, and that upset her further.

"I wanted to surprise you," he said evenly, gripping the wheel with both hands.

"You have. Where are we going?" She clutched the handle of her door, whether in support or poised for flight she didn't know. The latter was an absurd notion, since the car was traveling at the speed limit.

Suddenly that speed diminished and Ryan pulled up on the shoulder of the road. Everything around them was dark as pitch. Though he couldn't see her fear, he could feel it in the vibrations that came his way.

"I rented a place in Vermont for the night. There's a beautiful—"

"You *what*?"

"Rented a place. What's the matter, Carly?" he asked, bewildered and slightly frightened by her reaction. She had to have known what the evening would bring, and he'd only hoped to make it more idyllic. "I thought you'd be pleased." Mixed with the greatest gentleness was a note of hurt in his voice. "There's a beautiful inn in the middle of the woods with cottages strewn all around. I rented one of them. You'll like it. The inn has a terrific restaurant, and if we don't feel like going outside, they'll bring food to us. I stayed there once before. Right after my divorce, when I needed to get away. It was lonely then. I've been looking forward to being there with you."

"A . . . cottage?" she whispered, beginning to feel foolish. If he was planning on doing her harm, he could as easily have done it right here in the dark without having to fabricate a story about an inn in the woods, a cottage and room service. Moreover, if he was lying, he had to have been an actor of Oscar caliber to exude such sincerity. "You rented a cottage?"

"Yes. The thought came to me while you were in the Bahamas, when I had nothing to do but daydream. I'd been wondering when I could get you up there. Yesterday, when you agreed to go out with me tonight, when you seemed as . . . eager as me . . . I called and booked the place."

"You did?" She didn't know whether to laugh or cry, unbelievably relieved and at the same time incredibly excited.

"Like I said—" he reached out to stroke her cheek with the back of his fingers "—I wanted it to be a surprise. Instead, I seem to have scared the hell out of you. Why, Carly? You don't have any cause to be scared with me."

The hurt was in his voice again, and Carly hated herself for putting it there. She tipped her cheek toward his hand, covered that larger, stronger one with her own. "I know," she murmured, then turned her face and kissed his palm. "I know, Ryan." She inhaled the musky scent of his skin and gained strength. "But I can't help myself sometimes. And tonight, well. . . ." Her eyes met his over their hands; even the darkness couldn't dim their gleam of longing. In a final gesture of apology for all she'd thought but not expressed, she leaned forward with an invitation that Ryan accepted instantly.

With both hands he framed her face, kissed her deeply, then pulled back. "You'll come with me?"

"Yes."

He kissed her once more before letting her relax back in her seat and starting the car. Again he held her hand, this time more gently and with reassuring warmth. They'd driven for another half hour before either spoke, and then it was Carly whose eagerness got the best of her.

"How far is it?"

"Another hour and a half."

"And you didn't think I'd ask questions?" she teased.

"I half thought you might have fallen asleep, what with all that booze. Actually I should have gagged and blindfolded you." At her helpless shudder, he squeezed her hand. "Just joking, just joking. Don't like surprises?"

"Not much." Particularly regarding gags and blind-folds. But she couldn't dwell on that when her thoughts were on a mysterious cottage and the fact that she'd be spending the night there with Ryan, waking in his arms. "Ryan! I don't have any clothes!"

"I do," was his smug reply.

"That's fine. So while you're dressed freshly in jeans and a sweater, I'll be wearing a wrinkled silk dress?"

His laughter shimmered through the car. "I've got clothes for you too."

"Clothes for me?"

"I went shopping this morning." He raised one brow and darted her a glance. "Hope I guessed right on sizes."

She laughed. "I hope you did, too." Regardless, she was pleased as punch that he'd shopped for her, that he'd taken the time, that he'd thought everything out. Abduction schemes took great planning, whether evil minded or not. And since this one was so very clearly benevolent, verging on the divine, she fully appreciated it.

Tucking Ryan's hand between both of hers, she laid her head back against the seat and closed her eyes, clearing her mind of all but the most exciting of thoughts. Ryan naked . . . how would he look? *Her* naked . . . would he be pleased? She turned her head to the side and peered at him. His profile was every bit as strong as she already knew his body to be. When he cast her a quick smile, she felt her insides quiver.

And quiver. The ride seemed endless. They paused at one toll booth, then a second. She was grateful to be sitting. Her legs felt like rubber, as if she'd just completed a twenty-mile run. In a sense, she had. The decision she'd reached was a momentous one. She prayed she was doing the right thing.

Leaving the highway at last, Ryan turned onto a local road that took them more deeply into the heart of Vermont. The way was dark. Only the occasional car crossed their path. Had Carly been alone, she might have been terrified. A breakdown here, and a person was truly helpless. But she wasn't alone. Ryan was with her. As though reading her thoughts, he gave her hand a quick shake.

"Hungry?" he asked quietly. "We could stop for something."

"No. I'm fine," she whispered, heart pounding.

Several minutes later they turned in at a private lane. An elegant country home loomed before them, strategically lit by a rash of spotlights and seasonal bulbs. "The inn," Ryan said and carefully directed the car around the main building and onto a narrow path. "The cottages are around this way."

"Don't we have to check in?"

"I did by phone this afternoon. They're expecting us. They've left a key at the door."

As he spoke, the headlights of the car fell on a small cabin, its front light as welcoming as the golden glow from within. Braking, he killed the engine. Then he was out of the car and at her side to help her out. His arms lightly circled her. He studied her face, lit by the warm porch beacon, his gaze shifting rapidly over her in excitement, apprehension and a bit of disbelief that she was actually with him.

"Carly, are you sure?" he asked. The faint tremor in his limbs was telling. She realized that she hadn't been alone in the frustration of the drive. He touched her face tentatively, tracing her features with an unsteady hand, nervously smoothing her hair back from her cheek. "I know I'm probably rushing you, but I want you so badly." He hesitated. "Frightened?"

"A little," she whispered.

"That makes two of us." He took a broken breath. "You know that you don't have to do anything you don't want."

Her breath came in short gasps. Not even the cold night air could check the flow of heat suffusing her limbs. Her body was hot and alive, aching for Ryan's. The height of her own arousal was as frightening as anything—and they'd barely begun! She never dreamed she could feel this way. "I know."

"We'll take it slow, okay?"

When she swallowed and nodded, he brought her to his side and led her to the door, where he left her for an instant to lean toward an old oak swing suspended from the porch overhang. "They said they'd put the key on a nail." His hand searched the back of the swing. "Here it is." Then the door was open and he led her inside, where she saw that the glow that had beckoned came from a warm fire blazing in the hearth.

"Oh, Ryan," she exclaimed softly, "this *is* beautiful." They were in a small living room. A cushiony sofa and two equally soft chairs stood on either side of the fireplace. Before it lay a thick area rug.

Placing the most promising whisper of a kiss on her neck, Ryan slid her coat from her shoulders. "Let me go out for the bags," he breathed against her skin. "I'll be right back."

Not daring to look behind, Carly stepped toward the fire. Its warmth filled the void where Ryan had been, yet without him by her side, she couldn't help but have a moment's unease. Although she'd sworn she wouldn't get emotionally involved with any man, she'd done it. She was here, in an isolated cabin in the woods, with Ryan, and despite everything that told her she was courting trouble, she couldn't help herself. It was almost as though the loneliness she'd suffered over the past months had been nothing more than a preliminary to needing Ryan. Almost. . . .

She heard the trunk of the car slam shut, then Ryan's footsteps on the stairs, the porch. The cabin door closed, a bolt clicked. She wrapped her arms around herself, terrified in that instant of what she was about to do, half wishing she was back alone in her apartment where everything was safe and secure and predictable.

Then Ryan came up from behind and slid his arms around her, and she knew she didn't want to be alone. She wanted to be with him more than anything in the world. His body was her safety, his arms her security, his warm breath by her ear as predictable as his gentle words.

"Don't be frightened, babe. We'll do it right this time. Eyes open. No dark shadows." Slowly he turned her, speaking with infinite tenderness. "I don't know what it is that haunts you, but tonight is ours. I won't let anything come between us."

Carly felt herself captured and held. "Oh, Ryan," she whispered, "You're so good. So patient. I don't want anything to come between us either."

"It won't. You'll see. It'll be as beautiful as anything you've ever known." His deep voice quavered under the same restraint that held his body taut. Lowering his head, he sought her lips, kissing them slowly, then with greater urgency as her response to him burgeoned. He devoured every inch of her mouth, his tongue stroking hers, plumbing deeper for her essence. When he finally drew back, they were both short of breath.

He cleared his throat and cast a reluctant glance to the side. "They left us champagne, I think. Would you like some?"

She shook her head. She was high on Ryan alone, and the ache deep inside her demanded something headier than even the finest of bubblies.

"Carly," he whispered, adoration obvious in his face, "Carly." His hands caressed her back, bringing her even closer. He kissed her softly, lingeringly, once, then again. "What would you like?" he asked, seeming strangely to gain patience, knowing she was his at last.

At first Carly didn't know what to say. The last time things had just . . . happened.

"Tell me, sweetheart," he urged in a whisper. "I want to know what you like."

She'd never been one to verbalize her feelings when it came to making love. But everything with Ryan was so different. And her need was so great.

"I like it when you touch me," she responded in a shy voice.

"Like this?" he asked, moving his hands on her back.

"Mmm." But she wanted more; the quickening of her breath told him so. His hands roved farther, caressing her shoulders, sliding down her sides to her hips and her thighs, inching upward and inward.

"Like this?"

Her answer was a soft moan. He watched the pleasure on her face, felt the way her body arched into his, and though her hands gave no caress but simply clutched his shoulders for support, he felt more aroused by the minute. Not that he'd started out cold; the heat had been building for hours, no, *days*. The evening's festivities with Carly by his side had been a potent aphrodesiac, the two-hour drive further intoxicating. Knowing what was coming, wanting it, needing it, yet being forced to sit and suffer simply thinking about it mile after mile, had been a sweet torment on which he now took revenge.

"Let me take your dress off," he whispered.

Her pulse leaped, and she nodded, her gaze held steadily by his as he put several inches between them and worked slowly at the buttons, then the belt of her silk dress. His eyes dropped as he slid the fabric from her shoulders and let it slither to the floor. She was wearing a lacy slip that outlined her curves, clinging to her pert breasts, her slim waist, her gently flaring hips.

"So lovely." His voice was a thick murmur as he took in all before him, and it was Carly's turn to be aroused by her lover's pleasure. His fingers slid over the silken fabric, moving upward from her thighs to span her waist, then cup her breasts. His thumbs rolled over their crests until her nipples strained outward. Shaken by a jolt of raw desire, Carly bit her lip and moaned, letting her head fall back and her eyes close as she sagged forward against him, her legs suddenly useless.

But Ryan refused to let passion claim her so easily. "Carly," he whispered, "look at me." He had to repeat it before she complied, her eyes dazed and heavy lidded. "You like that?" His thumbs continued their devastating caress.

"Oh, yes," she whispered.

"What else, babe? What else would you like?"

Breathing shallowly, she struggled to concentrate.

There was one thing she wanted badly. "I'd like you to undress," she heard herself say, and would have been appalled at her forwardness had it not been for the rasping shudder that shook Ryan's body.

"God, Carly," he cried, wrapping her in his arms, crushing her hips against his hardness, "you're so special!" He'd said it before; he couldn't say it enough. There was an innocent passion about her that nearly drove him mad. Sensing an imminent loss of control, he stepped back and took several deep gulps of air before shrugging out of his jacket and tugging at his tie.

Deprived of his support, Carly sank to her knees on the thick rug, mesmerized by his every movement as though he were a god—more and more with each piece of clothing he removed. Tossing his tie carelessly onto the chair, he attacked the buttons of his shirt and threw that too aside. She had only time enough to begin to marvel at his broad, hair-strewn chest when his hands went to the buckle of his belt, then the fastening of his pants and its zipper. He'd stepped out of his shoes in time to thrust the pants from his legs, taking his socks off with the swoop. Then he stood before her in nothing but a slim pair of briefs that did nothing to hide the turgid rise of his sex.

Carly held out her hands then and he came to her. With a strangled sigh, she buried her face against the lean plane of his stomach and held him tightly, tightly, her breasts cushioning his tumescence. She ran eager hands over the taut muscles of his buttocks and down the backs of his thighs, aware of the throbbing against her and incited by it.

If she'd been worried about unwanted thoughts intruding as they'd done once before, her fears were unfounded. Her mind was filled with Ryan, to the exclusion of all else. His masculine scent filled her nostrils.

The feel of his hard muscle delighted her hands. She pressed warm kisses to his waist as her fingertips ventured beneath the band of his briefs. Then, with the boldness of one possessed not by the ash-strewn past but a very fiery present, she slowly drew the fabric down his sinewed legs, discarding it at last and sitting back on her heels to look at him.

He was magnificent, proud in his maleness. Trembling, she tipped her head back to meet his gaze. As she did, she touched him, her fingers encircling his rigidity, stroking his shaft of straining silk.

"Sweet Jesus," he choked, closing his eyes for an instant, then looking down at her again before grasping her arms and tugging her roughly to her feet. "God, Carly, this was supposed to be slow." His fists were bunching up her slip. "But you're unbelievable." She raised her arms and the slip went in the direction his own clothes had gone. "Slow," he gasped. "Slow and easy." His hands were anything but as they fumbled with the catch of her bra and stripped the gossamer fabric from her flesh. Holding her firmly against him, he slid his hands into her panty hose, exploring the texture of her femininity for an instant before peeling the silk from her limbs. When she was naked too, he clutched her to him and buried his face in her neck. Then, muscles trembling in anticipation, he lowered them both to their knees.

His hands framed her face, holding it away from him. "Slow . . . and . . . easy." He repeated the litany once more, though to no avail. He was clearly at the end of a tautly held rope, but no more so than Carly, who was so abundantly aware of his nakedness against her that it was all she could do not to attack him. "Carly. . . ."

"I need you, Ryan," came her whispered plea. Her arms wound around his neck, her body arched into his.

"I can't hold . . . babe . . . I need. . . ." His mouth was inches from hers, his breath catching. He slid his hands down the backs of her thighs and drew them apart, lifting them over his own spread ones. "Lord, I don't . . . think I can wait. . . ."

She felt his hardness and sucked in a tiny cry. "Don't wait! Don't . . . wait!" In one breath-stopping moment as she settled onto him he thrust deeply; her cry of ecstasy merged with his in echo of their bodies, now one.

They stayed very still then, savoring the sense of filling and being filled. Carly whimpered her pleasure; Ryan held her all the more tightly.

"You feel . . . so . . . good." He managed a throaty rasp. Angling her body the slightest bit back, he caught her gaze, then let his own lower to the spot of their mating. Carly's followed and she experienced an overwhelming sense of rightness. Their skin was, oh, so close, his hair-spattered, hers ivory smooth. With his sex buried deep inside her, their fit was snug and perfect.

He pressed her bottom still closer, then slid his hands up her sides until his thumbs grazed the rock-hard tips of her breasts. Sucking in a hard breath, she closed her eyes, felt herself falling backward, landing ever so gently on the rug with Ryan above her, his face reflecting her own dire need. She flexed her muscles and began to move under him. Bowing his back, he withdrew nearly completely, then thrust more deeply than he had before.

"That's it, sweet . . . more . . . yes, ahh, yes. . . ." His urgings brought her to the wild edge of sanity. The flame was lit; the heat burst forth. This time, though, Ryan was at the center of the flame and Carly had nothing to fear. Ever hotter she burned, spurred on by Ryan's impassioned movements. She arched and strained, craving more and more of him. He gave her everything she wanted and then some. When at last her body exploded into brilliant fragments of ecstasy, he gave a hoarse cry and arched a final time into his own mind-shattering climax.

The spasms seemed endless, a timeless sharing of rapture. When, after long moments of suspended delight, Ryan finally collapsed against her, they lay together in the sweet aftermath of heaven. Their hearts pounded, their limbs were drained of the power that had driven them so fiercely moments before.

He moaned, his breathing ragged. She ran her hands over his damp skin, holding him to her, reluctant to release him even when he levered himself up to gaze down at her.

"You're beautiful, babe. Do you know that?"

She shook her head and blushed, still unable to speak. Not so Ryan. Sliding off to her side and gathering her to him, he propped himself on an elbow.

"That was magnificent. A first."

She knew what he meant and said as much through the eloquent fingers she lifted to his face. He caught a wandering one in his mouth and nipped at it. His eyes were the richest of browns, toasting her with their warmth. Then, he slowly mouthed three words. "I . . . love . . . you."

Her own eyes widened, first in joy, then in fear. It was the latter that took momentary control. With her breath lodged in her throat and her expression one of stunned denial, she shook her head, but Ryan was fast to hold it still.

"No, no. Don't fade out on me, Carly. I won't expect anything from you. I just need you to know. That's all."

"But you can't . . ." she breathed feebly "I can't. . . ."

"It's all right," he soothed, his eyes worshipping her with the love he'd professed. A soft smile broke through the darkness of his beard. "Don't say anything. Just know what I feel. Okay?"

It was his expression, so deep and filled with adoration, that stifled her fear. In his arms she felt safe and protected and, yes, loved, as she'd never felt before. For the moment she couldn't think to question that love or to brood on its ramifications. The here and now were far too precious. Very slowly joy spread through her, bringing a soft smile to her lips.

"Okay," she whispered. As Ryan relaxed back on the rug, she closed her eyes and nestled against his chest. Gradually the heartbeat by her ear steadied and her own pulse slowed.

"It wasn't supposed to be like this," he murmured, deep in thought, hypnotized by the low flicker of flame in the hearth and the sacred warmth of the woman in his arms. He shifted her gently to better hold her. "I had it all planned. We were going to sit by the fire and talk, drink a little champagne and usher in the New Year simply enjoying each other's company." He looked down at her. "Because I do. I do enjoy your company." When she propped her chin on his chest and sent him a chiding look that said she'd caught him with his hand in the cookie jar, he had the good grace to blush. "I mean, sure, I wanted to make love to you, but if you hadn't wanted to we could have just lain here all night and I would have been happy."

Given the urgency of his tone, Carly half believed him. "I wouldn't have been, but thank you for saying that," she whispered.

He squeezed her. "What do you mean, you wouldn't have been? Was my body the only reason you came up here with me?"

She rubbed her flushed cheek against his chest. Her laugh was warm and soft against his skin. "Of course not. But I knew what to expect. I knew it was inevitable. I wanted it." Facing him again, she was suddenly serious. "I've never been this way with anyone, Ryan. I mean, there haven't been many men, *any* men other than my husband, and even with him I wasn't this way."

His heart soared. "What way?" he asked softly, needing to hear it from her.

She averted her eyes, shy in the face of his soul-searching gaze. "Forward. Aggressive. I've never undressed a man."

A ripple of fire surged through him, and he hugged her. "God, you're amazing!" he growled. "And there I was thinking you were reticent!"

She had nothing to say to that. The fact was that Ryan brought out things in her she hadn't known existed. Already she was tingling inside again. She slid her foot down his calf, sandwiching her leg between his two. Her hand moved gently across his chest. She savored the sensation of his firm skin, his soft pelt of hair beneath her fingertips. He was everything she could have asked for in a man, and her body sang. She touched him slowly, wonderingly, her fingers shaping his hipbone, slipping over the smooth valley beyond. Opening her eyes, she relished what she saw, a terrain of uncompromising maleness that was even now responding to her touch.

A low sound came from the back of his throat, followed by her name in hoarse question. Spreading her palm flat over his breast, she raised her head to find the light she'd rekindled shining bright in his eyes.

Ryan deftly shifted her body over his, moving it sensuously until she lay comfortably astride him. With a hand beneath each of her arms, he held her higher.

"Kiss me," he ordered thickly and met her lips with his open mouth, drinking her sweetness with a thirst that belied his recent quenching. There had been women in the past; he couldn't make claims to the same innocence as Carly. And, for his experience, his appreciation of her was all the greater. Here was one woman he knew he'd never, never tire of.

Stroking her slender length, he deepened the kiss, sucking her tongue, plunging his beyond it to the darkest hollows of her mouth as he couldn't do to her mind. If he'd had his wildest wish, she'd have returned his vow of love. But he knew she wouldn't lie about something like that. And he also knew she wasn't ready. So he meant what he'd told her; for the present, it was enough that she knew what he felt.

"Oh, babe," he muttered, his body on fire once more. The touch of her breasts on his chest, her belly on his, her most feminine parts on his most masculine—he suddenly ached as deeply as though he'd been celibate for years. "I want you again. Lord, Carly, I want you again."

She smiled softly, with a trace of smugness totally new to her, and inched her pelvis in a slow rotation. "I know." Then she slid her knees against the rug and, framing his hips, raised herself to take him in.

This time was the slow and easy Ryan had sought before. It was a more leisurely exploration of muscle and flesh, a more conscious mutual seduction, a taunting to the brink, then withholding and rising again, until they scaled a heart-stopping peak together.

Long after, when Ryan could finally muster the strength to move, he hauled himself from her side.

"Where are you going?" she whispered, unable to bear the thought of his warmth leaving her.

He knelt over her and placed a soft kiss on her lips. "Not far, sweet. Just to build up the fire and make us more comfortable."

Curling up on the rug, she watched him add another log to the fire. When he disappeared into an adjacent room, she realized that the only things she knew of the cottage were what she could see from where she lay— the few furnishings nearby, a small desk by the wall, the rug and the fireplace. Her cheeks grew all the more pink at the thought of the rush they'd been in, and she felt a moment's irrational modesty when Ryan returned. His arms were laden with pillows and a quilt, yet he couldn't resist pausing to look down at her delicate form.

Expelling a slow breath, he shook his head in amazement, then was on his knees, punching the pillows into a comfortable mass, spreading the quilt over her legs. If Carly was abundantly aware of her own nakedness, he was not of his. She marveled at his ease of movement, finding pleasure in the fluidity of his leanly solid lines.

The crackling of the fire accompanied a loud pop as he uncorked the champagne. When he came down to sit cross-legged before her, he held two filled glasses. Clasping the quilt to her breasts, she shyly sat up and took the glass he offered.

"What, uh, what time is it?"

His grin was filled with mischief. "Ten after midnight. I'm afraid we missed the moment."

A rich rosy hue glossed her cheeks and she looked down. "Maybe we didn't. . . ."

He chuckled, suspecting as she did that the New Year had arrived as they'd hit that last climactic peak.

"What a way to go!" he decided. "I don't believe I've ever done it quite that way."

She laughed softly, self-consciously. "Me either."

Ryan tucked a finger beneath her chin and brought her face up. "I wouldn't have had it any other way. Happy New Year, babe." He held out his glass.

Eyes dewy with tears of happiness, Carly brought her glass up. "Happy New Year, Ryan. May it be a good year."

"A special year," he added, holding her gaze as their glasses touched with a single soft, sweet ring. He held his glass to her lips and she sipped; she held her glass to his lips and he sipped. Then, as though to seal their wishes, each sipped from his own glass, putting his lips where the other's had been.

Tearing his gaze from hers at last, Ryan inhaled deeply. "Not bad." He swirled the bubbly liquid in his glass. "Not bad at all." Then he looked back at Carly. His eyes caressed her every feature, skimming the slender line of her neck, falling to her hand that clutched the quilt. Very gently he reached out and pried her fingers open, letting the quilt fall to her hips. "Your body's beautiful. I don't want you to hide it from me."

Smiling amid another rush of color, she let her gaze drop. "I guess . . . I'm not used to . . . it's been so long."

"I know. But I love everything about you. Please believe that."

Her gaze met his. "I do," she whispered.

Putting first his glass then hers on the rug, he stretched out by her side, drew her into the crook of his shoulder and pulled the quilt over them both. With his free hand, he gathered both of hers to his lips and softly kissed her fingers, then placed them against his heart.

"You took your wedding band off," he murmured. He held his breath as he waited for her response. It came quietly.

"Before you picked me up tonight."

"Was it hard?"

She thought for a minute, frowning slightly. "No. Strangely. I thought it would be, but I just . . . did it. I guess the time was right."

"Does it bother you now?"

"No. I loved Ma—my husband." Somehow she couldn't get herself to say a name that wasn't the right one. Not to Ryan, who deserved so much more than a fabrication. "Nothing can change what we had." She looked up at Ryan. "I think he'd know that."

"I'm sure he would," Ryan answered, proud of her conviction.

"Does it bother you when I talk about him?"

"Of course not. Why should it?"

She tried to find the proper words. "Some men would be jealous."

"Of a man who's dead?" When she flinched, he held her tighter. "How can I be jealous, Carly? He was your husband. I'd feel worse if you said you didn't love him. And you're right. Nothing can change what you had. Nothing *should* change it." He lowered his voice to little more than a whisper. "I don't want to replace him. I want my *own* place in your heart. There's room, I know there is, for him *and* for me. But I can wait," he whispered, taking her face in his palms, threading his fingers into a riot of auburn waves. "As long as I know that you're here for me now, that you'll be with me back in Cambridge, that I can look forward to seeing you at night, waking up beside you in the morning—" When she would have protested, he put a thumb to her lips.

"Whenever you can. That's all. Whenever you can." He took a breath. "I love you, Carly. I love you so."

Carly's eyes filled with tears. "Oh, Ryan."

"Shh." His thumbs smoothed the tears away. "Just be with me now, okay?"

Knowing her heart would have it no other way, she forced a tremulous smile and nodded.

Thirteen

NEW YEAR'S DAY DAWNED BRIGHT AND CRISP, though Carly and Ryan didn't see much of it. Having made love on and off for most of the night, they slept until well past noon, when Ryan put in a call to the main house for a hearty brunch, which they ate in bed.

"This is positively decadent," Carly commented. Ryan had just removed the large tray from the sheets and was climbing back beneath the covers with her.

"Decadent is fun. Besides, we owe it to ourselves. When was the last time you spent the day in bed?"

"Two years ago. I had the flu. My bones were aching then too." The last was drawled with such meaning that Ryan rose deftly to the occasion.

"Is that a complaint? I'll have you know that it takes two to tango." His eyes took on a lascivious gleam. "I seem to recall *your* waking me a couple of times there."

"Shh." She drew the sheet to her nose. "You're embarrassing me."

"No need to be embarrassed. You enjoyed yourself, didn't you?"

The sheet fell back. "Mmm. And you?"

He grinned. "What do you think?" Tucking her into his arms, he lay back more thoughtfully, speaking again only after a long silence. "Carly?"

"Mmm?"

He paused, debated, then went ahead. It needed to be said. "You hadn't been with a man for a very long time. You couldn't have been protected."

Tipping her head back, she studied the look of concern on his face.

"I didn't do anything, babe. I should have, but—"

She touched a finger to his lips, and left it there to stroke the thickness of his mustache. "It's all right. It's as safe a time for me as it'll ever be." Her period had ended two days before.

"You're sure?"

"Um-hmm."

"Would it upset you if you did become pregnant?"

"Now?" She felt a sudden stab of pain, knowing that to carry Ryan's child would be glorious yet dumb, really dumb. She might have set aside Matthew's wedding band and in that sense released a part of the past, but much as she'd denied its intrusion on her time with Ryan, the past was still a future threat. "I think it would, for now. I'm not ready, Ryan."

"You do want to have children some day, though."

"Oh, yes," she breathed. "Very much."

His features slowly relaxed. "Then we'll talk about it another time."

As he'd done before, he was implying quite a future for them. And as she'd done before, Carly wasn't ready to accede. She knew how much he wanted a family; they had talked about it more than once. Then she'd passed it off more easily; now, though, having shared all they had in the past hours, she found it harder to ignore. Ryan loved her. He wanted her to bear his children. She wondered just how long he was prepared to wait.

"Hey." He squeezed her arm. "Wanna go for a run?"

"A run? Now?"

"Sure. Beats decadence, doesn't it?"

"But we haven't got any running things."

He pondered that for a minute, then smirked. "Hmm. You're right. That was the one thing I forgot when I went shopping." He paused. "Oops."

"What is it?"

"Jackets. I didn't think about jackets either. I bought sweaters and jeans."

She sent him a speculative grin. "And shoes?"

In answer, he offered a slightly sheepish grimace.

"I'll look cute prancing around in freezing temperatures with a sweater and jeans and high heels."

He tossed the problem easily aside. "No sweat. We can buy what we need when the stores reopen tomorrow."

"Tomorrow?" Her grin faded. "Ryan, I wasn't planning on *today,* let alone tomorrow."

"Come on, Carly. What's back there? It's a holiday weekend. No work, no school. Why not spend one more day with me?" His lips thinned and he murmured beneath his breath, "God only knows when I'll get you back here!"

His sudden fierceness made a point that Carly couldn't ignore. When she returned to Cambridge, there would be other things to face. Given her druthers, she'd stay in this lovely dreamworld forever. But since forever was out of the question, she compromised.

"Just till tomorrow," she cautioned.

"If you say."

She sighed and spoke with heartfelt reluctance. "I

do. I'll have to spend most of Sunday getting ready for school."

He stared at her long and hard, then gave a single nod. "As long as you won't mind my hanging around while you work."

Once before she had refused him on the grounds that she would never get any work done. Now she yielded. Not that working would be any easier with the constant temptation of his presence, but she had refused him so much and he had been so good about it.

She forced a scowl and feigned annoyance. "As long as you *let* me work. Agreed?"

He grinned. "Agreed. See what a good fellow I am?" Reaching behind him, he dragged out a pillow and batted her over the head before making his escape to the bathroom.

Carly yelped, then sat up, closing one eye as a piece of lint vied for space with her contact lens. Head down, she tried to remove the lint. It was the contact that came out first. She was still working on the lint when Ryan returned.

"Hey, is something wrong?" he asked, sinking back down on the bed. He thought she was crying and was instantly contrite. He'd only been playing; he wouldn't hurt her for the world.

When she looked up he was perplexed. Though there was no sign of tears, her face was decidedly lopsided with one eye squeezed tightly shut.

"It's okay. Just my contact."

Amazed, he looked down at her forefinger, the pale pad of which held a small gray disk. "Your contact! I didn't know you wore them."

"All the time," she murmured, slithering past him off the bed. She wasn't sure if she was more worried about dropping the small lens or opening her bright blue eye.

"Give me a minute." She closed the bathroom door behind her.

It took only a minute for her to clear her eye of its irritant and restore a balance of gray. Her taut fingers grasped the edge of the sink while she scrutinized her mirror image. "Close," she whispered, muttered an oath, then recomposed herself to return to Ryan.

Mercifully, it was to be the closest call she would have in Vermont. The rest of the day, and the next, were unqualifiedly wonderful. With Cambridge, and so much of the real world, at a distance, Carly relaxed and enjoyed everything about Ryan. They talked and made love and slept, shared the local paper and its crossword puzzle, dressed up for dinner at the inn and, after buying a few necessities on Saturday morning, took a long walk in the woods.

Even without the snow craved so desperately by every innkeeper in the county, Vermont was beautiful. The forests, shorn of all but their evergreen finery, presented winter at its most striking. Endless clusters of pines and firs undulated across the landscape, stretching their graceful spikes heavenward as though in communion with their creator. Underfoot, dried leaves crackled in reminder of what had been and would be again in time. And through it all wafted the spicy, sprucy scent of fresh air.

Sitting with Ryan on a high boulder not far from the cottage, Carly marveled at the utter serenity of the vista. Its palette was a blend of grays, blues and greens. She had only to squint to soften the lines of the scene, and then she was reminded of the canvas she'd so recently bought. When she told Ryan about it, his response was immediate. It was the opening he'd sought.

"I want it."

"You what?"

"I want it. For my place."

"You're kidding. Surely you want something bolder—"

"No. How big is it?"

It was quite large; she indicated the vague dimensions with her hands.

"See! It'd go perfectly in my bedroom. What do you think?"

"I don't know," she teased. "I've never seen your bedroom."

He threw his arm around her shoulders and gave her a playful hug. "You will, babe. You will."

It was late Saturday afternoon when they finally headed back to Cambridge. The ride home was nearly as quiet as the one up had been, though a kind of peaceful satisfaction replaced the simmering expectation of that first night.

Ryan's thoughts were filled with the wonder of Carly. Driving distractedly, he reviewed everything they'd shared and done during their two-day spree. Casting the occasional glance her way, experiencing the now-familiar tugging at his heart that the simple sight of her brought, he knew that he loved her more than he'd ever loved another being. It had been the best New Year's ever; he felt more positive than he had in years.

Carly, too, felt positive. New year. New woman. Robyn Hart might have had so very much along the way, but Carly Quinn had Ryan. She wondered if she'd known, when she had removed her wedding band Thursday afternoon, just how different she would be without it. At the time she had been cued by propriety; somehow it hadn't seemed right to party with Ryan wearing another man's ring. If there had been deeper motivations, she hadn't recognized them at the time. Now she did. Though she wouldn't allow herself to envision a long-range commitment to Ryan, or any man for that matter, she felt for the first time that she was truly forging a new life. The events of the past two days spoke loud and clear. She had cast a vote for Carly Quinn in the most elemental way possible.

The winter sun had long since sunk below the horizon when they reached Cambridge. Ryan found a space around the corner from their building, shouldered his overnight bag, in which Carly had stowed her dressy things, tossed the hanger bearing his suit over the same shoulder, and threw his free arm around her. Slowly they walked toward home.

Carly wasn't sure when she grew uneasy. At first she thought it was simply her reluctance to see the two-days' idyll come to an end. As sure as she was that Ryan's feelings toward her wouldn't change, she knew that the time they'd shared in Vermont, totally free of work and worry, had been unique.

Then they passed a parked car whose driver, a man, was sitting quietly, staring in his rearview mirror. By habit she looked twice. It was unusual in an area such as this, where people seemed always on the go, to see one as idle. Perhaps he was waiting for someone. Forcing aside suspicion, she concentrated on the security of Ryan's arm around her shoulder.

Then they passed another car, the occupants of which—two men wearing suits and trench coats—lounged against its door.

She looked straight ahead, but the image of the men remained. It was odd; though they didn't look sinister, they seemed distinctly out of place in the neighborhood. There was something about the way they waited, something deliberately casual, deceptively alert. . . .

Uneasy, she looked at Ryan in time to see him shoot a quick look behind as they progressed up the court-yard walk.

"Who do you think they are?" she asked, feigning nonchalance as best she could.

"Beats me." He seemed to ponder the matter for another instant, then dismiss it, for by the time they entered the front foyer his frown was gone.

Not so Carly's. She cast a cautious glance inside while Ryan stopped to pick up his mail, then she raised apprehensive eyes to the third floor as soon as they entered the atrium. If Ryan noticed her hesitation when he gently nudged her on, he interpreted it as an exten-sion of the reluctance he felt himself. His smile was gentle and reassuring.

"Come on, babe. Let's get these things unpacked."

He led the way, passing the second-floor landing to go straight to her place. Several stairs short of the third floor he slowed, then came to a halt. Slightly behind, Carly stopped as well, instinctively reaching for his arm in support.

"Someone broke in!" she cried. The front door of her apartment stood ajar. She stared at it as she tried to deal with the sudden avalanche of possibilities. One seemed worst thàn the next, and she began to tremble. "Oh, God. . . ."

Ryan took the few remaining steps at a clip, dropping his things by the railing without once taking his eyes from her door and moved forward. In his mind any violation of Carly was a violation of him; while she felt fear, he experienced a surge of raw anger.

Carly, meanwhile, had a split second's mind-flash of a gunman behind that door waiting to blast whoever stepped through. Terrified, she opened her mouth to yell to Ryan when, to her astonishment, the door opened and a very agitated Sam Loomis emerged.

Ryan stopped short. Sam's gaze shifted from Carly to Ryan and back. It took him a minute to speak.

"Are you all right?" he asked, tension evident in his voice.

Carly ran up the stairs. "*I'm* all right, but *what happened*?" Her eyes were wide and filled with fear. "Who . . . ?" She darted an anxious glance at her door. "Did someone break in?"

Sam took a deep breath, let it out in a whoosh. "No one broke in."

"How did *you* get in?" Ryan demanded sharply. Digging into his pocket, Sam held up a single key, which hardly pleased Ryan. "How did you get that?"

Sam and Carly exchanged a glance. It was Carly who spoke, eyes glued to Sam's, heart pounding. "I gave it to him. It's a spare. What happened, Sam?" She imagined a world of things, one more bleak than the next.

"I was worried."

"You were *worried*?" Ryan barked, barely restraining his fury. It was bad enough that when it came to Sam and Carly *he* felt excluded. It angered him to find that Sam had invaded the space that should have been theirs alone.

Sam lowered his head and spread a hand across his brow to rub both temples with a thumb and finger. When he looked up, he'd schooled his expression to one of deference. He addressed himself to Ryan. "I tried to call Carly yesterday afternoon, then again last night and all day today." He shifted his gaze to Carly. "You said you were planning to spend New Year's Day here." She hadn't quite said that, but he knew she wouldn't disagree. They were in this together. "When I couldn't reach you, I guess I panicked."

"I'll say," Ryan muttered.

Carly put a hand on his arm. "It's all right, Ryan." She sounded far more complacent than she felt. "I'm sorry, Sam. We were in Vermont." There was an urgent question in her eyes as she asked, "There wasn't something special you wanted, was there?"

Sam deftly read between the lines and smiled comfortably. His eyes held gentle apology. "Just to wish you a Happy New Year. That's all. I should have assumed you'd taken off, but you've never done that before." His last words were spoken with meaning.

"I know." She thought of the men outside, realized that they would be from Sam's office *and* that Ryan would realize it too. She moved quickly to avert his suspicion, rationalizing that it was as good a time as any to reveal Sam's position, particularly with Sam there to help her out. "You're just not used to leaving work at work," she scolded, then explained to Ryan, "Sam's with the U.S. marshal's office. He gets carried away at times. Finds it hard to leave his white charger at the stable."

Ryan's eyes were dark and unreadable. "The marshal's office? Then those are your henchmen parked out front?"

Sam glanced at his watch. "Actually, we were supposed to be somewhere half an hour ago. I'd better run." As he sidestepped Carly he gave her arm a squeeze. "Glad you had fun. Talk to you later."

"Sam?" Carly moved to the railing to follow his descending figure. "How about you? How was the Ritz?"

He flashed her a wide grin. "Ritzy." Then, raising a hand in farewell, he was off.

When Carly turned back, Ryan was gone. She went to

the door of her apartment to find him standing in her foyer carefully scanning the premises. Stepping forward, she eyed him quizzically.

His slow sweep of the room continued. "Anything look out of place?"

"Of course not. That was *Sam*, Ryan. He wouldn't touch anything."

"Can't be too careful," he muttered, taking off down the hall. As Carly stood stock-still, he perused the bedroom, then, backtracking past her without a word, the kitchen for outward signs of disruption. "Everything looks okay," he said, returning to her at last. "What's with the Ritz?"

With his hands low on his hips and his dark eyes unyielding, he waited. There was an imperiousness about him that she'd never seen before. It might have bothered her had she not been as sensitive to his feelings. But she knew that the jealousy and resentment he felt were largely her fault. If Ryan knew the truth, the *whole* truth, he would easily understand Sam's concern.

"Sam and his wife spent New Year's Eve at the Ritz. It was the first time they've left their daughter overnight. She's barely two."

"Sam's married?"

"Yes, to Ellen."

"Oh." That made him feel slightly better and the tiniest bit foolish. "And he has a daughter?"

"Uh-huh."

He nodded at this, his mind moving on. "How do you know them?"

Carly didn't correct the "them"—in a sense, she knew both Ellen and Sara, too. Feeling uncomfortable, she forced herself to explain. "Sam went to school with one of my brothers. We've known each other for a long time. When I moved here last summer, he jumped right in as an older brother once removed." It sounded very legitimate. She held her breath, releasing it only when Ryan's features slowly began to relax.

"Older brother once removed?"

"Um-hmm."

"That's why you gave him your key?"

"He was the only person I knew when I came here. It was Sam who helped me find this place and get settled. At the time it seemed logical that, of anyone, he should have my spare." That much was very definitely the truth. Not that Sam had ever used the key before. He'd kept it locked in his files, preferring to ring the bell and call up from downstairs as any other visitor would do. The fact that he'd been worried enough about her to take the key from its place, *and* to bring along three of his cohorts, brought home with stark precision the true nature of their relationship. She had to struggle to keep her voice steady. "Just in case . . . you know, just in case I locked myself out or something. . . ."

Ryan stared at her a minute longer. Then, tipping his head to the side, he let out a deep breath. "Damn it, that guy bugs me." He thrust his fingers through his hair, leaving it disheveled, in keeping with his frustration. Turning his back, he stalked several paces, halted with his feet set in a broad stance, tucked his hands in the back pockets of his jeans and eyed the ceiling. "I know you'll say that I'm jealous, and I am." He swiveled around. "He comes between us." He held out a hand when she opened her mouth to argue. "You've told me there's nothing between you two romantically. And it helps to know that he's got a wife and kid at home. You're not the type to fool with married men. I know that. But, hell—" he threw his hand in the air "—he

calls and upsets you, he scares the living daylights out
of both of us by barging into your apartment—"

"He didn't barge in. He had a key."

"Don't remind me," he murmured, then seemed to
lose his momentum, for he shook his head and spoke
more quietly, almost to himself. "What is it about him
that sets me on edge?"

Drawn as much by his upset as by her own guilt,
Carly went to him. "Maybe it's just that he was here
before you were," she offered softly. She put both
hands up to his shoulders. "It'd be natural for you to
distrust him. But you've got to trust me and believe
that you've got nothing to fear in Sam. He's been worried about me since I came, getting after me to date and
all. He feels a responsibility toward me. Whether it's
right or not, it's meant a lot over the months."

Soothed by her tone, Ryan grew more gentle. "Then
I should be grateful to him, shouldn't I?"

She nodded, thinking how true that was. And she
hated herself for not being able to tell him everything.
But Sam's appearance had been a poignant reminder
that her future was still precarious. Given the choice
between hiding part of herself from Ryan and subject-
ing him to the fears with which she lived, she still had
to opt for the former. Someday, perhaps, she would tell
him. . . .

After a late dinner in the Square, they spent the night
at Ryan's place. If his passion was particularly intense,
Carly welcomed it in reinforcement of all they'd shared
in Vermont. Deep down inside she knew that he
wouldn't quickly forget Sam, or accept him, for that
matter. In compensation, she gave of herself more than
she ever had, responding to his fierceness with a high
fire of her own.

Sunday morning they ran together. They joked about the variety of activity they'd had in the past few days, wondering if their running time would be better or worse for it, speculating on the long-range effects of lovemaking on hamstrings and quads and other more private bodily spots.

When they came in to shower though, Ryan in his place, she in hers, she was quite serious. Crossing directly to the phone, she called Sam.

"I was wondering when I'd hear from you," he teased.

"I haven't been alone. Listen, Sam, are you sure there wasn't anything more to your worries? Was there any news from Chicago?"

"On a holiday weekend? Are you kidding? No, there was nothing. Hey, I really am sorry about being there like that when you and Ryan came back. Did he calm down?"

"In time. I told him a little about you. You know, about Ellen and Sara and—" she emphasized each word "—how you went to school with my brother."

"Did he buy it?" came the quiet rejoinder.

She sighed. "I think so. I feel awful about lying."

"Do you want to tell him?"

"Not yet."

"Any special reason?" When she didn't answer, he went on. "I'd say you're *very* serious about him. You had a good time in Vermont, didn't you?"

"Oh, yes."

"Are you in love with him?"

"In *love* with him? God, Sam, I haven't known him very long."

"It can happen like that."

"Not to me," she argued forcefully. "There's too much at stake. Love wasn't in the game plan."

"Still—"

"No!" Then she lowered her voice. "No. I can't think about love yet. It's enough that Ryan is patient and good and a wonderful companion." *And lover,* she thought, but couldn't quite say it, though she knew that Sam knew that she and Ryan hadn't gone to Vermont to roast chestnuts.

"Well, I'm glad of that, at least." He caught his breath. "Oh, damn, Sara's screaming and Ellen's across the street. I've got to run."

"Sam?"

"Mmm?"

"Should I . . . do you want . . . I mean, if I take off again. . . ."

"No, Carly." He grinned. "You're a big girl. You don't have to report every little weekend tryst to me. I really jumped to conclusions far too quickly. From now on I'll know to call *Ryan's* number before I panic."

"He'll love that," she muttered.

"He'll just know I'm concerned." He covered the phone and yelled a muffled, "I'm coming, baby! Daddy's coming!" Then he spoke directly into the receiver again. "Gotta go, Carly. Take it easy."

"Sure, Sam. And thanks."

"For what?"

"For worrying."

He chuckled. "Any time, hon. Anytime."

No, Ryan, I *don't* agree with you," Carly declared. Wearing her long terry-cloth robe, she sat on the sofa with her legs tucked up beneath her. It was a lazy Saturday morning, and she was thoroughly enjoying a colorful discussion with Ryan. "You can talk until you're blue in the face about the civil rights of your client, and I'd still argue in favor of the first-amendment rights of the press. That reporter saw a story, researched it, wrote it, and the *Globe* printed it. There's nothing wrong with that."

Ryan's long frame was folded into the chair across from her. In the week since their return from Vermont, he'd spent more time in her place than his own, particularly as of the Monday before when the movers had left him without a stick of furniture. Carly had teased him at the time, accusing him of having planned her seduction to coincide with his needing a place to sleep, but she hadn't minded. She was grateful for an excuse to have him around.

He crossed his ankles on one of her low sculpted tables and scowled at her. "Nothing wrong with that? What about the principle that a man is innocent until proven guilty? What about the danger of trial by the media?" He thumped his chest indignantly. "My client was proved not guilty in a court of law. Which means he's innocent!"

"Watch it, Ryan. You're spilling coffee all over the place." She leaned forward to put her own cup down and hand a napkin across to him, then watched him distractedly blot drips from the navy velour of his robe. "Innocent—" she quietly resumed the discussion, settling comfortably back once more "—only in the formal sense that the jury wasn't convinced beyond a reasonable doubt that he was guilty. That doesn't necessarily mean he was entirely without guilt."

Ryan crushed the napkin in his fist. "In the eyes of the law it does."

"But doesn't the public deserve more? I mean, you're a whiz of a lawyer; you can get people off right and left. Either the jury isn't convinced, or there's a technicality on which the verdict is overturned or you plea-bargain before the whole thing begins. But what about the public's right to know? You've told me the facts of this case, and you agree that your client may have cut corners here and there in the construction of that building. Okay, so a jury wasn't convinced there was malicious intent. Don't you think that the public deserves a warning? Don't you think that a reporter like Mahoney has an obligation to set out the facts as he uncovers them? After all, the A.G.'s office didn't do much of an investigation itself, and it had been receiving complaints for months."

Ryan sat forward, clutching his coffee cup. "That's not the point. The point is that my client's business has been adversely affected by not only the original series of articles but by slanted press reports of the trial. The press cannot be given the power to make or break. It's not God. It's not judge and jury. And it sure as hell isn't elected by the people!"

"But it is responsible."

"That's debatable."

"Come on, Ryan! Do you really think—" the phone rang but she ignored it "—that Mahoney had a personal motive in ruining Walfleet Construction?"

Ryan thought about that for a minute. "Personal? As in inflated sense of self-importance, maybe." Another ring. Ryan's voice softened instantly. "Want me to get that, babe?" It was as though he'd been playing a part and suddenly reverted to himself. Though Carly was coming to be used to it, at first she'd been stunned by the way he could turn on or off at will. What she realized was that he was strong in his beliefs, and he enjoyed the discussion for discussion's sake. She was finding that she did too.

"No, I'll go." She rose from the sofa. "But I still think you're wrong. I've known my share of newspaper people and the ego thing was minimal." When the phone rang again, Ryan shooed her with the sweep of his hand. She continued talking as she walked, thankful that given her detachment from this situation she was free to express views so close to her heart. "Investigative reporters work hard. For every one story that pans out, they've hit dead ends on four or five others. It's an ugly job—" She picked up the phone well after the fourth ring. "Hello?"

"Carly?" came the cautious voice on the other end of the line. With one word alone, its nasal quality gave it away.

"Sheila! I was beginning to wonder if you'd ever made it back from Chicago. How are you?"

"Great!" Sheila answered lightly. "But I've been really busy since I got back. How are you? Have a good trip?"

"How did you know about that?"

"Carly, *you* told me," she scolded with playful indignation. "More than once. The Bahamas, Jim and Sharon and the kids, lots of sun. God, was I drooling."

"Oh, the *Bahamas*." It seemed like an eon ago. She'd been thinking of her more recent trip, that glorious one with Ryan. Standing at the door of the kitchen from where she could see the object of her desire, she grinned. "I had fun. But it was good to get back." Her smile grew more catlike when Ryan pushed himself from the sofa and approached.

"You sound strange. What's happening?"

"Nothing." Carly kept her eyes on Ryan, who moved close up and pressed her slowly back against the wall. His essence, clean, male, and unique, taunted her senses. "Just . . . the usual," she managed in a mildly strangled tone.

"The usual sounds weird. Am I interrupting something."

Ryan was nibbling on her earlobe, marveling at his phenomenal attraction to this woman. He loved every minute he spent with her, intellectual arguments such as the one they'd been having included. She was supremely bright, stimulating both in bed and out. Oh, yes, questions remained; he knew there were things she hadn't told him. Quick to talk of her childhood and even her married years, she seemed to fade out after that. At times when she thought he wasn't looking he still caught that haunted look in her eyes, and he couldn't forget their first few times together and the fear he'd sensed in her. Then, of course, there was Sam. Something about him—a certain air of authority regarding Carly—went beyond simply the "older brother once removed" syndrome. All too often Ryan found himself daydreaming at work, trying to solve the puzzle; yet when he was with Carly, it flew from mind. Even now, as he pressed his lips to the soft pulse beneath her ear, he could think of nothing else.

Carly cleared her throat. "Not really. We were just, uh, just having an argument." Frustrated, she sent Ryan a quelling stare. "You called at an opportune time."

" 'We'? Who's 'we'?"

"Ryan and I." When the man in question ran his tongue down the slender column of her neck, she closed her eyes and tipped her head to ease his access. Her voice was more of a purr. "We were just having coffee."

"Then you're still seeing him?"

"Um-hmm."

"A lot?"

"Um-hmm."

"Does that mean that I can't stop by for a few minutes this afternoon?"

"This afternoon?" Coming to attention, Carly put a hand on Ryan's shoulder to hold him off for a minute. Her eyes held the question, which he answered with an accommodating nod and a whispered explanation. "I've got to stop in at the office for a couple of hours."

She had several things to do herself, particularly now that she seemed to be feeding two mouths more often. Not that she minded; for every time she cooked for Ryan, he took her out another. She hadn't eaten as well in years. "Sure, Sheila. This afternoon's great. But I've got a few errands to run. How about making it after three?"

"After three you got. See you then."

When Ryan took the phone from her and hung it up, she looped her arms around his neck. "That should be nice. Maybe you'll get a chance to meet her. How late will you be?"

"I should be back by four. Think she'll still be here then?"

"Knowing Sheila, yes. She loves to talk."

Arm in arm they walked back to the living room, where they stopped. "This place looks better," Ryan remarked.

"What do you mean?"

"More lived-in. Look, the newspaper's all over the place, there are coffee cups and empty plates. And I like the clay piece on that wall." On the Saturday they'd shopped in Vermont, in addition to buying clothes . Ryan had insisted on picking up a small handcrafted plaque that had caught Carly's eye. It was textured, stones intermeshing with clay in a distinctly modern arrangement that was warm and interesting. "Between that and the driftwood you adopted in Rockport—"

which had found a fitting resting place on one of the shelves of the wall unit "—your decor has taken on a more personal note."

She poked an elbow into his ribs. "Hah. That's just because you like seeing *your* fingerprints on things. I know your type," she teased. "Has to have a hand in everything."

He turned her into his arms and eyed her more solemnly. "When it comes to you, you're right. I like seeing evidence of the times we've spent together."

"Spoken like a true lawyer," she quipped, but her voice lacked the lightness she'd intended, sounding soft and wispy instead.

"Mmm." He kissed her once. "And if this lawyer doesn't get dressed and to work, he's apt to be out on his ear." He paused, then spoke hesitantly. "Hey, you're sure you don't mind going out with the Walkens tonight?" Cynthia Walken was a partner of Ryan's; it was her party to which they'd gone on New Year's Eve.

"Of course not. We owe them an invitation. They both seemed very nice . . . not that I had much of a chance to talk with either of them that night."

Ryan's grin cut through his beard in a devilish way. "We were in a hurry, weren't we?"

"Um-hmm."

"We'll have to try to be more patient this time."

"I should hope so."

He held her closer. "Know what I could go for?"

"Don't even think it, Ryan Cornell!" Carly exclaimed, pushing herself from his arms and making ceremony of gathering the scattered sections of the newspaper.

Ryan stood with his hands on his hips in a righteous pose. "How did you know what I was going to say?"

"Because I know you," she said, not in the least intimidated by his stance. "And I know that one-track mind of yours. Now, are you going to leave so I can get something done?"

He gave her a wicked grin and strode toward the bedroom. "As soon as I get some clothes on. You weren't thinking of sending me out in the cold like this?"

Eyes glued to his retreating form, Carly knew she didn't want anyone else to see how gorgeous he looked in a rich robe that stopped just short of his knees, broadcasting the longest of muscled calves. "I'll give you five minutes. Then . . . out!"

It was more like ten, for she made the mistake—the very pleasant mistake—of joining him in the bedroom, where he quickly made her forget all those other things she had to do. His kisses were long and lingering, heating her as they always did. She would have thought she'd get used to this, but she never did, so she couldn't help but yield to his fire for those few final minutes before he left. Even then it took a tepid shower to still her ache. The knowledge of Sheila Montgomery's impending visit helped. As always, Sheila was a timely reminder of what her life really was . . . and what it wasn't.

"So, tell me about Chicago. How was Harmon?"

Sheila sat back on the sofa and let her gaze wander around Carly's living room. "Harmon is Harmon."

"What does *that* mean? Are you two on or off?"

"Off."

"You don't sound upset."

She tossed her raven-black hair over her shoulder in a gesture of indifference. "I'm not. He can be a pill some times."

"But you were so excited when he called. You spent Christmas with him, didn't you?"

"Oh, yeah. But he split after that. He wanted to go skiing." She shrugged. "That mattered more to him than me. It's just as well. I found other things to do." She changed the subject, idly fidgeting with a throw pillow. "Tell me about you and Ryan. Thick as thieves, are ya?"

Skipping over the more intimate aspects of their relationship, Carly told Sheila of the days before New Year's, of New Year's Eve itself, of Vermont, of their return. Sheila seemed to want to know everything—whom she'd met at the parties, the name of the inn where they'd stayed, what exploring they'd done there, what they'd ordered for Ryan's place—and she showed enthusiasm even when Carly feared she was rubbing salt on the wound. But Sheila asked, following one question fast with another, so Carly answered, finding a strange kind of satisfaction in giving Sheila, who'd known her in that other world, this proof of her new life.

By the time Ryan arrived, Carly was beginning to feel decidedly guilty about talking so much about herself. She was relieved by the knowledge that Ryan would redirect the discussion. Sure enough, after depositing a large bag and a bouquet of flowers on the kitchen counter, he extracted a dark bottle from the bag, ferreted out three glasses from Carly's cabinet, filled each with mahogany-hued liquid, then joined the women in the living room.

"Sherry, ladies? It's about that hour."

Sheila was about to speak up in favor of a rum and Coke when she caught herself and smiled shyly, suddenly more subdued. "Thank you. This is lovely."

Carly cast her vote of agreement through the smile she gave Ryan. She'd seen the flowers, and though she didn't want to make a big thing of them in front of

Sheila, her smile spoke her thanks for that gift as well.

Ryan settled into a free chair. "I'm glad to finally meet you, Sheila. Carly tells me you were away?"

"That's right." She gripped her glass tightly. "I had to take care of some things back in Chicago."

"You haven't been here long, have you?"

"I transferred to the Boston office a little less than two months ago."

"What office is that?" he asked politely, causing Sheila to look in alarm at Carly, not quite sure what to say. It was Carly who spoke, trying to sound as nonchalant as possible.

"I'm sorry. I thought I'd told you. Sheila works with Sam. That's how we met."

It was Ryan's turn to look surprised, and the slightest bit dismayed. At first Carly feared he had suspected something of a strange coincidence in Sheila's occupation. Then she reminded herself of Ryan's displeasure at anything involving Sam Loomis, and she forced herself to relax.

"I didn't know," he stated thoughtfully. Evidently coming to the conclusion that a grudge against Sam shouldn't extend to Sheila, he smiled. "It must be interesting work."

"Sometimes. Sometimes it's pretty boring."

"Isn't any job? Tell me about yours. What kinds of cases are you working on?"

Carly sat back and listened while Sheila recounted several of the assignments she'd had since she'd come to Boston, then, at Ryan's prodding, spoke of some of the more exciting cases she'd handled in Chicago. She had enough sense not to mention Carly's case, taking her cue from Carly's impromptu fabrication of how they'd met. When she asked Ryan about his practice, he obliged with easy conversation. At least Carly thought it was easy, though Sheila seemed less than relaxed. She wondered if there was something about Ryan that made her nervous; Sheila Montgomery was not usually one to shy from men. She didn't have long to speculate though before the downstairs buzzer rang.

Sending a "who in the world could that be" look Ryan's way, she went to the intercom. "Yes?"

"Carly, it's Tom Cornell. Is my brother there?"

Carly paused for a minute, then couldn't quite suppress a grin. She made sure to keep her back to Ryan and Sheila. "He's here. Want to come up?"

"You bet."

She pressed the release, then opened her front door. Only then did she turn back toward the living room. Ryan was wearing a maddeningly innocent expression. Sheila seemed more on edge than ever.

It was to the latter that Carly addressed herself, a mischievous twinkle in her eye. "Relax. You'll like Ryan's brother, Sheila. He's nice."

Within moments, the tall, blond-haired man appeared at the door, greeting Carly with a warm hug— which she hadn't expected but which she supposed she should have, given the strength of Ryan's feelings and the fact that he was sure to have told his brother he was practically living with her—and casting a gaze toward Ryan, whose message on Tom's answering service was simply that he should stop by sometime after four-thirty. He was about to ask what he'd wanted when his gaze fell on Sheila. He stood very still for an instant before daring to dash a pleased, if questioning, glance at Carly.

Taking his arm, Carly led him down into the living room. "Tom, I'd like you to meet a friend of mine, Sheila Montgomery. Sheila, Tom Cornell."

Eyes glued to Sheila, Tom walked around the low tables, took Sheila's hand and raised it to his lips in as courtly a greeting as Carly had seen. She snuck a glance at Ryan to find that he too was amused, then focused back on Sheila, whose eyes were round and more lively than they'd been all afternoon.

"This is a pleasure," Tom said, his voice smooth as velvet and every bit as alluring.

"For me too," Sheila breathed. "I've seen you before."

"Twice."

"You remember?"

"I remember."

Ryan cleared his throat. "I didn't know you'd be by today, Tom," he said with a meaning the other couldn't miss. "Have a seat. Would you like some sherry?"

"Sherry?" Uncomprehending at first, Tom dragged his gaze from Sheila's face to the glass in her hand. "Ah, no. No thanks." Then he shifted his gaze to Carly. "Don't have any beer, by chance?"

With a suspicious look, Carly redirected the question to Ryan, who accommodated her by tossing his head toward the kitchen. "Let me take a look," she said, turning. Sure enough, a six pack sat at the bottom of the bag Ryan had brought. He'd come prepared, she mused, tugging one of the cans free and returning to the living room. "It's not quite as chilled as it should be."

"No problem." Taking the beer from her, Tom smiled. His attention was quickly back on Sheila, whose own had never left him. From where she was sitting Carly could feel the electricity between the two and wondered if it had been the same between her and Ryan. *Had* been? *Continued* to be. She didn't wonder;

she knew. Even now, when she met his gaze and he winked, she felt the charge.

. Much later, together in bed, Carly and Ryan would laugh at how it had been. Proud of themselves for having brought together two people so very obviously attracted to each other, they hadn't minded that they'd felt utterly superfluous during that time in her apartment. Nor had they minded when they'd had to excuse themselves to dress for a dinner date. Deftly taking the hint, Tom and Sheila had left . . . together. It was perfect.

Fourteen

SHEILA SAT AT HER DESK THE FOLLOWING MON-day feeling strangely disconcerted. She half wished she'd been assigned to the courtroom; at least then she'd have had something to keep her mind busy. As it was, blank report forms lay before her. She took the first, rolled it into the ancient typewriter that had come with her closet of an office—it galled her to think of being on the fifteenth floor without even the tiniest window—struck several keys and promptly chipped a fingernail. Muttering a choice oath, she snatched the paper from the typewriter, crumbled it into a hard ball and slammed it into the wastebasket. Then she sat back in her chair and attempted to file her wounded nail into an acceptable shape.

After a minute she despaired of that and let her hand fall. It came to rest against the purse hanging on the back of her chair. Instinctively her fingers curled around the fine leather, and she pulled the soft pouch onto her lap. It was lovely, as well it should be, she mused, given the amount she'd paid for it. Though a large satchel had always been part of her outfit, she'd never had one quite as nice. A small smile curved her lips. The car was nice, too, a bright, new, shiny Mazda, the sporty model she'd admired from afar for so long. Driving it this weekend, she'd felt elegant, special, important . . . not that she'd had all that much time to drive around.

Her thoughts turned to Tom and her smile grew more poignant. Tom Cornell was something else—very different from the men she'd known, oozing with sexuality yet restrained and respectful. They'd gone to dinner together on Friday night, to the theater on Saturday. Though she'd been awed by the latter, Tom had taken it all in stride, seeming to enjoy her enjoyment as much as the play itself. On Sunday he'd taken her out for brunch, then back to his house where he'd shown her his computer with the enthusiasm of a young boy. Computers had always bored her; she'd never understood their workings and therefore had found them thoroughly intimidating. But Tom's enthusiasm had been catching. Under his patient tutelage, she'd sat at the keyboard responding to prompts, giving commands, making the machine do remarkable things. Together they'd created a game on it, then spent hours playing it. She'd had fun.

And Tom Cornell hadn't even made love to her.

"Sheila?" Her head shot up. Greg Reilly was leaning around her half-open door. "Busy?"

She threw a disparaging gaze at the papers on her desk. "I should be, but I'm not. These things are hard to get into."

He straightened and came in. "Case reports? I know the feeling. Things are pretty slow at my desk too. Must be Monday mornings. Wanna waste a little time with me?"

He didn't need to coax her further. "Sure," she said,

pushing the papers back on her desk in a symbolic gesture. "Why not."

He grinned and propped a thigh on the desk corner. "So, how's it going? We missed you while you were away."

"Come on," she chided. "Anyone can do what I do."

"Not the way *you* do it. Sam put Henshaw on the Plymouth County case; she came near to brawling with our witness."

Sheila chuckled. "Theresa Rossi is a handful. One week with her was plenty. I'm glad I was away. Poor Henshaw."

"How was your trip, anyway?"

"Great."

"Do you miss living in Chicago?"

She shrugged indifferently.

"How do you like Boston?"

"I like it. It's cozy."

"Cozy. That's a new one."

"It's an easy city to get around," she explained impassively. "Not overwhelming like New York."

"Have you had a chance to meet people here?"

"A few."

"Anyone special?" He phrased it in the way of an interested suitor feeling out the competition. When she simply shrugged again, he changed the subject. "So." He sighed. "How's your apartment?"

"It's okay."

"Warm enough? Some of those landlords get pretty stingy with the heat."

"It's fine."

He sensed a wariness in her and wondered if he'd lost his touch. Fearing that he was trying too hard, he relaxed and let his gaze fall quite naturally to the soft wool dress she wore. It was loose fitting and simple, with a boat neck and wing sleeves; its red color set off her black hair and pale complexion well. "I like your outfit. Is it new?"

She smoothed the gentle fabric, then tipped her chin up with a hint of defiance. "I went on a shopping spree last week. I felt I deserved something new and bright to carry me through the drab winter months."

"You never look drab, Sheila. I have to say that for you. The office has never been more colorful."

Looking into his eyes, she couldn't help but wonder just what had brought him into her office. Yes, his gaze was warm, but not in the way of typical male appreciation. He'd never been terribly solicitous before. There had never been the slightest spark between them. He was the right age and very definitely good-looking, but he had always been standoffish, Sam's assistant in every sense. His sudden interest made little sense.

Unless, she thought with a jolt, unless he suspected. . . .

"You're kind to say that," she said demurely, then took on an expression of worry. "I only wish Sam felt that way. He distrusts me for some reason. I have no idea why."

"He doesn't distrust you," Greg improvised. "He's just a tough guy to get to know. He plays by every rule. Believe it or not, it was months before I saw him crack a smile." That was the truth.

"Really? But I thought you two were close."

"Not at first. It was political pull that got me in here. He resented that."

Where his studied attempts at flattery had gotten him nowhere, this honest confession seemed to break through Sheila's reserve. Her expression opened and she angled back more comfortably in her seat.

"How did you get him past it?"

"By working my tail off."

"I was afraid you'd say that." She shook her head. "I'm doing the best I can. It doesn't seem to faze him."

"It fazes him. Believe me. He's noticed."

"Hmmph. Could've fooled me. He seems angry every time I come near him." She widened her eyes innocently. "Do you think he's got something against the Chicago office?"

"Nah."

"Then it has to be me." She looked dejected. "I'm doing something wrong."

"You're new. That's all. Give it time."

Give it time. That was what they all said, she mused. Give it time, and you'll meet Mr. Right. Give it time and you'll make it up that ladder. Give it time and you'll have all those things dreams are made of. Well, she'd tired of waiting.

"So there's hope?" she asked, going along with the game.

Before Greg could respond, a knock came at the door, followed seconds later by the appearance of the very man under discussion. "Greg, here you are. Got a minute?"

Greg knew well enough to jump. He'd seen that tense look on Sam's face only once or twice before; it meant trouble.

"Sure."

Sam was gone as quickly as he'd come. At the door, Greg gave Sheila a parting wink, then made a beeline for his office.

Sam stood before the window, head bowed, fingers rubbing his forehead. When he heard Greg's footsteps, then the door closing, he turned.

"What's up?" Greg asked.

"I've just had one hell of a go-round with John Meade

in Chicago. He wants Carly Quinn back there for a couple of days. I tried to get him to come out here but he won't." He gave a weary sigh. "I'm going to take her."

"You?" Normally such a job would fall to one of the underlings in the office. As chief deputy, Sam was in demand.

"Yeah. She'll be really upset at having to go at all; the least I can do is to soften it up some. She likes me and trusts me. It might help." Allowing Greg no time to comment, he raced on. "Mazur and Stenmar will keep overall track of things. I want you to cover my desk though. And you'd better watch Judge Feldstein; if she gets any more threats, we'll have to put someone on her."

"Sure thing."

"Everything else is pretty well set. If all goes well I can be back by Wednesday night."

"Isn't it risky—your going with her? If someone sees you together and makes the connection. . . ."

Even in as little time as he'd had, Sam had thought it all out. Actually, he'd thought it all out before, when the trip to Chicago had been no more than a vague possibility. "We'll be together without being together. She won't have to know me, but I can keep her in sight all the time. Someone from Hoffmeister's office will meet the plane in Chicago and take over from there. When I've seen that she's in good hands, I'll find my own way to the state's attorney's office." He shook his head and raised troubled eyes heavenward in a plea for strength. "She is not going to like this. Not a bit." Lowering his gaze, he murmured, "Neither is Ellen, for that matter."

"Ellen will understand."

"Yeah. Unfortunately, Wednesday is our daughter's

birthday. It's gonna take a whole *load* of understanding!"

There wasn't much Greg could say on that score. He'd met Ellen only once, just before Christmas. Though he and Sam had grown closer in the past weeks, he wasn't exactly in a position to offer personal advice. All he could do was to reassure Sam that he'd be on top of everything crossing his desk, which he promptly did. He was rewarded with an appreciative nod.

"When will you be leaving?"

Sam had already scooped up his blazer and was tossing it over his shoulders. "As soon as I can get home to pack a bag and pick up Carly." He grimaced. "She's not gonna like this. . . ."

"Some great novels are semiautobiographical. Jonathan, tell me what you see of Hemingway in *A Farewell to Arms.*"

Jonathan, a rangy sixteen-year-old at the gawky stage, looked down at his notes. His deep voice came with deliberation. "I think that the war part is his. Didn't he fight in World War I?"

Carly sat on the front of her desk with her legs crossed at the ankles. "Uh-huh." She said nothing more, waiting patiently for an elaboration. It was Deborah, attractive and poised, who spoke up.

"The love story is fictitious. He didn't get married until after the war, and that marriage ended in a divorce."

Carly nodded. "That's true."

"But he had been in love," one of the other boys argued. "He remarried before the book came out."

A third, Brendan, joined the fray. "Sure, and his father packed it in the same year."

" 'Packed it in'?" Carly gave each word its due.

Brendan shrugged. "Killed himself. Maybe Hemingway had a fixation on death. To kill Catherine off that way—" The bell rang and there was a moment's hiatus.

Carly rose. "That's it. For tomorrow, think about the tragic quality of that last chapter. A theme. Two pages. And there will be a full test on Friday." At the last there were several sighs and a muffled moan, then all sound of complaint was lost in the gathering of books and papers and the slow dispersal of students.

Carly, too, closed her notebook and set her book atop it before stooping to get her bag. When she stood, she caught her breath. Sam was standing at her door.

"Sam! What a nice surprise!" Then she noted his expression. "Uh-oh, what's wrong?" But she knew; *she knew.*

"Meade called this morning. He wants you in Chicago."

"Oh, no . . ." she whispered.

"Just for a day or two. He wants to go over everything with you in hopes of avoiding that new trial."

"When?"

"Now."

"Now? I can't leave now, Sam!" she exclaimed, then looked frantically around. "I teach. I can't just—" she gasped "—just take off!"

He came closer and spoke very gently. "You have to. You haven't any choice."

All color drained from her face. It was bad enough running out on her job. . . . "But what about Ryan?"

"What about him?"

"I . . . he . . . we've been practically living together. If I just disappear, he'll be hurt and angry and suspicious. I can't leave him without an explanation. What'll I say?"

Tucking her books into the crook of his elbow, Sam

grasped her arm and guided her toward the door. There wasn't any time to waste; they had little more than an hour to make their plane. "You'll leave a note and say that an emergency's come up at home and that you'll call him. Now, should you speak with the headmaster?"

Carly stared dumbly at him, then looked straight ahead, seeing nothing of the corridor through which he propelled her steadily. "The headmaster. Uh, yes." Forewarned as she'd been, the turn of events was no easier to accept. She couldn't believe what was happening. Her life had been so pleasant. . . .

An hour later she sat on the plane. Beneath the wide brim of her hat, her hair was pulled straight back into a sleek chignon. She wore dark glasses over her colorless contacts. Only after the craft was airborne did she remove the hat and glasses. Her bright blue eyes stunned Sam; even anxiety-clouded, they were brilliant.

"Sorry I couldn't do better for clothes," she whispered, a wry twist to her lips. "I threw out all my Robyn things last summer. Gauzy blouses, floppy blazers—they were too artsy, too whimsical for Carly Quinn."

"You'll do fine," he murmured appreciatively. "I can't believe how different you look. Two things—eyes and hair—it's amazing."

"I feel strange."

His eyes widened in alarm. "Sick?"

Frowning, she tapped her head with her forefinger. "Crazy. Like I'm playing an absurd game. You know, charades or something."

He eyed her sadly. "It's no game, hon. But it'll be okay. Trust me."

She did trust him, and given the upset this trip was

bound to be, she needed every bit of help she could get. "Thanks for coming, Sam."

"No problem." He raised a finger to his lips and tossed his head meaningfully toward the rest of the plane.

Nodding her understanding, Carly turned her head toward the window where only the clouds could see her heartache. "RYAN?" Clutching the phone, she spoke timidly.

"Carly! My God, what happened? I couldn't believe it when I found your note! Is it your dad?"

She hated herself for what she was doing but felt, and not for the first time, that she was controlled by others. "Yes."

"His heart?"

She cringed. If all was well, as she assumed it was, John Lyons was playing golf with his brother in Phoenix. She'd called him there a few days earlier, before Ryan had come home from work. "Yes. His heart."

"How is he?"

"He'll be all right. It was just a scare. I think I'll stay with him for another day or two. You found the key, didn't you?"

"Right in my mailbox." He managed a half laugh. "How do you think I got in?"

She'd called her own number, just assuming he'd be there. "Right. That was stupid of me. I guess . . . I guess I'm not myself."

"You sound awful. Damn it, I wish you'd waited. I would have gone with you."

"I couldn't wait, Ryan. The call came early this morning, and I caught the first flight out."

"Want me to come? I can be there in the morning."

"No. No. Really. It's not necessary. It was just a scare. I'll be okay once I get over the shock."

"Then let me have the number so I can reach you. Or the address." If he couldn't be there he wanted to send something—flowers, candy, *anything* to cheer her up. As it was he felt thoroughly helpless.

"Ah . . . no." She tried to think quickly, but it wasn't easy with her heart torn in tiny pieces. "Listen, I'll call you again tomorrow night. Besides, I'll be at the hospital most of the time. I don't know when I'll be back." She swallowed hard, aware of a cold sweat on her palms. "Ryan, I miss you."

"I miss you, too, babe. Are you sure there's nothing I can do?"

"I'm sure. Just take care of things back there, okay?" Her voice cracked, and she knew she had to get off the phone quickly.

"Okay. Carly, I love you."

Hot tears trickled down her cheeks and, in that instant, she knew that she felt the same. "I . . . I'll see you soon," she whispered, then added a choked, "Bye-bye," and hung up the phone.

"Okay, let's go over this one more time."

John Meade stood over her, her inquisitor. Brozniak, his assistant, leaned indolently against the far wall of the office, relentlessly staring, saying nothing. Had it not been for Sam's reassuring presence, Carly would have screamed. If she'd thought a full day of quizzing on Tuesday had been bad, this Wednesday morning was unbearable. She'd barely slept for two nights and was nearly at her limit. Not to mention the fact that her scalp ached. Lacking the patience to blow her hair straight and let it hang long as Robyn Hart used to do, she had pulled it tightly back into a bun for the third day running. Now, for the first time, she could fully appreciate the beauty of letting it curl free and soft in the manner of Carly Quinn.

"I met Peter Bradley when I first came to work at the *Tribune*," she droned. "He was a staff photographer. I was a reporter."

"Had you ever seen him before that?"

"No."

"But you'd heard of him?"

"Yes. He'd won any number of prizes for photojournalism. Nothing like a Pulitzer, but local things. I'd always admired his pictures."

The prosecutor's eyes narrowed. "Admired?"

She scowled back. "Yes. Admired. They were striking, more dramatic than most of the other newspaper stuff."

"Had you ever bought one of his photos?"

"No."

"Had you ever cut one from the paper and framed it?"

"No!"

Meade ran a hand over the few remaining hairs on the top of his head. "Okay. You'd never met him."

She shook her head and spoke slowly, feeling as though she were enunciating for a dimwit. "Not until I started at the *Tribune*."

"How well did you know him then?"

"Not very. I saw him in passing from time to time. It wasn't until I joined the investigative team that we actually worked together." She sighed and raised pleading eyes to the state's attorney. "John, do we have to go over this again? I've already told you as much as I can."

Meade picked up on the slight catch in her voice. "Then there's something else—something you *can't* tell us?"

"No! I've told you! Peter and I were *friends*. That's it!" Annoyed and tired, she looked away. "I just don't see the point in all this. You're looking for something that *isn't there*. If Culbert's lawyer thinks he can prove something, let him try."

"Unfortunately, if it comes to a trial, the burden of proof is on the state. All Mancusi has to do is to plant a seed of doubt in the minds of the jurors. *We're* the ones who have to prove there was no deep emotional involvement between you and Bradley."

Frustrated beyond belief, Carly nearly went wild. "But there was!" she cried. "Nothing romantic, maybe, but we were very good friends. We worked together, sometimes ate together or took in a movie together. You have to understand the kind of camaraderie that develops when you work with someone on something like the arson probe. In a sense you become co-conspirators. You know a story's there and that there may be danger involved, but you believe strongly enough in your cause to go after the story.

"It was a team that did the initial investigation. I was just one member of that team. When things began to get sticky, most of the others bowed out. Our editor felt that we couldn't prove a thing. I disagreed. Most of my investigation was carried out without the formal sanction of the paper. The publisher was scared. One state legislator was involved; no one knew who else might turn up."

She took a breath. "Peter Bradley was the only person willing to go out on a limb to help me. He read my notes and came to believe as strongly as I did. For that I owed him a lot. So maybe Mancusi's got a point. Maybe my testimony *was* jaded by Peter's death."

Meade's eyes were hard and chilling. "Did you ever lie on the stand?"

"No."

"Did you ever so much as stretch the truth?"

"No!" She squeezed her eyes shut and rubbed her forehead.

"Then what we've got to do is to anticipate whatever it is Mancusi's going to produce."

"Manufacture," she corrected angrily, eyes flying open.

"Okay." He sighed. "Let's take it from where you left off. You first worked with Bradley when you joined the investigative team."

"Yes," she gritted. "He was the one we requested when we needed pictures." She had to have said it ten times before.

"Weren't there others?"

"Staff photographers? Of course."

"But you only worked with Bradley."

"I didn't say that. He was the one we *requested*. If he was busy someone else was assigned."

"He was always your first choice."

"Yes." Her head was splitting.

"Why him?"

"Because he was good!"

"He was also very attractive."

She glared and said, "So's Sam," then swiveled in her seat. "Are we making it, Sam?"

Despite the tension of the moment, Sam had trouble suppressing a grin. He admired her grit, always had. "No, Carly, we are not."

Satisfied, she whirled on John defiantly. "Whether or not a man's attractive doesn't mean a thing."

Meade didn't blink. "Sam's married. What was Bradley's excuse?"

"He was gay!" she blurted before she could stop herself, then, realizing what she'd said, she stiffened.

All three men did the same. It was Sam who came forward, kneeling by her chair. "What did you say?"

In mental pain, she frowned, wishing she could take back the words but knowing it was too late. Her voice was a mere whisper. "I said, he was gay."

Understanding the agony she felt at betraying a man so close to her once, he spoke very softly. "It's true?"

Knotting her hands in her lap, she nodded.

Meade exploded. "Well, why in the hell didn't you say something sooner!" he thundered. "Damn it, what was the big secret?"

At that moment Carly positively detested John Meade. She spoke very slowly, with a quiet force that made Sam proud. "It's not your business or anyone else's what Peter Bradley's sexual preference was. He chose not to broadcast it in his lifetime; I wanted to respect his wishes after his death. It doesn't have any bearing on whether or not Gary Culbert or Nick Barber are guilty of arson-related murder. And anyway—" she lowered her voice "—you can't prove it one way or the other."

The state's attorney was not averse to trying. "Did he have a lover?"

"I assume so."

"Who?"

"I don't know."

"You know, but won't tell—"

"John," Sam broke in, standing once again, "take it easy."

Carly put her hand on his arm, but her eyes had never left Meade's. "No, it's okay, Sam. I won't tell because I can't tell. I just don't know. Peter was very sensitive about the whole thing. I didn't learn about it myself until we were working together on the arson investigation. There were long hours and lots of pressure. One day it just slipped out, maybe because he knew I'd keep it in confidence." Her voice grew low and bitter. "Some confidante I turned out to be."

"It needed to be said, Carly," Sam reasoned gently. "For your sake, in more ways than one."

"Sure. I'm off the hook, but Peter's on."

"Don't you think he would have felt it a good enough cause?"

"I don't know," she murmured miserably.

"Aw, come on." Meade scowled. "Times have changed. Gay liberation's brought them out of the closet."

She stared. "Not all of them. Not Peter. He felt frightened and guilty. He said his parents would die if they knew. He didn't want to hurt them that way. Which is just one of the reasons I should never have spoken, one of the reasons you all should forget what I said."

Meade rolled his eyes and mumbled, "My God, you'd think this were a tea party. Listen, Robyn," he stated forcefully, "you seem to be missing the point, which is that Gary Culbert has filed a motion for a new trial based on evidence suggesting that *you* were having an affair with the deceased and therefore may have been less than an objective witness."

"I was *not having an affair* with the deceased."

"Then you were emotionally involved—"

"Of course I was emotionally involved!" she cried, clutching at the back of her chair as she turned to face the pacing prosecutor. "I'm a human being! When I witness death first hand it affects me! *But that doesn't make me any less of an objective witness!* When I was on the stand, I told what I did, what I learned, what I saw. That's all!"

Sam touched her shoulder. "It's okay, Carly. Relax."

"I'm sorry, Sam," she murmured brokenly. "This is

just so absurd. We're going round and round in circles, getting nowhere. If it's proof that John wants, he'll just have to pay some witness to perjure himself. Evidently that's what Mancusi's done." She turned to glare at Meade. "Your time would be better spent trying to find out who *that* witness is and discrediting *him*." Defeated, she sagged back in her seat. "Beyond that, I don't know what to say."

Sam turned to the prosecutor. "I think she's had enough, John. She just doesn't know any more."

Meade stared long and hard at Carly before relenting, and then only after darting Brozniak a meaningful look. "Okay. That's it then." He looked at his watch. "You folks want to join us for lunch?"

Food was the last thing Carly wanted, the first being to get on a plane and leave Chicago far, far behind. Attuned to her needs and well aware of his own, Sam answered. "Thanks, John, but I think we'll be on our way." He dug a crumpled piece of paper from his jacket pocket and scanned it. "There's an early afternoon flight we can catch. Give me about ten minutes' lead, then send Carly along with Marie." He turned to Carly. "I'll see you on the plane. Okay?"

She forced a wan smile and nodded, then watched him shake hands with the two men and leave. Without him, she felt suddenly more vulnerable, fearing for an instant that Meade might take the opportunity to grill her further. Standing awkwardly, she smoothed her skirt.

"I'm sorry I couldn't help you more."

"You helped us."

Something in his tone sent a shaft of fear through her. "You're going with the homosexuality thing?"

Meade was surprisingly gentle. "Only if I have to. Believe it or not, I understand and admire your feelings. And I'm not inhuman myself. If there's any other possible way—*including* investigating Mancusi's witnesses—I'll do it. But you've got to remember what's at stake here. A new trial will mean a huge expense for the state, not to mention the manpower involved. More important, if there *is* a new trial and Mancusi manages to cast doubt on your credibility as a witness such that a jury is swayed, Culbert may go free. You don't want that any more than I do." He paused. "I'm not really your enemy. Your enemy is up there in the slammer, and I'm just doing my best to try to keep him there."

Carly dropped her chin to her chest, then took a deep breath and raised very weary eyes. "I know, John. It's just that it's difficult for me to have to deal with all of this again. Leaving Chicago last July was one of the hardest things I'd ever done. I felt like I'd been given a life sentence for a noncrime. But I've adjusted. Things are going well for me. I don't want it all spoiled." Seeing Marie at the door, she extended a hand to John. "No offense, but I hope I won't be seeing you."

He grinned. "No offense taken. For the record, I hope the same. Sam'll keep you posted."

"He always does," she said with a rueful sigh, then, with a perfunctory nod toward Brozniak, she took her leave.

When they arrived back at Logan, Sam waited while she repaired to the nearest rest room, switched her contact lenses, loosened her hair, dampened it, and finally, using her blow dryer from her suitcase, let it dry curly. When she emerged, she felt almost normal.

Shaking his head, a grin on his face, he stared at her in amazement. "I can't believe the difference. I mean, you were gorgeous enough the other way, but this way you're . . . you."

"It's funny, but I *feel* like me, too. Now, if I can get over the next hurdle. . . ."

"Which is?"

"Seeing Ryan." She was a bundle of nerves. Not only was she strung taut over all that had happened in Chicago, but, realizing now the depth of her feelings, she was all the more burdened by guilt.

"You spoke with him last night?" Sam asked, steering her toward the parking garage.

"Oh, yes." Her sigh was wistful. "I told him my father was better and I'd probably be flying back on Thursday. I didn't dare say I'd be in today; he would have insisted on meeting the plane. Anyway," she rationalized more lightly, "now I can surprise him." The thought of it caused a thread of excitement to weave slowly through her discouragement. She caught sight of a wall clock. "Hey, you may be able to make Sara's party after all."

"If the traffic's with us, may be."

The traffic was with them. Carly was home by four. Dropping her bag on the bed to unpack later, she showered, put on a pair of slacks and a sweater, took a steak from the freezer and made a huge salad. Then she called Ryan at his office. Or tried.

The receptionist answered promptly. "Miller and Cornell."

Heart pounding, Carly made her request. "Mr. Cornell."

"One moment, please."

It was more than one moment—Carly counted every second—before Ryan's secretary finally picked up the phone. "Mr. Cornell's office."

"This is Carly Quinn. Is Mr. Cornell there?"

"I'm sorry, he's not in his office. I expect him back shortly. May I take a message?"

"Uh . . . uh, yes. Would you tell him I called?"

"Certainly. That's Carla—"

"Carly. With a *y*. Carly Quinn."

"And the number?"

"He knows it."

"Fine. I'll see that he gets the message."

Replacing the receiver, Carly sank into one of the director's chairs by the kitchen table. She felt deflated. Not only had Ryan not been there, but also she'd felt like a stranger when she'd called the place so very dear to his heart. Wondering why she'd never been to his office, she realized with a jolt that it wasn't for lack of invitation. Ryan had suggested it several times; on each occasion she'd declined the offer. In a small way it had to do with her aversion to lawyers, in a larger way with her aversion to exposure. The former was truly absurd, she knew, given her love for Ryan and the respect she'd felt for those of his partners and associates she'd met. And as for the latter, it had dwindled noticeably in the past few weeks.

Pushing herself from the chair, she wandered into the living room and perched on the windowsill overlooking the river. It was dusk. Even as she watched, one, then another, pair of headlights flicked on. Chewing nervously on the inside of her cheek, she glanced at her watch and wondered when Ryan would call. Then, resting her head back against the window frame, she tried to relax.

Indeed she was more confident now about "being seen," and in large part she had Ryan to thank. It was strange; before she'd met him she'd thought of security only in the physical sense. But there was more. She realized now that part of her public reticence had been induced by self-consciousness, by the fear that her disguise was so transparent that anyone and everyone would see through her.

Ryan had changed that. When she was with him, Carly Quinn had a full identity; his love, it seemed, provided the final piece missing from the puzzle of her daily life. He believed in her, so she had to believe in herself.

Her future was something else. Now that she'd admitted to herself that she was in love with the man, things were more complicated. To confess her love and still hold back the truth of her past was unacceptable. Yet she couldn't tell him of that past. Not yet. The Barber-Culbert case was still far too active. And she knew Ryan. If she told him she loved him, he would push for a commitment she was simply unable to make with that other still hanging over her head.

Glancing again at her watch, she crossed the room and sifted through the mail Ryan had brought in during her absence. When she found nothing but meaningless ads and not-so-meaningless bills, she thrust the pile down and paced to the television. Flipping it on, she retreated to the sofa. She rarely watched television. It bored her. But she was unsettled enough to try anything.

It didn't work. Within ten minutes the television screen was black and she had gone in search of her needlepoint. That helped for a time, though more to keep her hands occupied than her mind, which seemed suddenly prone to review the events of the past two days in grand detail. She recalled landing at O'Hare and being driven into the city, passing sights that were heart-wrenchingly familiar, yet different in a "you can't go home again" way.

It had actually been enlightening. She'd felt awkward, a stranger, in the city she'd thought of as home for so long. It was *there* that she'd felt conspicuous and in disguise. And rightfully so, she realized. The woman who had returned to Chicago was only part there. Her heart had remained in Boston.

Her mind skipped around, and for a moment she was in her hotel room again—that cold, lonely place with a bodyguard in the adjoining room. Shivering at the thought, she set down her needlepoint, wrapped her arms around her middle and relived those intense, exhausting hours in the state's attorney's office.

Her stomach knotted, then unknotted, then twisted again. She looked at her watch, leaped up from the sofa and moved aimlessly around the room before checking her watch again.

It was nearly six. Ryan should have called, she reasoned impatiently. Curling into the armchair, she hugged her knees to her chest and tried to define *shortly.* That was when his secretary had said he'd be back, and that had been ninety minutes ago. She swallowed and propped her chin on her knees, realizing that he'd probably been held up in court, or had bumped into a colleague on the way back to the office, or had simply taken a detour along the way.

Another twenty minutes passed. She shifted in her chair, eyeing her front door with trepidation as she began to wonder if something might be wrong. What if he'd been hurt somewhere—if he'd been in an automobile accident or, more bizarre but nonetheless possible, if one of his less reputable clients had attacked him. He wouldn't just *not call.* Would he?

After another thirty minutes of silence, her thoughts took a gruesome turn. She imagined Gary Culbert's henchman making the connection between Ryan and herself and setting out to silence her by injuring him. It would be one of the lowliest forms of emotional black-mail, and it would work in a minute.

She shuddered and moaned, squeezed her eyes shut to exorcise the image and ran her hands up and down her arms to ease her inner chill. The phone didn't ring. The door didn't open. She began to feel as though her world was caving in on her.

Fifteen

HEAD DOWN, RYAN CAME UP THE COURTYARD walk, let himself into the building and dispiritedly started up the stairs. It was after eight. The past two nights she had called at nine. He had missed her once today; he prayed she would call again.

If he'd had her number he might have called her back as soon as he'd returned to his office. But he didn't have her number. She hadn't given it to him. He'd thought to call Des Moines for information, but . . . *Johnson?* It had to be one of the most common names in the book.

That first evening after she'd hung up, he'd scoured her apartment for an address book. There had been nothing. No jotted scribbles tacked to a bulletin board. No crumpled listings of friends or relatives. No evidence of her world before Boston. He'd even flipped through her mail in the hopes of finding a handwritten return address, but still he'd struck out. It was like Christmas again. Then he'd simply phoned the wrong place; perhaps, he told himself, he wasn't looking in the right place now. Nonetheless he couldn't quite shake the eerie feeling he had.

Climbing slowly to the third floor, he thought about the power of desperation. This morning, wanting to contact her and having run out of alternatives, he had actually swallowed his pride and called Sam Loomis, who, after all that, was away on business.

Flipping Carly's key from his key case, he fumbled distractedly with her lock. He'd barely pushed the door open an inch when he paused. The light was on, slivering gently into the hall, yet he was sure all the lights had been turned off before he'd left early that morning.

In the instant he conjured three possibilities. The first, that someone had broken in, drew his muscles taut. The second, that Sam Loomis, the only other person with a key, had stopped by, would have set his teeth on edge had he not known Sam was out of town. It was the third that got his heart beating double time. Holding his breath, he pushed the door open, then burst into a broad grin at the sight of Carly curled in a chair across the room.

He slammed the door behind him and tossed his coat on the sofa in passing. "I didn't realize you were home! I thought you'd called from Des Moines!" He was on his haunches in front of her before he realized that the wide-eyed look she wore was not one of delight, but terror. His grin vanished, his pulse rate faltered. "Carly?"

"My God!" she exclaimed in a hoarse whisper, pressing a hand to her chest to still her thudding heart, "I thought you were a thief! It sounded like someone was picking the lock! I've been waiting so long for you to call—I didn't expect you *here*!"

"I didn't expect *you* here," he countered, taking her

cold hand in his. "I assumed you were still in Des Moines."

"Didn't you get my message?"

"The message said you'd called. That was all. I was furious when I got it— I couldn't have missed you by more than half an hour. Had my secretary been there, I would have wrung her neck for not forwarding you to the office where I was. But she'd left for a dental appointment, so all I could do was hope that you'd call again at nine. I've been stewing for the past three hours."

"So have I," she whispered, and suddenly something snapped inside her. It had been building from the moment she'd seen Sam at her classroom door on Monday and had been fueled by the extraordinary tension she'd been under since then. That, and missing Ryan and hating herself for having to lie to him and realizing in these past few hours how much she loved him. . . .

As he watched, her composure crumbled. Her eyes filled with tears, her chin began to quiver. Before she had time to do more than fall into his waiting arms, she was crying. Endless sobs shook her body. She clutched at the lapels of his coat. "Oh, God, Ryan . . ."

"Shh. . . ." He pressed her head to his chest and rocked her gently. "It's okay, babe. It's okay. Shh. . . ."

It was a while longer before she could catch her breath enough to talk. "I'm sorry," she gasped, blotting her cheeks. "I didn't mean to break down like this."

He held her away and saw the dark smudges under her eyes. "You look exhausted. You couldn't have slept the whole time you were gone. How is he, Carly? There wasn't a—"

Setback. Her father. "Oh, no. He's fine." She grew self-conscious. "I guess everything just built and built till I couldn't hold it in anymore." She sniffled. "I wanted to surprise you today, and when you didn't call back I began to imagine all kinds of awful things."

Ryan caught her face between his hands with sudden vehemence. "I've missed you." Then his lips were on hers and something burst within them both. He couldn't kiss her hard enough or deep enough; she couldn't take enough of him or give enough of herself. Hands were everywhere, clutching, stroking, reassuring with a fervor not to be denied.

Shifting her to the floor and moving down over her, Ryan kissed her neck, then shoved up her sweater, tore aside her bra and took her ripe nipple in his mouth, sucking strongly and drawing it to a peak before moving hungrily on to its mate.

No less feverish, Carly blindly grappled with the buttons of his vest, then his shirt, spreading the material, running her hands over his warm flesh in wordless stake of her claim.

The air was rent with moans and hoarse urgings. Carly tugged at Ryan's belt and attacked the zipper of his trousers, while he ravaged the fastenings of her slacks. Parting only long enough to strip off their lower garb, they returned to each other in a fluid motion that joined their bodies fully.

With a growl of possession, Ryan surged against her. He was without gentleness, for Carly's writhing body demanded force, and he wasn't sure if he could have taken her any other way, so desperately did he need to put his mark on her, to weld her to him, to make up for the loneliness of their time apart and clear every thought from her mind but the fury of his love. If he was punishing her for having flown so suddenly, so be it. He was out of control, mastered by his own rampant desire.

Carly took it all and then some with unabashed greed. Her body held his, tightened around him to keep him, rebelled each time he withdrew by capturing him all the more deeply at the next thrust. She had never felt such a powerful need to be bound to another person—or to blot every thought from her mind but the frenzy of Ryan's formidable strength.

The climax they reached was simultaneous, hard and mind-shattering, punctuated by loud cries of exultation. Bodies slick, they collapsed on each other, gasping for breath, moaning at the sweet pain each bore.

When finally he rolled to her side, he gathered her to him in an embrace every bit as fierce as their coupling had been. There were no apologies. The stinging spots on his back where she'd dug her nails told Ryan that she'd taken him as forcefully as he'd taken her. He found great satisfaction in that.

It took Carly longer to get her bearings. Raising her head at last, she blinked. Held snug against Ryan's chest, she lay on the rug at the foot of the chair in which she'd been sitting. Her sweater and bra were bunched somewhere just above her breasts. Ryan's shirt and vest flared from his shoulders.

"I can't believe we did this," she whispered.

He grinned down at her, his breathing still heavy. "Decadent again. But I love it." He placed a kiss on the tip of her nose, then, when she raised her lips, on her mouth. "I did miss you. If you ever, so help me, *ever* take off on me that way again, I'll make you sorry you did."

She saw the teasing in his eyes and hoped it would last, for she knew that there well *might* be other times when she would have to take off. Unable to think of that now, she sat up, tugged her sweater to her waist, then looked at her naked lower torso indignantly. "Look what you've done to me, Ryan Cornell. I'm a mess!"

"You're not a mess. You're gorgeous."

She glanced at his own naked body and smiled. "So are you." Then, reaching for her clothes, she began to dress. "Ryan?"

"Hmm?"

"I'd like to see your office sometime."

He lay on his back, arms pillowing his head, unfazed by his nakedness as he watched her reach beneath her sweater and ease herself into her bra. "You would?" His voice was higher than usual; something pleased him. She wasn't quite sure whether it was what she said or what she did. Before she'd decided, he sat up with a grin, reached behind her and fastened the bra's catch. Then he relaxed back once again.

"I want to be able to picture where you are when you're working." Balancing first on one foot then the other, she slipped on her panties and straightened. "And I want that secretary of yours to be able to picture *me* when I call."

Ryan savored the flashing of her eyes, so different from the gut-wrenching look he'd seen there when he'd first come home. "She'll feel awful about the mix-up," he murmured distractedly, watching her step into her slacks, zip the zipper and fasten the tab. "She's really very good." Sitting up again, he caught her hand. "Where're you rushing to? I want to hear about your father."

"My father's fine and I'm rushing to the kitchen. Aren't you hungry?"

"Sure. But we could go out. You just got back."

"I've been back since four. I took a steak out and made a salad before I called you." She slanted him a knowing look. "Don't tell me you've been eating at home all week." Her teasing hit its mark. If she'd learned one thing about Ryan it was that he had no inclination to cook. Oh, he did make coffee, and a mean cup at that, and he was more than willing to work beside her in the kitchen following her directions. On his own, though, he was a lost cause.

He reached for his briefs and pulled them on. "Eat at home? Uh, no. Not exactly."

"I didn't think so. Well, neither have I, so I thought we'd have a quiet dinner here." She hesitated. "Is that okay?"

Ryan shook his head, but in amazement that she could think otherwise. "It's more than okay. I'd like that, babe."

Carly was mesmerized as much by the velvet warmth in Ryan's tone as by the adoration in his eyes. She'd heard it before, seen it before, but never like this, knowing what she felt in return, knowing that it was nearly, nearly within her grasp.

Raising tremulous fingertips to his lips, she traced their firm contour, so smooth within the soft bristle of his beard. Then, eyes round and teary, she dropped her hand and offered a broken, "I'll get dinner. It won't take long," before fleeing to the kitchen.

Ryan stared after her for a minute. She loved him. She *had* to love him. There was no other explanation for the way she looked at him, the way she spoke to him, the way she responded to him, the way she demanded from him—and yes, she did demand. In her quiet, gentle way she demanded strength and comfort, companionship, understanding and appreciation and passion. She seemed attuned to his every need, satisfying him as he satisfied her. *She had to love him.* But she hadn't said so. Not once.

Retreating to the bedroom, he put on the jeans he'd

left in her closet. Hanging up his suit and shirt, he grabbed his sweat shirt, went into the bathroom to wash up, emerged after several minutes in the process of tugging the sweat shirt over his head and caught sight of her suitcase lying on the bed where she'd left it when she'd first come home.

He smiled, pleased to know that her thoughts of him had taken precedence over all else. Even now he could hear her in the kitchen opening and closing the refrigerator, rattling silverware and china. Thrusting his arm through the second sleeve, he straightened the sweat shirt and approached the bed. He rubbed one long forefinger over the leather of her case, admiring it even as he dreamed of the matching set they'd buy for their travels together.

Then something caught his eye. Frowning, he reached toward the baggage-claim tag attached to the metal fastening of the shoulder strap that stretched from one end to the other of the case. CHI. Chicago? Had she returned from Des Moines via Chicago? But no. Tags were marked with destinations.

Affixed to the traditional handle at the top of the bag was the tag he sought. He turned it over. BOS, indeed. The return-trip tag. Located where it was in a corner, the first must have been missed by the airport employee who would normally have torn it off before putting a new one on.

Ryan dropped the tag and looked up. Boston to Chicago, then back to Boston. And Des Moines? He had no idea how she'd gotten *there*; he only knew that something was odd.

Enveloped in flames, she was suffocating. Through the inferno's roar, she heard Peter's voice, "It was your idea, all yours!" then Matthew's, "I yelled for you but you didn't hear!" She turned first to the left, then the right, then completely around in search of escape, but there was none. There never was. Paralyzed by terror, she stared at the snakes of fire coiling menacingly at her feet.

Carly bolted upright in bed. The flames were gone. The night was black and silent. Only Ryan lay unknowing witness to her suffering, and he stirred slowly by her side, reaching for her in his sleep, coming more fully awake when he felt her trembling. Groggy, he lifted his head. "Carly? What's wrong?"

"Just a nightmare," she managed to whisper, then forced herself to lie down, curl in a ball facing away from him and pull the covers over her bare shoulders.

As Ryan drew her back against him, his grogginess vanished. "You're all sweaty. It must have been some nightmare."

"Mmm."

"What was it about?"

"Oh, the same thing it always is. Fire."

"Your husband's." He still couldn't remember if it was Matthew or Malcolm and was too embarrassed to ask.

"Mmm."

"Must have been your trip that brought it back," he murmured into her hair. "Being with family, and all."

Carly felt like a rat. Though she didn't lie, she didn't tell the whole truth. It occurred to her that come the day Ryan did find out, he would have a right to be positively furious.

"Hey," he said softly, "maybe you should put something on. You're really shaking."

"I'll be okay. It was just the fright. Give me a minute."

He had to give her several before she finally began to relax. Holding her, gently caressing her shoulder, his arm crossing up between her breasts, he couldn't help but think back on the puzzle of the tags. He hadn't asked Carly about them; one part of him was frightened of what her answer might be. Rather, he talked with her over dinner as though nothing was wrong. But something *was* wrong. In himself. Along with confusion and hurt, there was anger. He managed to push it to the back of his mind when he was with her and she seemed so loving and sincere, but it was there, emerging at times like tonight when she'd fallen asleep in his arms after they'd made love and he'd lain awake brooding long after.

Aside from the fact of the luggage tags, there wasn't much to put his finger on. It was weird—the lack of as common an item as an address book, the absence of details of four years of her life, a haunted look, nightmares. Taken alone, no one thing would have aroused his suspicion. But together, with new things all too often joining the list, something didn't add up. And it irked him. He was angry at her for not trusting him enough to confide in him, and angry at himself for not having the courage to confront her.

But she meant so much to him, and he was so afraid of losing her, that he didn't dare jeopardize the status quo. And so the anger built inside him, having nowhere to go but deeper into his gut. As he lay in the dark with her, holding her quiet now, her cuddling body close to his, he wondered how long he would be able to keep it buried.

Sheila hung up the phone, shivered more in aftermath of the call than the weather, pulled her collar higher around her, then looked cautiously around. Shrinking into her coat, she opened the phone-booth door and quickly began to walk up Chestnut Street toward her car parked about half a block from her apartment.

"Bastard," she muttered to herself. "In such a rush." Absently she kicked at the slush underfoot, leaving a path of elongated footsteps behind. It had stormed all Wednesday night and half of Thursday, giving the metropolitan area its heaviest snowfall of the season. With more than a foot of new white stuff on the ground, everything had been closed on Thursday. It had been beautiful; she'd walked through the Common that afternoon, admiring the crisp cleanness of the scene, the muted silence, the brisk fresh air. By Friday the comings and goings of the city had resumed. Now it was Saturday. The streets were wet, the snow dirty, the sidewalks spattered with mud. Thursday's winter wonderland was nothing but a pleasant memory, now tarnished, as was she.

With a determined thrust of her chin, she quickened her step. Reaching the car, she climbed in, started the motor and took off. Fifteen minutes, two near-skids and numerous oaths later she pulled up at Carly's place.

Carly was waiting just inside the front door. When she saw Sheila wave, she trotted down the front path, slowing only to negotiate the snow-glazed steps with care before climbing into the passenger seat.

"Nice car, Sheila!" She looked around, admiring the elaborate dashboard, the racy floor shift, the fine leather appointments. "I'm surprised you want to take it anywhere in this weather."

"Cars are like people. If they sit around all day, they get fat and rusty."

"People don't get rusty," Carly teased.

"Well, fat then. But cars get rusty. Their batteries die. They get scratched by trucks trying to squeeze down streets that are too narrow. Besides, life's too short. You've got to enjoy it while you can." She plastered a bright smile on her face. "So, where are we going? Chestnut Hill?"

"If you don't mind."

Sheila gave a throaty laugh as she pulled away from the curb and executed a neat, if illegal, U-turn. "I think you've got that backward. You're the one who's doing me a favor by taking me shopping."

"You're taking me; I won't *touch* my car."

"Did it always bother you to drive in the snow?"

"It's not the driving that bothers me," Carly said, turning her head to follow the progress of a child in the playground trying to maneuver down the snow-covered slide in a rubber tube. "It's the thought of losing my parking space." The child fell sideways into the snow. "I wasn't sure how the walking would be for school yesterday, so I drove. Let me tell you, I spent half an hour trying to find a space when I got home. Ryan warned me. He was right."

"How is school?"

"Okay. Of course, I missed more than half the week, between Chicago and the snow. The storm was actually a blessing. I don't think I would have been much good for teaching Thursday morning—"

"Chicago?" Sheila was racking her brain, wondering how she could have missed it. "I didn't realize you'd gone to Chicago." So *that* was where Sam had been. She'd wondered. Greg had simply said he'd had to take off. They really *didn't* trust her.

Carly looked at her in surprise. "You didn't know?"

"How would *I* know? They don't tell me anything." Her bitterness came through in her tone and was further emphasized by her pout. "Sam and Greg play their little games. I think they get a kick out of keeping secrets. It makes them feel important." She stepped on the gas at a traffic light turned green. "Hey, am I going the right way?"

"I think so," Carly said, "but this may be a case of the blind leading the blind. We could end up in Chelsea." The road looked right, according to Ryan's directions, but Carly's thoughts were on what Sheila had said and she felt impelled to respond. "I think you're too sensitive. Some secrets are necessary. And believe me, the last thing they do is to make the keeper feel important."

Sheila cast a quick glance toward Carly. "You haven't told him yet." Carly shook her head. "Feeling guilty?"

"Guilty is putting it mildly. I feel like a heel in the first degree. When I had to take off like that—"

"Whoa. Stop there. I want to hear all about Chicago." And rightly she did. She listened carefully to everything Carly told her, asking more detailed questions when Carly was prone to rush.

"What kind of time are they talking about, anyway?"

Carly frowned. "What do you mean? Wait." She peered out the window, looked at a road sign to the left. "I think we have to go up that hill and follow the road to Newton Corner."

Sheila did it, then got right back on the track of the conversation. "When will you know about a new trial?"

"I don't know. The motion has to be heard before the original trial judge. According to John it could take anywhere from two to six months."

"That long?" Sheila asked thoughtfully.

"Maybe I should be grateful. It gives me plenty of time to decide what to do about Ryan."

"What do you *want* to do?"

Carly made a frustrated sound. "There's one part of me that would like to throw myself into the guy's arms, tell him how much I love him, agree to marry him and have his kids and live happily ever after. Is that Center Street? Make a right there. We follow it for a few minutes."

"Why *don't* you throw yourself into his arms, et cetera?"

"How can I, Sheila? He doesn't know about who I was and what I did. How can I agree to marry him and then subject him to the anguish of all this?"

"If he loves you enough he'll accept it. Does he?"

"I think so. Yes. But that's the problem. He would accept it all right; whether I can live with the knowledge of what I'd be putting him through is something else." Her voice grew more strained. "Of course, that's taking for granted that I do tell him everything."

"Don't you want to?"

"I think I have to. I don't see how we can have a trusting relationship without it."

They lapsed into a silence then, each lost in her own thoughts. The car made its way through the streets of Newton, tree lined and brilliant with its blanket of snow. It was Sheila who spoke first, with caution.

"Maybe you shouldn't tell him." When Carly sent her a disbelieving stare, Sheila said. "At least, not right away. I mean, if you think he's going to be sensitive about it—"

"It's *me* who'll be sensitive."

"Same difference. Why ruin things?"

Carly shook her head. "Oh, Sheila, I don't know."

"What have you got to lose by keeping it to yourself a little longer? If the guy loves you for who you are, it doesn't really matter who you've been." She gained momentum. "And then there's the issue of breaking your cover. Are you sure you want to do that?"

"I trust Ryan," Carly said.

"I know. But things slip out. If you tell Ryan, there's always the chance he would say something to someone else."

"He wouldn't."

"Not intentionally. But by mistake? All it sometimes takes is a drink or two."

"He's not a drinker."

"Well, I'd still think twice." She shrugged. "But it's your affair."

The silence that filled the car this time was riddled with tension. Unable to believe the cynical twist in Sheila's attitude, Carly stared at her for a minute before shifting her gaze to the window. She tried to tell herself that Sheila might be jealous of what she had going with Ryan, but it didn't do much to ease the hurt.

"Hey, Carly." Sheila reached over and squeezed her arm. "I'm sorry. I didn't mean to come on so strong. I'm sure Ryan is trustworthy. Go ahead and tell him, if that's what you want to do."

What Carly wanted to do was not to think about it anymore just then. "Well, I'll see." She sighed, then pointed. "Make a left here. It'll take us to Beacon Street."

"Are we almost there?"

"Another couple of minutes, I think. I've only been here once before, and that was with a friend from school who didn't stop talking the entire way. She was driving; I'm not sure if I was paying attention to where we were going." She frowned, then nodded. "This is right. At the next set of lights make a right. What'll it be—Bloomingdale's or one of the smaller specialty shops at the mall?"

"Smaller specialty shops?"

"They're a little more expensive. Maybe we should stick with—"

"Let's try them," Sheila declared, smiling smugly.

Carly wasn't as positive. "Are you sure? You're talking about a formal gown. It's bound to cost—"

"No problem. I plan to splurge. Tom Cornell might just be worth it."

Two hours later, after having shelled out a frightening sum for a bright red silk and chiffon off-the-shoulder number at Charles Sumner, Sheila was as exuberant as ever, full of smiles as they wandered through Filene's. "I do like that dress. Didn't it look great?"

"It's perfect on you, Sheila—the color, the style. You'll look smashing at the party. Too bad you've got to drive all the way back here to pick it up when the alterations are done, though."

"I don't mind. I wasn't about to pay someone to alter it after what I paid for the dress!"

Carly threw her a glance, amazed that after paying what she had Sheila would think twice about a negligible alteration fee. Actually, Carly was stunned she'd been able to afford the dress at all. "What the hell," were Sheila's exact words when, after no more than a cursory glance at the price tag, she'd given the saleswoman the nod.

Carly regarded her speculatively. "Tell me you've come into an inheritance or something."

"No inheritance," was the terse reply, but Sheila's attention was on the nail-polish counter. She picked up one bottle, assessed its color next to her skin, shook her head and put it back. "I've just decided that it's my turn to enjoy life for a change."

"Does that mean you enjoy Tom?"

"You bet." She picked up two more bottles, discarded one quickly, studied the other.

"You saw him last night?"

"Um-hmm." The final bottle met the same fate as its

predecessors. "Hey, I'm hungry." She swung around and narrowed a gaze toward the interior of the mall. "How about some lunch? My feet are about to resign and my throat's gonna close up in a minute if I don't get something wet past it. I don't know how all these people do it. They must have been trained to shop. I guess I missed out on that particular class. But I am starved. There has to be something good around here for—" she straightened her shoulders and lowered her voice to a drawl "—patrons of elegant specialty shops."

Carly couldn't help but laugh. Here was the Sheila she knew and liked, the Sheila who was lighthearted and irreverent. "There's a Charlie's Wildflower on the upper level."

"Say no more." Sheila linked her elbow with Carly's. "Let's go."

Tom Cornell carried the two snifters—one with brandy, one with rum and Coke, back to the sofa, handed the latter to Sheila, then eased his long frame down next to her. "That was a super dinner, Sheila. You're a great cook."

"Comes from living a life without maid service," she quipped. "Actually, I learned to cook from my Uncle Amos."

"*Famous* Amos? I *thought* he was from the West Coast—"

"Not Famous Amos," she chided playfully. "*Uncle* Amos. He was as much of a nanny as I ever had. He took care of us while my mother worked."

"Didn't *he* work?"

"Uh-huh. At keeping sober. He didn't always make it, mind you, but when he did, he was wonderful." She laid her head back against the sofa. "I can remember one time—it was Paulie's birthday."

"Paulie's the third—"

"The fourth," she corrected with a grin. "You're getting there, Tom. Anyway, it was Paulie's birthday and, so help me, there wasn't an ounce of nourishment in the house. My mother wasn't one to worry about little things like food."

"What did she worry about?"

"Men. And clothes."

"And her kids?"

Sheila tossed that one around in her mind. "I guess she did. But you're getting me away from my story. It was Paulie's birthday and we didn't have any food. So Uncle Amos went to the store and brought back six bags of stuff." A sly smile played at the corners of her lips. "To this day I don't know where he got the money. Well, maybe I do, but his intention was good. He cooked the most delicious beef something-or-other—"

"Beef what?"

"I don't know. When I asked him, he said to call it Uncle Amos's Beef."

"Sounds better than beef something-or-other. Why didn't you?"

"Because i'd already had experiences with Uncle Amos's Chicken and Uncle Amos's Fish. Anything 'Uncle Amos' consisted of whatever he felt like adding to the pot at a given time. He was a natural. I stopped worrying about names and started watching him work. I think I learned more from him than from any other person."

"Is he still back there with your brothers?"

She took a gulp of her drink and looked wistfully toward the fire. "We've all split up."

"What are they doing?"

She shifted her gaze to Tom's face. "My brothers? You don't really want to know."

"I do. Maybe if you talked about them more I'd be able to keep them straight."

She studied her glass. "There's not much to keep straight. Jay is the star; he's working an oil rig in Prudhoe Bay. It goes downhill from there. Billy is washing dishes somewhere. Sean is serving one to three for auto theft. And Paulie, well, Paulie has been a senior in high school for several years now."

"And through it all you came out smelling like a rose?"

Her expression was somber, her voice low. "I don't know if I'd say that."

"Well, I would. Look at you. You've got an apartment in one of the greatest areas in town, a new car, a successful career." When he saw the pain in her eyes, he was touched. "You're really something, Sheila, do you know that?"

Snapping from her darker thoughts, she blushed. "I'm not. You keep saying that, but I think it's because you've never dated a policewoman before."

"You're not a policewoman." He slid closer. "You're a deputy U.S. marshal."

"And if I were a policewoman? What would you think then?"

"I'd still think," he murmured against her lips, "that you were the smartest, the prettiest, the funniest sexy lady to enter my house in years." He kissed her slowly, savoring the taste of rum on her tongue.

Sheila relished every minute of it, then couldn't resist a barb. "If I'm so sexy, how come I've never seen your bedroom?"

"Has that been bothering you?"

"Not bothering me. Puzzling me."

He slipped his arm around her shoulder and gathered her closer. "Would you like to see my bedroom?"

She tipped her head to the side and answered on a sing-song note. "Some day."

Tom couldn't believe it. He had paced himself so carefully, had waited for her opening, and she was turning him down? "Not now?"

"I can't."

"Why not?"

"Because I have to get back to Boston. I'm on duty at six tomorrow morning."

"You've got to be kidding." When she shook her head decisively, he let out a breath. "I don't believe it. I fall for a woman who has to go to work at six o'clock on a Sunday morning?"

"Not *every* Sunday morning," she said apologetically. "I'm really only doing my boss a favor tomorrow. He called just before you picked me up to ask if I could fill in for one of the others who has the flu. I couldn't really say no. He's been down on me enough lately."

"Is this the Loomis guy you mentioned?"

"Uh-huh."

"He must be a slave driver."

She shrugged. "A witness in custody needs protection twenty-four hours a day. So does a judge whose life has been threatened. For that matter, a federal fugitive doesn't only run from nine to five. *Someone*'s got to do the work. And *that*—" she broke into slapstick to cover for a world of bitterness "—is what's awful about dating an agent of the U.S. marshal's services. Now, if you'd been sensible enough to fall for a secretary or a bank teller or a teacher like your brother did. . . ."

Tom grinned. "Ryan's fallen, all right." He sat back and spread his arms across the sofa back. "He's hooked."

"Really likes her, does he?"

"Really *loves* her. I haven't seen him this crazy since—no, I take that back—I've *never* seen him this crazy about a woman."

"He was married before, wasn't he?"

"To a sweetheart from the suburbs."

"What happened?"

"Things just didn't work out. They called it quits over a year ago."

Sheila considered this. "Is he heavily into alimony payments?"

"Not really. He got a good settlement. Alyssa's family is loaded. Ryan may be doing well, but she has more than he has any day."

"He is doing well?"

"You bet, and he has himself to thank. He's worked hard." Tom snickered. "I'm getting the impression those days are over, though. He used to spend every waking hour in the office. Now he spends them with Carly." His voice dropped. "Not only the waking ones at that."

"They're living together?" Sheila asked, growing even more alert. Carly hadn't mentioned anything about *living together*.

"Welllll—" he stretched out the word and made a wavering gesture with his hand "—maybe not formally. Ryan's still got his place downstairs. Of course, there's no furniture in it."

"So he sleeps upstairs. Very clever." She downed the last of her drink and gazed into the fire with studied nonchalance. "Tell me about his practice."

Tom eyed her curiously. "What about his practice?"

"What kinds of cases does he handle?"

"Oh, white-collar, blue-collar, ring-around-the—"

"I'm serious, Tom."

"You're thinking of needing a lawyer?"

She swung her head sharply around. "Of course not!"

"The best of us do sometimes," he rejoined in a calm voice that held a certain bait.

Sheila took it. "You have?"

Holding her eyes, he told her of his collision with the law, then grew momentarily tense. "Does it bother you?"

She laughed aloud, feeling an even greater affinity with him for what he'd just told her. "How can you even ask that after hearing the rundown on my family? And my brothers are only the tip of the iceberg. There are cousins doing God knows what."

"But you got your clearance and escaped all that. You're in law enforcement."

"So's your brother. Does he love you any the less for what you did?"

"He was pretty damned mad when it happened."

"But he still loves you," she stated with abrupt force. "Yes."

Her ferocity died as quickly as it had arisen, replaced by an even smile. "Then who am I to criticize?" She paused. "Lucky for you Ryan's in the profession he is. What are some of the other cases he's handled?"

Tom scowled. "If I didn't know better, I'd wonder whether you were more interested in Ryan than me."

Instantly she relented, leaning forward to press a kiss to his chin. "That's what *you* have that Ryan doesn't have." At Tom's blank look, she laughed. "A chin. His is hidden under a beard. Why does he wear it anyway?"

She'd been only trying to make conversation and was startled when Tom provided a pat response. "To cover a scar, I believe. A souvenir of one of his earliest cases."

"Really? Tell me."

"No way. It's Ryan's business."

"Was he in a fight?" she asked excitedly.

"Uh-uh."

"Someone attacked him? Oh, Lord, Tom, this is getting juicy. Was it his own client?"

"Sheila, it was years ago. The beard's been on so long I don't even remember what the guy looks like with a skin face."

"Does he hold a grudge?" She stroked her lower lip with the tip of one finger. "*Is* he the vengeful type?"

Without a trace of warning, Tom pounced, sliding her sideways on the sofa, pinning her shoulders to the cushion. "If we have enough time to talk about Ryan, we sure as hell have enough time for ourselves." Lowering his head, he kissed her deeply.

At first Sheila responded. Everything about Tom appealed to her, except the fact that she'd met him too late. It was this thought that made her gently lever him away.

"Tom," she gasped, "we can't."

His hands were on her breasts, kneading their fullness, playing electrifying games with her senses. "Why not? I'm quick." In demonstration of his readiness, he inched his body upward on hers.

Holding him off was the hardest thing Sheila had ever done. The feel of his arousal fueled her own. But something nagged at her. A strange kind of guilt. She liked Tom Cornell, really liked him. Of all the men she'd met in recent years, he held the most potential.

Unfortunately, as of this afternoon, she had other plans for her body.

Sixteen

rETURNING FROM THE COURTHOUSE, SAM HAD just swung through the door of the U.S. marshal's office when his secretary waved him in. The phone was in her hand, the hold button blinking. He quickened his step. "For me?"

"Bill Hoffmeister on your line."

Turning into his own office, he shrugged out of his coat and picked up the phone. "Bill?"

"How're ya doin', Sam?"

"Not bad." The coat landed on a chair to the side; Sam took the one behind his desk. "What's up?" He'd had a strange feeling that something would be. And it wasn't unusual. Witnesses were placed in his care because of active threats. In most cases, he simply took new developments as they came. But the link between Bill Hoffmeister and himself was Carly, and she wasn't the run-of-the-mill criminal-turned-stoolie. It had been over a week since he'd returned with her from Chicago. He had been uneasy wondering if he would get a call.

"I'm not sure. It may be nothing, but I thought you should know. Barber's been talking."

Sam sat forward. "Barber? I thought our threat was from Culbert?"

"It is. Barber's a nobody in the chain of command. He doesn't have money or pull. As a torch, he blew it. But he's pretty confident about getting that new trial. And he's pretty confident about beating the rap."

"Maybe it's the macho in him talking."

"Could be. Could be that he's got to tell himself that or he'll go crazy. Could be, though, that he heard something from Culbert."

"I thought they were separated."

"They are. But you know the internal communication network in prison. Word passes."

"Where did you get yours?"

"From another inmate. He was shipped out to stand trial in Alabama and one of my men made the trip with him. He was feeling his oats, spieling about the guys he left behind. For obvious reasons, my man let him talk."

"Was there anything specific?"

"No. A guy like Barber follows directions. If he's told to do something, he does it. If he's told to believe something, he does. Well, he believes that he's going to be walking the streets before long. *Someone* must have told him that." He hesitated. "I thought you should know."

"I should." Sam rubbed the tense muscles at the back of his neck. "The question is what do I do. I hate to put someone on her. It'd really mess up her life."

"If someone gets through to her, her life will be messed up worse. But maybe we're both jumping to conclusions. So far there's been no sign of anything fishy from Culbert. He hasn't sold anything—his house or his car—to come up with money, and there haven't been any withdrawals from his bank account other than what his family usually draws. Of course, there may be an unlisted account somewhere. And if Mancusi's got power of attorney. . . ."

"Mancusi wouldn't dare. He's a lawyer."

"So was Culbert, and a sleazy one at that. Which means that he may have some tricks up his sleeve we don't know about."

Sam sat back in his chair. "Okay. Listen, I think I'll run all this past Carly. I know it'll make her nervous, but maybe if it does she'll agree to have someone watch her. At least she'll be on the lookout herself for anything strange." As if she wasn't already. She had told him about Ryan's homecoming on the day they returned from Chicago. For those few instants, when a key had jiggled in her lock, she'd been terrified. She was *always* on the lookout.

"Sounds fair. If I hear anything more, I'll let you know."

"Thanks, Bill."

He pressed the button to disconnect the line, then buzzed for his secretary. "Angie, is Greg around?"

"He left a little while ago to get some records at City Hall. He said he wouldn't be long."

"Thanks." Pressing the button for an outside line, he called Rand Academy and left a message for Carly to call him back. Then he sat back in his chair, analyzing his options. When Greg returned forty minutes later, he immediately broached the topic. "How's it going with Sheila?"

Greg set his files down on his desk. "Not bad. She's pretty closed about herself, but I'm working on it." He perched on the front of his desk, facing Sam. "She's really not bad once you get her talking. She's as wary of us as we are of her. Scared as hell of you. It may be a simple case of transplant adjustment."

"Transplant adjustment." Sam chuckled dryly.

"That's a novel term. But it could fit, I suppose. Is she happy in Boston?"

"She says she likes it well enough. She's been dating a guy. According to the receptionist, he's been calling her a lot lately. She always brightens when she gets his messages."

"Name?"

Greg hesitated for only an instant. "Thomas Cornell."

"Cornell? Any relation to Ryan?"

"Brother."

Sam sighed. "At least she's in good hands."

"I hope so," Greg replied cautiously. "He was in some kind of scrape involving embezzlement a while ago. His brother managed to settle the thing quietly. There's been nothing since."

"How deeply is Sheila involved with him?"

"I don't know. Couldn't be all *that* deeply. She invited me to her place for dinner tomorrow night."

"She did?" Sam arched a brow. "You *are* making inroads." Then he sobered again. "So what do you think—is she trustworthy?"

He gave a throaty laugh. "I'll let you know Saturday."

When Sam's phone buzzed, he waved Greg back to work. "Yes, Angie?"

"Carly Quinn's on the line."

"I'll take it." He pushed the blinking button. "Carly?"

"Sam? I just got your message. How are you?"

"Fine. Listen, I wonder if I could pick you up at school and we could go somewhere to talk." Once they would have gone back to her place. With Ryan coming and going so much, though, more neutral ground was preferable.

"Is something wrong?" she asked, tensing instantly.

"Not really. I just wanted to discuss something."

"What is it?"

"We'll talk later."

"Sam. . . ."

"Four-thirty?"

She sighed. "Four-thirty."

Sam was waiting in his car when Carly left the administration building. Trotting down the walk, she slid quickly into the passenger seat and he took off.

"What's wrong?" she asked, eyes glued to his face.

"Let's go get a drink."

"Sam! Tell me!"

He managed to put her off until they sat in the quiet booth of a small bar on the outskirts of the Square. Then, over beers, he related the conversation he'd had that morning with Bill Hoffmeister.

"Oh, hell!" she whispered. "I knew he'd try something!"

"We don't know that he has. But forewarned is forearmed."

"Which means?"

"I may want to give you a tail."

She slammed her palm to the thick wooden table. "No!" With a fast glance around, she lowered her voice. "I can't, Sam. Not now. Things are going too well with Ryan. It would ruin everything."

Sam sighed wearily. "I thought you'd feel that way, which is why I haven't put anyone on it yet."

"Do you think there's a real danger?"

"No. But I'd hate to overlook something."

"I'll be careful. I always am. And besides, Ryan is with me practically all the time I'm not in school."

"That's one plus." He leaned back in the booth and eyed her more thoughtfully. "Three months ago you would have reacted very differently to what I just told you." His words were gentle, devoid of criticism. They spurred Carly on to express her own thoughts.

"You're right. You were also right about my needing to be involved with someone. Before I met Ryan, I was afraid of my own shadow."

Sam was shaking his head. "Don't underrate yourself. You were never afraid of your own shadow. More nervous, perhaps. And very definitely more isolated."

"Still," she argued, "he's given me something. More fight, maybe? Then again—" her brows knit "—maybe he's just complicated things. Sometimes I want to tell him everything, sometimes I don't want to tell him a thing. As long as he's in the dark, I can't possibly have a bodyguard. There's no way I could explain one. But if I do tell him and there's someone around all the time, he'll be frustrated and it'll be that much harder on me. He's only human." Her voice softened. "So am I."

"I'm glad, Carly. What you're saying is that other emotions have surpassed fear in your life. And that's important. You *are* human. You do have a life to lead. It's not right that you should be a prisoner of your fears."

"I'm not saying they're not there. I'm scared to death."

"I know." He smiled gently. "But there's more."

She nodded. "I love Ryan." Her voice began to waver. "Problem is there are times when I'm torn apart. Reconciling what I feel for him with . . . with all this other stuff. . . ."

"You're doing a fine job so far. Listen, how's this. Why don't we sit on the guard for a while. Hoffmeister will let us know if he learns anything more. I'll have my people keep a lookout for strangers. I can also have someone ride through the streets near your place and the school from time to time. The police would be glad to send a patrol around."

"I don't want that."

"I don't have to give them details. It's enough if I tell them that the marshal's office is working on something sensitive. They'll keep an eye on the general area without ever knowing your name or address."

She took a deep breath. "I guess that sounds okay." Then she smiled apologetically. "I do appreciate all this, Sam."

He winked. "What are friends for?" He took a last swig of his beer and licked the froth from his lips. "Hey, why don't we go out sometime. The four of us."

"You and Ryan and Ellen and me. She'd love meeting you. She feels she knows you so well."

"I'd love that too," Carly said. She frowned when a thought came to mind, but in a minute it was gone. "No, it'd do him good."

"Do whom good?"

"Ryan." Her eyes sparkled mischievously, a welcome change from her earlier worry. "He doesn't trust you."

"Doesn't trust *me*? Mr. Clean? Your local Boy Scout in long pants? The Lone Ranger without a mask?"

Through a grin, she said, "He's convinced we have something going on the side."

Sam arched a brow. "Does he know about Ellen?"

She nodded. "And Sara. But you have to understand that the man's law firm does its share of divorce work. He's seen cheating like you and I have never dreamed of."

"I think," Sam observed, his eyes narrowing, "that he's jealous."

"He is. He admits it." There was a certain pride in her tone that caught at Sam's heart.

"He must love you very much."

Her smile was private and exquisitely gentle, her soft-spoken "He does" totally superfluous.

As fate would have it, Ryan was in the foyer tugging his mail from its slot when Sam walked Carly to the door. Sam saw him first and stopped, but Carly urged him on. She badly wanted to smooth things between these two men who, each in his own way, meant so much to her.

She pushed open the door. "Ryan! Hi!"

His head came up from the pile of letters he'd been skimming and a broad smile broke out on his face, only to be tempered seconds later when he caught sight of Sam in tow. "Hi, babe," he said more quietly than he might otherwise have. His wary gaze slid to Sam.

"Sam and I just went for a drink." Honesty seemed the best approach—that, and taking the bull by the horns. "He suggested we all go out for dinner sometime. How about it?"

"Sounds fine," Ryan said evenly.

Sam spoke from behind. "I'll check with Ellen to see when we can get a sitter, and I'll give you a call."

Carly turned back to him for a minute. "Great. I'll wait to hear from you."

Only Sam saw the deeper message in her gaze and knew that despite the brightness of her manner she hadn't forgotten the reason he'd sought her out today. He nodded and, with quiet goodbyes, left. When Carly faced Ryan once more her expression was wiped clean of tension.

"Have a good day?" she asked, getting her own mail before passing through the door he held.

"Busy," he answered succinctly, not quite sure what to make of Sam's taking her for drinks, much less his dinner invitation. "How about you?"

"Busy."

They started up the stairs in silence. When Ryan finally spoke, his tone was vague. "Listen, I think I'll go to my place to change. Do you want to go out for something to eat?"

She stopped, looking up at him. "You're angry."

"No." He, too, stopped. Discouraged, he took a deep breath, then let it out slowly. "It always bothers me when I see him. I know it's wrong, but I can't help it."

"That's why we should go out with Ellen and him." Hooking her arm through his, she resumed the climb. "I know how you feel, but this may be the best thing. If you get to know Sam you'll see that he's really a nice guy."

"I'm sure he's a nice guy. It's his motives I'm not sure about."

"Ryan," she scolded gently, "we'll be with his wife. He loves her very much. You'll see that."

On the second-floor landing they stopped again. Ryan's scowl took on shades of self-reproach. His voice was gruff. "Ach, I'm a beast. Of course we'll have dinner with them." His gaze grew more direct. "Anyway, I'd rather you see him when I'm there than when I'm not."

"It was only for a drink," she said very softly.

"I know. I know." He shifted his briefcase to his left hand and threw his right arm around her shoulder. "Kiss me. That's the problem. You haven't kissed me yet."

She shook her head firmly. "I'm not kissing a bear."

"But if you kiss the bear, he turns into a prince."

"That's a frog."

"You wouldn't want me to croak, would you?"

She closed her eyes for an instant. "You're impossible. Have I told you that before?"

"Many times," he said without a shred of remorse.

She sent him a chiding glance. Standing on tiptoe, she kissed him lightly before breaking away. "Go change and then come up. I'm broiling swordfish."

"You smell like beer," he called after her, but the anger was gone from his voice and she relaxed.

An hour later, she was still relaxed, sitting back in her chair drinking the coffee Ryan had brewed. The table was strewn with dirty plates, which neither of them had the desire to clear.

"Tell you what," Ryan began, turning sideways and propping his stockinged feet on the lower rung of her chair. "If I go out to dinner with Sam and his wife, will you come to a dinner with me?"

"What dinner?"

"There's a convention here next week of the National Criminal Defense Attorneys' Association."

"My God, that's a mouthful."

"Wait'll you hear the rest. There's a banquet on Friday night."

She screwed up her face. "A banquet? As in dressy?"

"Nah. Trial lawyers don't know how to dress. "You know that." They'd already been through Carly's aversion to lawyers, though she'd made a joke of it and had never elaborated on its cause.

"I thought I did, until I met you."

"Is that a compliment?"

"Yes."

"Then, I thank you. But we're skirting the issue. Will you go?"

"To the banquet? I don't know, Ryan. All those lawyers in one room." She was teasing him, but only half so. Ryan excepted, lawyers still gave her the creeps.

"It'll be boring. I can't argue with you about that. But think of how awful it'll be for me if I have to go alone."

"Do you *have* to go?"

The cord in his neck jumped when he grimaced. "I'm speaking."

Eyes widening, Carly sat forward. *"You're speaking? How can you *do* this to me, Ryan?"* She knew she could never refuse him, given the circumstances. He knew it too.

"I agreed to go out with Sam and Ellen," he reminded her.

It was the clincher. She was lost. "All right. But on one condition."

"What's that?"

"That except for the time you're on the podium you stay with me. I won't be left alone to fend for myself in that crowd."

Taking her hand, Ryan swung it gently between their chairs. "What did you ever do before I came along?" he teased.

"I didn't go partying with hordes of shifty lawyers, that's for sure!" she retorted, but her gruffness was mostly for show. "What are you talking on, anyway?"

His eyes danced. "What every lawyer longs to know—how to make friends and influence people."

"You are not," she scolded, squeezing his hand.

"Actually, I was planning to speak about ethics and the image of the criminal lawyer."

"That I do approve of. A much needed topic of discussion."

He tipped his dark head and spied her through half-closed eyes. "Anything else good to say about my profession?"

"You're in it."

A chuckle reverberated in his throat as he leaned forward and smacked a rewarding kiss on her lips. "All the right answers. Smart lady. . . ."

* * *

With her Creative Writing class over and the mid-morning break under way, Carly returned to her office to change notebooks and found a message on her desk. The sight of the pink slip sent an involuntary chill through her, bringing thought of yesterday and Sam's call. But this call wasn't from Sam. It was from Ryan. Lifting the phone, she quickly call him back. This time, when she identified herself to his secretary, she was instantly recognized.

"Oh, Mrs. Quinn, I'm sorry about what happened last week. I should have put you through. I had no idea—"

"It's all right." Carly smiled, her voice kind. "You had no way of knowing. I just assumed Ryan would realize I was home."

"Well, you have my apology anyway. Here, let me put you through to him now. Hold on."

Within seconds Ryan was on the line. "Carly! That was quick. I wasn't sure how soon you'd be able to get back to me."

"I'll have you know that I'm forfeiting coffee and doughnuts to make this call," she teased.

"No problem. I'll stuff you with them all weekend. Listen, since it's Friday, I thought maybe you could get away a little early and take the subway in to meet me. You can see the office, we can do something fun around here, maybe get some dinner and then drive home together."

The thought of riding the T sent a ripple of apprehension through her. It always did, though she knew that with so many people around she was probably safer than ever. But the thought of meeting Ryan, at his office no less, was enough to quell her fears. "Oh, Ryan, that sounds great! Wait a minute." Balancing the phone on her shoulder, she studied her calendar. "I have an appointment with a student at three. I could come in right after that. Say, around four?"

"Perfect. Do you know how to get here?"

"Uh, no."

He gave her directions, which she jotted down.

"Sounds easy enough."

"It is. We're on the thirty-fourth floor. The reception-ist will be on the lookout for you."

A wave of warmth washed over her. "I'm sure I'll have no problem. See you then?"

"You bet." He threw two quick kisses over the line. "Bye-bye." Then he hung up the phone and sat back in his chair, eminently satisfied.

He'd been tough on Carly this morning, waking in a mood reminiscent of the bear she'd called him yester-day. They'd run as usual, though the paths were messy and the pace slower and less rhythmic. He'd come into the office brooding, feeling torn and frustrated, realiz-ing that the thing he wanted most in the world was for Carly to be his, totally and forever. There was still one part of her that mystified him, but he was helpless to do anything about it or about the fact that he needed her more with each passing day. Knowing that she would be coming to him this afternoon cheered him immeasurably.

Carly, too, hung up the phone with a smile on her face. Belatedly she blew an answering kiss toward the phone, then took a deep, satisfied breath. She'd been aware of Ryan's mood that morning, and hadn't asked about it simply because she hadn't wanted to buy trou-ble. There were some answers she couldn't give him, and she was torn apart by guilt. She wanted to meet him this afternoon, she *had* to meet him this afternoon, if for no other reason than to show him how much she cared. Short of confessing her love, it was the best she could do.

Her student left by three-thirty. Stuffing her bag with books and papers, Carly was into her coat and boots and out the door by three thirty-five. Intending to take a cab into the Square, she had the good fortune to bump into one of the other teachers, who offered her a ride.

The T wasn't as crowded as it would have been an hour later. Slipping into a seat, she hugged her bag to her and looked around at her fellow riders. Most of the faces were benign; a few unsettled her. It was to these few that her gaze returned from time to time as her imagination went to work. She was beginning to wish she'd taken a cab after all, when she caught herself and recalled what Sam had said the evening before. It *wasn't* right that she should be a prisoner of her fears. She did have a life to lead, and she had every right to lead it in peace. At the moment she was on her way to see Ryan, and it galled her that anything should dampen the excitement she felt.

Lifting her chin in defiance, she stared at the faces in the transit car. To her surprise, not a one stared back. Most were blank, impassive, enduring the trip as a limbo between here and there. As comfortable as she'd been alone in public for ages, she relaxed.

By the time the car disgorged itself at Government Center, she was feeling strong, even gutsy. One part of her dared anyone approach her with intent to harm; that part was tired of waiting and had thrown off the shackles of intimidation. The other part was, very simply, looking forward to seeing Ryan.

"I am not wearing tights!" Ryan's voice rang out loud and clear through the cluster of customers at the photographer's shop. Several heads turned his way in amusement before returning to face similar difficulties.

Trying to suppress her own grin, Carly coaxed him gently. "You'd look great in tights." Then she lowered her voice to a near whisper. "I've seen you in less."

"Yeah," he whispered gruffly, casting a fast glance at the other customers before dragging Carly into a corner, where she alone could see the flush high on his cheeks, "but this is a public place. A picture is something tangible, with a negative and everything. Think of the possibilities for blackmail."

"Come on, Ryan. Romeo and Juliet would be terrific!"

"That's fine and dandy for *you* to say, since *you'd* be all covered up in some—" he gestured vaguely "—some kind of flowing gown. No. *Not* Romeo and Juliet."

With a sigh, Carly turned her sights on the bevy of other samples that plastered the walls. She could afford to be flexible; her mood was incredibly light.

From the moment she'd set foot in the hallowed halls of Miller and Cornell, she'd been treated like royalty. Not only had the receptionist indeed known her, but everyone else, from Ryan's secretary to the copyists and word processors, had greeted her with warm smiles. Ryan had shown her from office to office, introducing her to other lawyers, reacquainting her with people she'd first met on New Year's Eve. And through it all he was so obviously proud. It endeared him to her all the more.

From the office, they had walked to a nearby art gallery where Ryan had seen a painting he wanted her opinion on for his apartment. She had loved it. He bought it, plus a small bronze statue of a pair of lovers, which Carly had thought to be nearly obscene. But she hadn't argued then, any more than she was about to argue now.

The photographer's shop specializing in novelty portraits was in the lower level of the Quincy Market. It was Carly who had peered down through its door and then had been drawn back after browsing through several other shops. She didn't have a picture of Ryan. She couldn't think of one she would rather have more than of the two of them dressed in period costume as lovers from another time.

"How about Henry VIII and Anne Boleyn," Ryan suggested. "I'd do fine with the beard."

"But you'd need too much stuffing and you'd *still* have to wear tights. Besides—" she grimaced "—he had Anne beheaded. Ahh." The grimace yielded to a romantic smile. "Rhett and Scarlett."

Ryan shook his head. "He didn't give a damn. I do. Look. Tarzan and Jane. Now *there's* a costume."

"It's nothing!"

He grinned. "I know."

"Ryan, don't be crude. I won't be Jane. Tarzan was always taking off on vines, leaving her behind to fend for herself in the jungle." Her gaze shifted. "That's a cute one." She pointed, a bright smile on her face. "You'd make a great Raggedy Andy."

"To your Ann? Come on, babe. Those two are made of rags. They couldn't make it—"

"Shh. Okay. Forget Raggedy Ann and Andy." Her arm was linked with his, their hands clasped in his pocket. Carly tugged him farther down the row of sample photos. "George and Martha Washington?"

"D-u-l-l. How about Antony and Cleopatra?"

"I hate asps."

"Ling Ling and Hsing Hsing?" The glance they exchanged was mutually dismissive. "Whoa, who's that?" Ryan asked. "Ma Barker and her boys?"

"That's for families. Besides, we have only one boy here and I *refuse* to play his mother. *Ever.*"

They looked further, suggesting and rejecting several more in turn. Then, simultaneously, they saw the one they wanted. Carly looked at it, tipped her head, leaned closer. Ryan stared in fascination, growing more reckless by the minute.

"That's it," he murmured in her ear, never once taking his eyes from the photograph. "Us against the world. I love it!"

So did Carly. Outrageous. Infamous. Dramatic and daring. What did it matter that they had died so violently? Lovers under fire, they died together.

She nodded and grinned, feeling reckless as Ryan. "Bonnie and Clyde. Let's do it!"

"What a treat!" Sheila exclaimed. "I usually have to walk home. Not that I mind it; the exercise is great. It can be awful in lousy weather, though. Come to think of it—" she frowned, forgetting for the moment that she was supposed to be bright and appealing, which implied uncomplaining "—the weather's been progressively lousy since I got here."

Greg negotiated a left from Park to Beacon with ease. "You picked the wrong season to arrive."

"I'll say. I think it's been rainy or cold from day one, not to mention this latest. I don't understand it. We had much more snow in Chicago, but things didn't seem to stay so messy so long."

"Bostonians don't handle snow very well. It used to be worse, though. A real political issue."

"Oh?"

"Certain neighborhoods were up in arms, claiming

that others received preferential treatment when it came to plowing."

"Was it true?"

"Yup."

"But it isn't anymore?"

"Oh, it is. It's just that the uproar has died down." With a crooked grin, he said, "You're new. One of the first things to learn about Massachusetts politics is that it's totally political. A little pull goes a long way."

"As in getting jobs?" she teased.

"Right. Mind you—" he held up a hand "—I took the civil-service exam and was more than qualified for the position. But a few well-placed phone calls didn't hurt. Had strings not been pulled for me, they would have been pulled for someone else." He cleared his throat. "Anyway, *you* happen to live in the right area. Any number of pols live on Beacon Hill. Your streets may be narrow, but they're usually well plowed." At her pointing finger, he made a right. "Did you have any trouble getting your car out?"

"Oh, no. A good shovel, scraper and brush did wonders." She laughed, a high nasal chuckle that sounded good-natured enough. "Not to mention elbow grease. Oops. Hold on a minute. There's the market. Would you mind pulling over for a second so I can run in and get same shallots?"

Braking at the corner, he raised both brows. "Shallots? Sounds complex."

"Complex? *Me?*" She sent him her most captivating smile and slid out of the car. Several moments later she returned with a large brown bag in the crook of her arm.

"All that is shallots?" he asked. She laughed again, and he decided that the sound of mischief and allure made her nasal voice not all that bad.

"I guess I needed a couple of other things too," she explained sheepishly. "And while we're on the subject, I'd better warn you that my apartment is nothing fancy. I mean, I contemplated renting a suite for the evening at the Meriden just for the sheer luxury of the surroundings, but I wanted to cook and they wouldn't let me near their kitchen. Somehow I don't think they would have appreciated my checking in with Tupperware for luggage."

Greg couldn't help but laugh. For whatever her faults, the woman was entertaining. "No, I don't think they would." Starting the car again, he drove on. Two blocks later, Sheila pointed to a parking space.

"Why don't you take that one. My place is only six doors up. We won't find anything nearer."

Greg neatly maneuvered into the space, then came around to take the bag from Sheila and help her out. He was pleased that she waited for him; many of the women he knew were more aggressive in their liberation, making a point of helping *themselves* from the seat of a car. Not that there appeared to be anything old-fashioned about Sheila. But the touch was nice. It made him feel masculine.

Gently holding her arm to guide her over occasional patches of ice on the sidewalk, Greg looked down at her. "Where *do* you park your car? Around here?"

She tossed her chin forward. "Over there."

"Which one?"

"The burgundy one. In front of the white Rabbits?"

"The Mazda?" His eyes widened and he quickened his pace for a better look. "Not bad, Montgomery. Not bad at all." Dropping her arm, he leaned low to peer inside the darkened window. Then he straightened and ran his free hand along the sleek front curve of the car. "It looks new."

"It is."

He shot her a glance. "Did you drive it east?"

"Uh-uh. I bought it here."

His gaze returned to the car for a final covetous once-over. "Ve-ry clas-sy."

She dipped her head, a pleased smile on her lips. "Thank you, sir." Then she slipped her arm through his. "But if you stand and stare at my car much longer those shallots are going to freeze. Where will our Shrimp á la Turque—" the words were given a distinctly foreign treatment by her tongue "—be then?" With a gentle tug on his arm, they were on their way once more.

Moments later, Sheila pushed open the door of her apartment, flipped on the lights and turned to ease the bag from Greg's arms. "Please. Make yourself comfortable." She ran down the few stairs, leaving him alone on the landing overlooking her all-inclusive single room. "I'll put these away and then get us a drink. What'll it be?" she called over her shoulder. "Scotch? Bourbon?"

"Scotch is fine." Draping his coat on the rack just inside the door, he propped his elbows on the wrought-iron railing and studied the apartment. Though small, it wasn't bad, he mused. Vaguely U-shaped, it had the open kitchen in which Sheila now puttered as its principal area. In the right arm of the U stood a simple wood table and chairs. At the U's base were a wicker love seat and two matching chairs. In its left arm, quite surprisingly, given the usual choice of a sofa bed for a studio apartment, was a double bed, tucked against the wall but very much a part of the room.

As Sheila had said, there was nothing fancy about the apartment. Its style was eclectic, the furniture second-hand. What held the whole together, though, was the predominance of cherry red. It stood out in a cloth draped over the table and in similar fabric gathered on a rod across the single high window. It lay on the floor in the form of a throw rug beneath the wicker works, whose cushions matched. It was broadcast from the two framed rock posters above the nonworking fireplace, which held a slightly withered poinsettia. And most obviously, it covered the bed in sheets, quilt, lacy pillow covers and dust ruffles.

"Like red, do you?" he called, straightening and starting down the steps with one hand in the pocket of his slacks.

"Love it!" Her back was to him; only as he came closer did he see that she was arranging a small bunch of red and white carnations in a simple glass carafe. "It's bright and daring. It demands notice." Turning, she whisked around him and put the carafe on the center of the table. "Sometimes the shades clash, but this place is so dark and drab that it needed *something* to give it pep."

Greg looked around and shrugged. "Funny. It didn't even occur to me to think of dark or drab."

"Are you kidding? Maybe the dark covers the drab. I've got lights plugged into nearly every outlet and I still feel like it's constantly midnight."

"That's because you're below street level."

"I suppose. Still, gray brick on every wall? If I were ambitious I'd paint it all white. God only knows why anyone would go with yuck gray."

"Your red does a lot. I like it."

Hands propped on her hips, Sheila took a deep breath as she perused the room. "Well, this is only the beginning. From here I'll take a one-bedroom above ground, then a three-bedroom several stories up, then

the penthouse, then a mansion in the country, then
. . . who knows!" Her grin had broadened with each
step.

Greg wondered how she was going to manage it on
an agent's salary. "Are those dreams, or plans?"

Her grin vanished, her head shot around and, for the
first time in a while, he saw the sharpness in her eyes
he'd once commented on to Sam. She was really a
stunning woman, with her flowing black hair, her slender curves, and, yes, those snapping eyes that spoke of
mystery and fire. Of its own accord, and taking him
slightly by surprise, his body tautened.

Simultaneously hers relaxed and she broke into a
gentle smile. "Dream or plan? A little of each, I guess."
She opened a cabinet and extracted bottles of Scotch
and rum, and two glasses.

Greg lounged against the counter by her side. "What
do you want from life, Sheila?"

She turned to the refrigerator for Coke, the freezer
for ice. "In what sense?"

"Work, for one thing. What are your long-range
plans?"

"I just got here. How can I think that far ahead?"

"Tell me dreams, then. What do you want to do?"

She made a face and struggled to separate the ice
cubes from their bin. When the cold chips resisted her
fingers, she turned to Greg for help. "Can you give
these a try? This freezer stinks. The temperature is so
uneven that the ice all sticks together."

Greg reached in and fumbled unsuccessfully for a
minute. "Got an ice pick or a knife or something?"

She took a knife from the drawer and handed it to
him. After several hacks, he had freed enough cubes to
fill their glasses. Standing back, Sheila let Greg fix their
drinks and hand her hers. Then she led him to the

wicker love seat, kicked off her heels and, tucking one leg under her, sat down.

"Tell me about you, Greg," she coaxed. "What do *you* want from life?"

He hadn't exactly planned to talk about himself, but since she seemed interested, he said, "I'd like to work my way up the ladder in the marshal's service. When and if I decide to leave, the experience I'll have had here will stand me in good stead to do other things in law enforcement. At some point I'd love to go to Washington."

They talked about that for a while, with Sheila asking question after question, seeming intrigued by the thought of a career in the nation's capital. When she got up to fix dinner, Greg followed her into the kitchen and talked with her as she worked. He felt surprisingly relaxed, more so than he had expected, given the supposed "unsettling" effect that he was to be investigating. Strangely, as the minutes passed, he felt less and less the investigator and more and more the man. She had a way of doing that, a subtle way, a seemingly innocent way.

It was in her eyes, those eyes that could be so sharp, yet seemed now direct and latently sensual, eyes that lingered on his or fell to focus on the warm pulse beat at his neck or studied his fingers as they curled around his glass. It was in her voice, sometimes bubbly, sometimes serious but strangely sultry in its nasal kind of way.

As they talked through a dinner of shrimp, steamed rice and artichokes in butter sauce, Greg began to wonder what it was that had originally bothered him about Sheila. Nervous energy? If there was nervous energy now, he couldn't see it. Rather, he saw a woman who was composed and poised, mature and apparently unaware of how truly attractive she was. Her sense of humor erupted often, but it was finely tuned to his own. She listened, questioned, spoke as little about herself as possible. By the time they'd polished off dinner and a bottle of wine, he was unbelievably titillated.

Conversation waned. Sheila sipped kahlua-laced coffee, her eyes holding his over the rim of her mug. Then her gaze fell to his throat, and she was captivated by the curling tufts of hair that had escaped once he'd loosened his tie and unbuttoned his shirt collar.

Greg Reilly was a very attractive man, she decided. Tall and well built, he claimed to have been something of a jock at Boston College. She believed him. Though he'd also said that his involvement with sports was now limited to membership in a weekend basketball league, he had easily retained his lean physique and fluidity of movement. With dark wavy hair, deep blue eyes and a faintly ruddy complexion, he was an Irishman to do Boston proud.

"Sheila?" His voice held a sudden warning that brought her eyes instantly up from their intent study of him. "Do you know what you're doing?"

She neither pled innocence nor smiled, but spoke in a soft, sure voice, her eyes steady on his as she lowered the cup to her lap. "Yes."

"It's not very smart."

"Why not?" she asked gently. "We're adults."

"Adults who work together."

"Um-hmm."

"It can complicate things."

"I don't see how," she said in the same quiet voice. Its very guilelessness was a potent stimulant to Greg's growing awareness of her warm body, so near and apparently willing. "You're an attractive man. If you find *me* attractive. . . ." Her voice trailed off, her eyes asking the question.

Greg set his mug on the floor. Then he propped one knee by Sheila's hip and, with his other leg stretched to the floor, he half knelt over her. When she tipped her head up, he spread his fingers under her thick fall of hair and supported her head while his gaze caressed her features.

"I find you attractive," he conceded tightly. "Too attractive. Believe it or not, this wasn't what I had in mind when I came over here tonight."

"Does it matter?" she asked, "Some of the best things just . . . happen. There's nothing complicated about our finding pleasure in each other. You know what you're getting; so do I. One night. No strings attached." Her breath had begun to come faster as she'd spoken. She waited a minute for Greg to say something. When he didn't, but continued to drink her in with his eyes, she knew the battle was ninety-nine percent won. "Greg," she whispered, looking up at him beseechingly, "don't make me beg."

He didn't need to hear more. The lure was too great, and he was far too hungry. He was no saint, had never claimed to be one. Nor had Sam Loomis made sainthood a prerequisite for this particular assignment.

Taking her head between his hands, he captured her lips in a deep, heated kiss. When he finally dragged his mouth from hers and held her back, he saw that her eyes were closed, her lips still parted. He took them again, and again, finding her essence as intoxicating as the artful promise of her body.

Arms circling his back, she moaned softly when he released her lips, and opened her eyes to his. "Take me to bed, Greg," she breathed on a whisper. "Please . . . now. . . ."

She didn't have to ask again. He was aroused, bewitched and more than willing to take his satisfaction from her warm, eager body.

Only later, much later, did he realize that the name she cried at the moment of her climax wasn't his.

Seventeen

CARLY COULD HAVE SWORN SHE WAS BEING FOL-
lowed; the prickles at the back of her neck told her so.
With a sharp glance behind, she quickened her step,
she recalled the last time she'd felt this way, nearly
three months before, when she'd run into Ryan. Tonight he wouldn't be there; he had a late meeting and
would be out until ten.

After all these weeks of feeling so secure, she wondered why she should have the willies now. But, of
course, it had everything to do with her talk with Sam
last week, and the fact that, through the weekend,
she'd had to suppress it all. Her every thought then
had been of Ryan. He was tense about something, and
when she'd asked him what it was, he had shrugged
and mumbled something about a preoccupation with
one of his cases.

She didn't believe him. There were those random
times—she would be sitting on the sofa doing needlepoint, or standing at her dresser combing her hair, or
waiting in the kitchen for the coffee to drip—when she
would look up to find him studying her enigmatically.

She wondered whether he suspected something of her past or whether he was growing impatient about the future.

The present wasn't in doubt. When they were together doing things, they were totally compatible. But he never mentioned marriage, and now that she thought of it, he hadn't said he loved her in days.

Running up the steps to the courtyard walk, she cast another look behind. She saw no one. Perhaps it was her imagination again. Then again, perhaps it wasn't. With each passing week, the judge's decision on a new trial grew closer. If someone wanted to permanently prevent her testimony, the time was right.

Fumbling with the lock, she finally let herself in, grabbed her mail and ran up the stairs. Once inside her own apartment, with the bolts safely thrown and the alarm system on, she stood listening to a silence broken only by her thudding heart. Instantly the emptiness of the place closed in on her, and she realized how much she'd come to depend on Ryan's presence.

Dropping her things on a chair, she went to the kitchen and picked up the phone. If she called Sam and told him of her fears, he would insist on assigning her a guard. But she desperately needed to talk, and there was only one other person who knew enough to allow her full freedom on that score. The phone rang eight times. She was ready to hang up when it was finally answered breathlessly.

"Hello?"

"Sheila? I'm sorry. Did I get you from somewhere?"

"Oh, Carly! No! I just this minute walked in!"

"Listen, I really need to talk to someone. Can you come over?"

"Ah . . ."

"You have plans?"

Sheila thought quickly. Tom had asked to meet her for a light supper, and much as she'd been looking forward to it, instinct told her this was more important.

"Nothing I can't change."

"Are you sure? Hey, I'm really sorry—"

"Don't be silly! Give me half an hour, okay?"

Carly breathed a sigh of relief. "Thanks."

True to her word, Sheila arrived thirty minutes later. Carly buzzed her in, then waited at the front door as she ran up the stairs.

"Thanks for coming," she said as soon as the other was inside.

"Is something wrong?" Sheila asked, dropping her leather pouch on the chair and her coat over its arm.

Carly ran a hand through her hair, lifting the bangs from her brow. "Not really. I'm just nervous. I had to talk with someone. Come on. Let's sit down. How about a rum and Coke?"

Sheila grinned. "I'd never turn down one of those." She walked with Carly toward the kitchen. "What are the nerves about?"

"My imagination, most likely. I sometimes think I'm going out of my mind. When I was walking home from school today, I was sure someone was following me. I mean, no one was. It was barely dusk. But there I was, one eye over my shoulder, scurrying through the slush like a zombie."

"You could *never* look like a zombie," Sheila said, chuckling. "And I'm sure you were imagining the whole thing. Has anything else happened?"

"Sam's been in touch with Bill, and they're trying to keep on top of anything Culbert might try. If I'm not around for that new trial, the outcome might be very different for him. And for Barber. Actually *he* was the one Sam was talking about last week." She handed the drink to Sheila, who was regarding her intently.

"Barber? Barber's a nothing."

"That's what they all say." She poured herself a glass of wine. "But I guess he's the one who's been talking about the new trial and the possibility of getting off."

"You're kidding!"

"Don't I wish!"

"What's he saying?"

Carly headed for the living room. "Nothing specific. Just that he plans to be walking the streets before long." She sank onto the sofa. Sheila followed closely.

"He doesn't say how?"

"If only. Then we might have more to go on."

"So what does Sam say?" she asked more cautiously.

Carly sighed. "Sam says that if I want he could assign someone to cover me. But that's the *last* thing I want. Ryan would know everything. As it is, he doesn't like Sam. I can just imagine what would happen if either Sam or someone else from the office were to squire me around town. It would be so disruptive." She hung her head. "When I let my mind wander, I go mad. Can you imagine if my cover is breached and they decide to give me a new one?" She looked up then, torment etched in each fine feature. "I don't think I could go through it again, Sheila. New name. New place. New occupation. New friends. No Ryan."

Sheila reached over and gently patted her knee. "Don't think about that now. There's no cause for alarm yet. Your cover is really solid. Just because some bozo in prison is talking big doesn't mean he's got anything to back it up."

But Carly wasn't easily mollified. Her voice quavered. "I really love Ryan. There's no way I could leave him. It was different in Chicago. Sure, I had a home and a career and friends. But there was never anyone special like him. He was exactly what was missing in my life. I can't conceive of a future without him. So help me, even if there *is* some awful danger, I think I'd almost rather live with it than give up everything!" Her voice dropped, weighed down by an element of defeat. "A person can only run so far."

Sheila sat back quietly for a time, watching her. She sipped her drink thoughtfully. "You're a very lucky woman, to have found someone like Ryan."

There was a note of wistfulness—no, harder—in her voice that, even amid her own turmoil, Carly couldn't ignore. "I'm sorry. I've been going on and on feeling sorry for myself. You're right. I am lucky." She paused, then ventured on. "How about you? Are things looking up?"

"Oh yes," Sheila answered quickly. She thought back to the Friday night before and felt a ripple of satisfaction. Things had gone just as she had so carefully planned. Greg was on her side; she had an ally in the office. She had pleased him, and he hadn't been that bad himself. Through the night he'd taken her repeatedly. He was forceful and imaginative in bed. If she'd had to sell herself to someone, she could have done much worse.

"How about Tom?" Carly asked, and Sheila's satisfaction was dimmed by a wave of regret. "You're seeing a lot of him?"

"Uh-huh. He's quite a man." She meant it. While, for the time being at least, her body might be Greg's, Tom was the one who captivated her thoughts. "Very different from Ryan, but every bit as charming. He has a fantastic house. Did you know that?"

"Ryan told me a little about it." Ryan hadn't found it quite that "fantastic," but the time he'd spent there hadn't been under the best of circumstances. "I understand Tom's got a good business going now."

Sheila nodded. "Computers. He's taught me a lot about them. They're not really so bad. Oh, they don't pick up the dirty laundry or do boring case reports or—" she glanced down "—fix rum and Cokes, but they're pretty clever when it comes to things intellectual." She drawled the last for every syllable it was worth.

"Do you think there's any future in it?"

"In computers? Sure—"

"In Tom. You and Tom."

Sheila's flippancy vanished. She grew serious, almost troubled. "I don't know. I hope so. But there's so much. . . ." When her voice trailed off, Carly's picked up.

"He's free, and he's clever and good-looking, and he has those muscles and a wallet."

She'd been teasing, but Sheila didn't crack a smile. "But will he love me? I mean, really love me. Will he be able to accept me for what I am and what I do?"

"He doesn't mind your work, does he?"

Sheila's half laugh was dry. "Only the times I have to be home early for a six o'clock assignment the next morning."

"But his work hours are flexible. You could work around that."

"I know." Work hours were the least of her worries. "Well—" she gave an exaggerated sigh "—we're doin' all right, anyway. But back to you. Do you feel any better?"

"Yes. Talking about it helps."

"Want my professional opinion?"

"Sure."

"I think that you ought to relax and forget about all

this. No one's chasing you. No one knows who you are. No one's going to come after you. Hell, if either Barber or Culbert tried anything, they'd only be in worse trouble afterward."

"They haven't got much to lose," Carly reminded her pointedly. "Barber had a record. He's no stranger to prison. But I can't imagine Culbert cares much for it."

"Look. He's not stupid. He knows what would happen if he tried to harm you. He'd have to cover his tracks pretty well. How can he do that? He's in jail."

"He can hire someone—the same thug who came after me last time. I wouldn't be so worried if that hadn't happened." She snorted. "I wouldn't be *here* if that hadn't happened."

"But you are here. And you're safe. Take my word for it." She hesitated, but only for an instant. "You do trust me, Carly, don't you?"

"Yes."

"Then, please. Relax. Enjoy Ryan. Enjoy life. You never can tell," she ventured brashly. "Someone could get to Barber or Culbert before they get to you."

It was a thought that made both of them smile. Only Carly felt guilt at her reaction.

Early the next morning, Sheila strode into Sam and Greg's office. Greg looked up from his work and smiled.

"I wanted to talk with him," she whispered, cocking her head toward Sam, who was on the phone. "Do you think he'll be long?"

Sam looked up, shook his head and motioned her forward. She idled slowly toward Greg's desk. "Hi."

"Hi, yourself," Greg answered softly.

"I missed you yesterday." She'd come looking, only to find that he was out of the office for the day.

"We're trying to arrange security for a trial that's

coming up next month. I spent most of the day in Bristol county."

"Ah." She nodded, and looked shyly at her fingers gripping the edge of his desk. "I was hoping you'd come over last night."

Though her voice was little more than a whisper, Greg sent a cautious glance toward his boss before looking back. "I didn't get in until late."

Again she nodded. "I enjoyed myself."

He knew what she was referring to and wasn't sure how to respond. Since leaving her apartment early Saturday morning, he'd been bothered. It wasn't his style to stand in for another man, and one part of him was livid that he had. The other part, the same part that had prompted him to slake his hunger for her over and over again that night, looked at her now and saw her as she'd been then—naked, warm, and willing to do whatever he asked of her.

"So did I," he murmured at last.

"Sheila?" Sam's voice broke into their conversation. When her head spun around, Greg felt strangely relieved. She immediately crossed the room.

Guardedly, Sam nodded toward the free chair by his desk. Sheila had never sought him out before, simply taking her assignments and completing them with little ado and, apparently, more than adequate competency. "What's the problem?"

"Carly. I got a call from her last night. She was terrified. I spent several hours with her."

"Why was she terrified?"

"She imagined someone was following her on her way home from school."

"Why didn't she call me?" He felt a slight hurt, but schooled it carefully, along with a mild sense of guilt.

"She felt that you'd insist on putting someone on her,

and she didn't want that. She needed to talk, and since we're close and I'm one of the few people. . . ." Awkward, she cast a glance at Greg, who appeared to be listening to every word. She assumed he was aware of the situation, though she had never mentioned it to him herself.

"It's okay," Sam assured her, appreciating her caution. "Greg knows what's going on." He had taken him into his confidence about Carly even before he'd gone off with her to Chicago.

Sheila smiled a crooked apology toward Greg. "I wasn't sure how much to say. . . ."

"It's okay," Sam said again. "Was she really upset?"

"Yes. She knows it's her imagination, but she's been on edge since she spoke with you last week. "She's adamant about not having a guard because she feels that it would interfere with her life. It occurred to me that, since we're friends anyway and all, I could help. I mean, I know there are other things you've got for me to do, but if you decide to put someone on her, I might be the best one for the job."

Sam studied the woman standing before him. He had thought of the possibility many times and, as yet, had held off. He wasn't sure why, though she was right. She *was* the perfect one for the job, given her friendship with Carly and the fact that she could easily blend into Carly's daily life. As it was, he had already assigned a man to the case, an agent who, as of Monday morning, had silently kept watch over Carly as she'd gone to and from school. It appeared from what Sheila had said that he hadn't been quite that invisible.

He picked up a pencil and absently tapped its eraser against the desk. "You've got a point. She wouldn't have half as much explaining to do with a friend by her side. Of course, there's still Ryan."

Sheila was about to comment on her own relationship with Tom and the fact that that, too, might work out well, when she recalled that Greg was hearing everything she said. "Ryan already knows me and knows that Carly and I are friends. Assuming I fade into the background when the two of them are together, it wouldn't be much of a problem."

Sam shrugged. She had thought it all out. "Well—" he sighed, giving the pencil an idle move "—let me think about it. Maybe I'll give her a call and feel her out about the whole thing."

"She'll fight you," Sheila argued in a last-ditch effort to plead her case. "She went so far as to say that even if her cover is blown she won't budge. I think she's nearing her limit, and her involvement with Ryan isn't helping matters. He may be putting pressure on her for some kind of commitment." It sounded good. "The poor woman's being torn apart."

That Sam could believe. "I know. It's tough on her."

When Sheila would have jumped in to say that she could make things easier, she caught herself. She'd already made her point. Subtlety was in order. The decision had to be Sam's.

"Okay," he said. "I'll let you know what I decide." His tone reeked of finality. With a nod, Sheila turned, sent a gentle smile Greg's way and left.

In the wake of her departure, silence filled the room. It was Sam who broke it, though Greg was right on his wavelength. "How did it go Friday night?"

"Okay. She's nice."

"Is that an endorsement?" He had to admit that she had seemed more subdued, more serious than usual. Perhaps she was settling down. If something about her still bothered him—an unspoken intensity, a strange if subtle urgency—maybe that was *his* problem.

"I . . . think so."

"But you're not sure."

Greg had grown suspicious when Sheila had spoken of Ryan's acceptance of her. It would certainly be convenient—Ryan and Carly and Sheila and Tom. But that was his own ego speaking, and it had little to do with the facts of Sheila's ability on the job.

"I guess I'm sure," he said at last. "She's serious when it comes to work. She was the one who came up with the lead that netted Phillinski while you were in Chicago. She's good with informants, handles them well. Phillinski had been running the feds in circles for two years." He frowned. "No, any doubts I might have are personal."

"She's a lousy cook," Sam speculated, but Greg was quick on the rebound.

"She's a *great* cook. Claims she learned everything she knows from her old Uncle Amos. He recalled the amusing dissertation that had been delivered along with a midnight snack. "Sheila's a character. She lives in a subbasement apartment, which she hates, but she drives a brand new Mazda, which she loves. She serves me Chivas Regal, then helps herself to a rum and Coke. She talks as freely about having come from poverty as about the mansion in the country she plans to have one day." He took a deep breath, then, perplexed, let it out. "She *is* a character."

"Do you think she'd be okay guarding Carly?"

Greg shrugged. "I don't see why not. If they spent all that time together in Chicago and are still friends, Carly must be aware of her eccentricities. Sheila's good company once you get used to her."

Sam thought back to Sheila's arrival in Boston. "That's what Carly's been telling me from the start.

Maybe she's right. Maybe I'm too conservative for my own good."

Greg wondered the same about himself. No strings attached, Sheila had assured him, and he wanted it that way. She might have been great in bed, but it didn't change the fact that she stirred nothing else in him. So why did it bother him that she had used his body as she dreamed of Thomas Cornell? It bothered him because of the weird feeling he had that, though he'd been in the dominant position, she had been calling the shots.

Carly sat in class feeling worse by the minute. She'd had it again this morning—that awful sense of being followed. Neither Sheila's pep talk nor a night in Ryan's arms seemed to have made a dent in her paranoia. Her stomach was in knots. She felt decidedly drained.

By lunchtime she discovered one source of her problem. She had gotten her period.

By early afternoon she had the answer to the other. Sam had called. She phoned him back as soon as she returned to her office.

"How could you have done that, Sam?" she cried when he told her about the man he'd had following her.

"I thought about it all weekend and decided that I'd feel better knowing you were covered, at least during those times you were most exposed."

"But I was terrified! I felt your man on my tail from the start!"

"I know, Carly, and I'm sorry. He tried to be discreet, but I think you have fine-tuned antennas in that lovely head of yours. Anyway, I've pretty much decided to let Sheila cover you. She wouldn't be on it full-time. We don't have sufficient evidence of a problem to justify that. But she could walk back and forth from school with you, or drive you if you want, then go with you if you have things to do after—"

"What'll I tell Ryan? He knows Sheila and I are friends, but he's apt to suspect something strange."

"Do you leave with Ryan in the mornings?"

"Sometimes. Sometimes he gives me a lift."

"Then I could have Sheila waiting, watching from her car. If you're alone, she'd be there to join you. If you've got Ryan, you won't need her. And there's no problem in the afternoons. Ryan works."

"I suppose."

"See? An easy solution to a problem that probably isn't any problem at all. I'll keep up the patrols around your place. You weren't aware of those, were you?"

"No."

"Good. I'm sure Ryan wasn't either. Sheila will start tomorrow morning. For tonight, I'll let the same agent—"

"No, Sam. He doesn't need to follow me. I don't care who he is, but he makes me nervous. I'll be all right. It's just one night."

"You're sure? I mean, the whole purpose of this is for your peace of mind."

"And yours," she reminded him tartly.

"Right. Well, that's an idiosyncrasy of mine you'll just have to put up with. But I will pull Ben now if you'd rather."

"I'd rather."

"Then it's done. Give me a call if Sheila gets on your nerves."

"Sam, Sam, Sam. You're still down on her?"

"She may be a damn good deputy, but I don't care what you say, she'll always be a flake to me."

Carly sighed and closed her eyes, feeling lighter of

mind but very tired of body. "Well, if I have to have a bodyguard, I'd rather Sheila than anyone else."

"You've got her." His voice grew mischievous. "Have fun."

She smiled wanly. "Thanks."

She should have felt better, but she didn't. The afternoon dragged on. She moved gingerly through two classes, then several student conferences, than a department meeting. By five, when she would have started home, she felt terrible.

Lifting the phone, she called Ryan. He was in conference, but she was quickly dispatched through.

"Carly?" His voice was low and accompanied by the hum of others in the background. "Is everything okay?" She rarely called him at work. He couldn't help but worry.

"Everything's fine," she said quietly. "I, uh, I just thought I'd stick around here for a while and clean up some work. Do you think you could swing by for me on your way home?"

"You sound tired."

"I am."

"I can get away in an hour. Is that too late?"

"No. That's fine."

"You stay in your office. I'll come for you."

"I can wait at the—"

"I won't have you waiting anywhere. If I'm held up in traffic, at least I'll know that you'll be getting something done. Okay?"

"Okay."

"See you then."

"Bye-bye."

The extreme softness of her voice conjured up an image of the vulnerability Ryan had seen in her so often at the start of their relationship. He hadn't seen it as much lately; she seemed more confident, more content. Now, though, he was as affected as ever by it. Replacing the receiver in its cradle, he realized that regardless of how frustrated he might be about whatever it was she hid from him, he would never, ever be immune to her pain.

By the time an hour had passed, Carly had mixed feelings about Ryan's good intent. True, she was in her office, sitting, off her feet. And true, she had gotten some work done, albeit not as much as she might have wished. But she had also discovered that the rest of the school had grown very quiet. And while she doubted she had the strength to walk home, more than anything she wished she were there now, tucked in bed with a heating pad, safe and sound.

By six-twenty she'd begun to fear that he had been tied up longer than expected. The switchboard was off; he couldn't get through if he tried. She was about to try him, when she heard footsteps in the hall. They were steady, confident. She wanted to believe they were Ryan's, though with carpeted rooms at home, she couldn't be sure she recognized the sound. They came quickly closer, with neither hesitancy nor stealth. Sitting very still, eyes on the door, she waited. When Ryan poked his head in, she let out her breath.

He kissed her gently and helped her gather her things. "You do look beat," he said with concern, as he shut the door of her office and guided her down the hall.

When she was finally in the car, she put her head back and closed her eyes, trying to concentrate on anything but the cramps that were painfully constant.

"Want to go out for something?"

"I think I'd just like to lie down for a while."

He turned to study her face, which looked all the more pale in the dim streetlight. "Don't feel well?"

"Just cramps. I got my period this morning."

He reached out to caress her cheek with the back of his hand and felt utterly helpless. "I'm sorry, babe. Is it bad?"

She managed a noncommital reply, but nothing more. Taking his cue, Ryan started the car. Within five minutes they were home. Carly headed straight for the bedroom, kicked off her shoes and curled in a tight ball atop the quilt, coat and all. She was only vaguely aware of a shift in the mattress when Ryan sat down.

He reached for her coat, working at the buttons, finally easing it off and laying it aside. "Want to get undressed?"

She shook her head. "Not yet."

He spread an extra blanket over her feet. "Can I get you anything? Aspirin? Warm milk? A hot-water bottle?"

"Don't have a hot-water bottle," she mumbled against the quilt. "There's a heating pad though. Under the bed."

Without rising, he groped for it, plugged it in and watched her unfold herself enough to place it on her thigh. "Why there? Isn't it your stomach?"

"When I get cramps, my thigh aches."

"Is it always like this?"

"For years it was, then it got better." She moaned softly and shifted position. "This is the worst it's been in months."

"Should you call a doctor?"

"No. He warned me. I'll be okay."

"Warned you?" There was mild panic in Ryan's voice. He felt very male and very out of it. "What do you mean, warned you? What did he warn you about?"

"The IUD. When I got it a few weeks ago. He said there was a chance my period would be worse."

Ryan breathed a pithy oath. "Get rid of the damn thing. I don't care about birth control."

"Well, I do." She smiled gently up at him and put a hand on the tensed muscles of his arm. "Ryan, it's okay. Really." She started to get up. "If it'd make you feel better, I'll go sit with you in the living room."

He pushed her down again, leaving a protective hand to rub her back. "It'd make me feel better to see *you* better. Isn't there anything that helps?"

"Peace." She eyed him in gentle chiding. "And quiet."

"That's a hint."

Closing her eyes, she burrowed deeper into the quilt. "Mmm." It was as much a groan as anything else. When she felt him begin to rise, she reached out to stop him. "No. Don't go. Just lie with me a little."

He leaned low and placed a kiss on her cheek. "Let me change. Then I'll be back."

She nodded and, trying to tune out the pain, focused on the quiet sounds of his undressing. First he slipped his suit jacket from his shoulders and let it fall to the bed. There was near silence as he tugged at his tie and worked at the buttons of his vest, then a swish as it separated from his shirt. She heard the rattle of his belt buckle, the dull click of a button, the rasp of his zipper, the rustle of his trousers. Moments later there was the clatter of wood hangers in the closet, one of which he removed and on which he began, piece by piece, to hang his suit. She pictured him standing by the bed in his shirt, his tie draped down either side of the fabric that tauntingly bared his chest.

She moaned again, louder this time, and Ryan was

instantly on a knee, leaning close. "Is it worse?" he asked in alarm.

The sound she made was a poor imitation of a laugh. "I don't believe it," she whispered hoarsely. "I'm lying here listening to you strip and it's totally erotic, but I hurt so much I can't feel a thing."

Ryan stretched out on the bed and took her ever so gently in his arms. "I wish there was *something* I could do."

"This is fine," she murmured against his chest. The faintly musky scent of his warm skin momentarily numbed her brain against that other, more visceral discomfort. In a gesture totally devoid of sexual intent, she ran her hand up his chest and hooked it around his neck. Her thumb fell to caress the point beneath his jaw where beard ended and skin began. After a minute, she tipped her head back and studied the spot. "It's soft here. I never noticed before."

"We all have our weak points." He cleared his throat of its thickness.

"Not weak. Very nice." Her thumb ventured into his beard, her eye following its gentle exploration. "What's this? A scar?" She felt the faint ridge and, on closer examination, saw the slightest line where no hair grew. When he was upright it was invisible. Only now, with his head back against the pillow, could she see it.

He quickly looked down at her, obscuring the breach. "A little one. It's nothing."

"Where'd you get it?"

"An accident when I was younger." He wasn't sure why he didn't tell her the truth, but suspected it had something to do with the frustration he felt inside. If she wasn't opening completely, he didn't have to either. Juvenile perhaps, but he couldn't help himself. Another time, he might have feared she would prod deeper. Already, though, she was shifting position, trying to get more comfortable. "Here—" he eased her out of his arms "—why don't you rest. I'll go see what I can scrounge up in the kitchen."

"Just give me a couple of minutes and I'll get you something."

"You will not." He was tugging on his jeans. "I lived alone for over a year. I'm not completely helpless. Besides, I don't think you'll be good for much for a while. Maybe I can get you some soup or something."

"Uh-uh," she groaned, shaking her head. "I'll just lie here. That'll help."

It didn't help much. She moved restlessly on the bed in an attempt to find a comfortable position. In essence the only relief she got was from the movement itself, which, for those brief instants, masked the pain. Finally she pushed herself up from the bed and, no longer able to bear anything binding around her body, changed into a long-sleeved nightshirt.

Ryan appeared at the bedroom door just as she was attempting to pull the bedcovers back. "Let me help you!" When she slid between the sheets, dragging her heating pad along, he tucked her in. "Why didn't you call?" He glanced at the clothes she'd strewn on the chair. "I could have given you a hand."

"A woman has to do some things alone," Carly murmured, attempting a joke that fell flat.

"Not in my book. A relationship's for sharing. Both the good *and* the bad."

"Ryan. . . ." Her moaned protest stemmed not only from the need she'd had for privacy but also from her own sense of guilt. But she wasn't in the mood for a lecture. Not tonight. Not now. Eyes closed, she burrowed more deeply into the covers.

His voice was soft in concern by her ear. "How about some aspirin?"

She shook her head. "It doesn't help."

"Then something stronger? Maybe if I call your doctor—"

"No. I have my usual prescription, but I hate to take it. It knocks me out."

He tucked an auburn wave behind her ear. "That might be the best thing."

"No," she answered with a vehemence that was instantly spent. She went on more weakly. "I'll be all right. I mean, it's not like I'm unique. Women have been going through this since the beginning of time."

His lips brushed her brow. "But if there's something that can make it easier. . . ." His voice trailed off with the shifting of his thoughts. Slipping an arm under the covers, he searched for her hand and gently took it in his. "I suppose it's all for a good cause," he said quietly. "Your body's working. Some day it'll work a little differently." She opened her eyes in time to see his ardor. "That'll be when you have my baby."

He said it with such quiet conviction that, for an instant, she couldn't think, couldn't breathe, couldn't so much as blink or swallow. It was a beautiful thought but staggering in its implications.

"Ryan, I can't—"

"Don't say a thing," he whispered. His gaze touched her features one by one, pausing at her brow to follow the progress of his fingers as they smoothed her bangs from her damp skin. "I have to believe that some day you'll be mine, Carly."

"I am yours."

He shook his head, his eyes profoundly sad. "Not yet. Not completely. And I promised I wouldn't push." He spoke with quiet urgency. "But there are times when I can't help myself. When I have to say what I feel. Because I do believe it, babe. The two of us—we were meant to be. I don't care what else might have happened in your life. It has no bearing on *us.*"

But it does, Carly screamed silently, then lowered her lids in anguish. Curling more tightly into herself, she moaned. "Maybe I should take something after all. I feel like I could crawl into the nearest hole and die." What she wanted to do was to crawl into the nearest hole with Ryan, pull it in after them, and escape together to another dimension. In lieu of that, she would take a pill.

"Where?" he asked.

"The medicine chest. The small prescription bottle on the top shelf. It may be behind something. I haven't taken anything in so long." Lapsing into silence, she thought of how, since she'd first come to Boston, she had avoided taking anything that might leave her less alert. But she had Ryan now to be her eyes and ears, and she desperately needed to sleep.

Ryan was a long time in the bathroom. He stared at the bottle in his hand, looked back to the shelf and, seeing no other prescription, studied the label again. "Percodan?" he called out.

"That's it," she managed. "One."

He rolled a yellow pill into his palm, snapped the top back on the bottle, then, frowning, stared at the label again. "Percodan. One every four hours for pain. P. Demery, M.D." So the directions read, and Ryan had no problem with them. What he did have problem with was the fact that the prescription was made out to an R. Hart and came from a pharmacy in Chicago.

Very slowly he replaced the bottle in the medicine chest, filled a glass with water from the sink, and returned to Carly. Eyes closed, she didn't see the way he stood looking at her for long, long moments. She barely moved when he sat down on the side of the bed, and opened her eyes only when he lifted her and urged the pill into her mouth. She seemed distracted, far away, which was a very good thing. He needed time to decide what to do.

Eighteen

WEDNESDAY NIGHT RYAN WORKED LATE. HE DID the same on Thursday. Had Carly not had Sheila with her, she might have had more time to worry. But Sheila *was* with her, and, beyond that, there was school and plenty of paperwork, what with the third marking period nearly over.

If Ryan was more tense than usual, she attributed it to fatigue. Both Wednesday and Thursday nights, when he came home late, he seemed content just to stretch out on the living-room sofa and close his eyes. On both occasions she had to wake him to get him into bed, and then he was too groggy to talk.

By Friday morning, though, she was beginning to sense something else. He wasn't looking at her. Not directly at least. It was as though he was the one with something to hide.

They ran. They showered. They dressed, talking from time to time about one inconsequential thing or another. Then he made a point of reminding her about the dinner they were to attend that evening.

"I haven't forgotten," she said softly. They were

standing in the kitchen, leaning against the counter drinking coffee. "What time do we have to be there?"

He scrutinized his shoes as if debating whether to have them shined on the way to work. "Cocktails are at six. If we get there at six-thirty, we'll be fine."

"Are you sure? If you need to be there earlier—"

"Six-thirty's plenty." He took a deep breath, stared at the window and absently sipped the dark brew. "Listen, if you'd rather not go, it's no problem."

Hurt and puzzled, she answered slowly. "You're speaking. I wouldn't miss it."

"I know how you hate lawyers. It's bound to be boring."

"Would *you* rather I not go?"

Closing his eyes, he dropped his chin to his chest. "Don't be foolish," he muttered. *"I'm* the one who'll be bored stiff. I hate these things. Your being there is apt to be the only thing that gets me through."

"Funny. You don't sound thrilled about it. What's wrong, Ryan? What is it?"

For the first time that morning, he met her gaze. His eyes were expressionless, his voice steady. "Nothing."

"I don't believe that. You've been walking around here like you have the weight of the world on your shoulders." She put a hand on his arm. "Please, Ryan. I can't stand the tension."

"Maybe I should move out."

She caught her breath. "That's not what I want."

"What do you want?"

"I want you to talk, to tell me what's bothering you. What's that you were saying the other night about sharing—both the good *and* the bad?"

His eyes suddenly sharpened and Carly knew she'd hit a nerve. "Is that what *you* do? Talk? Discuss? Open up freely, with no reservations at all?"

"I . . . I. . . ."

He put his mug down on the counter with a thud. "It goes both ways, Carly. I won't pressure you. Don't pressure me." Turning, he stalked from the kitchen, grabbed his overcoat and briefcase from the living room and was gone.

Carly placed a trembling hand on her stomach. She felt as though she'd been kicked, left with neither breath nor the strength to move. She didn't know how long she stood, rooted to the same spot in the kitchen, when the downstairs buzzer rang. For an instant, her eyes brightened. She wondered if it would be Ryan wanting to apologize, to say he was simply tired or had a troublesome case or was coming down with a cold. When she heard Sheila's nasal twang, she was disappointed.

"Hey, buzz me up!"

Carly did it, then began to put her things together for school. By the time Sheila arrived, Carly had her coat on. Her forced smile of greeting was as much of a tip-off as her otherwise stricken expression.

"Uh-oh," Sheila said, taking several books to relieve some of Carly's load. "You guys had a fight. I sat in my car and watched Ryan storm out of here a minute ago and, man, was he boiling."

"Sheila. Please. I don't need this now." They started down the stairs, walking in silence for a while. When they got to the bottom, Sheila spoke more gently.

"What happened?"

Carly took a deep breath and shrugged. "I guess I got caught at my own game."

"What do you mean?"

"I mean," she said, pushing the front door open, "that Ryan's been brooding about something for days now. It's been worse lately and was horrible this morning. When I asked him about it, he said that if I don't share with him, he doesn't have to share with me." She swallowed hard. "I hadn't realized he'd been that bothered . . . or maybe I've realized it and just chosen to look the other way."

Sheila said very little as they walked down the path. When they got to her car, she propped her elbows on the roof and eyed Carly across the burgundy gleam. "So what are you going to do about it?"

Carly was no less direct. "I'm going to tell him."

"Everything?"

"Yes."

"You're sure?"

Nodding, Carly opened the door and slid in, speaking again when Sheila was in the driver's seat. "I have to." She reasoned aloud. "It was one thing keeping my secrets when our relationship was super. I didn't want to rock the boat then. Now it turns out that the boat's being rocked by the very fact of my keeping those secrets." She took a long, tortured breath and let it out as an evanescent mist against the window. "I don't see where I have any other choice."

Sheila started the car and headed for Rand. "You could stall. See if it'll pass. Make it up to him in other ways."

Carly's head turned quickly. "What ways?"

"Oh, you know," she hedged, vaguely intimidated by Carly's sharp look, "doing little things that he likes." She wrinkled her nose and managed a one-shouldered shrug. "Food. Sex. That kind of thing."

Carly looked away muttering, "I couldn't do that. I'd feel like even more of a crumb than I do now. Besides, that'd be avoiding the issue." She pressed two fingers to her forehead and squeezed her eyes shut. "I knew I'd have to tell him one day. It was only a matter of time.

Sam said it once; when the time was right, I'd know it. Well—" she sighed, opening her eyes and looking straight ahead "—the time is right now. We have Ryan's speech and that dinner tonight, but after that I'll tell him."

Though firmly made, the decision weighed heavily on her mind all morning. Ryan phoned during her lunch break, timing his call perfectly to catch her in her office. Her heart skipped a beat at the sound of his voice, but she wasn't sure quite how to respond. "Hi, Ryan," she said softly, cautiously.

"Babe, I'm sorry. I was a bastard this morning. I've been furious at myself since I got in here." His voice lowered to a husky whisper. "I love you. I just wanted you to know that."

Slow tears gathered at Carly's lower lids. She gave a convulsive swallow. "I know. I love you too."

The silence on the line was profound, with Carly as startled by her confession as Ryan. "You what?"

It seemed the most natural thing in the world to say. "I love you."

"So you finally decided to tell me." His voice was lower, almost gruff, but there was a thread of humor in it that Carly recognized instantly.

A smile came to her lips and slowly grew. "Uh-huh." It wasn't even worth denying his implication that she'd known for a long time, or asking how *he'd* known.

"Damn it, Carly, this has to be the cruelest thing you've done to me yet! I have an afternoon of appointments lined up starting in five minutes. There's no way I can get out there now!"

"I didn't expect you to come out," she said. "I only have a few minutes myself. I just wanted you to know how I felt." Her voice softened all the more. "It's a start."

Suddenly his tone matched hers. "It is, babe. And we'll make it work. You'll see."

"I hope so." Even as she said it, an unbidden shiver coursed through her. In her mind, if nothing else, she was committed to telling Ryan everything about her past. If only telling him would make it all go away.

Shortly after Sheila saw Carly safely into her apartment, Ryan came home bearing a bouquet of roses and a smile warm enough to melt even the coldest of hearts. But Carly's heart needed no melting. Accepting the roses with a smile to match his, she flowed into his outstretched arms and murmured the precious words against his lips.

"Tell me again," he ordered after a kiss that left her short of breath.

"I love you," she breathed. "I love you."

He searched her eyes, found that they echoed her words, and let out a long breath. "I was worried you wouldn't say it to my face, that you'd lose your nerve or have second thoughts in the course of the afternoon."

"Come now, Ryan," she teased. "Where's your faith?"

"My faith has been raked over pretty rocky ground lately," he said, His sober expression wiped the grin from her face.

"I know. But I do love you. You've known that for a while."

"Yes." He kissed her again, this time slowly and with a thoroughness that reached to her soul and back. Carly arched closer, loving the feel of his tall, lean body, loving the strength of him, loving the way his arms circled her back in total possession. No longer did she fear the fire he created. Together like this, they *were* the fire, prepared to consume anything and everything that came across their path.

When he released her, it was with a reluctance she shared. "I wish we didn't have to go tonight."

"I know," she whispered, "but we do."

"I could always call in sick."

"You could not. You're the *speaker*, Ryan. You can't let all those wonderful people down. Besides—" her grin wasn't to be contained "—those wonderful people need to hear what you have to say."

He gave her a squeeze. "You're full of it."

"No. I'm serious. Just think. They've come from all over the country. Your talk may be the most important one they'll have heard all week."

"You *are* full of it."

"We won't know that unless we go."

He cleared his throat. "We'd better get dressed then?"

She nodded. "Society can only arrive so late."

The evening started out well enough. Armed with drinks and each other, she and Ryan circulated through the predinner crowd. More accurately, she observed in a moment's grace, the crowd circulated around them. It seemed that Ryan was indeed well-known in the legal community—and sought after, if the number of people who approached them was any indication.

Several members of Ryan's firm were in attendance. Carly was pleased to see these familiar faces in what was to her an otherwise anonymous and potentially threatening group. At several points she was amazed that she was there at all; three months before, she would never have dreamed of appearing like this, so open to speculating eyes. But with Ryan beside her, sometimes with an arm lightly around her waist, other times simply rubbing shoulders with her, she managed to control the urge to hide her face and run.

He held to his promise of keeping her by his side, except for those moments when he was on the podium. What she hadn't expected was that he would be seated at the long rectangular head table, and that she would be seated right beside him. It was heaven; it was hell. His presence was a constant comfort, even as her insides churned at the thought of being in the public eye.

Through dinner, he kept a close watch on her, talking softly with her during those times when the judge on her other side felt obliged to eat. As for herself, she barely tasted the filet mignon before her.

"You're not eating," Ryan whispered at one point. "Don't like the fare?"

"The fare's fine," she replied as softly. "It's the table I don't like. Why is it that the head table is always long and straight, and on a *stage,* no less. Everyone else has a lovely round table. I feel like we're on display."

"We're important people," he teased, feeling incredibly buoyed by the events of the day.

She plucked at a minuscule piece of lint on his sleeve. "I'd rather be less important. You didn't tell me we'd be stuck up here."

"I didn't know. Smile. They're all looking."

She plastered a smile on her face. "When do you speak?"

"Right after this course, I think. Relax, babe. It's not that bad."

"Aren't you nervous?"

"Nah. I've spoken before groups larger and more important than this one."

She passed an eye over the crowd, then ran her gaze down the length of the head table. "This kind of thing always reminds me of The Last Supper." Stifling a shiver, she looked out at the throng. "Wonder who'll play the part of Judas?"

"No Judas. They're friends, Carly." Beneath the table, he ran his hand along her thigh and leaned closer. "I doubt any of the Apostles were thinking what I am now."

A more natural grin softened the lines of her lips, and she met Ryan's gaze with the warmth he would always inspire. "You have a dirty mind, Ryan Cornell. What do you think they—" she tossed her head toward the crowd "—would think of *that*?"

"They'd be jealous. They are jealous. You may not have noticed, but a number of my illustrious colleagues have been staring at you covetously," he drawled, squeezing her hand when a nearby gavel rapped.

Swept up in the excitement of Ryan's imminent speech, Carly thrust his words into the recesses of her mind. Meanwhile, in a far corner of the room, one of those colleagues was indeed staring at Carly, not with covetousness but the intense curiosity of one trying to place a face. Again and again, as Ryan spoke, the man's gaze returned to her. When recognition finally dawned, it was followed by puzzlement. Not until the address was over, several other speeches and awards given, dessert downed and the dinner adjourned, did he make his move.

The crowd milled in large groups. He wound his way through them to the front of the room where, off the stage now, Ryan stood with Carly by his side. They were surrounded by people. He waited, studying Carly intently, biding his time until the crowd thinned.

Glowing with pride both in Ryan's speech and in his audience's enthusiastic reception of it, Carly didn't see the onlooker at first. Her smile was more relaxed than it had been all evening as she listened to Ryan graciously accept congratulations and thanks and comments on the points he had made. Only when two lawyers moved aside to make way for several others did her gaze bounce off the man waiting several yards away. With Ryan, she turned her attention to the newcomers. But something had jarred her. Her smile faded. For an instant her mind flashed the image of another place, another city, and she felt a sense of unease.

Puzzled, she let her eye wander. Within minutes it settled on the face of the man who stood watchfully to the side, and her pulse lurched. For as long as she lived, she would remember that face along with every detail of the Chicago trial. It was that of Mancusi's assistant, the young associate who had sat at the defense table on the far side of one Gary Culbert.

"Uh, Ryan?" she whispered, tugging at his sleeve, heedless of what she might be interrupting. "I'm going to run to the ladies' room. I'll be back, okay?"

A flicker of concern crossed his face at the sight of hers drained of color. But she managed a smile, and he accepted the fact that she might simply be fatigued. "Sure, babe. We won't stay much longer. Why don't I meet you at the door?"

So much the better. "Okay."

Without another glance at the man whose presence terrified her, she turned and wound her way through the crowd, finding relief for her shaky legs on a cushioned stool in the powder room. She took several deep breaths, raised a trembling hand to her forehead, propped her elbow on the counter and closed her eyes.

Back in the ornate dining room, Ryan had neatly

wound up the conversation and was about to make his escape when a man approached and extended his hand.

"Frank Pritzak, Mr. Cornell. That was a very impressive talk."

Ryan nodded, noting that this man seemed more somber faced than the others who'd come by. "Thank you." He frowned. "Pritzak. That's an unusual name. I'm sure I would have remembered it if I'd heard it before. You don't practice locally, do you?"

"Chicago."

A tiny alarm went off in Ryan's mind, but he schooled his expression to one of calm. "Chicago." He nodded. "Are you with a firm?"

"Mancusi and Wolff. We handle mostly criminal work, just as you do." He went quickly on. "I was curious about the woman you're with. She looks very familiar."

"Oh?"

"Has she spent time in Chicago?"

"She's from San Diego."

"Has she been here long?"

"Long enough."

He stared off in the direction Carly had gone. "She looks very much like a woman who testified in one of our cases last summer. She was on the other side. State's witness. I believe she was relocated by the government after the trial. But—" he straightened "—if your woman's been here, I must be wrong."

Ryan stood, heart pounding, waiting for the man to go on. When he did it was on a note of perplexity.

"Funny. I was sure it was her. I suppose the hair's different. The woman I knew had long straight hair. And the eyes. She had blue ones." He chuckled. "Never could mistake those. They stood out across that courtroom like nothing else." He shook his head in admiration. "She was one tough lady, Robyn Hart. It was an arson trial. She'd been a reporter investigating the story for the local paper. Before that, she'd lost her own husband in a fire." As though realizing he was rambling, he cast an apologetic smile Ryan's way. "She was a beautiful woman, even if she *did* screw up our case. Your woman's just as beautiful." He clicked his tongue against the roof of his mouth and narrowed one eye for a moment longer. "Same face. Hmph. I guess I'm just a sucker for the pretty ones." Then, with a philosophical shrug, he relaxed his features and stuck out his hand. "Anyway, enjoy her."

It took every bit of self-control Ryan possessed to shake the other man's hand with a semblance of composure. His limbs felt stiff, his insides frozen. Even his "Thanks" sounded wooden.

Turning, he headed for the door, where he scanned the lobby until at last Carly appeared. He wasn't sure what to say or do; his hands felt like ice. He retrieved their coats and silently led her to the car.

Unaware of the conversation that had taken place in her absence, Carly breathed a sigh of relief as Ryan drove off. "You did well," she said. "They loved you."

"Good crowd, for lawyers."

There was an edge to his voice that she might have easily attributed to sarcasm had she been listening. But she wasn't. Her thoughts were dominated by her own attempt to recover from what had to be the closest call she'd had with true and utter exposure since she had assumed the identity of Carly Quinn. Hands clasped tightly around her purse, she turned her thoughts to what she had to say to Ryan as soon as they got home. After what had happened tonight, it was all the more imperative that she tell him. As each revolution of the wheels brought them closer to Cambridge, the terror she had felt at seeing a face from her past slowly turned to apprehension.

Amid her own tension, she was oblivious to Ryan's. They drove, then arrived home, in silence. Only at Carly's open door did Ryan speak, his tone one of well-modulated nonchalance.

"Listen, I'm going down to my place to make one or two calls. I'll be up a little later."

Simultaneously disappointed and relieved, she nodded and watched him retreat down the stairs. Her gaze clung to his dark head, bowed in concentration, and she wondered, fleetingly, what calls would be so important at an hour like this.

Closing herself into her apartment, she glanced at her watch. Ten o'clock. Not that late at all. The better part of the night was ahead.

Stomach knotting, she changed into a pair of jeans and one of the sweat shirts Ryan had left in her closet, then sank into a chair in the living room to await him. Fifteen minutes later he hadn't come. Heading for the kitchen for some tea to settle her stomach, she wondered what the outcome of the night would be. He would be angry and hurt. But if he loved her. . . .

Another fifteen minutes passed and she grew restless. It was the waiting that was so bad. She half wished she had blurted it all out in the car on the way home, but Ryan had been as quiet as she. She assumed he'd been preoccupied thinking of the dinner. Perhaps he'd been thinking about something one of those people had said. What *had* they said? She tried to remember, but realized that she'd been concentrating solely on Ryan.

Sipping her tea, she shifted in her chair, then stood and wandered around the apartment, waiting, wondering. Who *was* he calling? Another glance at her watch told her it had been forty-five minutes since he had left her at her door. It wasn't like him to stay away for long. For that matter, it wasn't like him to need to use his own phone. Hers had been more than adequate from the start.

A small smile curved her lips as she thought back on those first encounters. She had been intrigued by him then, if a little frightened. But he had quickly put her at ease, taking things ever so slowly and gently, as was his style. This morning, ah, this morning she had seen a side of him she would rather forget. He had been cold and angry, but it had been her fault. She shouldn't have kept things from him for so long. He was too intelligent, too perceptive not to sense that there were some things she never discussed, some things she kept hidden from him.

She sighed. As soon as he arrived, she would tell him.

But he didn't arrive. The slim gold hands of her watch rotated slowly. Eleven. Eleven-ten. Eleven-fifteen. Eleven twenty-five. She told herself to be patient, but her nerves didn't listen. They jumped and jangled, jolting at any tiny sound. There was no sound, though, of a key in the lock. Finally, unable to bear the suspense any longer, she hurried to the kitchen and dialed his number.

The phone rang. And rang. Nine. Ten. Eleven times. She hung up. Maybe he was in the bathroom. Maybe he was, at that moment, on his way up. Crossing to the door, she put her eye to the viewer and watched in anticipation, heart pounding, palms pressed flat to the cold metal expanse.

When enough time had elapsed to eliminate the possibility of his having been en route when she'd called, she raced back to the phone and tried again. By the eighth ring she wondered if something was wrong. Heedless of the safety factor that three months before would have kept her cowering behind her locks, she left the front door wide open and, barefoot, dashed down the stairs. She knocked on the door, then pounded more loudly, then pressed a finger to the bell in a nonvocal cry for help.

After what seemed an eternity, she dropped her hand and, turning, slowly made her way back upstairs. She locked the door, set the alarm, then slumped in utter disbelief against the wall.

She didn't understand. Ryan would never run out without telling her. He knew she was waiting. He'd said he would be up. After his delight when she'd said she loved him, the flowers, embraces filled with such promise, it didn't make sense.

All she could do was to wait, which she did, huddled in a corner of the sofa as midnight passed and one o'clock became two, then three and four. By dawn she was frantic. It had been one thing when she'd been able to tell herself that a legal emergency had called him out, though she had no idea what kind of legal emergency would do that at such an hour, and she had even less idea why he wouldn't have let her know. But with the passage of more than eight long hours and still no word, she had to assume that something was wrong. It was then, with the first rays of light spilling onto the rug, that her imagination went to work.

Her first thought was that there had been some family emergency that had taken him out so suddenly. Perhaps one of his parents was ill. Perhaps Tom was in trouble again. In either case, he would surely have called. He would never have left her alone and expecting him momentarily. Especially now, when he knew that she loved him.

Her second thought, one that filled her with sudden dread, was that he knew more about her than that she loved him. She recalled the something that had been bothering him, the something he had passed off as a vague "nothing." What if he'd little by little put the pieces together, what if he'd purposely left her, what if, what if he'd finally given up. What if—her blood froze— the man at the dinner had said something.

Trembling, she pressed a fist to her mouth to stifle a cry, for there was a third possibility, coming fast on the second. If, indeed, Ryan had somehow learned the truth about her, he might be in danger. If one of Culbert's men had been following her, Ryan might have been snatched up as a hostage, or a source of information. She imagined him suffering unspeakable tortures and ground her head against her knees to force the thought from her mind.

Instinctively she had known that to tell Ryan the truth would be to risk his safety. There had been good reason why neither her father nor her brothers had been told where she lived; the less they knew, the less they would have to offer an evil-minded hunter. But Ryan knew just about everything to do with her present life, and if he also now knew about her past. . . .

For a moment she thrust aside that possibility and focused on his returning to her with a viable excuse for his absence. Perhaps her secrets *were* better kept, for his safety if nothing else. But that was self-delusion, she knew. Ryan was endangered by simple association with her, whether he knew the truth or not.

With a helpless shudder, she conjured up all kinds of terrifying thoughts. In one, they would be trapped inside her bedroom while deadly gas poured in through the heating vent. In another, their car would be rigged to malfunction when it reached a certain speed on the highway. It would easily pass as an accident. She could see the headline now: "Prominent lawyer and girlfriend killed in freak accident on the Massachusetts Turnpike."

A car bomb would be very effective, as would an ambush on a deserted country road some peaceful Sunday afternoon. They wouldn't have a chance.

Then her eye caught the flicker of sunlight on the frame of the picture that stood on the lacquered shelf against the living-room wall. If they were armed with machine guns of their own, they could protect themselves, or try, as Bonnie and Clyde had done. But Bonnie and Clyde had died.

With a cry of despair, she jumped from the sofa and slammed the picture face down. Shaking all over, she thrust her fingers into her hair, closed her fist and tugged, as though trying to pull from her mind every ugly possibility that lurked there. But it was no use. Ryan was gone, and she didn't know what to do.

She knew what she *wanted* to do, but she waited. To call Sam and dump her tale of woe on him, given the distinct possibility that Ryan had simply left on his own, seemed premature. Unsteady, she brewed a pot of coffee and waited. And waited. And waited, until even that particular humiliation seemed nothing compared to the possible danger Ryan might be in.

Sam was home, as she had prayed. "Hello?"

"Sam?" Her voice was tremulous.

"Carly? Is that you?"

Tears suddenly filled her eyes. "Yes. Sam. . . ."

"What is it, hon? A problem about tonight?" He had been frankly surprised that Ryan had agreed to their dinner date so readily. "Listen, we could make it another—"

"No. It's not that. Well, it is, I guess—" Her voice cracked and she broke. "Oh, God, Sam! I don't know where Ryan is! We went to a dinner last night and got back here and he went downstairs to change and said he'd be up after he made a couple of calls and he never came." Her soft sobs filled the line. Sam had to wait until she'd quieted to speak.

"Did you argue about something?" he asked gently.

"No. Well . . . in a way . . . yesterday morning. But we patched that up. And he brought me flowers. And it was going to be all right because I was going to tell him everything." She began to cry again.

Sam tightened his grip on the phone. "Take it easy, hon. I'm sure there's some explanation. Want me to come out?"

She sniffled. "I hate to ask you. I know it's Saturday. But I'm so worried. I keep imagining all kinds of terrible things. I don't know what to do."

"I'll be there, Carly," he said firmly. "Just stay put. And, please, hon, don't worry. We'll find out where he is. There's got to be some explanation."

That was what she kept telling herself for the forever it seemed to take Sam to arrive. By the time he did, she had composed herself enough to tell him everything, from the events of the day before and the startling presence of that face from Chicago, back to smaller things, things of a more personal nature that might help him help her. She spared nothing, from Ryan's growing frustration, to his wanting her to have his children, to her fear that he had simply dumped her.

"I won't believe that until I hear it from the horse's mouth," was Sam's forceful response. "I saw the way he looked at you the other day. The man's in love. A love like that doesn't just go away."

Carly crossed the room and picked up the photograph she'd turned over earlier. Looking at Ryan's image, so manly, so strong and protective, she felt the deep pain of yearning. "I hope you're right."

"I am. There has to be some explanation for all this. We'll try to get something on the guy from Chicago, but you say Ryan didn't talk with him."

"Not that I know of."

"And the guy didn't speak to you, so I doubt he made the connection."

"I don't care about him! It's *Ryan* I'm worried about!"

"Okay, hon. Okay. Now. Where might he be?"

"I don't know!"

"Think, Carly. Any lead you can give me might help."

Clutching the photograph to her breast, she turned. "I've gone over and over it in my mind. I've been through everything. If he went on his own, he might be just wandering somewhere. If he was forcibly taken away—" she couldn't help but shudder "—he could be anywhere." Her voice broke and Sam stood quickly. "Where are you going?"

Downstairs. Where did you say he parked his car?"

Relieved at the thought of doing something concrete, she ran for a pair of sneakers and a coat. "I'll show you."

The BMW was gone.

As Sam led her back inside, he tried to bolster her spirits. "If he was abducted, his car would probably still be there, so that's one vote against violence. Let's check his place."

"But I don't have a key."

Extracting a small case from his back pocket, Sam winked. It took him no more than a minute to pick the lock. "Why don't you have a key? He has yours, doesn't he?" He pushed the door open and went in, Carly following closely.

"There was never any need. There's nothing here."

Looking around the bare living room, Sam straightened. "So I see. I thought he ordered furniture."

"He did, but, aside from the bed, it was all custom-made. It won't be ready for another two or three weeks."

With a nod, Sam proceeded to go over the entire apartment in search of a clue as to Ryan's whereabouts. "Nothing," he announced, then sighed. "Well, at least there's no sign of violence here either."

Back in Carly's apartment, he contemplated the options. "Okay. Assuming he was upset and went somewhere just to think things out, where might that be? Would he have gone to his parents' house?"

She shook her head. "I don't think so."

"Or his brother's?"

"Maybe, but I doubt it. He'd want to be alone."

"Were there places the two of you went together?"

She shrugged, eyes glued to the floor, hand closed tight in her pocket around the spare key she'd taken from Ryan's kitchen cabinet. "We used to take drives—up toward Rockport and Gloucester, out along the old Boston Post Road." She paused for an instant, then spoke her agony. "If it were me and I wanted to go somewhere, I'd go back to the place we stayed in Vermont." She looked up, daring to hope. "That might be where he went. He said he'd been there right after his divorce when he needed time to get away and think."

Sam was scribbling in the small notebook he'd taken from his pocket. "Okay. Give me the name and address." As soon as she'd done so, he put in a call to Greg. From where Carly stood staring glumly out the living room window, she caught snatches of the conversation. She jumped when Sam materialized behind her.

"We'll check out Vermont. And his parents' and Tom's and his office. I've also got someone going to the airport, train station, bus depot." He took a breath. "I'll head into town to coordinate everything. Where's Sheila?"

"I think she's with Tom."

"Good. That'd answer one question. Can you call her? I don't think you should be alone." At the widening of her eyes, he spoke very gently. "Not for safety's sake, hon. I just think you could use the company."

"I hate to bother her. She's been busy enough following me around all week."

"That's her job. This she'll do out of friendship." He tossed his head toward the phone. "Go call her. I'll wait until I know she's on her way."

With lingering reluctance, Carly put through the call. Sheila was indeed at Tom's house—with no sign of Ryan—and promised to be over as quickly as she could. Knowing that, Sam left.

When Sheila arrived, Tom was right on her heels. "He insisted," she explained by way of apology when Carly's worried gaze flew back and forth between the two.

"Damn right I insisted," Tom announced, but kindly. At the sight of a forlorn Carly, he went to her. "He's my brother," he said softly, then very gently put his arms around her in offer of comfort. She was stiff at first, yielding only gradually to his warmth. "I'm worried too. There has to be some explanation for his disappearance. I can't believe he'd knowingly put you through this pain. He loves you very much."

Whether bidden by his heartfelt words or by the

strong arms that offered a support she badly needed, tears formed in her eyes, gathered in large pools, then began a slow trickle down her cheeks. She tried to check them, and bit her lip to stifle the sobs threatening to erupt, but Tom wouldn't allow it.

His arms tightened. "Cry, Carly. It's all right. You can't keep it bottled up. It'll only hurt more."

She wept softly, hands clinging to the light wool of his sweater. "It hurts."

"I know. But it'll be okay. Sam will find him, and until then, we'll be with you." Over her head, he cast a glance at Sheila. Tears were in her eyes too. He had no way of knowing that her thoughts were of his tenderness, his goodness, and her own awful lack of those qualities. She returned his sad smile before going to stand, deep in thought, before the window.

"I love him," Carly whispered.

"I know."

"What if he doesn't come back?"

"He'll be back." Very gently he began to rub her back, coaxing warmth into her chilled body. "You'll see. He'll be back."

Sam had the same conviction, but his reasoning ran along different lines, as he sat brooding at his desk. Ryan Cornell had flown to Chicago that morning. Chicago. Strange coincidence. Though he had a head start on them, he would be found and followed; Bill Hoffmeister had already put his best men on the case. If by some chance Ryan wasn't on the up-and-up, they would soon know it and obtain whatever evidence they needed to pursue the case.

He had been on an early flight and would have already landed. No doubt Hoffmeister's men were checking on car rentals and calling every hotel in the area. If things went well, they would locate him before he made his contact, *if* that was what he'd gone to Chicago to do. In any case, Sam would be there to meet his plane when he returned to Logan.

Brows furrowed, he closed his eyes and thought of Carly. How could he live with *himself*, knowing how he'd encouraged her from the start! But he was jumping to conclusions. He had no proof that Ryan had gone to Chicago with evil intent. Not yet. Hell, he'd cleared him himself. It just didn't make sense. The man had no motive whatsoever—unless, having discovered Carly's secret, he'd been so enraged at her deception that he'd lost his marbles. But Ryan Cornell? Cool, levelheaded, straight-as-an-arrow Ryan Cornell?

Lifting the phone, he dialed Carly's number. When a man answered, he was taken aback. Then he put two and two together.

"Tom?"

"Yes."

"Sam Loomis. I'm Carly's friend."

"Sure, Sam. Any word?"

"Yeah. We've got a lead on him."

"Where is he?"

"I'd rather not say yet." He wasn't sure how fully Carly had filled Tom in on the scenario, and, on the chance that she'd simply told him Ryan was missing, was reluctant to spill anything else. Not to mention the fact that if Ryan was into something, there was always a chance Tom might be somehow involved. "We're working on it." He paused. "Is Sheila there?"

"Right here."

That was a relief at least. "How's Carly?"

"Pretty unhappy."

"Can you reassure her at all?"

"I've been trying."

"Well, tell her that he seems to be well." The airline had reported that he had checked in alone, that yes, he had looked tired and rumpled, but that there was no sign of anyone coercing him to make the flight. "And that as soon as I know anything more, I'll call."

"I'll tell her."

"Thanks. Hey, and tell her that if *she* gets a call or anything, she's to let me know immediately."

"Where are you?"

"At my office. She knows the number."

"Okay. And Sam, thanks. We really appreciate all you're doing." He sounded genuine enough to Sam, whose gut instinct was to trust him. Particularly with Sheila there.

"Carly's pretty special," Sam said in closing. "I only wish I could do more."

Tom hung up the phone. Carly was at his elbow, eyes round, face ashen. "What did he say?"

"They have a lead." Urging her to the sofa, he sat down with her. Taking both of her hands in his, and he spoke gently. "He couldn't say anything more, except that he thinks Ryan's fine."

Carly's relief was short-lived. "If he's fine, why would he run off like that? Where is he? What's wrong?"

"We don't know that yet. It may be nothing but a misunderstanding."

"There wasn't any misunderstanding! Ryan clearly told me that he'd be back up after he made his calls." Shoulders slumped, she looked away. "I don't understand, Tom. I just don't understand."

He pushed a lock of hair back from her face. "You look exhausted. Did you sleep at all last night?" She shook her head. "Maybe you should lie down."

"I can't sleep."

"Then rest. Here on the sofa."

She looked up at him, taking solace in his concern. "I'll be all right." She gave his hand a feeble squeeze. "I'm glad you're here, Tom. I felt so alone."

He quirked a boyish grin. "Hey, what's family for?"

"I'm not exactly family."

"You will be. Take my word for it."

Leaving her curled in a corner of the sofa, he returned to the kitchen where Sheila stood, head down, leaning against the counter. "What else did Sam say?" she whispered, lifting her gaze at his approach.

He shook his head, his own discouragement showing. "Nothing." Then, in need of comfort himself, he put his arms around her and drew her to him. "Ah, Sheila. Sometimes we think we understand someone so well, and then. . . ." He hugged her tighter. "I never would have dreamed Ryan would go off like this. Carly means more to him than anyone in the world."

Eyes closed against his shoulder, arms firm around his back, Sheila struggled with her own warring devils. Tom was so good, as Ryan had seemed to be. But he was right; people weren't always what they seemed. Even the smallest thing—a moment's greed or anger or frustration—could chart an irrevocable course.

It appeared that Ryan had embarked on such a course. For her own sake, even more than for Carly's, she had to know which one it was. For that reason among others, Sam's assigning her to stay close to Carly was propitious indeed.

Nineteen

R YAN SAT ON THE PLANE ON SUNDAY AFTERNOON,
a fist pressed to his jaw, his eyes fixed on the blanket
of clouds below. It all fit. He should have put the pieces
together sooner. Had it not been for Pritzak, though, it
might have gone on forever. It appeared that Carly
wasn't going to tell him.

He thought back to all the signs. The fear in her eyes
that first night when, frightened in the dark, she must
have thought she was being followed. The slip of her
husband's name. Her reticence to speak about those
years since Matthew had died. The nightmares. Her
quickness on legal issues, her aversion to lawyers, her
vehemence when they had discussed the case he considered taking against the *Globe*. Her sudden disappearance, then the tag on her luggage. The absence of
an address book that might identify her. Even the stone
wall he'd run into trying to call her in the Bahamas.

The newspapers he'd read in the library yesterday
had told him as much as he needed to know. Even the
pictures had been revealing. No, Pritzak hadn't been
imagining the similarity. True, Robyn Hart's hair had

been long and straight, while Carly's curled naturally. And her eyes—Robyn Hart's eyes had apparently been blue according to Pritzak. But then, so were Carly's. Contact lenses could do wonders. It had never occurred to him to question why he'd never seen her without them.

He understood now why her pills had been made out to R. Hart, why that phone call had come for Robyn so long ago, why the needlepoint pillows and wall hangings all bore tiny robins in their corners. And he understood now her relationship with Sam Loomis.

Squeezing his eyes shut, he rubbed his throbbing temple. Having spent Friday night driving around Boston and Saturday night walking the streets of Chicago, he hadn't slept more than a couple of hours in the past sixty. But all the driving and walking in the world hadn't eased his agony. He might now know exactly what Carly had to hide, but the future of their relationship was as shaky as ever.

He had wanted her to come to him. But she hadn't. And he wasn't sure if he could continue to live with her, knowing she didn't trust him enough. But could he bear to live without her? That was the crux of his worry. He cursed the fate that had sentenced him to such pain.

In the end, the anger and hurt he felt were nothing compared to his love for Carly. His time in Chicago had given him a glimpse of all she had suffered before she met him. At least now he knew what enemy he fought. And he loved her. If he could make her life easier, that was what he had to do. He could only pray that one day she would love him enough, trust him enough to confide in him and make his life complete.

The plane landed in an early evening mist. Hauling his small bag from the overhead compartment, Ryan waited with the rest of the passengers until the deplaning began. He walked slowly, head down, into the terminal. When a hand clamped onto his arm, he stiffened.

"Let's go," Sam commanded softly enough not to attract attention.

He tried to shake the hand loose, but it cut into his arm with a strength he would never have guessed the other man possessed. "What's this about?" he barked.

"A few questions."

"What for?" Again he tried to pry loose, but Sam's grip only tightened.

"Let's not make a scene. I just want to talk with you."

"You should have done that a hell of a long time ago!"

Ignoring the outburst, Sam walked quickly down the corridor, then tossed his head to the side and guided Ryan into a small room where they were joined by Greg Reilly and another, more burly-looking, man. With the door closed firmly and his arm suddenly released, Ryan glared at the threesome, finally homing in on Sam.

"What's going on?"

"You were in Chicago."

"Obviously."

"What for?"

"Use your imagination."

"I am. And I don't like what it's saying. So I want to hear it from you. What were you doing in Chicago?"

"Walking."

"Tell us something we don't know. We've had a tail on you since last night."

"Haven't your men got better things to do—like protecting Carly?"

"That's what we are trying to do. What else did you do in Chicago?"

Ryan simmered. "I learned things I should have known weeks ago."

"Like what?"

"Hell! You know it all! You're the one who set it up!"

"What did you learn in Chicago?"

Hands on his hips in a stance of disgust, Ryan looked around the room. There was a desk, a phone, a few chairs. Far nicer than the usual interrogation room. But the men hovering around him were every bit as hostile as the local jailer. He'd seen plenty of them in the past, though as lawyer to clients in trouble, he'd been spared the worst of the guards' ire. Now he felt on the hot seat, and he was livid.

"What is this, Loomis?" he asked, eyes narrowing. "What do *you* think I did in Chicago?"

Sam didn't bat an eyelash. "I think you might have made contact with someone working for Culbert."

Of all the things Ryan had expected him to say, this wasn't one. Stunned, he tried to understand. "Made contact . . . Culbert? You think *I* might try to harm her?"

"You ran out awful quick Friday night right after you saw that guy at the dinner."

Incredulous, Ryan stared. "Goddammit, I'm in love with the woman! I wouldn't do anything to harm her!"

"You already have," Sam said with deadly force, heedless of the surfacing of his personal feelings. "She was crushed when you didn't show."

With the knifelike thrust of pain into his gut, Ryan closed his eyes. "God, I didn't want to do that," he whispered hoarsely.

"Why did you? You knew you couldn't get a flight out till morning."

"I knew," he said. Feeling suddenly weary, he sank into the nearest chair. "But I couldn't face her. Not with what I'd learned. Not with all those mysterious pieces finally falling into place. Not with the hurt I felt."

Head down, he didn't see Sam motion for the other two to leave. Only when the door closed quietly did he glance to the side and find that they were alone.

Taking a seat opposite him, Sam spoke more quietly. "Tell me everything you did, Ryan. Everything from the time you left her Friday night to the time you boarded that plane in Chicago this afternoon." He lowered his voice even more. "I love her too, y'know. Not in the way you do, but she's a very special person."

Ironically, though Ryan might have been wildly jealous at such a confession a week before, it was now the thing that most effectively broke his resistance. It was a show of trust, something he needed desperately.

Marginally encouraged, he began to speak. "I went down to my place and paced the floor for a while. I felt sick. Absolutely sick. It occurred to me to hire an investigator and send *him* to Chicago, but if what I'd been thinking was right and she was in the Witness Protection Program, I didn't want to do anything to risk her cover. Even the best investigator can be bought."

Sam sat, silent and patient, watching intently as Ryan's lower lip covered the upper then slid slowly down. "I knew what I had to do—what I had to find out for myself. And I didn't want to wait. I thought about leaving Carly a note, about concocting some story about an emergency trip, but I didn't want to lie." His gaze sharpened. "There'd already been enough of that. I was furious at her. Maybe subconsciously I wanted to hurt her back by making her sit up there waiting. It was stupid. But I didn't know what else to do. Anyway, I drove around for a while, stopping every so often just to think. By dawn I was at the airport. I was on the first flight out to Chicago." He looked up. "Is she all right?"

Sam nodded. "Tom's been with her. And Sheila."

"Sheila." Ryan gave a coarse laugh. "I bought that story too—about their meeting through you. I should have realized there was more to it. But I was blinded by everything I felt for Carly."

"Not too blind to begin to question."

Ryan's lips thinned. "No. Not after a while, at least." Then his tone grew urgent. "You have to understand. I want to marry her. I want to have children with her. But she held back, and I couldn't understand it. There were so many things I didn't understand—little things, little contradictions. Once I got to Chicago, I went to the library and pored over old newspaper articles. Pritzak—that guy at the dinner Friday night—mentioned her name and the gist of the case. It wasn't hard to find. Everything jelled."

"And then?"

"Then I walked around, just as your men said. I've been trying to decide what to do ever since."

"Have you?"

In that instant, as Ryan's gaze met Sam's head-on, any hostility that might have existed between them in the past vanished. They were suddenly allies, on the same side of the fence, each wanting the best for Carly.

"I'm going back to her. I'll just have to be patient, I guess. Maybe someday she'll tell me on her own."

"She was going to Friday night."

"What?"

"She'd already decided. She was going to tell you everything."

"She told you that?"

"Uh-huh."

"And I ran out."

"Uh-huh."

Ryan wore a look of self-disgust. "What an idiot I am."

"No. I probably would have done the same thing, given similar circumstances. Maybe we're both idiots."

Feeling strangely calm now and at ease with the man he'd distrusted for so long, Ryan lapsed into a moment's thought. "That night after New Year's, when we came back from Vermont and found you there—"

"I thought she was in trouble. Until she met you, she hadn't dared stray from her place, let alone go somewhere for the night. I thought someone had gotten to her."

"And that mysterious trip a few weeks ago. Her father wasn't sick, was he?" The light dawned. "I tried to reach you, but you were out of town too. I didn't even make the connection."

"I took her to Chicago to meet with the state's attorney. We only had a few hours' notice. She wasn't happy about going. It wasn't pleasant for her."

"The papers said that Culbert's lawyer filed for a new trial. Will there be one?"

"I don't know. The judge is considering the motion. But Carly can tell you all about that. Maybe you ought to get home. I doubt she's had any more sleep than you have."

A look of anguish crossed Ryan's face. "She may not want to see me after I ran off the way I did."

"She'll want to see you. She was frantic that one of Culbert's men did you harm."

"Does she know where I was?" he asked more cautiously.

Sam shook his head. "I didn't say anything. When I thought you might have been . . . well, let's just say that I've been putting her off all weekend. She'll be very glad to see you."

Ryan stood. "I hope so." Then he extended his hand. "Thanks, Sam. I appreciate everything you've done for her."

Sam met his grasp firmly. "She's an easy one to do things for. She asks for so little."

"Do you think there's any danger?"

"I don't know. Culbert and Barber are both restless. They've got great hopes for this new trial. We'll have to wait and see what the judge decides. Obviously, if something should happen to Carly in the meantime, their chances for a new trial will be that much better." He frowned his frustration. "All we can do is to keep an ear out and investigate anything that looks fishy."

"Like guys who fly out to Chicago for kicks?"

"Like those."

With a weary smile, Ryan opened the door. Instantly Greg and his sidekick came to attention, but Sam was quick to hold them back with an upraised palm. Passing them, he walked Ryan to the garage.

"Want me to come?"

"Thanks. But no. Carly and I have a lot of talking to do. It's enough that you and I understand each other. I'll take care of her. You keep your eyes peeled."

"Roger," Sam said and, turning, rejoined his men.

Ryan didn't go straight home. He needed a few extra minutes to digest his discussion with Sam and think through things one more time. When he arrived in Cambridge it was dark. After parking, he walked toward the building, his sharp eyes on the third floor windows that were Carly's.

They were dark.

Heart pounding, he took the stairs two at a time, knocked on her door, then rang the bell. Unable to wait, he fished in his pocket for his key and let himself in, only to find the place deserted. Puzzled, he tried to think. Tom might have taken her out for something to eat. Or she might have gone to Sheila's. Neither thought pleased him. He wanted to see her *now*. Having thought everything out, he was as ready as he'd ever be. And after two long days, he needed her.

Dejected, he retraced his steps to the second floor and let himself into his apartment, determined to unpack and clean up, then go back and wait for her.

Flipping on the lights, he saw nothing but loneliness—wall-to-wall carpet as stark without furniture as he felt without Carly. She was his color, his comfort, his joy. Without her, his life was empty.

He didn't turn on the bedroom light, choosing not to be reminded of that void in his life, but dropped his bag on the bed and began to undress. Then he heard a tiny cry and froze. There in the darkness, lit only by the palest hint of moonlight, was a small bundle of arms and legs and long hair that curled over hunched shoulders.

"My God . . . Carly?" He was across the room on his knees in an instant, prying her rigid hands from her mouth.

She cried his name then and threw herself into his arms, clinging to him with a strength that belied two days with little food or sleep. "Ryan," she sobbed. "I thought you weren't coming back."

"Oh, baby," he moaned, "I'd come back. I love you. Don't you know that?"

"There's so much I have to tell you," she managed in a broken rush. "I'm not who you think. I was somebody else before . . . in Chicago . . . a reporter. Robyn Hart. I testified for the state on an arson case and when someone tried to kill me they put me in the Witness Protection Program."

"I know. I know."

For an instant she was still, only intermittent gasps breaking the silence. Then she drew her face from his neck and stared up at him. His cheeks were wet. Bewildered, she raised a finger to touch his tears.

"You know?"

He pressed her hand to his bearded jaw. "I spent the weekend in Chicago."

"Ch-Chicago?"

Shifting her onto his lap, he settled back into her corner. Holding her tightly but gently, he told her everything. "I'm sorry to have left you that way Friday night. I was hurt and confused. I didn't know what to do. Sam met me at the airport today. He half thought I'd made contact with Culbert in Chicago."

"With Culbert? How could he think *that*?"

"It's his job. He's protecting you. I must have looked pretty strange when I disappeared, to go to Chicago, no less. But we got everything straightened out. He said Tom and Sheila were with you."

"I sent them home."

Thoughts of her safety were foremost in his mind. "You shouldn't have."

"I couldn't take it anymore. I needed to be alone."

Ryan frowned, as though just then realizing where she was. "How did you get in?"

The night couldn't hide her sheepish expression. "Sam picked the lock when we first went looking for you." Her voice dropped. "I stole the key from your key board. Do you mind?"

"Of course not. I should have given you one sooner." He glanced off into the darkness. "Your Sam. He's not such a bad guy after all."

For the first time since he'd returned, Carly felt the horror of the past begin to recede. Tension very slowly seeped from her limbs. The ice that had encased her senses grew moist. "I missed you so, Ryan. I can imagine what you must have felt when I raced off to Chicago with Sam."

"Thank God I didn't know then that you were with him. I didn't figure that out till a little while ago. I think I would have gone mad if I'd known."

"I half wish you had. Maybe this would have all come out sooner."

He held her back and gazed into her eyes. "But you were going to tell me? Before I left?"

Reaching up, she kissed him softly. "Friday night. I waited and waited, but you didn't come."

"Will you ever forgive me?"

"Will *you* ever forgive *me*?"

"There's nothing to forgive," he whispered. "You were frightened. I can now understand why. I only wish I'd been able to share some of that fear with you."

"But I didn't want that. Don't you see? It's bad enough that I have to live with it, but to impose it on someone else makes it even worse."

"I love you, Carly. That gives me the right to know, the right to share *everything* with you."

She wasn't sure she totally agreed, but couldn't think about it with his lips suddenly sipping hers. The knowledge that he was here with her, safe and loving, made her mind whirl. A soft moan slid from far back in her throat and she opened her mouth, craving more than his gentleness offered.

He needed little encouragement. Her invitation touched off a spark, igniting his passion like a match to dried leaves. With a shudder, he kissed her more deeply. Their lips meshed, their tongues dueled. He sought from her every bit of her sweetness, and, brimming with it, she gave eagerly.

He groaned, shifting her to face him, easing her legs

around his hips. "Do you know how much I need you? Do you know how much I love you?" Pressing his hands against her buttocks, he showed her how his body ached, and she thrilled to the fact even as her own body matched his yearning.

Sliding his hands beneath the band of her sweat shirt, he touched the slender span of her back and, finding no barrier, sought her breasts. He held their fullness and kneaded them, aware of their swelling at his touch. Deftly whipping the sweat shirt over her head, he feasted his eyes on what he'd felt.

"Your breasts are beautiful," he said thickly. "See how the moon catches them?"

Carly looked down. Her breasts were high and full, gleaming softly in the silver light, their tips waiting for his touch. She would never have believed she could be further aroused by the sight of her own body, but at that moment her body gloried in Ryan's searing gaze. Dear God, how she'd missed him. Even aside from his passion, she had missed their conversations, his quiet companionship, his caring. Two days—and she'd had a glimpse of what life would be like without him. She prayed it would never come to be.

Excitement shot through her when he lifted his hands. With thumbs and forefingers alone he touched her nipples, rolling them slowly, tugging them taut. Closing her eyes against the sweet torment, she cried his name and arched closer.

"You're mine," he whispered. "These are mine. When I touch them they respond as though they were made for me."

"I think they were," she managed in a strangled gasp. "No one's ever made me feel the way you do." Needing to touch him, she ran her hands over the fabric of his shirt, lauding the swell of his chest, its firm muscle, the symmetrically ridged contour of his rib cage. They fell past his belt to graze the hardness beneath his zipper. There she caressed him, spreading her palm over his strength, closing her fingers around his tumescence as much as the straining fabric would allow.

Ryan's hands fell to the delta of her womanhood. Slowly, devastatingly, he massaged her there. "So warm," he murmured against her lips moments before his tongue plunged into her mouth. One kiss followed another, and the intimate petting went on. Releasing him only long enough to unfasten his belt and lower his zipper, she slid her hands under his shorts to his hot flesh. He convulsed helplessly, urging her into a tighter, more erotic grasp, his breath coming in tortured gasps as, increasingly, was hers. When he could bear no more, he made a low sound.

Slipping his arms under her to hold her to him as he stood, he carried her from the dark of the bedroom into the brighter living room. She eyed him warily.

"But the bed. . . ."

"This room's too empty," he explained. "I want to fill it with you."

His words thrilled her, his very presence still new and imbuing her with untold relief. That he was safe seemed a dear gift; that he was back loving her was incredible.

Her feet slid to the floor when he stopped in the middle of the room, and she saw the same hunger in his eyes that she felt in her body. Only then letting him go, and never once taking her eyes from his, she stripped off her jeans and panties in one quick move, then finished the work she'd begun on his pants.

Fumbling in his haste, he had his shirt barely unbuttoned when she finished. Swallowing hard, he watched her slip to her knees and press her head to his stomach. She turned her face from side to side, driven wild by his scent and the firmness of his skin. Her lips traced a fiery path over his hard muscles, her tongue a tool of rampant heat. When her mouth ventured lower, he felt his knees tremble. Ripping the shirt open, he thrust it aside, then collapsed onto his knees and took her to the rug with him.

But Carly had begun something she couldn't stop. Never in her life had she felt as uninhibited. She'd been blessed with Ryan's return; her gratitude knew no bounds. Every inch of his body was precious and desirable; she showed him this in no uncertain terms. The past days' agony had left her starving for him, and now her soul was bared and she was proclaiming it his.

Her lips sampled the haired plane of his thighs, moving from one to the other and ever upward. The swath of skin at his groin was smooth at the side. She nibbled her way in until once more her lips approached the core of his maleness. Hands never idle, she explored and fondled, cupping, gently squeezing, only realizing that he'd shifted her when she felt his breath between her thighs.

Arousal and excitement and passion took new meaning then. Holding him still with one hand while the other caressed him lower, she used her tongue in an exploration of silk. Intoxicated by the eroticism of the act, she instinctively sought more.

She barely felt the hands that bent her knee up. Somewhere in the background of her own heady daze, she was aware of encroaching kisses at the top of her thigh. She moaned her delight when his fingers slid against the source of her heat, forging deeper with each glide, slowly, tenderly opening her wide. Then, as his lips found her moistness and sucked gently, his hands shifted to cup the curve of her buttocks, caressing her intimately closer. She had to struggle to maintain her own gentle touch against the urgency that was building, filling her with nearly unbearable need.

She stroked him as he stroked her, matching the deep plunge of his tongue with searing swirls of her own. She attempted to devour him as she was being devoured, and rather than becoming less for losing part of herself in him, she was more.

Every muscle straining against the limits of the flesh, Ryan suddenly twisted, rising over her, coming down to take her lips in the kiss of a heavenly soulmate. At that moment he entered her. His hips surged forward, grinding her against the rug, his hardness a fiery prod electrifying the pathway to her womb.

Then, feeling the quick gathering in both their bodies, he held himself above her. "Look at me," he gasped in a hoarse whisper. She opened her eyes to the wealth of love he offered. "I love you," he mouthed, withdrawing nearly completely, then slowly, ever so slowly filling her again.

She caught in a breath, her eyes wide at the exquisitely gentle motion, but she knew that the excitement she felt went far beyond the simple mating of flesh. Her heart was Ryan's, her soul was Ryan's. She was naked before him, exposed and adored. As she mouthed his words in return, she felt a graceful crescendo begin in her body, rise higher, flame hotter, gain a force that finally exploded with a cry from her lips.

Ryan held himself on a wire-taut thread of control in a bid to savor the glorious sensation of her contracting around him. Eyes bright and passion fired, he marveled at her beauty as she arched in the throes of her climax. Head thrown back, her neck glistened. Her pulse throbbed. Her breasts shimmered. She gave him everything she possessed, making his life in that instant as rich and full as anything he'd ever known.

Then, slowly, she opened her eyes and smiled. It was his undoing. The very innocence she exuded stimulated him as much as her womanly intricacies. On trembling arms he bowed his back, withdrew one last time, then drove forward into a climax that stole every thought from mind but one, and that one was on his tongue at the supreme moment. "Carly!"

His body pulsed wildly, blindly, for what seemed an eternity of indescribable pleasure. Finally collapsing, he gasped for breath. "Ahh, Carly. . . ." It was a hoarse moan muffled against her hair. "You can't believe what that . . . was. . . ."

Her smile grew less innocent and more smug. She had a head start on him for composure. "I think I can."

Very slowly, his limbs heavy and languorous, he slid to the side, drawing Carly with him. Nose to nose they lay in quiet enjoyment of the sounds and feel of each other's life's breath.

"You're wonderful," he murmured at last.

"So are you," she whispered. "I do love you."

There was a slight tremor in the hand he raised to brush loose wisps of hair from her face. His fingers returned to trace her features, which relaxed and glowed with happiness. "When I first saw you that night in the courtyard, you looked so frightened. I wanted to protect you then. I wanted to see you smile the way you did just now." He sucked in a breath of remembrance. "That really turned me on."

She halted his hand in its wanderings and pressed it to her lips. "You mean that all I have to do is smile and . . . wham?"

"Well," he drawled, "I'm not saying that the rest of you didn't help. You're quite a lover."

"When one is stimulated by another who is just a little better, one always rises to the occasion."

"Tell me you teach that to your students."

She grinned. "Not in the same context, that's for sure. But I do believe it. Playing tennis, skiing, bicycling, writing, it's the challenge that works."

"Tell me about your writing, Carly. I read as many of your articles as I could find while I was in the library in Chicago. You were good. Do you miss it?"

Taking a deep breath, she rested her head back on his outstretched arm. "I haven't had a chance to miss it. When I was in protective custody all those months, I was too nervous and upset to think about anything much. Then, after the trial, when I moved here, I was too busy trying to get ready for school. When I wasn't working, I was preoccupied with sheer survival."

"I wish I could have spared you some of that."

"It wasn't your job to. I had to learn to live with Carly Quinn myself. A crutch would have done as much harm as good."

"But still, I hurt when I think of what you went through."

"I was the lucky one," she said quietly. "I lived."

"You're thinking of Peter."

"He was a wonderful person—talented and dedicated. We were just about ready to wrap up our story. We had gotten this last tip and felt that if we could *be* there, if we could get pictures, we would have irrefutable proof."

"Of Culbert's involvement?"

"More of Barber's. We'd already tied the two of them together pretty conclusively. We never expected Culbert to be there at the scene of the crime."

"You testified that he was."

"And he was. Peter had pictures. It was a deserted

old apartment building that would have cost untold millions to renovate without the insurance money Culbert was counting on. Barber set up the fire the way he always did—using a cigarette attached to a matchbook, which was in turn attached to a fuse and then something highly flammable like a plastic bag filled with cleaning solvent. It was perfect. The evidence self-destructed during the fire. There was never anything left afterward. Which was why Peter wanted to get pictures inside before we called the police.

"Culbert and Barber were outside in a dark corner talking. We thought we had time. We knew that between Barber's technique and Culbert's connections neither the police nor the fire department would find evidence of arson. So we wanted proof." She frowned, still disbelieving. "We were sure we had time. What we hadn't counted on was Barber lighting the cigarette when he did—or the entire building seeming to explode. By the time I could get to an alarm, Peter was trapped." She shivered and whispered, "It was awful. There wasn't anything I could do. By the time the firemen pulled him out, he had third-degree burns over ninety percent of his body. He lay in critical condition for a week before he died."

Ryan's arms tightened. "I'm sorry, babe. So sorry."

She took a shuddering breath, closed her eyes and reminded herself that it was over. Ryan's solid presence beside her helped. "The film was lost in the fire. That was one of the reasons why my testimony was so critical."

"Did you ever have second thoughts? In light of everything that's happened since, it would be only natural to have some regrets—"

"About Peter, yes. About the investigation itself, no. I felt too strongly about the issue of arson."

"Because of Matthew?"

"Uh-huh. Now that I think of it, I'm sure that much of the strength in my writing came from anger. I felt so helpless when he died. Writing was my vent." She spread a palm down the solid span of Ryan's chest. It wasn't a sensual gesture so much as a touchstone to the present. "The anger's gone now. Maybe testifying did that for me." She lowered her eyes. "But I suppose if I want to be completely honest I'd have to admit that there have been times when I've had second thoughts about testifying and being relocated. I had to leave my family and friends. It was scary coming to a new city alone, even with Sam to help me." She looked up and dared a smile. "But I've found you, so that made the whole thing worthwhile."

Ryan took her in his arms and rolled on the carpet until she lay atop him. "You're incredible. I can't say that enough. Since I met you I've been a human being. Before that I was nothing more than an automaton of a lawyer."

"That's not what Sam told me. He said you were brilliant."

"He did?"

"He trusted you from the start, regardless of what he might have thought for a while this weekend."

"This weekend." It's every detail contrasted sharply with the warmth of the moment. "Let's forget this weekend."

Resting her cheek on his chest, she nuzzled the soft skin by his nipple. "No. Let's not forget." Her head came up in a flash. "I want you to know who I am and where I've come from. I want you to love Robyn Hart too."

He lifted his head and caught her lips in a long, moist kiss. "I do. Because she's here." His hand came to rest on her breast. "She's in you. And I love you." His hand lingered to caress her, and where she had thought herself spent new fires blazed. "Carly?"

"Yes?"

"Take your contacts out. Let me see your eyes."

Her breath caught. It was the last thing she had expected him to say. She wore her contacts so constantly that she gave them little thought. When she looked up to protest, she saw the urgency in his eyes and understood that with the revelations of the weekend there was one more to be made.

"I want to see you as you were born." He ran his hands down the ivory warmth of her slender torso. "I want to see you as no one else does."

Her gaze lingered on his for a minute. Then, slowly, she pushed herself up until she sat astride him. Carefully she removed first one lens then the other, long lashes shading the eyes that studied the gray disks in her palm.

"Look at me, babe," he murmured huskily.

Strangely shy, she hesitated. Then, closing her hand loosely, she slowly raised her lids, to be rewarded by Ryan's soft gasp when her bright blue eyes met his. In a gesture of awe, he framed her face with his large palms.

"They're beautiful," he breathed. "Very beautiful. Will you do this for me each time we make love?" When she shook her head, he frowned. "Why not? You have nothing to hide from me now."

"I can't see you," she mumbled, chin tucked low again.

"What?"

When she tipped up her face, she spoke with greater determination. "I can't see you. Not the way I want." Her boldness gained momentum. "When we make love,

I want to be able to see everything about you. Clearly."
Her free hand swept slowly over his chest. "I can feel
you, how warm and hairy you are. I can feel this." She
rubbed the tip of her finger over his nipple and felt it
harden. "But it's a blur. I want to see it. I want to see the
way your eyes crinkle at the corners when you smile at
me. Your smile turns me on too. Did I ever tell you
that?"

"No," he rasped, suddenly and acutely aware of
where she sat. "Oh, babe." Grasping her under her
arms, he brought her forward until her breasts teased
his chest and her lips met his. "Make me yours."

It took little effort. Already Carly's body clamored for
his. Her kiss transmitted the message of her slowly
undulating hips, and it was amplified all the more by
the brush of their bellies against each other's.

Very carefully, her breath coming faster, she placed
her contacts on his chest. "Lie still," she commanded
in a purr, then propped her hands on the rug by his
shoulder and bent her head again. She kissed his eyes
and his nose, wove her way along his bearded jaw, then
finally took his open mouth with one that matched it in
heat and hunger. Drawing away at last, she spread her
hands over his torso and told him how much she loved
his leanness, his strength. When she felt him grow beneath her, she fell forward again and raised herself to
taunt him there.

But if she had planned to arouse him to a state of
subjugation, her scheme backfired. Before he would
ever reach the begging stage, she would take him of
her own free will. As lovers they were equals, with
desires as wild and needs as great.

When Ryan lifted her hips, she welcomed him eagerly, arching her back, sighing at the pleasure of his
hardness deep inside her.

"That's it," he urged in a moan when she began to move. His fingers grasped the soft flesh of her bottom and guided her, while her hands claimed the sinewed brace of his shoulders. She rode him well; he was a joy of a beast. Together they raced across a plain of rapture and scaled a multitude of passionate peaks, arriving at last on the highest, reaching out for its ultimate glory. At that moment they were one as fate had decreed. At that moment a forever together seemed the greatest promise of all.

But the moment passed. Pulse rates slowed, breathing eased. Damp bodies lay limp in the aftermath of the exertion. When Carly finally slid to Ryan's side, it was with a reluctance that went beyond physical lassitude.

Ryan let out an unsteady breath. Hooking an arm around her shoulder, he hugged her. He felt particularly blessed. Carly Quinn, Robyn Hart—both were his.

"Marry me," he whispered. "Marry me, Carly."

Her heart contracted. For a minute she couldn't breathe. It had all been so wonderful up to that point. Stricken, she managed to push herself up and grope for the lenses that nestled in the hair on his chest.

"I'd better get these back in," she murmured unsteadily, but the sudden rise and fall of his chest impeded her search.

He grabbed her wrist and held it firm. A tenseness ran through him but it was more urgent than angry. "I asked you something. Something important. The contacts can wait. I can't. Will you marry me?"

She swallowed hard and moistened her lips. "Let's, let's talk about it later—"

"No!" He bolted up, heedless of the tiny disks that fell to the rug. "We have to talk about it now," he insisted, but gently once more. "I want you to marry me. As soon as possible."

Needing a diversion, she felt for and located first one, then the other, of the lenses. But she was aware of Ryan's alertness, could feel it in the powerful vibrations seeming to emanate from his pores.

"Carly?"

"I can't."

Something snapped inside him, letting loose the anguish that seemed to have been gathering for weeks. "Why in the hell not?"

"Because it's too soon."

"For what?"

"For us to know."

"That's absurd. You say you love me."

Her head shot up, eyes searching blindly. "I do."

"And I love you," he barked. Then, realizing the contradiction of his tone, he gentled it. "There are no more secrets between us. So there's no reason why we shouldn't get married."

Tucking her chin low, she huddled into herself. "I can't. Not yet."

"Explain."

"Too much can still happen."

Ryan shook his head as if to clear it of nonsense. "What could possibly happen? We could have a fight? We could suddenly decide that we're incompatible? That's insane. I'm not saying that our marriage would be one endless bed of roses. No marriage is like that. We'll have our small differences; every couple does. But what we've shared in the past three months, what we had just now on this rug—that has to account for something!"

"You don't understand," she whispered, slowly raising her head. Her gaze held a mix of defeat, of fear, of anguish. "I'm still a witness for the state of Illinois. I'm not my own person. If they call, I have to go. Look at what happened a few weeks ago. Meade called Sam, and within hours I had to drop everything to run off to Chicago."

"What's that got to do with marriage?"

"There's the danger."

"*What* danger?"

"Culbert. Barber. Whoever out there thinks that he'd be better off with me out of the way."

Ryan stormed to his feet. "That's crazy! No one's taking potshots at you!" He paced halfway across the room, then turned and, mindless of his nakedness, cocked his hands on his hips. "You're one innocent woman! You couldn't harm a flea! You've already given your testimony. It's over. Done."

"No, it's not," she cried. "If there's a new trial, it could be just beginning."

"Baloney," he fumed, needing to quash that possibility. "There won't be any new trial. I've heard of Meade. He's known to be one of the most careful prosecutors in the country. Even Sam said he tried a solid case. Besides, there's no way either one of those bastards would go to the effort of seeking you out. It'd be suicide!"

In an attempt to minimize Ryan's sheer physical dominance, Carly rose. Her own frustration was seeking outlet. She wasn't any happier refusing Ryan's proposal than he was. "Come on, Ryan. Since when did thoughts of suicide deter a convicted killer? Let's not be naive. Barber and Culbert were both given stiff sentences. If they have to serve them, they'll be losing the best years of their lives. On the other hand, if they can wangle a new trial and somehow throw in a glitch, they'll be home free. What have they got to lose?"

He threw up his hands. "Damn it, Carly, you can't live your life thinking that someone's on your trail."

"Someone was once." Turning away, she hugged her arms around her. With the dredging up of a nightmare, she felt chilled to the bone. "I was walking home after work," she began in a tiny voice. "It wasn't long after the indictments had come down. I'd walked the same route for years. I knew every nook and cranny along the way. But I wasn't watching. I thought of myself as an innocent witness to a crime. I felt *impelled* to testify—because of Matthew and whatever—but I also knew it was the right thing to do. I never dreamed someone would try to hurt me. Things like that only happened in B movies. I didn't imagine...." Her words trailed off as her voice cracked. Only when she felt Ryan's gentle hands on her shoulders did she realize he'd approached.

"What happened, babe?" He sensed her need to tell him and, though his own insides knotted, he needed to know as well. If he was ever to convince her to marry him, he had to know what had happened.

She took a steadying breath. "It was an alley. Dark and narrow with a big dumpster in the middle and garbage strewn all about. I never saw him. Suddenly there was this arm around my neck and something hard sticking into my ribs." She gasped for air. "He dragged me back, back where no one could see us. I struggled, but he was very big and his arm tightened around my throat. I could barely breathe." She was panting softly. Ryan moved his hands in slow circles to remind her that he was there, that it was all in the past. But it didn't do much good. The memories were too vivid.

"He didn't say much and when he did it was in this low snarl to mask his normal voice." She was shaking. "I'll never forget those words. 'Think you're pretty smart, do ya?' he said. 'Din't no one ever teach ya not to play with fire?' Then he gave this horrid-sounding kind of laugh. 'Little girls get burned. They end up in an alley with a bullet in their brain.' "

"Oh, God," Ryan whispered into her hair as he brought her trembling body against his for support. He wrapped his arms around hers. "How did you ever get away?"

"I was so scared. So scared." She spoke quickly and in short bursts as though fearing that any minute she would run out of breath. "I knew it was the end. But I didn't want to die! So I started struggling again. I was desperate. I must have taken him by surprise. I surprised myself. Then I began to run."

"But he had a gun. Why didn't he use it?"

Her laugh, verging on the hysterical, held a none-too-pleasant ring. "He tried. But my legs were so wobbly that I was weaving around, running in this jagged pattern. And I started to scream. And scream. I didn't realize I was out of the alley until I heard the screech of brakes. Then I passed out."

Ryan's own legs were shaky. "Sweet Lord. Did the *car* hit you?"

"No. It stopped in time. But by the time the police got there and I'd come to enough to tell what had happened, whoever had attacked me in the alley was long gone."

"He was never identified?"

"No." Enervated, she sagged back against Ryan's strong body. As though only then realizing the point of her dissertation, she managed to turn in his arms. "But it happened. And I'll never forget it. That's why I was put into the program. That's why I don't think I'll feel really safe until these appeals and motions are settled. And until then—" her gaze held great sorrow "—I can't marry you. It's bad enough that I fear something might happen to you in the course of the battle if there ever was one. This weekend, I was so frightened. . . ."

He kissed her brow and pressed her head to his chest. "Nothing's going to happen to me. *Or* to you. I won't let it. Sam won't let it. Everything's going to be all right."

She had to look at him again to convey her urgency. "I want to marry you, Ryan. I want to have our babies. But I don't want either you or them to be hurt by the decisions I've made in my life. Can you understand that?"

"I hear you. I'm not sure I agree. If you want to put our marriage off for a couple of months, just until something gives regarding this new trial, I won't be happy, but I could live with it. As far as children go, though, you're talking of time, Carly. Even if we *were* to marry now, it'd take nine months before a baby arrived. By then a new trial would either have taken place or be ruled out. Are you telling me that even after that you're going to be nervous?"

"I don't know," she said honestly.

"But it could go on forever! You can't live that way!"

"I don't know how else to live," she whispered in defeat.

"Then you're a fool," Ryan muttered, releasing her, stepping back. "All of life has danger. Hell, one or the other of us could be killed in a car, an airplane, walking across the street—" When she gasped and reached out to erase those thoughts, he refused to be silenced. "Do you think you're the only one to ever be threatened?" he asked, eyes ablaze. "Well, you're not." He thrust out his jaw, tipped his head back and pointed. "See that scar? It didn't come from some little childhood accident. I was slashed!" He whipped the word at her, and it struck with deadly force. Her eyes widened. The muscles of her throat constricted. But Ryan was so intent on countering her self-pity that he ignored her pain.

"I was doing my father-in-law a favor by representing one of his friends in a divorce. Personally, I couldn't stand the woman. But she did have a right to representation. We were in the midst of messy negotiations when I happened to bump into her husband at a party. We were all in the same social circle—the one I divorced right along with my wife." When Carly simply stared, he went on. "This guy was drunk and angry and jealous of every other man in the room. And since I was visible evidence of his humiliation, he took it out on me. He accused me of having a personal interest in his wife," Ryan sputtered, then suddenly grew more calm. "I never did figure out if it was a steak knife or a grapefruit knife." Sighing, he turned away and stared blindly out at the night. "The plastic surgeon did wonders. But I was self-conscious. So I grew a beard. After a while I began to see it as a symbolic change. I haven't handled a divorce case since. That was ten years ago." He sighed heavily. "I never pressed charges. Same social circle and all. The fellow was obviously disturbed. He was contrite afterward." He snorted. "I got a great settlement for his wife."

When no sound came from behind him, he turned to Carly, who stood with a hand over her mouth. "Don't you see, babe? Nothing in life is a given. If you'd ever told me that I'd be physically attacked in a divorce case, I'd have thought you were crazy. But it happened. Two inches lower and I might have died. I gave up divorce work because I didn't want to have to deal with that pettiness, those irrational emotions. But the rest of my practice grew. Hell—" he chuckled dryly "—any number of my criminal clients have been far more dangerous than that man; *they* would have hit the jugular instantly."

Carly stood frozen, trying to absorb it all. "I didn't know," she murmured at last.

"Of course you didn't." He took a step closer. "Because it's behind me. Because I don't put that fear on a pedestal and worship it."

"I'm not—" she began in self-defense, only to have Ryan interrupt her with a conciliatory wave.

"I know. I didn't mean that. All I mean," he said slowly, "is that I live with whatever life brings. That's what you have to learn how to do."

Silence filled the room while Carly pondered what he'd said. "It's so hard."

"I know." He closed the space between them and took her face in his hands. "I know. But I can help. Please let me try."

"Will you be patient?" she whispered timidly.

"How patient?"

"Patient as in holding off on marriage for just a little while?" Despite his argument, there was an unease deep inside her that she knew she had to deal with before she could agree to marry him.

"That's asking a lot," he stated soberly.

"I know."

"Does it mean that in time you'll say yes?"

"If nothing happens—"

"None of that talk."

"Just a couple of months, until I know more."

He gave pretense of considering her proposal, though in fact there was no consideration to be made. He had already decided to take whatever she would give. Marriage in a couple of months . . . he could have done worse. "You're a tough negotiator, Carly Quinn."

But his eyes were warm and she knew she had won.

Feeling abruptly light-headed, she threw her arms around his neck and clung fiercely. "I love you, Ryan. Oh, my God!" Stepping back, she stared from one to the other of her open palms.

Ryan looked at her in alarm. "What's wrong?"

"My contacts." She dropped to her knees and began to gingerly pat the rug. "I dropped them. I don't know when. Was I here . . . or there. . . ." Sitting back on her haunches, she squinted across the floor. Then she looked up in dismay. "If I don't find them, I won't be able to leave this apartment!"

Ryan's grin was one of pure masculine pleasure. "I think I'd like that, babe. Mmm. I think I'd like that very much."

Twenty

CARLY'S RELIEF WAS IMMEASURABLE NOW THAT Ryan knew everything. She spent hours talking of her life after Matthew's death, those four years that she had previously avoided, and Ryan wanted to hear it all. Regarding the trial, they discussed what had been and what might yet be. She was able to share her fears and was all the more relaxed for it. More than once she told him so. On each occasion, Ryan simply gave her that smug "I told you so" smile and hugged her tightly. They grew closer by the day.

Sheila continued to cover Carly, making sure she was never alone, but, as the weeks passed, given Ryan's full awareness of the situation, there was less and less need. Ryan timed himself to drop Carly at school on his way to work, and though Sheila always picked her up afterward and saw her safely home, often coming in for a drink, Ryan was with her the rest of the time.

It was a late February day, cold but mercifully dry, when Carly mentioned her to Ryan. They were running along the river path, keeping a rapid pace to ward off the chill.

"I'm worried about Sheila."

"What about?"

"She seems tense."

"More so than usual?" he quipped with a smirk. Strangely, Ryan had come to share Sam's view of Sheila. He sensed the intensity in her and couldn't quite shake the feeling that, while controlled on the outside, she sizzled inside.

"Mmm. I thought things were going well between Tom and her."

"They are. As far as I know. They see each other often enough."

Sheila had told her that. But there were a lot of things Sheila hadn't told her. "Do you think they're sleeping together?"

Ryan slanted her a look of amusement. "That's none of your business."

"You're right," she countered, undaunted. "But what do you think? When we were in Chicago, she used to drop little hints. It sounded like she slept with every guy she dated. But something's different with Tom. She's quieter."

"Maybe she really likes him."

"He seems to like her." They'd been out as a foursome more than once. The attraction between Sheila and Tom was highly visible.

"He does. I know Tom. Funny, though, he doesn't talk about her much to me either. Like he's saving her for himself."

They ran on a bit before Carly spoke again. "Then that can't be what's bothering her. I wonder if she's bored with her work."

"She likes being assigned to you."

"I haven't needed her much lately. I think she's offended."

"Nah. Sheila's beyond that. Besides, Sam has her on other things. It's not like she's sitting around waiting for you to call."

"I wonder, though. When I see her, she's so full of questions. She wants to know *everything*. As if she's starved for conversation. It's weird."

"Maybe that's just her. Haven't you always said that?"

"Mmm," she agreed, "but still. . . ."

For the few days after that, Carly made a point of trying to coax Sheila to talk more about herself, but in vain. Sheila was as skilled in evasion as she was in handling courtroom security. For each question she had an answer, albeit a flippant or a humorous or a diversionary one, such that it took Carly a while to realize she'd learned nothing at all.

In the end, she decided that Sheila was simply drawing the line between deputy and witness, and in the final analysis Carly was relieved. Her own greatest source of strength and support now was Ryan; Sheila's role in her life was fast fading.

Or so she thought. Early in March Sam learned that the decision on a new trial was imminent. Within hours he received a phone call from Bill Hoffmeister saying that Gary Culbert had sold extensive interests in real-estate ventures in California and Hawaii. Sam promptly instructed Sheila to stick to Carly like glue.

Carly took the news with remarkable calm, but then, in her presence, Sam downplayed the worst of his fears. Her tension emerged during quiet times, when she would find herself chewing on her lip or shredding a napkin in her lap or staring out a window. When Ryan caught her at it, she confessed. Much as she regretted it, her fears had become his. Though she didn't know it, he was in constant touch with Sam.

As a bodyguard, Sheila was as diligent as any of them might have wished. She was always there when Carly was alone, whether at school or at home, but she kept a low profile, waiting to the side, ever watchful. Carly had begun to wonder whether she'd simply grown more sedate when, one afternoon, shades of the old Sheila surfaced.

Classes had just finished. As arranged, Sheila was there to walk Carly back to her office. Tipping her face up to a pale sun, she took a deep breath. "Hey, Carl, it's early yet. Feel like taking a ride?"

The March wind whipped through Carly's hair as they crossed the campus. The air held a promise of mildness conducive to spring fever. "A ride?"

"Into town. It's so nice out. We could drive around the North End and along the waterfront."

"Oh, Sheila, I don't know," Carly waffled, drawing open the door of the administration building. "I have a whole stack of papers to read through for tomorrow. If I get them done now, I won't have to worry about doing them tonight when Ryan's home." More than anything, she enjoyed sitting with Ryan in the evenings. Often he brought work home to do, and then she would relax on the sofa with him, sometimes grading papers, sometimes needlepointing, sometimes just watching him and counting her lucky stars.

But Sheila was at her most persuasive. "It won't take long. My car's never seen Boston in the spring." At Carly's scowl of skepticism, she backtracked. "All right, so it's not quite spring yet. But at least the roads are clear and dry for a change. And the air is fresh. And I do have a quick errand to do. Besides, we've been stuffed up here all day. We could use a break."

Carly laughed. "In case you haven't noticed, I work here. I don't feel 'stuffed up.' I like it."

"Well, I don't," Sheila announced, then softened. "Humor me, Carly? You haven't got any appointments. Let's take off—just for an hour?"

"Really antsy?" Carly teased.

"Yeah."

With a wistful glance at the papers piled high on her desk, Carly relented. "Okay. But just for an hour."

"No more," Sheila vowed, as she grabbed her coat and bag, then Carly's arm, and led her at a clip toward the car.

Moments later they were on Memorial Drive, headed toward Boston. "This is nice," Carly said, breathing the air off the ocean through her open window. "Ryan says it'll get cold again."

"Ryan's a killjoy."

"He's lived here a lot longer than we have." She sighed. "At least the worst of it's behind us."

Sheila nodded and sent her a guarded glance before taking the Massachusetts Avenue bridge to the other side of the river. Then they hooked onto Commonwealth Avenue and followed it in.

"I love this street," Sheila said. "So pretty with grass and trees in the middle. I can't wait till everything blooms in another couple of months. And look there." She pointed to the four- and five-story buildings they passed. "I bet one of those town houses is more impressive than the next. You know—high ceilings, elaborate wood moldings, beautiful oak floors, a fireplace in every room." Her eyes grew momentarily distant. "Someday. . . ."

Carly's own dreams centered around one spiral staircase. She smiled. "You'll have it someday, Sheila. Just wait and see. You'll have it."

Sheila snapped. "If one more person tells me to wait. . . ." When Carly looked at her in surprise, she grinned instantly. "Good things come to those who wait," she said, but in a mocking tone this time. "I'm waiting, I'm waiting." Moments later, she pulled to the side of the road. "Now it's your turn. See that bakery just around the corner? I'm going to run in and get some pastry for tonight."

"You're seeing Tom?"

"Umm. This place has strawberry cream tarts like you've never tasted in your life. Stay put. I'll keep an eye on you through the window. I won't be long." Before Carly could utter a word, she was gone, returning less than five minutes later with two small boxes.

"For you," she said, handing one to Carly.

Touched, Carly eyed her in bewilderment. "What's this for?"

"Dessert. And for putting up with my whims to take afternoon drives."

Carly smiled. "Your whims aren't all that bad. You were right. The break feels good."

"See? What did I tell ya?" Sheila started the car, tossed a quick glance over her shoulder, and pulled out. The shiny Mazda sped along Arlington Street, around the Public Garden, down Charles Street and up Beacon before veering off onto streets new to Carly.

"How do you find your way around here?" she asked.

"This is my home turf. I walk these streets all the time." As if to prove it, she made a sharp left, then a sharp right, then several more turns in succession. Before Carly knew what had happened, Sheila had maneuvered through the Government Center traffic and into the North End. There she drove more slowly, the better for them to appreciate the flavor of Italy in the clusters of small shops and homes fronting the narrow streets.

"Flavorful," Carly observed, eyes warm in survey of the vibrant window displays. "It's supposed to be great in the summer when the festivals start." They passed a bakery whose tempting aroma seeped into the car.

"You didn't see it last year?"

"Had no one to go with. Maybe this year with Ryan. . . ." Her voice trailed off, her thoughts daring to advance that far.

Sheila drove through to Commercial Street and on along the waterfront. "Speaking of Ryan, where's his office? Isn't it somewhere nearby? I've never seen it."

Carly looked from one street sign to the other. "Uh, State Street? I think—you make a right here."

Sheila followed while Carly directed haltingly. By a miracle Carly couldn't explain, given the fact that they approached from a direction totally new to her, they arrived at the new high rise that housed, among others, Ryan's firm. Pulling over to the curb, Sheila bent her head low to admire the structure.

"Nice place," she drawled. "How high up is he?"

Carly's gaze joined hers in scaling the earthen-hued walls. "Thirty-fourth floor. He has a gorgeous view. Hey, want to go inside? Ryan would love to—"

"Oh, no. We shouldn't disturb him."

"I'm sure he wouldn't mind." She grinned, eyes glued to the upper stories of the building. "Besides, I feel like a jimmy fanatic in an ice-cream parlor. I'm drooling at the thought that he's so close—"

Sheila's low whisper cut her off. "Oh, hell."

With a frown, Carly focused on the woman in the driver's seat. "What is it?"

When Sheila said nothing but simply stared toward the building's huge bank of doors, Carly shifted her gaze. It took her but a minute to see what Sheila saw. She stiffened instantly, her voice as tight a whisper as Sheila's had been. "My God. . . ."

"Do you recognize him?"

"Yes!"

"Then it's not me?"

"Oh, no," Carly wailed softly, raising a trembling hand to her mouth. "He's there. He used to lounge like that at the back of the courtroom. When I was testifying, I'd look back. There was always something sinister about him." Then, suddenly hit by the import of that single man's presence against the ocher stone of Ryan's building, she caught her breath. "Sheila?" she managed to gasp at last.

Sheila already had the car in motion. "You bet. We're getting out of here."

"But Ryan! Someone has to warn Ryan!"

"Once we've gone a little way, I'll call Sam."

"What if he's done something to Ryan? He was standing there so idly. Maybe he's done something already! Maybe Ryan's hurt!" She grabbed Sheila's arm. "We have to go back."

"No," Sheila said calmly. "Not back. We go ahead. Trust me."

Her tone held a ring of authority that Carly couldn't ignore. For the first time since they'd been together in Chicago, Sheila was in charge.

Slumping in her seat, Carly stared blindly at the floor. "How could he have known?" she whispered. "Everyone assured me my cover was tight. But he broke it. *How?*"

"Let's not worry about that yet. The most important thing is to get you away and let Sam pick him up."

"Who is he?" Carly asked, her voice high-pitched, directed more to herself than to Sheila. "The courtroom was always so crowded, but there were those people who stood out. Culbert's family glared. The press, too, though I knew most of the reporters. There was a little old lady in the back row, a kid who looked like a college student on the far right, two gray-haired men in the center . . . and him. *Who is he?*"

"Beats me," Sheila answered tersely. Pulling over to the curb by a pay phone on Cambridge Street, she grabbed for her purse. Carly knew there was a gun inside. "Wait here. I'll call Sam."

Clutching the door handle for dear life, Carly sat ramrod straight, looking out at the people who passed. She imagined the man at Ryan's building having communicated by walkie-talkie with someone who was even now on their trail. Glancing in the side mirror, she was horrified to see two young men eyeing the car. She held her breath when they passed, still admiring the sleek lines of the hood.

Then Sheila opened the door and slid in. "Okay. Sam's on his way to Ryan's office."

"What does he want us to do?"

Gunning the engine, Sheila pulled away from the curb. "We're taking off. You're going to be stashed away for a little while, at least until we find out who that man is and why he was there outside Ryan's building."

"And Ryan?"

"After Sam makes sure he's all right, he'll join us."

"Where?" She pictured the small house on the shore of Lake Michigan where she'd been squirreled away for four months. It had been quaint and cozy, as so-called safe houses went.

"Sam suggested a certain place in Vermont?"

"In Vermont! The inn?"

"Where you stayed over New Year's. You said you

loved the place. Sam thought you'd be comfortable there."

Carly grimaced. "Slightly different circumstances. I hate to taint it with this."

"Everything will be all right," Sheila soothed again. "Once Ryan's there with you, it'll be New Year's Eve revisited."

Carly doubted that. "But we can't just show up there."

"Sam's calling to make the arrangements. They'll have something. And if they don't, they'll make something."

Carly closed her eyes. "I can't believe this is happening. After so many false alarms, I really thought I was home free." She raised a hand to her forehead, only to snap her eyes open on a new thought. "I have to stop at home. I'll need some things."

Sheila took her eyes from the road long enough to glance at her watch. "Uh, I don't know. . . ."

"If I have to be holed up somewhere, at least I can feel like a human being. How long will we be staying in Vermont?"

"Not long."

"But you can't be sure. If Sam can't find that guy, it may be a while longer. The apartment's right on the way. It'll only take a minute." It seemed imperative that she stop. She needed the boost of a familiar place.

"What if someone's there?"

"Someone?"

"As in dark and dangerous?"

Carly sucked in a breath and shook her head to deny the thought. "Oh, God," she murmured, shaking. Pressing a fist to her mouth, she chewed on it. Her words were muffled. "I can't believe this is happening."

On Memorial Drive now, Sheila halted at a traffic

light. One look Carly's way told her of the woman's distress. As she watched, Carly grabbed the door handle and looked around as though contemplating escape. It was then that Sheila yielded. Anything to keep Carly from getting hysterical.

"I suppose we can stop at your apartment. If we stick close together, there won't be any problem. Sam may have already sent someone by the place. But we can't stay long. Just long enough for you to stick a couple of things into a bag."

Carly nodded, feeling numb. "What about you?"

"Me?"

"Your things. You're coming to Vermont with me, aren't you?"

She dismissed the problem with a wave of her hand. "I'll be all right. If we have to stay there for any length of time, Sam will have someone pick up my things. Come to think of it, that's what he could do for you. We really shouldn't stop—"

"I *have* to." Carly needed things of her own. What with everything she'd given up—and rebuilt—in the past year, she wasn't about to go anywhere without some familiar trappings of her identity.

Sheila concentrated on driving. When they arrived at Carly's building, Carly jumped out and ran ahead. She didn't think of the possible peril; one part of her actually wanted to be a decoy to draw danger away from Ryan.

The apartment was undisturbed, as neat as she'd left it that morning. While Sheila scouted around for anything suspicious, Carly stood in the middle of the living room trying to calm herself, to think clearly.

"Why can't we just stay here?" she asked when Sheila joined her.

"Because Sam says no."

"Then I'll call him," she suggested, starting for the phone.

But Sheila beat her to it, holding the receiver firmly in place. "Be sensible, Carly. Sam has his hands full trying to get that man."

"Let me call Ryan—"

"And tip someone off that you're here? If your cover's been blown, this line might be tapped."

"I don't want to go to Vermont."

"You have to. And the longer we spend here, the greater the danger will be." It took every resource Sheila had to project a semblance of composure. She was as nervous as Carly. "Now, go put some things in a bag. But be quick. We have to move." She watched Carly move slowly off. "Quick!" She glanced at her watch, then back at the retreating figure. Needing a shot of strength, she quickly poured herself a drink, downed it in record time, and was by the door when Carly emerged from the bedroom. "All set?"

"I don't want to do this." Dropping the bag on a chair, she wandered to the wall unit and lifted the clay plaque from its hook. "Ryan bought this for me in Vermont. It's always held special meaning." Hugging the plaque, she turned, eyes filled with anguish. "I can't believe all this is in danger."

"Not if we hurry. Let's go." Crossing the room, Sheila grabbed Carly's bag.

If Carly heard the impatience in her voice, she was too lost in emotion to heed it. She turned around again. "We picked up the driftwood in Rockport. The picture was done at the—"

"Carly! We're wasting time!" She forced a softness into her tone and spoke more slowly. "We have to leave. Now." She took Carly's elbow.

Understanding Sheila's plight and knowing that her

urgings were for the best, Carly didn't resist. She slid the plaque to the cushion of the chair as she passed and gave a final glance around the place she truly felt was home, before turning her back and leaving with Sheila.

Arriving home shortly after six, Ryan took the steps at a quickened pace. He was uneasy. As he'd walked from his car and glanced up, he hadn't seen any lights. True, it was barely dark outside, still. . . .

His key turned easily in the lock. He pushed the door open. "Carly?" He flipped on the light. "Carly?"

There was no answer.

He searched the apartment. She wasn't there. He tried to think of where she might be. She hadn't said anything to him about having late appointments or meetings, and she was always careful to let him know, especially now that she knew he would panic at any misunderstanding.

For a minute he wondered if he was simply uneasy about the strange meeting he'd had that afternoon. A potential client. An arsonist. Of course, given Carly's experiences and the emotions that now were his, he wouldn't accept the case. But somehow he sensed that his visitor had expected that all along. And it wasn't the arsonist himself who lingered in his mind as much as the man who had brought him in. Something about the way he talked. . . .

Lifting the phone, he dialed Sam's number. When the phone rang for an inordinately long time, he feared Sam had left. Then a man answered breathlessly.

"Is Sam Loomis there?"

"I think he just left. This is Greg Reilly, his assistant."

"I have to talk to him. It's Ryan Cornell."

Greg was instantly alert. "Hold on," he said. "Let me see if I can catch him."

Ryan held on for what seemed forever. Finally Sam came on the line. "Ryan. Any problem?"

"I don't know. I just walked in and Carly's not here. She's usually so good about telling me if she's going to be late. Do you know if she's with Sheila?"

Sam muffled the phone against his chest as he spoke to Greg. "Do you know where Sheila is?"

Greg shrugged. "With Carly, I assume. Or she may be done for the day."

"Try her number," Sam ordered, then returned to Ryan. "Greg's trying Sheila. Hold on."

There was no answer at Sheila's. Greg shook his head and put down his receiver.

"Sheila's not answering either," Sam told Ryan. "Maybe the two of them went somewhere?"

"It's not like Carly. She's almost always here to meet me. Besides, I had a weird meeting this afternoon."

"What meeting—wait. Let me come over. In the meantime you call the school and anyone else who might know where she is."

Ryan's hand was tense on the phone. "Bring your key. If the switchboard at Rand is closed I may drive over there. If I'm not here, let yourself in. I'll be back."

The switchboard was indeed closed. He called Bryna Moore, who hadn't seen Carly since that morning. He called Dennis Sharpe, who hadn't seen her since lunch. He paced the floor, wondering if he was making something out of nothing. Throat parched, he went to the kitchen for a glass of water, then was reaching for his car keys when the phone rang.

"Ryan? This is Sheila."

"Sheila! I've been worried. Is Carly with you?"

"No. That's why I'm calling. I went to pick her up at

school and she wasn't there. She left a note saying that she had to get away. I've been driving around trying to spot her car, but I don't know where to look."

"Oh, my God." At least there was a note. But why would she have to get away? "Christ, Sheila. Where have you looked?"

"I've been all over the school and in and out of Boston. She talked about Rockport, but I've been driving around here for an hour and I don't see any sign of her."

"You're in Rockport now?"

"I'm at a pay phone on the highway. I'm wondering, she talked so much about that place in Vermont. Do you think she might have gone there?"

"Maybe. I'll call there. I can't believe she'd take off. . . ."

There was a click. "My three minutes are up. Listen, I'll keep looking. I'm sure nothing's wrong. The tension may have just gotten to her. She may be mortified if you follow her."

"Damn it, I don't care." The phone clicked again. "Okay, Sheila. Call back if you hear anything." At least Sam would be there.

But Sheila didn't know that. She diligently wiped the smug expression from her face before she returned to the car where Carly waited.

"Ryan's on his way," she announced. "And Sam has an APB out for that fellow we saw."

"Then Ryan's all right?" Carly asked, needing that one bit of reassurance to counter her fears.

"Fine. He'll meet us at the inn."

Five minutes later, they crossed the border into Vermont.

* * *

Sam arrived at Carly's apartment to find it deserted. He and Greg waited five minutes, ten, fifteen. When Ryan didn't reappear, Sam called Tom.

"You haven't by chance seen Sheila Montgomery, have you?" he asked with more nonchalance than he felt.

"Sheila?" Tom echoed cautiously. "No. She said she had to work tonight."

Sam darted a glance at Greg, who had checked the assignment schedule just before they left the office. Sheila was not working. "Then Ryan?"

"Is something wrong?"

"I don't know. Ryan called me a little while ago saying that Carly hadn't come home. I'm at their place now. And Ryan's nowhere either."

Ryan, Carly, and Sheila. Three people who meant a lot to Tom. "I'm coming over," he said, promptly hung up the phone and was on his way.

Neither Sam nor Greg had learned anything more by the time he arrived. Ryan still hadn't shown.

"Okay," Sam said, walking slowly around the living room as he tried to organize his thoughts. "Ryan said that Carly hadn't come home. He thought she might be with Sheila. But she's not. And we can't locate Sheila either." He faced Tom. "You two didn't have plans?"

"For tomorrow. Not tonight."

Sam turned to Greg. "When was the last time you saw her?"

Abundantly aware of Tom, Greg was uncomfortable. "Uh, this morning. She stopped in at the office before meeting Carly at Rand." With fresh sweet rolls and coffee, no less. Sheila had been at her most enchanting.

"And she was to have stuck around there until Carly was done for the day," Sam said, stroking his jaw, deep in thought. "Damn it, I had a feeling. . . ."

"What feeling?" Tom asked, suddenly aware that there was more to Sam's concern for Sheila than might have appeared at first.

But Sam only shook his head. "And Carly. Where in the hell could she be?" He paused, trying to recall every word Ryan had said. "He said something about a meeting this afternoon. 'Weird' was the word he used. Know anything about it, Tom?"

"Hell, no. I don't keep track of Ryan's clients."

Sam turned to Greg. "See if you can get someone in his office. Find out who that meeting was with."

As Greg headed for the kitchen, Tom lifted the small clay plaque and sank into the chair, studying the piece. "This is crazy. Carly wouldn't up and run off. She and Ryan were closer than ever since he returned from Chicago."

"Then you know everything?"

"They both told me. I thought they had things straightened out. Even if Carly was terrified by something, she would have gone to Ryan first." He rubbed a small stone on the plaque, then stood and, as though he'd done it any number of times, returned the piece to its hook on the wall. "They bought this when they were in Vermont. They're collectors." He gestured toward the shelf. "Mementos of their life together." He eyed Sam. "This whole thing is weird. Do you think someone got to Carly?"

Before he could answer, Greg returned, the page of his small notebook filled with jottings. "Ryan had a whole *afternoon* of meetings. Smythe and Reading at twelve-thirty, Frazier at one-fifteen, Dunn at two, Walsh and Thiess at two-thirty—"

"Walsh and Thiess?"

Greg checked his notes. "The guy who gave me this

stuff said that the last was scribbled in. The names may be off. A last-minute thing, I guess."

"Thiess," Sam repeated, reaching for something he couldn't quite grasp. "That name sounds famil— uh-oh. . . ."

Tom was on his feet in an instant. "What is it?"

But Sam held up a hand and took his turn at the phone. When he returned, his expression was grim. "That was Meade in Chicago. Thiess is an alias used by a guy named Theakos. Horace Theakos. He's served time more than once. A reputed arson expert."

"Geeeeez," Tom breathed, running a hand through his blond hair, disheveling it all the more. "What does that mean?"

"That means that either your brother is on the take—"

"No way! He wouldn't harm Carly for the world."

"And he did call that meeting weird," Sam said, then raised his eyes and spoke with deadly gravity. "I think he's being set up. He may be in as much danger as Carly." On his way back to the kitchen, he shot a glance at Greg. "I'm calling out the troops."

He made one call, then a second and a third. Tom and Greg stared at one another. Finally Tom spoke.

"Where does Sheila fit into all this?"

Greg shrugged and avoided his gaze. "Beats me. She may just be shopping somewhere. Likes to buy new things lately. . . ." His voice trailed off, his thoughts taking a twist. The eyes he raised to Tom were more wary. "She does like to buy things. Where's she getting the money?"

"*I'm* not bankrolling her." Not that he wouldn't, given the chance.

"So where does she get it?"

"She saves," Tom replied defensively.

"On an agent's salary? I know what *I* make and there's precious little left over after taxes and the rent and food and gas. That new car of hers. . . ."

Tom's features were rigid. "What are you getting at?"

"She's come into a hell of a lot of money all of a sudden."

"Now wait a minute. You're suggesting—"

"That *she* was the one who was bought off."

"That's a goddamn lousy accusation."

The two men stood eye to eye. Fully understanding the enormity of his accusation—and its ramifications, should it prove true—Greg didn't flinch. "But it'd explain a lot. New car, new clothes, new bag, lofty dreams, but a dump of an apartment."

"Her apartment? You've seen her apartment?"

"Many times." His gaze narrowed, and though he knew he was inflicting pain, he needed to speak. "It'd also explain why she came on to me the way she did. A bosom buddy in the office—"

"Came on to you?" Tom clenched his fists by his sides. "What are you talking about?"

For the first time, Greg's tone softened. "She seduced me, Tom. While she wanted you. And if you think *you're* hurt, think of how I felt when she cried out your name when we made love."

"You're crazy!" Tom exploded. "Sheila's no easy lay. Hell, she's in love with me and still she—"

"Wouldn't go to bed with you?" Greg paused, finding no satisfaction in the other's stunned silence. "She didn't, did she?" The answer that never came was answer enough. "Then she did have some sense of morals, at least. If she knew what she was planning, and that she was trading her body for my loyalty, that's something. And loving you—which I'm sure she does—and feeling guilt—"

"What's going on here?" Sam growled, walking a tight wire himself.

Dragging his gaze from Tom's, Greg sighed. "I think we have a problem."

"What problem?" Sam asked, only to have the phone ring before Greg could answer. Retracing his steps on the run, Sam picked it up.

"Yes," he barked.

It was Ryan, sounding nearly desperate. "Thank God you're off the phone. This is the third time—"

"I know. I have everything working. Where in the hell are you?"

"I'm on the highway. Eighty-nine. Carly's in Vermont."

Sam's gaze flew to the far living-room wall and the plaque Tom had replaced. "Vermont? What's she doing there? What are *you* doing there?"

"Lord, Sam, I think it's bad. Right after I spoke with you, I got a call from Sheila."

"Sheila! Where is she?"

"She said she was calling from a pay phone near Rockport. She said that Carly hadn't been there when she'd arrived at school to pick her up. It didn't occur to me then that Sheila was supposed to be there all day. She said that Carly left a note for her saying that she needed to get away. She said she hadn't seen her and that she'd been looking all over, going to the places Carly had mentioned she and I had been. Vermont— you know, that cottage we rented at New Year's— seemed the obvious place. Sheila suggested it herself." He took a breath and raced on. "But I've been driving along and little things keep coming to me. That meeting I had this afternoon. A rush job. Two fellows, one of whom is accused of arson. But neither of them seemed particularly committed to retaining me. And one of them—not the one in trouble, but a guy with him—talked this funny way. Instead of 'didn't' he said 'din't.' I couldn't figure out why it bothered me—until I remembered Carly telling me about that guy who tried to kill her in that alley back in Chicago. I told myself that maybe it was a coincidence. But there's something else."

"What?"

Greg and Tom had come to stand in the kitchen, but Sam's every sense focused on what Ryan was saying.

"Right before I left I took a drink of water. I put the glass in the sink. It didn't occur to me till a couple of minutes ago that there was another glass there. One with the remains of a dark liquid in the bottom. Carly is meticulous. She'd never walk out in the morning leaving anything in the sink. And Sheila claimed she hadn't seen her." He paused, almost afraid to ask. "Check it, Sam. What's in that glass?"

Sam had already turned and was lifting the glass. He sniffed, then tipped it to his mouth to taste its tepid contents. "Rum and Coke." His eye caught Greg's, then Tom's as, with quiet urgency, he addressed Ryan. "How far are you from that inn?"

"About forty minutes." He'd been pushing seventy most of the way, praying the police wouldn't stop him.

"Okay. Keep going. I'll make some more calls, then move. Greg and Tom are with me. We'll take a helicopter. It shouldn't take long."

"For God's sake, hurry!" Ryan begged, then slammed down the phone and, leaving the phone-booth door rattling in his wake, bolted for his car.

"I still can't believe this is happening," Carly said, dazed as the lights of the inn appeared at the end of the drive.

Sheila said nothing, simply steered down the dark side road, heading straight for the small cottage that held such beautiful memories for Carly.

"Don't we need a key?" Reminders of that other trip. Then the key had been hooked behind the swing.

"I told Sam what you'd said about last time. He was going to instruct the inn to leave it in the same place. The fewer people who see you, the better."

But as the dim cottage light came into sight, Carly forgot to ask how Sam had ever thought to get the same one. "That's . . . my car. . . ." she stammered, perplexed. The yellow Chevette stood out in the night, a beacon of its own. "What. . . ."

Sheila pulled to an abrupt halt in front of the door. Without a word, she reached for her bag.

"Sheila, what's going on?"

It was only after she'd spoken that, in a haze of horror, she caught the glint of the small service revolver that emerged from the bag.

"Come on," Sheila grated. "Let's go see who's there."

"Someone stole my car!" Carly sucked in a breath. "That man, the one from Chicago, the one we saw before. He knows about Ryan. He knows about *me*. *He* must have!" She grabbed the other woman's arm. "Oh, no, Sheila! We can't go in! He'll be waiting! But how did he get my car?" she murmured half to herself, withdrawing her hand, raising it to her forehead.

Sheila spoke calmly and clearly. "I gave him the keys."

"You?"

Slowly and with deliberation, the gun turned on her.

Sheila's face was shrouded in darkness, her characteristically nasal voice nearly unrecognizable for its sudden venom. "Get out. Now. And don't try anything or I'll use this."

"I don't understand. . . ."

The sharp poke to her ribs made the first point, Sheila's grating tone the next. "You will. Now get out."

By the time Carly had managed to force her wobbly legs into action, Sheila was by her side of the car, clamping a firm hand on her arm, hauling her forward.

The door of the cottage opened and Carly instinctively drew back. There, silhouetted but unmistakable, was the same man who hours earlier had been at Ryan's building.

"Took you long enough," he growled.

"She wanted to stop by her place for some things," Sheila explained with a snort. "As if she'll need them. . . ." Pressing the gun to Carly's ribs, she pushed her on. The man stood aside, then closed the door firmly when the women were inside.

"That was dumb, stopping," he snarled.

Sheila's retort was cold. "She was getting hysterical. I had to do something."

"Wasted good time."

"We're all right."

"What's going on, Sheila?" Carly cried, unwilling to believe that Sheila, *Sheila,* had betrayed her.

It was the man who spoke. "Nothing that should not have happened a long time ago. You caused me a load of trouble."

"Who are you?" Carly whispered fearfully, eyeing the man whose ominous advance brought him directly before her. It was all she could do not to cower.

"Name's Ham Theakos," he announced with a kind of perverted pride. "Don' remember me?"

"From the courtroom—"

"From the alley."

If Carly had had any hopes for salvation, they were

dashed with his curt statement. "You?" she breathed, stunned.

His smile was ugly. "Me. You got away from me then. Won't happen now."

Carly looked wide-eyed from his harsh features to Sheila's. "This has to be a joke."

"No joke," Sheila stated bluntly.

"But *why*? What have I ever done—"

"You opened your mouth when you should not have," Theakos grated. "You stuck your nose in where it din't belong."

But Carly's eyes were glued to Sheila's. "*Why*, Sheila? You were supposed to be protecting me."

"I'm always protecting someone. This time I'm protecting myself."

"But we were friends."

"Hah! We were only friends because back in Chicago you had no one else. In other circumstances, you wouldn't have looked at me twice. But we were stuck in that house together, day after day, week after week, and it was only natural. *Real* friends? Never."

Shock raised Carly's voice an octave. "Then you had this in mind *from the start*? You *asked* for that transfer just so that—"

"Not exactly," Sheila interrupted, chin tipped up defensively. "Actually, it was much the way I told you. I was bored in Chicago. Nothing was working out there. I decided I needed a change and Boston seemed as good a place to go as any."

Try as she might to understand it, Carly couldn't. "Then you made this little deal—" she dared a glance at Theakos "—after you got here?"

"Remember when I went back to Chicago?" Sheila asked smugly.

"You went *looking* to do me harm?"

"Welllllll, that's pushing it a little. While I was there, seeing Harmon and visiting old friends at Hoffmeister's office, Ham, here, was snooping around looking for an in."

"And you gave it to him," Carly stated, crushed beyond belief.

"Why not? The price was right and there was cash up front. I'd had a good look at the way you were living. Pretty clothes. Fancy home. Super guy. You had everything. Now it's my turn."

"At my expense?"

"The way I see it," Sheila went on baldly, "we all have to compromise a little in life." Her eyes hardened. "I've done my share of compromising. Now I want a little of that luxury I've been looking at from the wrong side of the fence all my life."

"This isn't the way," Carly whispered, even as she sensed that Sheila was past remorse. "And what about Tom—"

Sheila stiffened. "What about him?" She didn't want his name brought into his. It had no bearing.

"He loves you."

"I love him."

"And you think that he'll really be able to live with you after this?" She couldn't suppress a shudder. Where she found the strength to think clearly, she didn't know. But something drove her on, perhaps the need for a temporary diversion from her very real terror.

"He'll never know."

"Do you believe that? Ryan won't take anything happening to me sitting down. Neither will Sam." A new thought bloomed. "That call you made—"

"Was never made. Not to Sam, at least."

Carly glanced again at Theakos. "Then you knew he'd be at Ryan's office."

"I called Ham from the bakery. He was waiting for my call at a phone booth near Ryan's building. He'd just come from a meeting with Ryan."

"With Ryan?"

The smile Sheila gave her then was enough to freeze her blood. "It's all pretty brilliant, if I do say so myself. Took a lot of planning, especially when you began to clam up on me after Ryan returned from Chicago." She cast a conspiratorial glance at Theakos. "But I think we covered everything. Ryan will be under suspicion simply for having met with Ham and his buddy. You will have been overcome at the thought that he might have been planning to betray you. It'd be perfectly natural that you'd commit suicide."

"Commit suicide? I'd never commit suicide!"

"Maybe not on your own," Sheila purred, "but with a little push and no one around to say differently, which reminds me." She turned to Theakos. "We'd better get moving. I called Ryan. He should get here just in time to find her hanging. He'll be the one to call the police. The distraught lover."

For an instant, Carly was utterly paralyzed. Remembrance of Ryan's Luis—whose death was still listed as a suicide despite Ryan's doubts—flashed through her brain. Sheila was right. They would never know. She had to move.

With a burst of energy born of desperation, she broke for the door, only to have Theakos haul her right off her feet and back. "Not so fast, l'il lady. First we need a note."

Carly struggled wildly against the arms that held her. "Let . . . me . . . go!"

"First the note," he gritted. "Every suicide needs a note."

She kicked back with her legs, but her captor was that much stronger than she was. She'd taken him by surprise in the Chicago alley; this time he was prepared. Her flailing arms hit air. "I'm . . . not writing . . . any. . . ."

He lowered his head until his thin lips were by her ear. "If you don't write it, we'll wait and murder your lover when he arrives. Then it'll look like a double suicide."

The fight left Carly instantly. "You wouldn't," she gasped, looking at Sheila, pleading for any last remnants of sanity. There were none.

"We would. Very easily." Extracting a piece of paper and a pen from the small desk against the wall, Sheila slapped them down flat.

Theakos shoved Carly forward, forcing her onto the hard wood chair. "Write what she tells you."

"This won't work, Sheila," Carly began, only to be stopped, then filled with dread, by Sheila's whimsical look.

"My beloved Ryan," she began to dictate. When Carly stared at her in horror, Ham pressed a gun to her neck.

"Write," he ordered. "If your boyfriend gets here before we're done, he's a goner. You wan' him shot?"

Carly tried to catch her breath. When Sheila rapped a long fingernail against the stationary, she tried to focus, but her eyes were flooded with tears. Shaking, she lifted the pen.

"My beloved Ryan," Sheila repeated, then waited until the words were written. "I never thought it would come to this. But I know what you're planning—"

When Carly dropped the pen, Theakos prodded her

again with the gun. Mustering shreds of strength, she retrieved the pen and wrote falteringly.

"I know what you're planning," Sheila continued, speaking slowly, pausing for Carly to catch up, "and I can't bear to live. I've never loved another human being as I love you."

"Sheila—" Carly sobbed.

"Write!" There was not the slightest hint of feeling in Sheila's voice. "I've never loved another human being as I love you. I'm so sorry. For both of us." She paused. "Just sign it, Carly."

The script was indistinguishable at points and blurred where Carly's tears had fallen. When she was done writing, Sheila lifted the paper and read it over.

"Not bad. Even those smudges. Shows how upset she was. Perfect."

Theakos snaked his hand into the drawer, heedless of Carly's recoiling when his arm grazed her breast, and drew out an envelope. "Put it in," he commanded. When, fumbling badly, Carly finally managed that, he directed her to put Ryan's name on the envelope. Then, propping the note in a visible spot on the desk, he grabbed her arm and pulled her from the chair. "Let's get on with it," he growled. "I got a plane to catch."

Twenty-one

bEFORE CARLY COULD UTTER THE SMALLEST cry, she was gagged with one of the scarves Theakos had pulled from his pocket. She jerked in pain when the knot caught her hair but Theakos only tugged it tighter. When her tongue fought against the stifling intrusion, her mouth went dry. She felt as though she was suffocating. Nausea welled up from the pit of her stomach. She swallowed convulsively, breathing fast and hard through her nose.

Driven by primal instinct, she struggled against the arms that pinned hers back, against a second scarf being bound around her wrists. She twisted and turned against Sheila, who tried to hold her still.

"Better hurry," Sheila managed to grunt. "She'll fight us all the way."

Theakos's answer was a snarl. "I've handled worse."

They were the words of a coldhearted killer. In that instant of stark realization Carly panicked. She whirled around. She reared back. Then she bucked against Sheila, toppling them both to the floor, but Theakos grabbed her before she could do more than roll to her knees. When she tried to pull away, he shook her hard.

"Goddammit!" Sheila yelled and raised a hand to hit her, only to be stopped by Theakos's meaty grip.

"No marks," he growled, glaring at Sheila as though she were a dimwit. "Can' be any outward sign of a fight. Why d'ya think I'm usin' scarves?"

Sheila scrambled to her feet. "I thought you liked the color," she grumbled, brushing herself off.

"Dumb broad." Theakos's quelling look applied the epithet first to Sheila then to a fast-breathing Carly, whom he tugged up.

Carly made frantic sounds, but, muffled by the gag, they remained deep in her throat. A cold sweat bathed her brow. Her body was a mass of tremors. But she continued to thrash against Theakos's hulking form, her legs scissoring and stabbing, landing with no apparent effect.

Theakos tightened his grip. "You tie," he gritted toward Sheila, then squeezed Carly with such sharpness that she grew faint.

Seizing the moment, Sheila quickly retrieved the scarf from the floor and, grasping first one, then the other of Carly's ankles, secured them fast.

Carly regained awareness as she was being carried toward the bedroom. At first she thought she was having another of her nightmares, but the bite of her shackles was too real, as was the bulk and bodily smell of Ham Theakos. She tried to scream, but couldn't. She thought she might vomit, but didn't. She writhed in his grip, thrashing her head from side to side, wearing herself out with her efforts but knowing that it was now or never.

When she hit the bed, she brought her knees up in an attempt to kick out at her captor, but he was too fast.

Sprawling half across her, he pinned her down so that her knees banged uselessly against his back.

"Get the cord," he ordered.

Panting in terror, Carly saw Sheila approach holding a thin nylon cord. She moaned and tried to roll away, eyes bulging, ever pleading. But the cord slipped over her head and, trussed as she was, she was helpless to stop its tightening.

Theakos hauled her up over his shoulder. "Now the chair."

When Sheila disappeared for an instant, Carly rammed her chin against his back. Defying the dizzying rush of blood to her head, she squirmed madly, but Theakos was unfazed.

Sheila returned with the wood chair Carly had sat on moments before.

He tossed his head. "Middle of the room."

She put it there, and Carly was set standing on it, held still by Theakos, who tossed the end of the nylon cord to Sheila.

"Over the rafter," was his gruff command.

Carly could barely breathe. Her gaze dimmed. She didn't want to die. Not now. Not when the future was so bright.

In her daze she was aware of Theakos's grumblings, of his low curse when Sheila repeatedly missed her goal. She wanted to laugh hysterically at the farce of it all. Such a well-planned murder to be thwarted by bad aim.

Then all thought of laughter died, replaced by the most soulful dread Carly had ever known when the cord successfully cleared the rafter and tumbled down the other side. She writhed in hideous desperation, thinking, in vivid flashes, of her parents, her brothers, of Matthew and, mostly, mostly Ryan. Ryan, who was her soulmate. Ryan, whom she loved more than life itself. Ryan, who would now be alone. A low cry of agony burst from her throat, but had nowhere to go. The cord tightened. She whimpered futilely.

Then a loud crash shook the cottage and before Carly could begin to understand, a blur of darkness barreled through from the other room. With the advantage of both speed and surprise, Ryan hurled himself at Theakos, knocking the burly man away from Carly.

Had Carly not been in a state of shock, her legs would have crumbled. But she stood rigid, trembling inside, eyes fixed on Ryan as he grappled with his husky opponent. Only when Sheila made a dive for the bed did she try to cry out, but it was too late.

Grabbing the gun that lay there, Sheila lunged back for Carly just as three uniformed policemen burst into the room.

"Drop it!" one yelled. All held large rifles cocked to fire.

"No, *you* drop it," Sheila cried, dragging Carly stumbling down from the chair with the gun pressed to her head. "Guns down, or she gets it."

All movement in the room ceased. The air was still, thick, the silence broken only by random gasps from Ryan and the man who lay half beneath him.

For an instant it was a standoff. But only for an instant. En route to the cottage, the troopers had been alerted to the identities and skills of Carly's abductors. Each of them knew that she would be dead if any one of them fired. And then there was Ryan who, ignoring their commands to stop, had raced ahead and broken into the cabin. His life, too, was now on the line. Slowly they lowered their rifles.

"Now back out," Sheila ordered, inching forward with Carly as a shield.

Theakos was on his feet, training his own gun on Ryan. Ryan's eyes never left Carly. When the police were in the other room and Sheila was watching each step from the door, she raised her voice. "Get out. And shut that door."

One by one the men left, closing the door behind them. Only then did Sheila release Carly with a shove that sent her toppling to the floor. Ryan was by her side in a flash, tearing at the noose, then the scarves that bound her hands and feet. Together they worked at the gag. When it was free and she could breathe, she collapsed against him, panting loudly, trembling uncontrollably. Face buried against his chest, she could think of nothing but the fact that he was there with her, that she was still alive. His hands moved convulsively, hugging her, then stroking her hair, shifting to rub her back, touching her face. For an instant he forgot the two with their guns. When Theakos spoke, he looked up in abrupt alarm, his arms crushing Carly to him as though he feared she would be taken away again.

But Theakos was looking at Sheila, his face distorted with rage. "You really done it." His gun jabbed the air with each word. "How in hell did the cops get here?"

"How would I know?" Sheila countered breathlessly. "I didn't expect this any more than you did."

"You were the brains," he roared angrily. "You had it all worked out."

"Something goofed."

"No kiddin'." He moved to the lamp and turned it off. The dim spill of light from the living room lent an even more sinister aura to the room. "I ought to shoot *you* and say I was set up too."

Sheila eyed Ryan and Carly. "But they'd know better. Are you going to shoot both of them and say I did it?"

"Not a bad idea."

"But dumb."

"She's right," Ryan said, trying to think clearly even though he felt as though he'd been to hell and back. Well . . . partway back.

"Shut up," Theakos growled, his attention still on Sheila.

But Ryan wasn't about to give up. "There are cops all over the place. You haven't got a chance. Attempted murder is better than murder—"

His words were cut off by the well-aimed kick Theakos sent his way. It caught him in the ribs, knocking him off balance. When Carly winced, Ryan regained his hold of her, pressing his mouth to her ear. "It's okay, babe. It's okay. Everything's going to be all right." But her trembling continued, and it was all he could do to control his fury at the two who had made her this way.

"So, brains," Theakos started in on Sheila again, "got any bright ideas?"

She scowled. "I'm thinking."

Her thought was disrupted by the blare of a bullhorn from outside, its words slow and distinct. *"Theakos and Montgomery. You are surrounded. Drop your weapons and come out with your hands up."*

"No . . . way . . . Jose," Sheila stated slowly and distinctly.

"Come on, Sheila," Ryan coaxed. "You can't win."

She gritted her teeth. "I can and I will. I haven't come this far only to spend the rest of my life in jail." She held up her free hand. "Let me think."

"Do it fast," Theakos grumbled.

"Theakos and Montgomery. You are surrounded. Repeat. You are surrounded. There is no means of escape."

Theakos shifted from one leg to the next. Sheila tapped a finger to her mouth.

"We have hostages," she murmured, thinking her

plan aloud. "We'll have to demand free passage somewhere." Her eyes lit. "Zaire. The United States has no extradition treaty with Zaire. And I've always wanted to see Africa."

Theakos cursed, his beady eyes darkening in disgust. Africa was the last place *he* wanted to see. Though the brunt of his anger was directed at Sheila, who had somehow bungled what should have been a simple murder, his wrath also spread to Gary Culbert, who'd been responsible for all this from the start.

"We'll ask for money," Sheila said. "Five hundred thousand, a plane and a pilot in exchange for two hostages."

Carly pressed closer to Ryan. She couldn't think, could barely comprehend Sheila's words. Her entire being felt numb. She wanted to sleep, to escape it all.

But suddenly Sheila was tugging at her, forcing her from Ryan's arms while Theakos placed his gun by Ryan's head. "Up, Carly," she ordered. "We have some dealing to do."

When Carly clung to Ryan, Sheila lowered her voice to a menacing whisper. "If you'd rather, we can kill you both now."

Carly managed to climb to her feet. She moaned when Sheila twisted one arm up painfully behind her. Ryan's reflex rush forward was halted by Theakos.

"If I have to kill you," he rasped, taking his cue from Sheila's psychological play, "I'll have nothing to lose in killing her too."

Ryan fell back to his seat on the floor. Aching, he watched Sheila nudge Carly forward. When Carly stumbled, Sheila hauled her roughly up. "I don't have to worry about marks, now," she warned, her tone more ruthless than ever. "Watch your step, Carly. If I go, you go."

Making her cautious way into the living room, she switched off the lamp as Theakos had done. The last thing they needed was to be in a fish bowl. As it was, there was plenty of light spilling in from outside, the flicker of red and blue lights heralding what was beyond. Holding Carly carefully before her, Sheila parted the light drapes. Though night reigned, it couldn't hide the line of bumper-to-bumper cruisers that obstructed the narrow drive. Sneering an oath, she tugged Carly to the door, then slowly opened it just far enough to call out.

"We have hostages here. They'll die if you try something."

"You are surrounded," the megaphone replied. *"You haven't got a chance."* Helmeted heads lurked behind every car, rifles pointed, primed and aimed.

"Then neither have they," she yelled back, tightening her hold on Carly, careful to stay covered herself. "If you want them alive, you'll do what I tell you."

"Send them out. Make it easier on yourselves."

Carly flinched when Sheila's shout battered her eardrum. "We want five hundred thousand in cash, free passage to the nearest airport, a plane and a pilot. And we want them by midnight. That gives you a little more than three hours."

Without awaiting a reply, she slammed the door, retraced her steps to the bedroom and threw Carly toward Ryan, who still sat on the floor, his back now braced against the foot of the bed. He caught her easily and enclosed her chilled form in his arms.

Sheila joined Theakos, who stood some distance from the bed, his gun pointed at the couple on the floor. "There," she said. "Now we wait."

"That was stupid, too," Theakos snorted.

"What was?"

"Midnight. Where they gonna get that kind of money at this hour of the night? The banks are closed."

Sheila tossed her head in a gesture of indifference. "Banks can be opened. The right call here or there can do wonders. Don't worry, they'll manage."

"And if they don't?"

"They can beg us for a time extension," she blurted crossly. Then, as though she'd exhausted her store of bravado, she stumbled through the darkness to a nearby easy chair and, for the first time, realized what had happened. Everything had gone wrong. Had things run as planned, Carly would have already been dead, and she'd be on her way back to Boston to fall into Tom's arms in despair at having failed to find Carly.

Tom. It was over. He would never love her now. She would never be free to love *him* now.

She looked over at Ryan to find him studying her closely, and her dismay turned to anger. If she correctly read the somber expression that even the darkness couldn't hide, he pitied her. "Have you got a problem?" she barked.

"Obviously I do," Ryan stated quietly. He rubbed his jaw along Carly's brow, pressed his hand against her head, holding her face to his throat. "I haven't got any five hundred thousand dollars."

She made a face. "Come on. You have a lucrative law practice, an expensive condo, a gorgeous car—"

"But no five hundred thou."

"Then your law firm can dig it up. The rent in that building must be hefty. I'm sure that Miller and Cornell has ample resources."

"The firm wouldn't yield to a ransom demand."

"Then your wife will. She's loaded." She smirked at the last. "I understand she's got a terrific house. That should be worth something."

"She's my *ex*-wife. And her money is hers, as is the house. You won't get anything from her." He paused, calculating. "I guess you'll have to hope Tom can come up with something."

"Tom's got nothing to do with this," she snapped.

"He's my brother. And he should be arriving here shortly."

Sheila blanched. "Here? But I only called you, and you must have left immediately. How would Tom know anything about this?"

"Tom was with Sam."

"With Sam? How would *Sam* know anything about this?"

"Sam was the first one I called when I got home and found that Carly wasn't there. I was already on my way when he and Greg—"

"Greg?" Sheila's eyes were wide with horror. She was oblivious to Theakos's slow simmering nearby.

Goaded by her obvious discomfort, Ryan went calmly on. "He and Greg went to Carly's place. Tom joined them there."

"Sam, Greg *and* Tom?" Sheila asked, then turned her eyes away and murmured, "I never dreamed they'd all get together. I never dreamed you'd go to Sam in the first place!" She looked back angrily. "I thought you distrusted him. That was what Carly said."

Carly tipped her head up to respond, but Ryan held her quiet. "She didn't tell you everything."

"I'll say," Sheila grumbled, eyeing Carly with an irrational hatred. When she raised her gun, Theakos uncoiled to stop her.

"Kill her now, and they'll be all over us in no time. Wait. You gave 'em a deadline. Just wait."

Sheila's lips gave an ugly twist. "She ruined everything. Don't you see? She ruined everything!"

"Not her," Ryan injected. "You. You weren't quite smart enough, Sheila. That's all there is to it."

Sheila leaped to her feet. "You . . . shut . . . up," she gritted, holding the gun, now aimed at Ryan, with both hands.

He was undaunted. "You know, Sheila. Some day, when Carly and I are happily married, I might be able to forgive you for what you've done to her." His voice grew sharper. "Tom's something. else. You might as well aim that gun at *him* and pull the trigger. He loved you."

Nearing his limit, Theakos threw his hands in the air. "Goddammit, I'm sick of hearin' that. Who in the hell cares if he loved her or if she loved him. You—" he pointed a finger at Ryan "—screwed that up by bustin' in here." The finger moved toward Sheila, though the eyes stayed on Ryan. "She can't go back. Whoever he is, the guy's history for her." Finally, Theakos shifted his narrow gaze to Sheila. "If you know what's good for you, you'll sit down and shut up yourself. He's trying to get you ruffled, or din't that occur to you?"

It hadn't. She'd been too busy trying to sort things out, trying to absorb what was happening. Suitably chastised, she slumped back into her chair and stared glumly at the couple by the foot of the bed. It wasn't fair—he in his business suit that was barely wrinkled despite the tussle he'd had with Theakos, she in her skirt and sweater, seeming fragile and all the more feminine for it. And the two of them, in an absurdly tense situation, looking like lovers at ease in a room glowing with vague flickers of red and blue. . . .

"How're ya doin'?" Ryan whispered, tucking Carly more securely in the crook of his shoulder.

She tipped her head back. "Okay." It was the first word she'd said since Ryan had saved her from what had seemed to be certain death. Her whisper was slightly hoarse, her throat was dry. "How did you get here so fast?"

He grinned. "I sped."

"You could have been killed that way."

"Uh-uh," he murmured in the same hushed tones she was using. "My mission was a good one. God watches out for his own."

"Is He still watching? I think we need help."

"It's coming. Have faith."

As though in answer, a faint hum arose outside the cottage. As it neared, it took on a choppy tone.

Crossing to the window, but being sure to stand carefully to the side, Theakos peered out. He saw nothing. But the sound couldn't be mistaken. "Helicopter," he grunted. "Maybe the banker."

It wasn't the banker. Within minutes, the bullhorn blared again. *"Sheila. It's Sam. Come to the door."*

Sheila sat in her chair, nostrils flaring, jaw tense.

"Sheila. Come to the door."

Still she made no move.

"Something can be worked out, Sheila. You've been under stress. We can make a case for leniency."

"Hah," Sheila snorted, talking to no one in particular. "That's a pipe dream if I ever heard one. He's been out to get me since I arrived in Boston. Now he's suddenly on my side?"

"He's right, though," Carly said softly. "There's always a chance—"

"Oh, keep still," Sheila grumbled, and for a while, everyone did.

Ryan held Carly tightly, biding his time. He knew that to make a break for it now would be suicide, for himself and Carly. There were two guns and they were in the wrong hands. All he could do was to put his faith in the troops outside.

"Sheila. It's Tom."

"Oh, God," she said, but her tone was beseeching.

"I have to speak to you."

She clenched her hand in her lap, propping the gun on her knee.

"Sheila. Please."

Had he sounded angry or commanding, she might have resisted him. But even the bullhorn couldn't hide his anguish. And it cut through her as nothing else could.

Bolting from the chair, she reached for Carly's arm.

"Whadya think you're doing?" Theakos demanded in a vicious growl.

"I'm going to talk to him," she replied shakily, as she pulled Carly up and headed for the living room.

Nudging Ryan up, Theakos quickly followed. "Don' do it. It's dumb."

"I have to."

"It's a trap."

They were in the living room now, with Sheila fast approaching the front door. "Tom wouldn't hurt me," she half-whispered, unable to think clearly.

Holding the gun to Ryan's back and pushing him forward, Theakos caught up. "You're crazy if you think that. He's lost you and he knows it. Hell, it was his brother's girl you were gonna kill."

"Sheila. I have to talk to you."

"And I have to talk to you," she whispered, barely aware that Theakos had taken up position at the side window. With Carly as her plate of armor, she inched the door open. "Tom?" Her voice quavered on the single name.

"I'm coming," was the quick reply and Sheila

scanned the glare of headlights and flashers for sign of him.

"Get him away," Theakos growled from the window, his own eye trained toward the mass of lights.

"It's okay," Sheila soothed.

"Get him away!"

A figure separated from the maze of cars, approaching slowly, arms spread wide to show that he was unarmed.

"Get rid of him!" Theakos yelled. His fear came from the sure knowledge that the man who approached was Sheila's Achilles heel.

"I want to talk—" Sheila began, only to be interrupted by Theakos's coarse threat.

"I'll kill him. You want that?"

Sheila cast a quick glance to the side and saw that while Theakos had his gun pressed to Ryan's neck, he could as easily shift it and shoot. Then she looked forward again to see Tom continuing his slow, steady approach.

Her hand trembled on Carly's arm. Somehow there seemed nothing more important than to talk with Tom, to try to explain.

"I'm going," she whispered.

"Don't . . . you . . . dare." Theakos paused. Everything was out of control. He didn't understand it. He'd killed before and gotten away free and clear. But he'd always been dealing with the low life. That was it. These people were different and they were going to kill *him*. "He takes one more step and I shoot," he warned a final time. The cold steel in his voice said he meant every word.

Again Sheila looked at Theakos, and suddenly she was frightened. She knew his type. There was a madness in him. There was a madness in *her*. She couldn't let Tom suffer because she'd been weak.

"Don't, Tom!" she yelled. "He'll shoot!"

But Tom kept walking.

"Stop him," Theakos growled.

"Tom! Please! No farther!"

Tom was on the front path and walking.

"Tom!" A hint of panic tinged her nasal cry. Then she heard Theakos's gun cock. Thrusting Carly to the side, she raced from the cottage.

The shot was deflected by Ryan, who batted at Theakos's arm split seconds before twisting and diving in Carly's direction. In the same instant, the night air was rent by a barrage of gunfire and splintering glass. Scrambling across the floor on his belly, Ryan covered Carly's quivering body with his own and pressed them both flat.

As quickly as it had erupted, all sound died. The silence lingered for an awesome eternity. Then there were the sounds of running feet, on the path, on the front steps, into the cottage.

"Carly?" It was Sam's voice.

Ryan raised his head. "We're here," he mumbled, half afraid to move farther. "What happened?"

Joined now by half a dozen troopers, Sam moved to examine the body that lay in a tumbled heap in the middle of the room where the force of bullets had blown it. Moments later, he was back, kneeling by Ryan and Carly. "Is she all right?"

Carly lifted her head and Ryan pulled her to a sitting position. "She's fine," he said, turning her to him and holding her convulsively. "She's fine." Without releasing his hold, he stood and glanced to the side. "Is he . . . ?"

"Dead."

"How's Tom?"

"Unhurt."

"And Sheila?" Carly whispered.

When Sam didn't answer, she tried to break from Ryan. But he wouldn't let her go. "It's okay, babe. It had to be. It's better this way."

"My God," she breathed. "Oh, my God." Again she tried to escape Ryan's protective hold. Though he refused to allow it, he began to move her toward the door.

The scene outside was gut-wrenchingly still. Police seemed all around, but Tom was alone, kneeling over Sheila's lifeless form.

An anguished cry broke from Carly's throat. This time, when she pulled away, Ryan released her. On trembling legs she ran forward, falling to her knees beside Tom, staring down at Sheila's bullet-riddled body.

"She was crazy and unconventional," Tom murmured brokenly. "There was always that mystery about her. But she was exciting and warm. I loved her."

"I know," Carly whispered. She put her arms around him, and in that instant, yielding to grief and terror, she began to cry. Slowly, Tom's trembling arms circled her and held her with the force of his own emotions.

Throat tight, Ryan watched and waited until at last they stood. Only then did he approach, slip his arm around Carly's waist and, with a firm hand on his brother's shoulder, lead them away from the place which, for all three, was best put behind.

When they left, Greg approached to gaze a final time at the woman who had, in her way, bewitched him, too.

The night was far from over. There were long hours spent at the local police station, then a weary drive home. It was dawn when at last Ryan and Carly returned to Cambridge.

"Want to sleep?" he asked as they entered her place.

"I don't think I can," she said tremulously.

Ryan smoothed a wave behind her ear. "Maybe you should try."

She shook her head. "I'd only have nightmares."

"But I'll be there to hold you."

"Oh, Ryan," she whispered, sagging into his arms, "it was so awful. I keep thinking of that cord and the guns. If you hadn't come just then—"

"I did come. That's all that matters."

She rubbed her face against his neck, trying to dispel other images. "I still can't believe Sheila planned it all." The hurt lingered, a raw wound festering with sadness. "All that time we were together she was so friendly. I guess Sam was right in distrusting her." She faltered, her voice dropping to a whisper. "I wish they hadn't had to kill her."

"She came out with a gun," Ryan reasoned gently. "They didn't know she would never have used it on Tom."

"Poor Tom . . . to see her die like that right in front of him. Will he be okay?" Tom had stayed with them during the questioning at the police station, then had returned to Boston with Sam and Greg.

"He'll be fine. It may take a while, but he'll be fine." Ryan paused. "He really came through for us, didn't he? He had to know the risk he was taking, coming forward like that."

Hearing the note of deep affection and admiration in Ryan's tone, Carly looked up. "He's a good man. You should be proud of him."

"I am," he said hoarsely, then buried his face in her

hair until he'd regained his composure. "We'll have to keep him close. He may need it for a while."

Lapsing into silence, he led Carly toward the bedroom. "Come on. Let's lie down. I just want to hold you."

Fully dressed, they stretched out on the bed. Ryan's body was as tense as Carly's. With their minds viewing and reviewing all that had happened, relaxation remained elusive.

"Ryan?"

"Mmm?"

"Will it be all over the papers? I don't want the publicity. Everyone will know who I am—"

"Shh," he soothed. "I spoke with Sam about that. There's bound to be something in the Vermont press, but it'll be minimal. With both of them dead, the case is over." He tucked in his chin and looked down at her. "Anyway, you're safe now. You know that, don't you?"

"I keep telling myself, but it's hard to believe."

"Believe it. Culbert will get his new trial all right, but it'll be for conspiracy to murder. And the sentence will be for a term after the one he's already serving."

"He could hire someone else."

"For what purpose?"

"Vengeance?"

Ryan shook his head with a conviction that gave his words extra force. "It was one thing when he thought he could wipe you out as a witness. But there'd be no point in it now. Even if he wanted to do something out of pure malice, you can be sure that he'll be severely restricted as to visitors and calls. He won't be *able* to do anything. Besides, chances are Theakos didn't have a chance to tell him your new name. He's probably being interrogated right now. We'll know more in time."

"Then I won't need another identity?"

"Hell, no." He grinned. "And if you did, I'd take it right along with you." His arms closed around her and brought her close. "We're in this together, whether you like it or not." His tone sobered. "I nearly lost you last night. I'm not planning on doing that ever again."

Slow tears formed in Carly's eyes. "Running into you on the walk that night was the best thing that ever happened to me."

"Me too, babe. Me too."

It was days before Carly could sleep through the night without waking in the throes of a nightmare. But, as he had promised, Ryan was always there to hold her tightly and gently talk her out of her terror.

To her relief, there was no mention of the events in Vermont in the Boston papers. When she felt sufficiently strong, Carly phoned her father and, censoring the most gory details, told him what had happened. He took it well, though he insisted on speaking with Ryan, who assured him that Carly was fine. Sensing that with Ryan his daughter was in good hands, John Lyons relaxed.

Carly took the rest of the week off from school, knowing that she would be unable to concentrate. Ryan worked for the most part in the apartment, spending hours on the phone, taking Carly with him when he needed to go into the office for an hour or two. They talked with Tom every day, convinced him to spend the weekend with them in a beachfront cottage on Cape Cod. It was a quiet, restorative time for them all, a time for healing, for counting blessings, for looking toward the future.

Returning to Cambridge on Sunday night, Carly was busy making dinner when she suddenly realized that

Ryan had been out of sight for too long. Curious, she wandered through the living room and into the bedroom. At the bathroom door she came to an abrupt halt.

He stood before the sink, the remnants of white lather on his jaw.

Stepping slowly forward, she reached to touch his newly shaved face. Only a mustache remained. At first glance it looked lonesome.

"Well," he said, eyeing himself critically in the mirror, "what do you think?"

Astounded, Carly took the ends of the towel and gently dabbed at the last of the lather. "I think . . . you look . . . as handsome as you did before."

"Then you like it?" he asked more tentatively, stroking the mustache, then his jaw before he closed his hand over hers.

"I love it." With every second she looked at him, he seemed to grow more dashing. "But why?"

He turned to her then, taking both of her hands in his and holding them to his chest. His deep brown eyes melted warmly into hers. "Because I have nothing to hide anymore. I want to see my scar." Only then did her eyes go to the pale ridge that underscored his jaw from ear to chin. "I want *you* to see my scar. It should be a reminder to us that life is never without its risks. Nothing is a given, Carly. We've both lived through ordeals, separately and together, and there may be others in the future. But we can't dwell on them. We'll learn to live with them, just as I'm going to learn to live with this scar."

"You look . . . so different," she murmured.

"You will too," he said confidently.

"What do you mean?"

Releasing her hands, he went to the bedroom closet,

dug into the pocket of a jacket and returned carrying a small box. "For you."

Carly stared at the box.

"Go on. Open it."

Trembling, she carefully lifted the lid, then caught her breath. On a bed of black velvet lay the most exquisite marquis diamond she had ever seen. "Ryan," she breathed at last and looked up at him again.

"I've been carrying it around for days. Had Tom not been with us this weekend, I might have given it to you sooner. Will you wear it, babe? Will you marry me?" Removing the ring from its box, he held it out.

Very slowly, Carly moved her left hand forward until the ring found a perfect niche on her third finger. Then, she threw her arms around Ryan's neck and in that instant knew that nothing in the world could keep her from this man she loved. Nothing at all.

Epilogue

WITHIN A WEEK AFTER, AND INDEPENDENT OF, the attempt on Carly's life, motions for a new trial were denied Gary Culbert and Nick Barber. Gary Culbert was subsequently tried and convicted on charges of conspiracy to murder and given a lengthy sentence to be served from and after the original. He served out neither. After three years' incarceration, he suffered a stroke and was transferred to a state hospital, where he died four months later. It was on that day that the United States Supreme Court denied his last appeal.

Sam Loomis continued to thrive as chief deputy to the U.S. marshal in Boston. Eventually when the United States' presidency changed hands and political parties, he retired from public service and took a prestigious position as head of security for a large electronics firm in the area. With Carly Quinn's file going inactive, he and his wife, Ellen, became close friends of the Cornells.

* * *

It took some time for Greg Reilly to recover from what he considered a major error in judgment on his part. Only with Sam's steady encouragement did he continue at his job, and then it was in a sober and dedicated manner. His hard work paid off. After two years and with Sam's glowing recommendation, he landed a Secret Service post in Washington.

Tom Cornell, badly shaken by Sheila's death, floundered for several months, keeping the latest of hours with the fastest of women in the hopes of burying his hurt. Realizing at last that he was getting nowhere, he rented out his Winchester home and took a traveling job with an international computer concern. In London some time later, he met a woman who, while not as unconventional as Sheila, was caring enough to restore his faith in the happily ever after.

Three weeks after Ryan proposed, he and Carly were married. It was a simple ceremony witnessed by both the bride's and groom's families, as well as by the numerous friends they had quickly come to share. They honeymooned in the Caribbean and returned, gloriously happy, to see to the installation of a large, open spiral staircase connecting upstairs and downstairs.

Though Carly continued to teach, she also began to write. Her earliest works were therapeutic pieces on fear and self-identity, pieces that went no further than Ryan's eyes and ears. As she regained confidence, though, she broadened her outlook to focus on articles of local interest, which found enthusiastic reception in regional publications. In time she was solicited to do an in-depth biographical study of a prominent member of the Boston community.

It was the start of a new career, and the timing couldn't have been better. For, after three years of marriage, and with the horrors of the past finally fading, Carly and Ryan had a son. He was a healthy boy, with his father's thick dark hair and his mother's bright blue eyes. And he was a joy to them both. Ryan was as attentive a father as he was a husband, loving his law practice but loving coming home more. As for Carly, she was in seventh heaven. What used to be the kitchen of Ryan's old apartment was converted into a large study for her. She quite happily arranged her writing hours to fit the baby's schedule, then those of the two other children who came in subsequent years. By that time, the Cornell family was firmly ensconced in a spacious home in Lincoln, with acres of fields, a profusion of maples, oaks and willows, the most beautiful pine grove, and a large golden retriever named Red. The house was modern and sprawling, with a master suite, twin sky-lit studies for Carly and Ryan, and for all the children separate bedrooms, each boasting a large needlepoint hanging with a tiny robin in the corner.

Over the years, many framed photographs joined that of Bonnie and Clyde. There were pictures of Ryan's family and of Carly's, many, many of their children, and the largest a portrait of Carly and Ryan on their wedding day. She would pick it up often and study it, mindful of the miracle that had made it possible.

But of the many, many fingerprints that Carly Quinn Cornell was to leave over the years, none were more gentle, more loving, more indelible than those on her husband.

"We have to stop meeting this way," Ryan would tease in his deep, sexy baritone when, on a spring afternoon, they savored a moment's privacy in an overgrown corner of their woods.

"Who chased who?" she countered, slipping her arms around his neck as his hands pressed her hips to his.

"Whom. And I only wanted to make sure you didn't get lost."

She cleared her throat, even then feeling the quickening of her pulse that his body never failed to inspire. "I am getting lost," she murmured more breathlessly, as she raised her lips to meet his kiss.

It had been that way from the first; it would always be that way. Some things, like fingerprints, never changed.